"Let me see what you saw."

He showed me, and LK hissed quietly behind me.

I wasn't just a serpent; I was huge and black, my head brushing the ceiling. My eyes were as black as my scales, and I was covered in intimidating spikes over my head and down my back, with a frill around the back of my head instead of a cobra hood.

I released Ronnie and fell to sit at the table, my head in my hands. "Oh dear Lord, no."

"More demonic than the Dark Lord," Ronnie said. "That thing was scary. Immeasurably big; I think it could take down the King easily. Immense destructive power, and so damn *dark* the center of it was like looking into the Abyss. Whatever you were, Lady Emma, it certainly scared the living shit out of me."

Books by Kylie Chan

Dark Heavens

WHITE TIGER
RED PHOENIX
BLUE DRAGON

Journey to Wudang

EARTH TO HELL
HELL TO HEAVEN
HEAVEN TO WUDANG

ATTENTION: ORGANIZATIONS AND CORPORATIONS
HarperCollins books may be purchased for educational, business, or sales promotional use. For information, please e-mail the Special Markets Department at SPsales@harpercollins.com.

HEAVEN TO WUDANG

JOURNEY TO WUDANG
BOOK THREE

KYLIE CHAN

HARPER Voyager
An Imprint of HarperCollins Publishers

First published in Australia in 2011 by HarperCollins*Publishers* Australia Pty Limited.

This is a work of fiction. Names, characters, places, and incidents are products of the author's imagination or are used fictitiously and are not to be construed as real. Any resemblance to actual events, locales, organizations, or persons, living or dead, is entirely coincidental.

HARPER Voyager

An Imprint of HarperCollins*Publishers*
10 East 53rd Street
New York, New York 10022-5299

Copyright © 2011 by Kylie Chan
Cover Design by Darren Holt, HarperCollins Design Studio
Cover images: figure by photolibrary.com; temple by Karen Su/Getty Images
Chinese characters supplied by author
ISBN 978-0-06-221034-0
www.harpervoyagerbooks.com

All rights reserved. No part of this book may be used or reproduced in any manner whatsoever without written permission, except in the case of brief quotations embodied in critical articles and reviews. For more information, address Harper Voyager, an Imprint of HarperCollins Publishers.

First Harper Voyager mass market printing: December 2012

Harper Voyager and) is a trademark of HCP LLC.

Printed in the U.S.A.

10 9 8 7 6 5 4 3 2 1

If you purchased this book without a cover, you should be aware that this book is stolen property. It was reported as "unsold and destroyed" to the publisher, and neither the author nor the publisher has received any payment for this "stripped book."

The Serpent lies on the carpet, alone.
The city lights shine through the windows.
It raises its head and tastes things gone;
it drops its head and returns to the sea.

The Turtle raises its head from the water;
the lake stretches around it.
People point and talk, excited.
It goes to the bottom and settles in the mud.

CHAPTER 1

Leo and I sat on the mats across from each other in the Fragrant Lotus training room. His dark face was rigid with concentration as he held the chi on his outstretched hands.

I held one hand on his forearm, watching as the energy flowed through him. 'Float it to the other hand.'

He lost it and it snapped back, hitting him in the middle of the chest. He bounced backwards but didn't fall; then sagged, leaning on the floor. 'This is so damn hard.'

'That was a pathetically small amount of chi for anybody to generate, especially an Immortal,' I said. 'You ate meat, didn't you?'

He didn't reply but his face said it all.

'Alcohol too?' I said.

'Not alcohol.'

I felt the answer through his arm. 'Well, I'm glad you've forgiven him.'

He pulled his arm away. 'That is none of your business and you're not supposed to be able to do that.'

I didn't pursue it. 'You have a choice here, Leo. Either give up trying to do energy work or give up meat, alcohol and sex. You can't do both.'

'But I'm a Shen,' he said, softly protesting.

'Shiny new and green as grass,' I said.

1

He grimaced.

The door flew open and my secretary, Chang, charged in and planted himself in front of us. 'They're taking away my job!'

Leo waved one hand and his wheelchair rolled to him. He pulled himself into it. 'You salute your Master when you enter. Where is your respect?'

Chang fell to one knee and saluted me and Leo. 'Lord. Lady.' He rose and gestured impatiently. 'They say I am no longer to serve you, ma'am. Stop them!'

Yi Hao came in, her expression desperate. 'I'm sorry, ma'am, I didn't expect him to react like this. I thought he'd be happy not to have to do it any more.'

I pulled myself to my feet and Leo held one arm out to steady me. 'Yi Hao was my secretary before you were, Chang. You had the job on a temporary basis; I explained it to you before.'

'I thought she couldn't be trusted.'

'That's why we're going down to the Earthly this afternoon. I'll find out one way or the other if she's trustworthy, and if she is she can resume her post.'

'Let him do it, ma'am,' Yi Hao said. 'I'll do something else.'

That stopped Chang and he stared at her.

'She's a tame demon, she doesn't have free will,' I said. 'If a human or Shen orders her, she must obey. She's seen that you want the job, so she's ceding to you, even though it'll make her miserable.'

'And the fact that you're making such a fuss about it proves that you're not worthy to do it,' Leo said. 'You need to release your attachments and accept circumstances with serenity and grace.' His face went strange. 'Where did that come from?'

'You were just connected to the universe while we were doing chi gong,' I said. 'Well, that's what it feels like anyway. Some of it rubbed off.'

2

'I think I'll spend more time connected to it then,' Leo said, musing. He glared at Chang. 'Cede the position. You deserve to be moved back in with Lok.'

'I don't want to serve the dog again!' Chang said, desperate. 'I'm better than that ...' He stared at us for a long moment, then fell to one knee and lowered his head. 'I will report to Master Lok immediately.' He rose, saluted us, and went out without looking back.

I exhaled a huge breath. 'Finally!'

'What if Lok doesn't want him?' Leo said.

'Then I'll put him to work in the gardens,' I said.

'Oh, good idea.' Leo concentrated, attempted to lift himself out of the wheelchair, and failed. 'Okay, I give up. Meet up with me again after I've been vegetarian for a few days.' He spun his chair to leave.

'Martin will understand,' I said.

'Martin's been trying to make me abstain,' he said without looking back. 'He said the same thing you did.'

'Don't forget you're driving me to Kwun Tong in an hour to meet with the Demon King,' I called after him.

'Don't go, ma'am,' Yi Hao said. 'Don't see the King. He's ...' She searched for the words. 'He will hurt you again.'

'Don't you want to be sure that I can trust you? That you won't turn?' I said.

'Not if it puts you in danger.'

'I won't be in danger. Half a dozen Celestials are coming along. We'll be fine.'

She shuddered and dropped her voice. 'Protect me, ma'am.'

I pulled her into a quick hug. 'Don't worry, I will.'

Leo drove me through Hong Kong's industrial area in Kwun Tong to the meeting place. We had to meet on the Earthly; I refused to invite the Demon King onto the Celestial Plane, and I wouldn't travel to Hell if I could avoid it. The streets were two lanes either way, passing between multi-storey factory buildings with the floor numbers painted in large letters on the sides, for easy lifting of objects up to the correct floor by crane.

Leo checked the building numbers carefully, and pulled into the right one. The entrance was large enough to allow two trucks to pass side by side. Just inside the ground floor on the left were three enormous lifts, large enough to hold the ubiquitous Hong Kong blue lorries. The ground floor was deserted, and the small grimy windows let in rays of sunshine that lit up the floating dust. Leo drove to the edge of the vast space of the ground floor area and parked the car next to the wall. Bricks were heaped against the back wall, strewn haphazardly on the concrete. Paint marked the floor, taking the shapes of the objects that had been sprayed with it.

The Tiger and several of the Wudang Mountain staff came into the building through the truck entrance, knelt to salute me, and waited quietly behind us.

'This is a bad place to meet,' Leo said softly. He was in his wheelchair behind me to my right. 'Difficult to defend.'

'He'll stick to the protocol,' I said. 'Not even the Tiger could teleport in. We're safe.'

'I wish I had your confidence.'

The noise of the traffic outside stopped and the only sound was the breeze whistling through the factory's broken windows. All ten floors of the building were empty.

Someone shouted and a red and gold palanquin appeared in the entrance. About twenty young men surrounded it: demons in human form. All of them appeared to be in their early twenties, of all races, tall and muscular and wearing only skin-tight black bike shorts. They were all impossibly handsome. Some carried the sedan chair and others flanked it.

'Is he insulting me?' Leo said.

'He's probably insulting both of us,' I said.

The Demon King stepped out of the sedan chair in Celestial Form. His perfectly white, strikingly beautiful face was surrounded by a huge mane of red hair that stood up on his head then fell down his back past his waist. His scaled armour and boots were red and gold.

The Tiger summoned an outdoor table and chairs, and I stepped forward to talk to the Demon King. He saluted me and I saluted back, then I gestured for him to sit. He bowed slightly and gestured for me to sit first.

I had an uncomfortable feeling of déjà vu and wished that John was doing this. Now that I was clear of the demon essence, I felt the King's dark nature even more intensely. He was sinister and charismatic, and I just wanted this done and to get out of there.

I sat at the table, and my staff repositioned themselves to the optimal configuration. The King's men moved to stand behind him, mirroring my own Retainers. The Demon King sat and smiled across the table at me, his face alight with warmth.

'You failed,' I said.

He raised one hand slightly. 'I forgot for a moment it was you, and straight to the point as usual. You're alive, Emma, and clear of the demon essence. I didn't fail.'

'If the Xuan Wu Serpent hadn't intervened I would have died.'

He dropped his head slightly and an expression of remorse swept across his face. 'I acknowledge that I caused you a great deal of suffering and that you nearly died.' He raised his head and saluted me again. 'I apologise most sincerely for my misjudgement, madam.'

'You owe me one, George.'

He waved one hand to indicate the demons behind him. 'These are a gift to make up for it. Enjoy them until they expire, then dispose of them.'

I glanced at the handsome young men. 'I think you underestimate me, Wong Mo.'

He shrugged. 'Okay. Worth a shot. Come and live with me and you can have as many of these as you like.' He leaned over the table and grinned. 'Three, four, at once, they're remarkable. You should try. How about I send you one or two just for a sample?'

'Give it up,' I said.

He sighed theatrically, his shoulders moving with the sound. 'Guess I'll just have to give them to the Mothers then. That's what they were originally bred for. I have to keep making them, they don't last long.'

I inhaled sharply. 'I'll take them then.'

He waved me down. 'No, no, if you're not going to use them as sex toys then don't bother. That's all they're good for, they can't even speak.'

'I'll still take them.'

He shrugged. 'Suit yourself.' He waved the young men forward. 'Serve the Dark Lady.'

The demons moved mechanically to stand behind my staff, seemingly unfazed by their fate.

'Will you still bring me Kitty Kwok?' he said. 'She needs to be stopped, and she's human. I can't do it.'

I nodded once. 'We made a deal. You cleared the essence from me; I agreed to bring her to you. You will have her.'

'Is there anything else I can do to atone for the pain I caused you, Emma?' he said, his face still warm and full of affection.

'Yi Hao, Er Hao.' I waved my two demon servants forward without looking behind me. 'These are my demons from One Two Two's nest. I want you to tell me if they are the original demons or copies; and if they are programmed to turn. I want your assurance that I am safe with them, because I love them dearly.'

He turned his attention to them and his face lit up. 'If

you can love these two demons then maybe there is room in your heart for one more.'

'You said you'd love me as snake broth,' I said.

He leaned back and his expression grew wry. 'You'll never let me forget that, will you? It was a spur of the moment thing, Emma, just competitive bullshit. You know I was talking out of my ass.'

'Will you check my demons for me?'

'I will.' He waved them closer. 'Come here, little ones, I will not harm you.'

'Or hurt them,' I said.

He nodded acquiescence. 'Of course.' He waved to them again and they sidled towards him. 'I hear you were willing to sacrifice the Tiger's wives — one of whom is your own best friend — for these two tiny demons.'

'The wives had the Tiger's whole army defending them. All these demons had was me,' I said. 'Any creature that chooses to seek humanity and attain the Tao is worthy of protection.'

'You need to concentrate on the bigger picture, sweetie. Ah Wu would have protected the humans before any demon.' He gestured towards the demons. 'Kneel.' They hesitated, and he spoke more brusquely. 'Down!'

Yi Hao approached and knelt before him. He put one hand on the side of her head and concentrated; she remained rigid with fear as he studied her.

'Demons are demons and they don't have a real life at all,' he said. 'Even if they choose to turn and pursue the Way, they're not worth anything.'

He snapped back, then waved Er Hao forward. She knelt and he touched her head as well, then released her. 'They're not copies. They're nothing special. No programming.' He glanced up at me. 'How were you identifying the copies if these ones were suspect?'

7

'Touch them loaded with shen energy ...' I hesitated. Had I told him too much?

'Don't worry, Emma, I don't have access to shen energy. You can tell me.'

'Touch them loaded with shen energy and you get a similar effect to a Shen touching them without protecting them. They go black.'

'And these little ones go black in response to shen energy as well?' the King said, turning his attention back to my demons.

'They do.'

'They shouldn't do that. They are probably the result of some of Simon's breeding experiments before his Mother was destroyed. Or ...' He leaned hungrily towards them. 'Maybe they're the spawn of that Mother he made himself.' He grinned at me. 'The one he made from your friend.' He put his hands on his knees. 'I would love to tear these two apart and see what's inside. They're fascinating.'

Yi Hao and Er Hao jumped to their feet and scurried to hide behind me.

'Don't worry,' I said, putting my hands behind me to touch them without looking away from the King. 'I won't let him hurt you.'

'We trust you, ma'am,' Yi Hao said, but her voice quavered with fear.

'Can I trust them?' I said. 'You said they were probably specially bred by One Two Two. Are they agents for Kitty or the Death Mother? Are they spies?'

'They are tame demons, and they are yours. They have been tamed with the Fire Essence Pill and cannot turn on you. You can trust them.'

'Go back to the others,' I said, and they ran back to my group. 'Tell the Tiger to summon tikuanyin tea for me.'

'Allow me,' the King said, and a pot and cups of priceless crackled green glaze appeared before us. He poured for both of us and raised his cup. 'Warn the Celestial about the demons those two have created, the ones that are programmed to explode. I never thought I'd see the like again, and here they are. So wrong. Probably just a small part of their arsenal, Emma, be very careful. They may have copies that are undetectable even with shen.'

'How badly do you want the Death Mother and Kitty taken down?' I said.

He carefully replaced his cup on the table. 'Badly enough to enlist your help. Particularly Kitty — she is an unknown quantity. I've never seen anyone do what she's done; she's well on the way to some sort of twisted Immortality. She can survive in Hell unassisted, but she's still human enough that I can't break my vow to Ah Wu and deal with her myself.' He lifted his teacup again and studied it. 'To be honest, she scares me. I think she has designs on my throne.' He gazed at me over the rim of the cup. 'She has links with the other Centres; being human, she has no limitations on her travel. She helped Six make those hybrid stone elementals using Western stones.'

'Will you assist the forces of Heaven to find and stop them?'

His blood-coloured eyes were intense. 'Are you speaking as a representative of the Celestial here? A simple ordinary human female, mortal, un-Raised, and only holding your title in a temporary capacity?'

I raised my teacup. 'That I am, Wong Mo.'

He took a swig of his tea. 'You're doing it again.'

I sipped my own tea: perfectly normal tikuanyin. 'Thank you.'

'I will have to walk a very fine line, Dark Lady. Assist you too much and I will appear weak to my subjects; they will see me as a puppet of the Celestial and turn against me. If I do not assist you enough, these two bitches could threaten my throne.' He placed the teacup on the table and turned it in his manicured fingers. 'One of the most delicate dances I have ever performed.'

'In this case we share a common goal,' I said. 'I don't want to see either of them on your throne either.'

He put his hands on the table on either side of the cup and inhaled deeply, throwing his head back and closing his eyes. 'Oh, but I would so like to see you on my side.' He opened his eyes and they burned into me. 'Even without the demon essence, you are so dark and powerful and destructive — so attractive and intriguing. No wonder Ah Wu found you irresistible; you appeal to both his demonic and Celestial sides.'

'You could tell me what I am as a show of good faith,' I said.

'I could,' he said. 'But I've already cleared you of demon essence. I think that's enough for now. I have your word.' He picked up his teacup and drank again. 'You have the phone. If I get any leads I'll send you a text or something. Right now I think Kitty's on the Earthly somewhere overseas, and the Death Mother is in Southeast Asia somewhere like Laos or Vietnam. You're still weak anyway, Emma. Rest and send in agents, and we'll both see what we can turn up on the intelligence side.'

He disappeared.

I rose and turned back to our group and the table also disappeared.

I sighed. 'Now what do I do with these demons?'

'Start a massage parlour for the Hong Kong ladies that pop across the border on the weekends to have their nails done. You'd make a fortune,' Leo said.

'Liu,' I said loudly. 'Find something for these demons to do, will you?'

'Sure thing, Emma. We'll use them for binding practice until they expire.'

I studied one of the young men carefully. Liu was right: the demon was so tiny, he would last a maximum of six weeks; and from the blank look in his eyes, he wasn't even aware enough to care.

The next morning Leo, Simone and I went shopping together in Pacific Place. Some things just couldn't be bought in Heaven, fashionable shoes among them. Simone told stories about school as we drove, seemingly uncaring as to whether anyone was listening.

'And so I told her that there's only one vampire left in the world, and he's a Retainer of the House of the North and lives in a graveyard in London,' she said. 'You should use the disabled space, Leo, you have the right. Use the label.'

'I'm not disabled,' Leo said, turning the car into a vacant spot in the Pacific Place car park.

Simone continued talking as we got out of the car. 'So she said, "Is he hot?" and I said, "If you like your guys short, skinny and old."'

'What did she say?' I said.

'She said, "But vampires are gorgeous!" I told her, "Never have been, and the last one left looks like a ferret."'

'He doesn't look like a ferret!' I said, then stopped. 'Okay, maybe he does.'

'You're being rude to poor Franklin behind his back,' Leo said as the wheelchair floated out of the boot of the car and unfolded itself.

'She's going over to London to take a look,' Simone said.

'Isn't that too far from her Centre?' Leo said as he levitated to sit in the chair, then wheeled it next to us.

'Nah, she's one of the Tiger's kids, she'll go with her dad on the next wife trip,' Simone said. 'So I have to warn Franklin: here comes another one, be ready with the girl repellent.'

'It'd be better if you just didn't tell people about him,' I said as we walked out towards the shopping centre.

'He asked me to,' she said. 'He loves blowing their romantic brainless little notions out of the water. He says it's the most fun he's had since he swore off, and that's more than two hundred years.'

'He's a vegetarian vampire,' I said with amusement.

'And he's not into girls,' Simone said.

'Well, not so much not into girls as not into anything,' I said. 'He's just asexual, Simone, he isn't interested at all. Most of them were like that. The sexy vampire thing is just the mythology that's grown around them.'

'That explains why he has no looks, charm or charisma,' Simone said.

'Not even any gay sparkle,' Leo said.

'Gay sparkle?' I said with disbelief.

'Gayer than me, and that's saying a lot,' Leo said.

'We are evil,' I said.

'No,' Simone said. Her face went slack and her eyes turned inwards, then she took Leo's and my hands. 'That's evil.'

She shared what she was seeing with her touch. Somewhere up ahead and below us in a maintenance area of the shopping centre, there were two large forces facing off with a third entity standing panic-stricken nearby. One force was dark and cold; one was demonic; and the third seemed to be human and scared out of its wits. We dropped our hands and ran towards it. Whatever was happening, the human was in peril.

We entered the underground corridor between the car park and the shopping mall. A stairway on the left led up to ground level; the standoff was below us. We went down the stairs, Leo making his chair float above them. At the bottom there was a door, and a grimy mop and bucket leaning against the wall. The area smelled of stale cigarettes and urine.

Simone pulled at the door; it was locked. She raised both hands with palms towards the door.

I put one hand on her arm. 'If you can unlock it without blowing it off its hinges, we'll have the element of surprise.'

She put one hand over the lock and the door opened. 'Blowing it off its hinges works both as a surprise and a warning.'

There was a corridor on the other side of the door, with plain concrete walls and floor and bare white-painted pipes through the ceiling. At the end of the corridor and facing towards us was a young European of about sixteen. He was the same height as Michael, with sandy brown hair, and didn't appear anything special. An older European man stood behind him, taller and slimmer with the same colour hair — probably his father. The third person was a young Chinese man, the same height as the younger European and heavily-muscled; he stood with his back to us in a long defensive stance.

Older man is human. European kid is a demon type I've never seen before. The one facing away from us is a half-Shen, seems reptile, may be one of Daddy's, Simone said.

'Stay back,' the Shen said to us without turning away from the young European. 'Leave now. I will protect you.'

The older man put one hand out. 'There's nothing to protect anybody against. My son won't hurt you. Please, whatever you are, just let us go.'

'I don't want any trouble,' the younger man said. 'I won't hurt anyone, I promise.'

I stepped forward to stand next to the Shen. 'Stand down,' I said without looking at him. 'I'm Emma

13

Donahoe, Regent of the Northern Heavens, First Heavenly General. This is Princess Simone Chen and Lord Leo Alexander. We'll handle this demon, you don't need to destroy it.'

The Shen stared at me. 'What the hell are you talking about?'

'I'm not a demon!' the young man shouted, his face fierce with fury. 'I'm not ... I'm not ...'

His father put his hand on the young man's shoulder and spoke soothingly. 'Don't lose it, Tom, deep breaths, you can do it. Hold on, lad, you can't change here. These people know what you are!'

The Shen and I both stepped back as the skin on the young man's face disappeared.

'Snake Mother,' Leo whispered behind us.

'Can't be,' Simone said. 'The only male Mother-type is the King himself.'

'What the hell are you people talking about?' the Shen said, turning to glare at me again.

I raised both hands. 'Okay. You.' I pointed at the older man. 'What's your name?'

'Ben O'Breen,' he said. He pressed his hand harder into Tom's shoulder and the young man's face returned to normal. 'I'm his father, and he won't hurt anybody.'

I raised one hand towards the Shen. 'What's your name?'

'Vincent Pang,' the Shen said. 'Your name is Emma? You know what I am?'

'Yes.'

'Then you probably know more about me than I do.'

I turned back to the Europeans. 'Ben, do you know what your son is?'

'I know that his mother was something vicious and powerful, and that we had to get away from her before our son turned into something similar,' Ben said.

'Was she Chinese or European?' I said, noticing Tom's slightly Eurasian features.

'Chinese,' Ben said. 'Do you know what she was? What he is?' His face filled with hope. 'Can you help us?'

'None of them has any idea what they are?' Simone said, incredulous.

'Strange as it sounds, I think that's the case,' I said. 'Tom's half demon. Vincent attacked him because that's his nature, being what he is.'

'What am I?' Vincent said.

'You're half Shen, and probably my half-brother,' Simone said.

He turned to stare at her. 'You can see what I really am?' He took a couple of steps back and appeared ready to run.

'Don't be ashamed,' I said quickly. 'Your father — if you share the same father with her — is the most powerful Shen in the Heavens, second only to the Jade Emperor himself.'

'All that stuff is real?' he said.

'Have you changed to a turtle or snake?' I said.

He hesitated. Admitting to changing to either was huge; it was understandable that he'd prefer not to share.

'Do you change, Vincent?'

He nodded once sharply.

'And you ask me if the Shen are real?'

He sagged against the wall and looked as if he was about to cry. 'I thought I was an experiment or something. I change into this horrible thing, and I have this urge to kill people like him.' He bent and put his head in his hands. 'I'm not a monster at all!'

Simone went to him and pulled him into a fierce hug, and he let go into her shoulder.

I turned back to Ben and Tom. 'Now, what to do with you two? Tom, when you change, what do you change into?'

15

'Can we take this somewhere where we can sit, rather than standing around here talking about it?' Simone said. She patted Vincent on the back. 'He's broken down and he's heavy.' She pulled back to look into Vincent's face. 'You have a family now, we can help you. Come with us.'

'Anywhere but the Shang,' I said.

Leo concentrated. 'Coffee shop upstairs at the Conrad is empty.'

'Ask LK Pak to join us, please,' I said. 'Let's go.'

CHAPTER 2

We took the glass lift up to the hotel and all entered the coffee shop. The staff were setting out the central display for the lunchtime buffet, moving quietly and with precision. A couple of foreign businessmen sat at a table next to the window, but apart from that the café was deserted.

After some searching through my bag I found a packet of tissues and handed them to Vincent. He took them with a nod and wiped his eyes, then blew his nose.

The waiter took our orders, and when he was gone I leaned on the table.

'Vincent, your case is simple,' I said. 'You're a lost reptile Shen and we'll take you in and give you a home. You have a family now.'

'I already have a family,' Vincent said. 'My parents brought me up in a housing estate in Lam Tin.'

'Both parents?' Simone said.

'Of course. When I was about fifteen, I changed. They were … They threw me out, they said I was evil. My father tried to kill me.'

'A Shen wouldn't do that,' Simone said. 'They'd be proud, not scared. I wonder why your parents reacted like that? Maybe one of them isn't your real parent?'

'We'll find out later. Whatever you are, you're safe and you have a home now,' I said. 'We will look after you.'

He bobbed his head. 'You've given me reason to live.'

'I hope that's not true,' Simone said.

'I had given up,' he said. 'I finally gave in to this horrible urge to hurt people and followed this poor boy and his father in the hope that the boy would end it for me.'

'That's our nature, to destroy demons,' Simone said. 'You were all lucky that we found you when we did.'

'Is that what I am?' Tom said. 'A demon?'

'You are something new and different and frankly more than a little scary,' I said. 'What do you change into, Tom?'

'I've done a lot of research into it,' he said. 'The closest thing I've seen is a thing called a lamia: front end of a woman, back end of a snake. I'm something like that — but they're always female, and I'm not.'

'You have the top half of a man and the bottom half of a snake, and the human part has no skin?' I said.

He nodded, his face full of misery.

'Simone, have a look at Ben, just to be sure that he's human,' I said.

Simone touched Ben's hand and focused on him. He didn't appear to be concerned by it.

'Not hurting him, and I'm touching him with shen energy,' Simone said. 'He's completely human.'

She stood and reached for Tom and I raised my hand. 'Wait until LK gets here. He's the expert.'

She nodded and sat again.

'You said your name's O'Breen?' I asked Ben. 'That's unusual, it sounds like O'Brien.'

'It's an ancient form of O'Brien,' Ben said, obviously something he'd said many times before. 'It's spelt differently —'

'Because it's an older form and slightly different,' I finished for him. 'I have the same issue. My surname's

Donahoe, and I'm always telling people how to spell it because —'

This time it was Ben who finished for me. 'Because there's only one letter different.'

'Freaky,' Simone said.

'My dad's doing our family tree,' I said. 'He reckons our family originally came from Wales, though, not Ireland.'

'Same here,' Ben said. 'I'm not Irish, I'm actually Welsh.'

'Seriously freaky,' Simone said.

'Tell me about Tom's mother,' I said. 'She was Chinese, and cruel? What was she like?'

'I met her when I was here in Hong Kong on business,' Ben said. 'About twenty years ago. She was small and sweet and smiled all the time, and I was completely smitten. We married and I took her back to Wales with me, and the minute Tom was born, she changed. She turned into the opposite of what she'd been here; she was manipulative, angry and — there's no other word for it — she was straight-up evil. I left her after I came home one day to find that she'd stolen the next-door neighbour's dog, butchered the poor beast on the dining table and was drinking its blood. Tom was with her, she was holding him, and their faces, their hands, were covered in blood...' He leaned on the table and put his head in his hands. 'Tom was only two years old. I grabbed him and ran. We went to London, but she found us and nearly stole him back. I ran further — I lived in Singapore for ten years until she found us again, then Kuala Lumpur, then Sydney, then back here. We've been on the run ever since. I just pray to God she never finds him because I know that if she does, she'll change him into something like her.'

'What was her name?' I said.

'Gloria Ho,' Ben said, and I sighed with relief.

'Could have been a name that Kitty used, though, Emma,' Simone said.

'I don't think so. Kitty's been here in Hong Kong the whole time; she hasn't had a chance to have a family in the UK,' I said. 'Someone else, not Kitty.'

'I'd be very surprised if she wasn't in Kitty's group, though,' Simone said. 'I wonder how many other overseas experiments they've been doing. And all without the Shen here in Asia lifting a finger to do anything about it. They'll be sorry when an army of hybrids turns up at the Gates of Heaven with the power of East and West combined.'

'Suddenly this sounds much bigger than just Tom and me,' Ben said.

'How much control does Tom have when he changes?' I said.

'I've never killed anyone,' Tom said. 'I have it under control.'

'Have you wanted to kill?' I said.

He looked away.

'Tom, look at me,' I said, and he turned back. 'I used to be something very much like you. But I had control, and I never hurt anyone. If you're the same, we have a place for you as well, where you'll be safe from your mother and we can help you to control this nature.'

'You *used* to be? You were cured?' His face filled with hope. 'I could be cured?'

I was silent at that.

'Tell him,' Simone said softly.

I shook my head.

Simone said it for me. 'Removing the demon essence from Emma involved burning it out of her. The Demon King made us pay a terrible price, and then he engulfed her in flames and burned her alive. He took off the entire top layer of her body, and most of her insides as well. Not just the skin, everything. Burned her eyes and

20

tongue out of her head, destroyed her lungs and throat — there wasn't anything left. That's why her skin's so smooth and strange-looking. If one of Heaven's greatest healers hadn't intervened, she would have died.'

Tom's face crumpled. 'It would be worth it.'

LK Pak, the Wudang Demon Master, arrived and sat to join us. He nodded around the table, then focused on Tom. 'I see what you mean.'

I raised one hand to stop LK before he spoke any further.

'Master Pak is an expert on demons, and hopefully he can help you,' I said. 'Before we begin: understand that you have free will, Tom. You must never, under any circumstances, offer to give that up to anybody. If you ask for someone's protection and offer yourself, you'll lose your free will and become something much less. It's like being an object, a possession, and it's worse than death. Do you understand? Don't ever ask anybody to protect you, or offer to serve them.'

Tom nodded, his eyes wide.

I turned to LK. 'Take a look. From what he said, he's a male Snake Mother, East-West hybrid.'

'Not possible, no such thing,' LK said, and took Tom's hand. His eyes unfocused, then widened. 'Well, shit. He's right. Never seen anything like him. What the hell did his Mother look like?'

'Last seen cutting up a dog and drinking its blood,' I said. 'Strong enough to spend a significant amount of time in the West.'

'What colour dog?' LK said quickly.

Ben thought about it for a moment, then said, 'Black.'

'Well, damn,' LK said with concern. 'She really drank the blood of a black dog? Damn.'

'Is the colour significant?' Ben said.

'The blood of a black dog is a demon ward,' I said. 'She's not supposed to be able to even touch it.'

21

'I never wanted to get messed up in all of this,' Ben said weakly. 'I just want somewhere safe and normal to bring my boy up.'

'Safe would be enough for me,' Tom said. 'I hate seeing Dad in danger. Especially when it's from me.'

'We will provide you with safety,' LK said. 'Just make sure never to submit to anyone's will, like Lady Emma said, and you'll both be safe.'

'Can you help me too, sir?' Vincent said.

LK rose, went around the table and held his hand out. Vincent took it; LK nodded and returned to his seat. 'Third or fourth generation.'

'But he changes!' I said.

'Can still happen, particularly if one of the biggest of us is involved.'

'So he's like … my great-great-nephew or something?' Simone said.

'Fourth or fifth cousin,' LK said. He turned back to Vincent. 'You are descended from a mighty heavenly Shen, and your powers have emerged after several generations, even though they were dormant in those before you.'

Vincent's expression was a mix of delight and disbelief.

'The English term for that is throwback,' I said. 'But three or four generations? Really? John's his grandfather, or great-grandfather?'

'Could be more than that; with the Xuan Wu the powers have laid dormant for up to six generations,' LK said. 'Look at Simone: the first-generation human cross and nearly as powerful as the Dark Lord himself.'

'But he'd never had a human wife before Michelle,' I said.

'So it was either his son or daughter that was Vincent's ancestor,' LK said. 'They're probably still around as well; we should check Vincent's ancestral tablets.'

Vincent winced. 'My family won't let me near them.'

'Then accept what you are with grace. You have a Heavenly family, and Lady Emma will care for you as if you were her own.'

'Lady Emma.' Ben studied me. 'When we were down in the basement, you said you were a General and a Regent. Forgive my bluntness, but you don't look like anything much.'

Simone, LK and Leo all flinched.

'Don't do that!' I said, sweeping my hand in front of me. 'I'm not going to explode and bite people's heads off just for stating the obvious! I'm middle-aged, short, plain and scruffy. He's right: I don't look like anything much.'

'One of the first lessons you learn at Wudangshan is that nothing is as it appears,' Simone said to Ben. 'It's the plainest, scruffiest and most ordinary-looking people who are the most powerful and deadly. The big, heroic, handsome types usually grow up selfish and conceited and generally never find the Way.'

'I'm the heroic handsome type,' Leo said.

Simone nodded to him, serious. 'I concede your utter gorgeousness and total irresistibility, Lion. You are the most handsome inhabitant of Wudang.'

Leo saw our guests' faces. 'We're just having fun, don't worry.'

'I'm not powerful and deadly,' I said.

Leo blew his breath out loudly and turned away.

I ignored him and continued. 'I'm very small compared to many of the residents of Wudang. Due to a weird set of coincidences, and a god who makes *really* bad decisions, I've been put in charge of a lot of stuff. I can't wait for him to come back so I can offload all of it back onto him.'

This time Simone made a disgusted noise. 'Like he'll let you.'

I ignored her as well. 'But you're right: I'm nothing terribly special. I've just been given a high-ranking job and I'm doing my best with it.'

'What level demon can you take down, Lady Emma?' LK said.

'Weapon or energy?' I said.

'Thank you for making my point for me.' LK nodded to Tom and Ben. 'She's Regent of the Northern Heavens and Acting First Heavenly General. She's smart, fights like a demon when her family is threatened, and completely loyal to Wudang.' He leaned back. 'We are all proud to serve her.'

'Oh, look, you made her blush,' Simone said with delight. 'That's way more fun than anything I could have done.' She grinned at LK. 'Way to go. I won't forget that. If you really want to freak her out, just compliment her.'

'I think one of the most popular pastimes on the Mountain is Emma-baiting,' I said. 'LK, can Tom go to the Celestial Plane?'

LK nodded. 'With an escort, he can.'

'Well then, our morning tea's here; let's enjoy it, then head up.'

'Where to?' Vincent said.

'Wudang Mountain in Heaven, home of all Martial Arts,' Simone said, watching his reaction.

He didn't disappoint. He grinned broadly and said, 'I can't wait.'

We landed on the main training square at the bottom of the stairs that led up to Yuzhengong — True Way — the largest building on the Mountain. It was a hundred metres long and fifty metres wide, a traditional bracket construction made completely without nails, with red pillars holding the gold-tiled, upturned roof five metres above the ground. The seven peaks of Wudangshan stood around us in a rough circle, joined by soaring bridges and walkways over the gorges between them. The three main halls — True Way, Purple Mist and Dragon Tiger — flanked the vast training forecourt of polished dark slate.

Ben, Tom and Vincent turned on the spot, admiring the view. True Way was one of the highest parts of Wudangshan, with only the Golden Temple higher on its own peak behind it. Some small meditation pagodas sat at the same level on other peaks, but they were impossible to reach without flight.

The mountains around us stretched forever, covered in pines. Clouds moved through the gorges below us, the sunlight from above making them shine. The sky was that impossible Celestial blue and the breeze was fresh with alpine scents from the gardens.

Ben took a deep breath and smiled. 'I feel more at ease than I have ever felt anywhere.'

Vincent was smiling too, his face streaked with tears. 'I feel like I've come home. I always felt there was a place for me somewhere that would be bright and wonderful and where I would be welcome.' He fell to one knee and saluted me. 'Thanks to you, I have found that place. If I were to die right now, I would die a happy man.'

I nodded to him as he rose, and wondered if the place that was my home would be possible to find, and if I would have to lose this place to gain it.

'That's astonishing. How do they do that?' Tom said. He was watching the Disciples working on the forecourt.

They were performing a level five staff set, the most advanced staff kata on Wudang. They had placed their staves upright, climbed up them, and were standing on the tips of the vertical staves with one foot, their hands clasped in front of them. They swapped from foot to

25

foot without the staff falling, then switched to one hand, doing a handstand on the end of the staff.

'Are there holes in the stone for the staves to sit in?' Ben said.

'No,' I said, 'it's a matter of balance and energy control.'

'Could I learn that?' Vincent said.

'If we don't have you doing that within a year I'll hand in my gold sash,' I said.

'I heard that!' Leo said. 'It's a bet!'

I strode to Leo, held my hand out and we slapped palms. I bent to whisper in his ear. 'You're supposed to be celibate at the moment, so no sexing him up to ruin his energy manipulation.'

'I'm with Martin right now so I wouldn't do it anyway,' he whispered back.

I straightened and studied him. 'It's that serious?'

'No,' he said, meeting my gaze. 'I am.'

My mobile rang in my bag and I pulled it out. It was Ronnie Wong.

'I hear you just found something very interesting, ma'am. I was wondering if you'd let this worthless small demon examine it? Is it really a male Mother?'

'East-West hybrid,' I said. 'Hold on a minute.' I turned to Ben and Tom. 'I have a gentleman who is an expert on demonkind who would like to have a look at you. Do you mind?'

Ben and Tom shared a look, and Tom nodded.

'We trust you,' Ben said. 'Do what you have to.'

I returned to the phone. 'Are you big enough to come up here unescorted?'

'That I am, ma'am.'

'Call me again when you reach the main gate.'

'Ho ak.'

'He's been in Hong Kong too long,' I said as I snapped the phone shut. 'Ho ak indeed.'

'Better than Hell,' Simone said.

'Vincent, do you know Ronnie Wong?' I said.

'No,' Vincent said.

'Ben? Tom? Do you know a gentleman by the name of Ronnie Wong? He runs a really small crappy fung shui shop full of paper effigies and Hell money out in Western District.'

Both of them shook their heads.

I looked down at the phone. 'Then how the hell did he know that we just found you?'

'Ask him when he gets here,' Simone said. 'Let's go to the admin area and sort out what we'll do with this lot.'

We walked along the path from the three main halls on the largest peak, heading east to the support areas. The buildings here were close together, mostly low, brick and single storey, except for the Imperial Residence — a two-storey courtyard house standing alone, flush against the stone side of the mountain — and the Armoury, which was one floor but had an exceptionally tall roof. We crossed a twenty-metre-long marble bridge, a perfect semicircle over the deep chasm between the peaks, to the administrative area: a cluster of small buildings housing offices and meeting rooms around a central larger hall — the War Room.

We went into my office and sat at the small conference table, and Yi Hao ran off to find the allocations for quarters in the residential area.

'If this is Chinese Heaven, then what about Western Heaven?' Ben said. 'Have you been there?'

'The Eastern Shen — the gods from here — have made intelligence-gathering trips to the West and encountered demons, but haven't met any Western Shen,' I said. 'Xuan Wu — the most powerful guy, the boss of Wudang — actually has a house in Kensington and spent years in London, and never met a single Western Shen.'

'It's possible they may have been avoiding him because he has a very dark nature,' Simone said. 'Xuan means dark, and he sort of changed sides and joined the Celestial.'

'But other Shen have been over there too, and tried to visit Western Heaven, and found nothing,' I said. 'It's like it's only demons over there, no Shen at all.'

'Not many of the Asian Shen have shown much interest, though,' Simone said with resignation. 'There's still the "Middle Kingdom" mentality. China is the central ninety per cent of the world and nothing else really matters.'

'Middle Kingdom?' Ben said.

'The Chinese characters for China are "Middle Kingdom", Dad,' Tom said.

'Oh.'

My phone rang and I answered it.

'Emma, this is Gold. We need an advanced energy worker over at the infirmary — Amy's in labour.'

'Where's Meredith?'

'Here, but we need you too. We have to deliver by caesar; she can't deliver normally and hold her shape. If she changes to dragon, she'll kill them.'

I snapped the phone shut, rose and bowed slightly. 'One of our dragons is about to give birth to human children and I'm needed to make sure that she stays in human form. If you'll excuse me, I'll be back later.'

'I'll take care of this,' Leo said.

'Thanks,' I said, and hurried out.

'Did she just say what I think she said?' I heard Ben say with disbelief behind me.

'I'm going to be an auntie!' Simone said.

CHAPTER 3

Gold held Amy's hand and smiled down at her while the staff gave the newborns their first bath. Amy smiled back at him, then around at everybody else.

'Do you have names for them?' Meredith said.

'Richard after Amy's father, and Jade after mine,' Gold said.

'How's the urge to change?' Meredith said.

Amy didn't reply, and Meredith nodded.

'We're nearly done here,' Edwin, the Academy doctor, said. 'You'll be able to change to dragon very shortly.'

'Will the wound still be there when I change back from dragon to human?' Amy said.

Edwin nodded. 'This much trauma and blood loss will lower your transformation ability.'

'You could always stay dragon and bottle-feed them,' Gold said.

Amy shook her head. 'I want to give them as much of a boost as I can. My human milk is the best for them. And if I cuddle them as dragon I won't be nearly as soft.'

'Can you give me an estimate on when I can release the meridians?' I said.

Edwin raised his hand and the forceps holding the suture appeared over the edge of the screen. 'I'm on the final layer, ma'am, less than three minutes.'

'You okay, Emma?' Meredith said.

'I can manage.'

'Do you want me to administer an analgesic so you can release the meridians?' Edwin said.

'No,' I said. 'If I pin down these meridians before I withdraw, the pain relief will last a good six hours, and I can come back then and top it up.'

'Don't hurt yourself, ma'am,' Amy said.

'Don't you "ma'am" me,' I said. 'Do you have any idea at all how good it feels to be able to contribute like this? With clean, pure, healing energy?'

'I can only imagine,' Amy said, then gasped and grimaced.

'Sorry,' I said, and returned my concentration to the meridians. I'd let one of them slip and she'd felt it.

'It wasn't anything, just a twinge,' she said. She turned her head to see Gold again. 'Did you manage to contact my father?'

'I told both your parents, and your father is bringing your mother up here to see them,' Gold said.

'My father and mother together? That's unbelievable,' Amy said.

'I think your mother's making a special effort because she wants to see her grandchildren,' Gold said. 'I spoke to her before him … You should have warned me she was so … so …'

'Did she go ballistic at you?'

'I think she'll rip my throat out if we don't get married within the next two weeks,' he said.

'But she doesn't know what we are, and that dragons and stones don't do that sort of thing.'

'Actually she does. She knew all along your father was a dragon. He told her I'm a stone, and that stones don't marry, and apparently it's made her even more determined to see it happen.'

'I'm done,' Edwin said.

Meredith took my hand and our consciousnesses touched; she still had Amy held down hard into human form. She studied the meridians alongside me and indicated the top point on the core meridian. 'Start here.'

'Don't let her intimidate you. We don't have to do it if it doesn't feel right,' Amy said.

I concentrated, and with Meredith's assistance pinned the energy into the meridians so that they stayed lit. I released them one at a time, moving slowly down the core to the area where they'd opened Amy up. Her body was shrieking with distress at what had been done to it, and I spread the energy from the meridians to soothe its panic and ease the nervous reactions. The energy flowed through the area, giving it a healing boost, and I carefully withdrew completely.

'It's something I've been meaning to ask you for a while anyway,' Gold said. 'Will you marry me, Amy?'

Amy shivered and her teeth rattled; a normal feeling of extreme cold that came when an energy worker withdrew after a major energy healing.

'Are you in any pain?' Meredith said.

Amy shook her head, her teeth stopping her from speaking.

'Is that a no?' Gold said.

Amy shook her head again, still unable to talk.

'I'm going to release you now, you can change back,' Meredith said.

Amy transformed into dragon, raised her head, then dropped it again with a huge sigh and closed her eyes.

'Natural sleep, no pain, leave her to recover,' Meredith said. 'In a couple of hours wake her up and see if she can change back to human.' She turned to me. 'Magnificent job, madam. You can take it easy now.'

I stood up and toppled sideways.

Meredith caught me. 'Oh, and congratulations, Master Gold. I think you just got engaged.'

'My father will kill me,' Gold said, his hand on Amy's back.

'Who is scarier: your father or her mother?' Meredith said.

'Oh, definitely her mother.'

'Then you made the right decision.' She hefted me in her arms. 'Come on, missy, you've been overdoing it lately and need some serious rest.'

I woke, and had a moment of confusion as I saw the ceiling above the bed. Where was I? I looked left and nearly panicked: I was on the Celestial Plane, in the Imperial Residence of Wudang Mountain. Then I remembered that I didn't need to be a snake, and I settled further under the silk. I was here. I had made it. But something was wrong; something bad had happened. Something terrible had happened and I couldn't remember what it was; only the dark feelings of misery and despair that it brought me.

I sighed deeply and remembered.

Nothing bad had happened. I was feeling the grief for something that was yet to come. I often woke like this, feeling the loss. Something awful was going to happen to us in the near future and I had no idea what it was, only that it hung over all of Wudang.

I centred my chi and put the feeling aside. I was living in the present, enjoying the peace of now, and ready for the future when it crashed over us.

The four-poster was made of ebony, black with the deep sheen of many years of care. The dark grey curtains were embroidered with silver depictions of turtles and bats — symbols of longevity and good luck. The bed was flush against the wall, with a raised twenty-centimetre barrier around three sides to hold the covers in place, the fourth side left open. The room around me was five metres to a side, the walls hung with elegant ink paintings of sea creatures. A black sofa and coffee table in front of the open fireplace gave it a warm, comfortable atmosphere. I slapped the mattress next to me. They'd put me in the Emperor's suite again, against my express orders. I'd commandeered a room in the servants' quarters attached to the Imperial Residence and they should have put me in there.

I rotated to put my feet on the silk rug, pushed them into the slippers sitting next to the bed, and wandered into the en suite bathroom. Fortunately Michelle had demanded modern Western fittings when John had built the bathroom for her, so there wasn't a squat toilet. However, there'd been a compromise about the decor and the entire bathroom was tiled with black marble, giving it a dated eighties look. I didn't care, I just used it and wandered back out again.

'You awake?' I said.

'You've only been out an hour or so,' the stone said. 'Ronnie Wong is in the gatehouse waiting for you. They've served lunch there so you can talk to him while you eat.'

'Any complaints about Tom being allowed in untamed?'

'Actually, no. General consensus is that he's so interesting they're willing to risk it.'

'If anybody puts me to sleep in this bed again before John returns, I will personally take their head myself,' I said as I pulled my clothes back on.

'Even if it's Simone?'

'Bah.'

The gatehouse sat on the hillside outside the wall that protected the Mountain, in a grove of small cypress trees and surrounded by a tumble of granite boulders as tall as a man. It was a basic village house: two-storey and rectangular with a tiled roof. A living room, kitchen

33

and dining room were downstairs, with two bedrooms and a bathroom above, all sparsely furnished because the administration of Wudang hardly ever met with demons there. It was too far for any but the largest demons to travel from Hell, and just the proximity to the Mountain scared them to death.

I walked in the front door and went into the dining room, Ben and Tom trailing behind me. Ronnie Wong and LK Pak were already there sitting at the table.

As soon as I walked in the door, Ronnie shot to his feet, knocking his chair over, and leapt backwards so violently that he knocked his glasses off. He stood spreadeagled on the wall behind him and stared at me, wide-eyed and trembling.

I backed up as well, then took a deep breath and controlled it.

'You okay, Emma?' LK said. 'You look like you saw a ghost.'

'I'm fine. I just had enhanced vision for a moment,' I said.

I moved away from Ben and Tom, but Ronnie didn't stop staring at me. It was definitely me, not Tom, that had freaked him out.

'It's me, Ronnie,' I said. 'What do you see?'

Ronnie retrieved his glasses, put them back on and peered at me. 'Emma?'

'You don't even need the glasses,' I said. 'What did you see?'

He picked his chair up and returned it to its place. 'I can't really describe it,' he said without looking at me.

I strode to him and he shifted uncomfortably away from me. I held my hand out. 'Show me then.'

'I'm not sure I want to touch you right now,' he said, looking at my hand as if it was something toxic.

'You've seen her serpent form many times; this can't be what's causing this,' LK said. 'Tell us what you saw.'

34

'Serpent form?' Ben said.

'It's a long story,' I said. I didn't lower my hand. 'Show me.'

'He can't show you, you're only a human. You need to be more than human to touch minds with a demon,' LK said. 'Don't risk the damage from trying.'

I reached out, grabbed Ronnie's hand and made the link.

He let his breath out in a long gasp, like he'd had the wind knocked out of him. 'Holy shit.'

'Did you just link to him?' LK said.

'Let me see what you saw, then I'll show you what I saw,' I said.

'What did you see?' LK said.

'I'll show you after he's shown me,' I said. 'Do it, Ronnie.'

'Wait,' LK said, and came to us. He put his hand on my shoulder. 'Good God, Emma, you really did that.'

'Take a seat, Ben, Tom, this won't take a moment,' I said. 'Help yourselves to the food if you like. The demon will be coming in a moment to take drinks orders.'

'This is it,' Ronnie said. 'Tell me if you need me to back off.'

He showed me, and LK hissed quietly behind me. I wasn't just a serpent; I was huge and black, my head brushing the ceiling. My eyes were as black as my scales, and I was covered in intimidating spikes over my head and down my back, with a frill around the back of my head instead of a cobra hood.

'Looks like a Serpent form of John's Turtle ...' I said, and my voice trailed off. I released Ronnie and fell to sit at the table, my head in my hands. 'Oh dear Lord, no.'

'More demonic than the Dark Lord,' Ronnie said. 'That thing was scary. Immeasurably big; I think it could take down the King easily. Immense destructive power, and so damn *dark* the centre of it was like

35

looking into the Abyss. Whatever you were, Lady Emma, it certainly scared the living shit out of me, and I'm big enough to sire spawn on a Mother.'

'You saw something too?' LK asked me.

I nodded into my hand.

'Are you concerned you're his Serpent?' Ronnie said, sitting next to me. 'Is that what this is about? I've heard stories.'

I wiped my eyes. 'If I'm his Serpent, then when he rejoins — well, that's it, isn't it? I'd be gone.'

'You're afraid of losing your identity into his?' Ronnie said.

'No, I'd welcome it,' I said. 'But for Simone, it would be the same as if I died. She'd gain him and lose me, and I'm like a mother to her. She's lost enough family members as it is. I really can't do it to her.'

'You may not have a choice,' Ronnie said.

I nodded.

'Show me what you saw,' LK said to me.

I raised my hands and each of them took one. I re-established the link and our minds touched.

LK was a human Immortal, not a Bodhisattva, so his soul didn't have the ringing purity of a Buddha, but he was connected to the Universe and one with Eternity. His soul smelled of mint-fresh shen energy, intertwined with constantly regenerating ching energy, tasting of firelight and summer heat. His chi enveloped both and moved with his breathing, full of the essence of sunshine and autumn leaves. His Immortal nature sang in tune with the Universe, and was at the same time as small as an atom and as vast as a galaxy.

'That I could attain such heights,' Ronnie said with awe.

'You have made the first step onto the Way,' LK said.

'It would take so long for me to travel there,' Ronnie said.

'You cannot travel to a Path, you are already on it,' LK said. 'And as you travel, time has less and less meaning. Eventually you are pure thought and time does not exist at all.'

Ronnie's essence was the dark roiling thickness of demon, but there existed strands within it of chi; he had cast off his nature and turned, and was attempting to attain humanity. He didn't taste of the foulness of demon; he was more like dark chocolate, deep and bitter, with the chi making sweeter and lighter strands through it. My heart went out to him; he'd turned hundreds of years before and still had achieved so little.

'Remember what I said. Time is an illusion,' LK said.

Ronnie nodded agreement inside my head.

I showed them what I'd seen when I walked in the door. I'd tasted LK's pure Shen nature and Ronnie's dark demon nature, made sour by his fear. I'd smelled Tom and Ben behind me; Tom's demon nature was similar to Ronnie's but in many ways different. Ronnie saw it as well and his mind glowed gold with the smell of spice and curiosity. Ben I saw as human; he was the only human there. Compared to LK his nature was earthy and rich, but he did have traces of something greater within him, like flashes of a deeper scent that came and went.

'You aren't supposed to be able to do that,' LK said.

'That's something I haven't heard anyone say in a very long time,' I said.

'No, Leo said it yesterday,' the stone said. 'And before you ask, I have no idea what you are.'

'You don't see people's souls, you taste them,' LK said. 'I've never seen anything like it. Usually we have a sight or sound analogue for the way we perceive the higher senses. Why are you experiencing them as smell and taste?'

'Probably because I'm a snake,' I said. 'We work off taste and smell more than anything; that's why we flick out our tongues all the time.'

'Snake?' Ben said weakly.

I released their hands and turned to speak to him. 'Many spirits on the higher plane are the essence of nature, weather and animals,' I said. 'Dragons, tigers, wolves, foxes — many types of animals. Reptiles as well, including turtles, dragons, and snakes like me.'

'Any cockroaches?' Tom said, amused.

'I'm glad we found you, Tom, you're smart and brave and have transcended your nature,' I said. 'Only demons take the form of insects; they're not intelligent enough to be Shen.'

'I'm starting to feel less and less like a freak all the time,' Tom said.

'Oh, we're all freaks, one way or another,' I said.

'Hear, hear,' LK said. 'Now that everybody's established how scary we all are, let's have a look at you, Tom.'

Tom's eyes widened and he sat back in his chair.

'Nobody's going to hurt you; we'll just look at you,' I said. 'No need to be concerned.'

I sat at the table and gestured around it. LK and Ronnie Wong could have been brothers: both appeared to be mid-thirties and were wearing plain white dress shirts and slacks and ugly plastic-rimmed glasses. 'LK Pak is the Wudang Mountain Demon Master; he's made an extensive study of the nature of demons. Ronnie Wong here is a Prince of Demonkind and exiled from Hell. He turned from the hosts of Hell and has aligned himself with the Celestial, but because of his nature and the strength of the seals he is still unable to enter Wudang uninvited.'

'I wouldn't go in anyway. One of your students might think I'm a threat,' Ronnie said with good humour.

'It is important at this point that you do not change to your demon form,' LK said to Tom. 'You would be destroyed.'

'I won't anyway,' Tom said. 'It tries to control me, and it thirsts for blood.'

I had a sudden horrible idea. 'Do either of you know a woman called Kitty Kwok?'

They both started and shared a look.

'I remember you mentioned a Kitty before, but it didn't click until you said it again,' Ben said. 'Not Kitty Kwok; she said her name was Kitty Ho, same as my wife's name. She came to visit us in Wales, said she was my wife's sister, and my wife welcomed her.' He grimaced. 'But the way they behaved wasn't like sisters at all. It was more like …' He hesitated.

Tom said it for him. 'Lovers.'

Ben nodded, his face full of misery.

'Did she ever experiment on you, Tom?' I said.

'Not that I know of,' Tom said.

'Did you have needle tracks?'

They shared another look.

'I accused him of taking drugs and he denied it,' Ben said. 'We had some huge arguments over it. He said he had no idea how the marks had got there.'

'Emma,' LK said, 'I hate to suggest this, but —'

'No,' I said.

'You wanted to find out what you are, ma'am,' he said.

'Don't even think about it,' I said. I rose and walked to the other side of the room. 'We are not going there.'

'What is it?' Ben said.

'Emma was filled with demon essence by Kitty Kwok and it turned her into a lamia, same as you, Tom. But she isn't half-demon like you; she is supposed to be all human —'

I spun to shout at him. 'I am all human! My mother has never cheated on my dad!' I turned away again. 'Don't even think it.'

They were silent. I turned back and saw LK's face.

'Oh, no, you don't,' I said. 'If you're talking to the Tiger about my blood samples you can stop right now. I was born in Australia. I'm not half-Chinese so I can't be half-demon. I resemble both my parents; it's obvious.'

'I wonder if they ever tried to hook you up with a demon?' Ronnie said.

Suddenly April's husband, Andy, was standing in front of me. I backed up until I was against the wall, breathing hard with loathing as he grinned at me, an expensive bunch of flowers in one hand and a set of car keys dangling from the other.

'Emma, it's okay, you're on the Mountain,' LK said.

I shook my head and snapped back. I was in the demon interview room on the periphery of the Mountain. I rubbed my hands over my face and returned to the table.

'What happened?' LK said.

'I had a flashback,' I said. 'Most severe one I've ever had.'

'PTSD?' Ronnie said.

I nodded, miserable.

'What's PTSD?' Vincent said.

'Post-traumatic stress disorder,' LK said. 'Used to be called shell shock. You have enough extremely bad things happen to you and your mind never completely recovers. I didn't know you suffered from this, Emma.'

'That's the first time it's happened in front of anyone else,' I said. 'Don't spread it around that I have this, please. I don't want anyone else to know about it.'

'Wouldn't dream of it,' Ronnie said. 'I have flashbacks myself. You go through enough, your brain keeps bringing it out and tormenting you with it because it can't make it go away.'

'You should both see someone,' LK said.

'I am,' I said.

'I've been studying human clinical psychology journals,' Ronnie said. 'I've even thought of studying psychiatry to add to my knowledge, but that would mean studying medicine and my physiology would come under scrutiny. Not a good idea.'

'That was a pretty severe flashback,' LK said.

'I remembered,' I said. 'I just saw Andy Ho ...' I stopped. 'I just saw Andy *Ho*, my friend April's husband. It was before he married her — I was back at the kindergarten, still working for Kitty Kwok. He was trying to date me, promising me all sorts of stupid stuff, claiming he was so rich and could give me a life better than anything I'd ever experienced. He was trying to give me a car.'

'But he was a demon,' LK said.

'He fathered a demon copy of Simone on April, and they generated a Mother copy of April as well,' I said. 'He was in league with Kitty.'

'Same name as my wife's family,' Ben said. 'Her name was Ho.'

'But you never mentioned him trying to date you before, Emma,' LK said.

'*I didn't remember*,' I said. 'I have no idea what the circumstances were around that flashback; I have no memory of him trying to date me. All I can remember is the terror and revulsion I felt towards him.' I shivered and hugged myself. 'Ugh, the idea of him even touching me freaks me out.'

'Some of the damage Kitty did to you may be permanent,' LK said. 'It's likely lost memories will continue to surface for the rest of your life.' He pulled a notepad and a pen towards him and flipped the pad open.

'They were filling me with demon essence in preparation for having a child with him,' I said. 'A child like Tom.' I turned to Ben. 'You and I have something in common; something that makes us different, and something these demons know about. I can't wait to find Kitty Kwok Ho Man Yee and have a very serious talk with her.'

'You need to track down whether you have any common ancestry or heritage and go find what it is,' LK said, scribbling notes on the pad.

'Where in Wales are you from?' I asked Ben.

'Cardiff, but my family originally came from the town of Holyhead. It's spelt "Holy" but pronounced "Holly". It's on an island off the west coast of Wales called Holy Island.'

'If that isn't the perfect name for the home of Shen then I can't think of one,' Ronnie said.

'I wonder where my ancestors came from,' I said.

'If they didn't come from the same place I will be very surprised indeed,' Ronnie said. 'I'd love to come along if you go. I've never been that far from my Centre and I'd like to see how long I could handle it.'

'Deal,' I said.

'Me too,' LK said, underlining a couple of points on his notes, then peering at Tom. 'If there's any new demons there, I want to see.'

'I'll take you,' Ben said. 'There are so many strange things on that island — ancient ruins, mystical stones — I'd love to show them to you.'

'Stone, find a week to clear in my diary,' I said. 'I have to go.'

'Give me some time to rearrange your appointments,' the stone said. 'Might be best to do it during term break.'

'Is there a village there? High up on a hill, with thatched cottages and lawns with low walls and flower gardens?' I said.

'No,' Ben said. 'There is a small group of houses high up on Holy Mountain, but no thatching any more, it's too expensive to maintain.'

'There really is a group of houses up on the mountain?' I said, incredulous.

'Yes. It's called Mountain,' Ben said.

'The village is called Mountain?'

'Welcome to Wudang Mountain,' LK said with humour, still taking notes. 'Which is also known as the Mountain.'

'So many coincidences,' Tom said.

'No such thing,' I said. 'Are you done yet, LK?'

'Nearly. This has been most interesting,' LK said, scribbling a few final points on the notepad.

Tom stared at LK. 'You've been examining me this whole time?'

'That I have,' LK said. He pushed the pad away and focused on Tom. 'You are fascinating, sir. If you don't mind, I'd like to have a brief look inside as well.'

'Inside?' Tom said.

'Inside your head,' I said. 'He'll flip through your thoughts and memories. It's an excellent way to see exactly what makes someone tick, but an unfortunate side effect is that they see everything else as well. You can't hide anything from them. You can trust LK to keep everything in confidence, but it's still up to you.'

'Dad?' Tom said.

Ben nodded. 'They might as well, son.'

'They'll see, Dad.'

Ben's expression darkened. 'And I don't think they'll be surprised. I'm not surprised myself any more. It's worth it if they can help you.'

Tom turned to LK. 'If you promise you won't share anything you see in me, you can do it.'

'I'll only share things that are directly related to your demon nature,' LK said. 'Other than that, you can trust me.'

He rose and moved to stand behind Tom. Tom stood up, but LK stopped him with a hand on his shoulder. 'Sit, relax. This won't hurt a bit.'

Tom sat back down and LK put his hands on either side of Tom's head, then raised his own face and closed his eyes, concentrating. Tom stiffened then relaxed. They remained silent for a while, then both grimaced at the same time.

'Sorry,' LK said. He released Tom's head, sat back down and scribbled some more notes.

Ben and Tom shared a look, and Tom shrugged.

What do you think they're hiding? the stone said. *I asked LK and he wouldn't tell me.*

Of course he won't, I said. *He gave his word. My guess is that she abused them and Ben's ashamed that he didn't protect his child from her.*

I see, the stone said. *What a horrible situation.*

LK pushed the notepad away. 'Go back to the apartment you rented in Hong Kong,' he said to Ben and Tom. He turned to me. 'Ma'am, provide them with an escort. It's quite likely that Kitty knows what's happened and may have an ambush set up for them.' He turned back to Ben and Tom. 'Gather all your belongings; you won't be going back there ever again. Then I suggest we find you a safe house somewhere on the Earthly, but well hidden. The Celestial is too dangerous for Tom. If he loses control over his demon nature he would be destroyed.' He shrugged. 'Perhaps one of the Follies?'

'The Follies are deserted, and human residents are returning; it would be too risky,' I said. 'How about one of the Twelve Villages?'

'Put them with the Rats,' LK said. 'They'd love to study Tom; it will open a whole new area of exploration for them.'

'Yeah,' I said. 'It might even inspire them to extend their intelligence beyond China's borders.'

'Rats?' Ben said.

'We have twelve villages in different parts of Asia, named for the twelve animals of the Chinese zodiac,'

44

I said. 'They aren't real rats, they're just people, and they specialise in intelligence gathering.'

'They're our spies,' LK said. 'They're based in Macau, in an urban area even though we call it a village. You'll be safe amongst the Rats; they have advanced security measures.'

Tell LK I'm hoping he's absolutely sure this kid isn't a plant, I said to the stone.

That's why I'm putting him with the Rats, LK said. *They'll handle him if he is. They'll be on their guard and actually hoping that he's one of these advanced copies.*

'Very well,' I said. 'LK, arrange the escort for the trip to the apartment, and I'll contact Rat Village and make the arrangements from this end.' I gestured towards the plates of Chinese vegetarian food that the demons had made for us, which had gone cold while we'd been talking. 'I'll have someone warm this up for us.'

A demon entered, bowed to us, and took a few of the plates off the table. Another demon took the teapot to fill it with fresh hot water.

'No chance of anything non-vegetarian, ma'am?' Ronnie said wistfully.

'Not on the Mountain, sorry,' I said.

'Do you mind sharing the info you just gathered?' Ronnie asked LK.

'Link up, I'll tell you,' LK said. They concentrated on each other and went quiet.

'So, tell me what kind of work you were doing while you were living here in Asia,' I said to Ben.

'I'm an engineer, aircraft systems,' he said. 'So I never had difficulty finding work anywhere we went —'

Simone appeared at the end of the room holding a large, black, flapping tortoise that sprayed muddy water in a wide arc with every movement.

'Emma, come up to the compound,' she said. 'I've found Daddy!'

'John?' I asked the turtle.

Simone was having trouble holding the struggling creature. 'It doesn't have any intelligence, it's just the animal.'

'Are you sure —'

'I know my own father!' she said. 'Now what do I do with him?'

'Meet me at the entrance to the Grotto,' I said.

'Oh, good idea,' she said, and disappeared.

'That was her father?' Ben said. 'I thought my wife was strange.'

'It gets better, I'm engaged to it.' I rose. 'I'd better head back up, she'll be waiting for me. Wait here for your escort, and I'll see you later when things have settled down.'

'I'll take it from here,' LK said. He picked up his chopsticks. 'Now, let's eat!'

'If you don't mind, Emma,' Ronnie said, 'I'll go find something a little more —'

'Carnivorous,' I said. 'I'll see you later.'

He saluted me and disappeared.

'Later, guys,' I said, and went out to jog up the winding trail that led back into the Mountain.

CHAPTER 4

Simone was standing outside the entrance to the Grotto, still holding the struggling turtle. 'I forgot you can't travel. His panic is easing but he's still fighting me.'

The Grotto entrance was a rock face on the hillside behind the Armoury, a plain grey wall of stone.

'Have you tried talking to him?' I said, putting my hand on the latch to make the wall disappear. The stone stairs down into the Grotto became visible as the rock faded.

'Yes, he's not replying. All that stuff with you and the Demon King and the demon essence must have really taken it out of him,' she said.

We started carefully down the steep stairs into the darkness.

'Where was he?' I said.

'Hanoi. There were reports of a giant tortoise that used to live in a lake there centuries ago — that it had returned. I had a free period so I wandered down there. God, it stinks — it's so polluted — but there he was, large as life. I couldn't believe it.'

'Can you do a light while you hold him?' I said.

She struggled to hold the tortoise with one arm around its shell, then made a ball of chi energy that floated to light the tunnel around us. 'Sorry, forgot you can't see in the dark.'

She hefted the tortoise in both arms again and we continued down. As we headed deeper into the Grotto, the air became colder. Condensation ran down the walls, making the steps slippery.

After two hundred metres, our breath formed fog and the air was still and bitterly cold. I jumped down the steps, trying to move faster to warm myself up. The tunnel opened into the cavern of the Grotto, so huge its walls and ceiling were invisible in the distance. The water before us shimmered in Simone's light. We stood on a ten-metre-wide ledge that jutted five metres into the underground lake. The lake itself was a kilometre long, two kilometres across and two kilometres deep, plunging into the core of the Mountain and making its centre water — fitting for the Xuan Wu.

The lake's fish came to the ledge, curious. They were three metres long, with white bodies and pink, lilac and blue fins, glowing with bioluminescence. One of them stuck its head out of the water and made gasping movements with its mouth, then spoke telepathically to us.

It's not feeding time, what's going on?

'This is Xuan Wu. I found him,' Simone said.

More fish appeared around the ledge, sticking their eyes out of the water with curiosity.

Put him in here with us, we'll look after him, the fish said. *Do you think he's hungry?*

'I'll be right back with some cat food for him,' Simone said. She lowered the tortoise carefully onto the wet black rock. 'Don't go anywhere, Daddy, this is your Mountain.' She put her hand on the back of his shell. 'Please stay here and come back to me.'

The tortoise walked clumsily to the edge of the water. He was sixty centimetres from nose to tail and, apart from his complete blackness and his feet instead of flippers, appeared to be an ordinary amphibious tortoise. He carefully slid into the water then poked his head out. The fish quickly moved back out of his reach. He ducked his head under the water and dived beneath the surface.

The fish that had spoken to us went under too, then came back up half a minute later. *He appears to be heading right to the bottom. We can't follow that deep.*

Simone dived into the water. *I'll see what he does.*

I sat cross-legged on the rock and waited.

Martin and Yue Gui, Simone's older brother and sister, came down the stairs and I stood.

'Yes, it's him,' Martin said. 'Can we go down and see?'

'Go right ahead,' I said.

They changed to tortoises, walked to the edge and slid into the water.

'Can you hear me?' I asked the fish.

Yes, it replied. *He's sitting right on the bottom, and the Princess is sitting with him. The other two are heading down as well; goodness, but they move fast.*

He's just sitting here with his eyes closed, Simone said.

Nothing happened for a couple of minutes.

They're coming back up, the fish said.

'Thanks,' I said.

No problem, ma'am.

'Do I know you?' I said. 'You sound familiar.'

The fish's voice sounded horrified. *Can't you tell who I am?*

'Sorry, no.'

I've been in your energy work classes since the school returned to the Mountain — that's a good six months now. You should know my voice; I've even spoken telepathically to you before. Its voice filled with humour. *I am mortally wounded.*

49

'If the wounds are mortal then please die quietly.'

The fish surged out of the water onto the rock and flopped around, splashing water everywhere. It opened and closed its mouth and its eyes rolled in agony.

'I said quietly.'

The fish stopped flapping, lay still for a moment, then rolled back into the water. It resurfaced and floated belly up without moving.

Simone, Martin and Yue Gui rose out of the water so that their feet were clear of it. The water ran out of their clothes, and they floated towards me, drifting to lightly land on the stone.

Simone glanced back at the fish. 'What happened? Is everything okay?'

The fish quickly flipped back upright and dived under the water.

'Is John still down there?' I said.

Simone nodded. 'He seems to have gone to sleep.'

'We can leave him there, bring him food; the fish will tell us if anything happens,' Martin said.

'Where did you find him?' Yue Gui said.

'There was this news report,' Simone said, 'about this lake in Hanoi that had a mystical giant tortoise living in it. The tortoise disappeared from the lake hundreds of years ago, but people claimed to have seen it in the last year — it seemed to have returned.'

'Ooooh,' Martin said, a drawn-out sound of understanding. 'I remember! Father got in so much trouble with the Jade Emperor, he was nearly thrown from Heaven.'

'What did he do?' I said.

'The Ming of China were planning to invade the Kingdom of the Viets — what is today Vietnam. Father didn't agree with their plans, so he took the form of a giant tortoise, and when the King of Vietnam was rowing for pleasure on the lake, Father surfaced and gave the King an enchanted sword that helped him to defeat the invading force.'

'Good Lord, he's the Lady of the Lake,' I said.

'Straight up,' Simone said.

'Did the King throw the sword back into the lake when the battle was done?' I said.

'Yes,' Martin said. 'It was Dark Heavens — of course Father wanted it back.'

'The parallels are crazy,' Simone said.

'No wonder he did his PhD thesis on Arthurian legends compared to his own,' I said. I shivered; the damp was seeping through my clothes and the long period of inactivity wasn't helping. 'Can we go back up? Do any of you want to stay here with him?'

'We can leave him; if he wakes the fish will tell us,' Yue Gui said. She linked arms with me. 'I hear you've had a busy day. Since we're here, we will definitely take you up on your generous offer of a Wudang Mountain luncheon.'

'How many times has Daddy nearly been thrown from Heaven anyway?' Simone said as we made our way back up the stairs. 'It seems to happen every ten years or so.'

'Sounds about right,' Martin said.

'Come to the Northern Heavens later this evening,' Yue Gui said over lunch in our private room attached to the officers' mess. 'Allow us to reciprocate by providing you with dinner, and you can inspect the rebuilding work on the Serpent Concubine Pavilion.'

'I can't tonight,' I said. 'Simone and I have a charity art auction on the Earthly. But I'll come in the next few days to have a look at the work on the Pavilion.'

'The Pavilion is gone and the gardeners have already moved in,' Yue Gui said.

'Do you have space for another gardener?' I said.

51

Martin unfocused, talking to the staff of the Palace, then snapped back. 'If he is strong and talented, then yes we do.'

'I have a Buddhist monk, a full Shaolin master — he fell from grace and worked as an assassin for a demon for a while,' I said. 'He's trying to return to the Path and needs employment.'

'Then the garden in the Palace is perfect,' Martin said.

'An assassin?' Yue Gui said with disdain. 'He should be incarcerated.'

'Kwan Yin has favoured him,' I said.

'Oh,' she said. 'Very well then.'

'He is sincere about redeeming himself,' I said. 'I can just see him attaining Enlightenment and then doing what they all do — coming straight back down to help the sorry rest of us, raking the gravel in the garden and imparting really cryptic koans.'

'How many Buddhas are there anyway?' Simone said.

'You have not studied the different Ages and their Buddhas?' Yue Gui said with surprise. 'Perhaps you should talk to Kwan Yin ... No, perhaps not.'

'Exactly. She says that numbers aren't meaningful and that I should find the Universe within myself,' Simone said. 'And that once I have embraced Unity, I will achieve Oneness with all of them.'

'They are pure thought when they are not assisting us,' Martin said. 'And thoughts cannot be numbered. They exist outside of this reality and are uncountable. So the answer to your question as to the number of Buddhas is: the answer is not meaningful.'

'I became more interested in the whole thing when Emma came back and told us about the Second Platform,' Simone said. 'But right now, I think coming to terms with the Tao is more important anyway.'

'You are lucky. You have Grand Masters on the

Mountain who can teach you in the ways of alchemy, internal energy work and self-cultivation to achieve Immortality. All of the different paths are laid out before you.'

Simone looked down at her food. 'The path I most want to travel is the one with my whole family waiting for me at the end of it.'

'We're nearly there,' I said. 'We're all here on the Mountain. It won't be long.'

'Why are you returning to the Earthly tonight?' Martin said. 'You are established here now, Emma, you don't need to sully yourself with Earthly activities.'

'And we just talked about Buddhas from the higher plane coming down to help us,' Simone said. 'As long as there are children being abandoned in China because they're either girls or disabled, I'll be down there helping them.'

'We both will,' I said. 'We have a long list of service organisations that we help out. Orphans, micro loans for small businesses, prisoners of conscience —'

'Political prisoners? That's perilously close to interfering in political matters,' Yue Gui said, tapping the table with her fingertips. 'You know we can't have anything to do with the way that humans choose to run their governance.'

'I haven't been warned yet, and until I am I'm continuing,' I said. 'We still have the apartment on the Peak, and we use it as a base of operations.'

'Sounds like you ladies are on a mission,' Martin said with humour.

'You could say that,' Simone said.

'Is John still there?' I said.

Their eyes unfocused, and they all came back and nodded at the same time.

Simone checked her watch. 'I have to go back to school.' She rose and kissed Martin and Yue Gui on the cheek, then turned to me. 'Are we free tomorrow night to have dinner at the Northern Heavens?'

'Tomorrow's Nanna and Pop,' I said. 'How about after Michael and Clarissa's engagement party?'

'It's a date,' Yue Gui said, pleased. 'Make Leo come this time as well; he is family.'

Martin concentrated on Yue Gui and they shared a telepathic communication. Yue Gui bent over the table and spluttered with laughter. 'Never mind. Di Di just told me why Leo's staying away from the North right now, and it's an excellent reason.'

'Do I want to know?' Simone said.

'You are very perceptive,' Martin said. 'And the answer to your question is: no.'

'See you later then,' Simone said, and disappeared.

Martin leaned his elbows on the table and put his face in his hands. He looked up at me and his eyes were dark with emotion. 'Hurry up and push him past the basics. I miss him horribly.' He leaned back and rubbed his hands over his eyes. 'Telling him to stay away was one of the hardest things I've ever done.'

I felt a rush of sympathy for him. 'Do you think he feels the same way?'

Martin leaned forward again and shook his head without looking up. 'It is not me but the one I resemble that he wants. But I am happy to be a surrogate for as long as he will let me.'

Yue Gui put her hand on Martin's. 'Oh, Di Di, I did not know. You should withdraw from this, you will only suffer.'

'This separation while he masters energy was a trial for me, to see if I was strong enough to end it,' he said. 'I failed. I don't want to be apart from him.' He shrugged. 'It's better to enjoy what I have than to deny myself altogether, isn't it? He's happy, I'm happier with

54

him than when I'm not, so I will let the future take care of itself and enjoy the present.'

'Does he know?' I said.

'Of course he does. He hopes that I will tell him not to come back because he knows exactly how I feel.'

'I'm counting on you to bring him round so that when John returns with enough intelligence, Leo won't want to be drained by him,' I said.

'It is a losing battle.'

Leo drove us to the Convention Centre that evening, with Michael in the front seat next to him. Simone and I sat in the back.

We all headed up to the main area together, to be greeted by David Hawkes, the taipan of one of the biggest multinationals in Hong Kong, and his wife, Bridget. David was one of the younger taipans, being only in his early forties, and one of the most talented members of the company family to come up through the ranks in a while. He was very tall due to his Scottish heritage, but his grandmother had been Chinese, giving him dark hair and eyes. Like most long-term Hong Kong residents he spoke with an accent that was a mix of English and American. Bridget Hawkes was small and slender with bright red hair. She appeared elegant and relaxed in her made-to-measure tailored suit, but I'd competed against her in dressage up at the Jockey Club and she was a fiendishly good rider on her massive warm-blood mare.

'Good to see you, ladies and gentlemen,' David said. He moved closer to speak softly to me. 'There's something strange going on here. Can you check it out?'

'What sort of strange?'

'There's this woman ... she wanders through the place with these men following her, and wherever she goes, everybody falls in love with her. Do you think she might be,' his voice dropped even further, 'a demon?'

'You see demons around every corner, David,' I said with amusement.

He smiled down at me. 'Wishful thinking, I know.' He glanced behind me and his smile widened. 'You didn't tell me you were bringing John!'

He strode past me and I turned to see. It was John, in his Mountain uniform, his expression puzzled.

I quickly moved to stop David. 'He may have amnesia. Let me talk to him first.'

I went to John and gazed into his eyes, putting one hand on his arm. He looked down at me without recognition. 'John, it's me, Emma. Do you know who I am?'

'What am I doing here?' he said.

I turned and called quietly to Simone. She was talking to Bridget about the function, oblivious that her father had entered. When she saw him, she rushed over to us. 'Daddy!'

John still appeared confused. 'Simone?'

'Let's take him over to the side and sort this out,' Leo said, looking around to ensure we hadn't attracted too much attention. A couple of people were watching with curiosity but hadn't approached.

David put his hand on my shoulder and spoke in my ear. 'Take him downstairs to the lobby level next to the harbour. All the shops there are closed and it'll be deserted. I'll cover for you.'

'Thanks, David.' I took John's arm. 'John, you need to come with us.'

John looked from me, to Simone, to Leo, then Michael, obviously made the decision and nodded.

We took him in the lift down to the small shopping mall under the Convention Centre. Floor-to-ceiling windows on one side looked onto an open area containing a large gilt statue of a bauhinia flower. A row of convenience stores, all closed for the evening, stood across from the glass. We found a bench and I sat next to John, with Simone on his other side. I took his hand. I wanted to give him a huge hug but was wary of scaring him away. Michael and Leo took up positions on either side of us, guarding.

Simone leaned on his shoulder. 'It's good to have you back, Daddy.'

'Simone. Your name is Simone,' he said. He looked at me, still confused. 'Michelle?'

'Oh, God,' Simone said quietly.

'No, it's fine,' I said. 'I'm Emma, John.'

'Emma?' He looked up at Michael and Leo. 'Lion? Tiger?' He looked at me again. 'Snake?'

'Welcome to your family,' I said with amusement. 'The Turtles are still in the Northern Heavens.'

'I don't remember anything,' he said, running his hand over his forehead. 'My name is John?'

'Your name is Xuan Wu,' Simone said. 'Emma calls you John.'

'That's not a very auspicious name — dark and war together,' he said.

'That's your nature: dark and war.' She threw her arms over his shoulders. 'And you're my father.'

He put his arms around her. 'That I know. That's something that will never change.' He took a deep breath into her shoulder. 'You're my little girl.'

'Daddy,' she said, muffled by his jacket.

He pulled back. 'I don't remember anything! Why do I see them as big cats, and her as a snake? Why do you glow with stars and darkness and blue and gold? How come I can see the past and the future and the world around me clearer than just vision? Why do I want to drown everything in ice-cold water and bring death to all?' His voice gained a frantic edge. 'What am I?'

'You're a god,' I said. 'You're the God of the North, and dark, and cold, and winter, and martial arts.'

'If I'm a god then how come I don't remember?' he said, challenging me, his hands still protectively on Simone.

'Do you trust me?' I said.

'You can trust her,' Simone said.

He studied me for a long time, his arms still around Simone. His eyes roamed my face. Then he nodded once, sharply. 'I can trust you.'

Simone exhaled with relief.

'Then trust me that you don't need the details right now of why you can't remember. It's a very long story. Just come home with us and we'll fill you in.'

His eyes unfocused. 'Something unbalanced is coming.'

'He's right, Emma,' Simone said urgently. 'Something very nasty is heading our way ...'

Kitty Kwok, flanked by two big Chinese bodyguards, came around the corner and stopped in front of us. I rose to face her, standing protectively in front of John and Simone. Leo and Michael moved behind me, mirroring Kitty's bodyguards behind her.

This is a good time to grab her and give her to the King, Leo said. *Get this done and finished.*

I nodded slightly. He was right. I summoned the Murasame but nothing happened; the sword didn't come.

'What have you done?' I said.

'Nothing. I just want to negotiate.' She raised her hands. 'I know what the King said. I want to offer you a deal.'

'Nice to be taken seriously for a change,' I said.

I didn't look away from Kitty and heard rather than saw John move to stand behind me on the left. He touched me on the shoulder and said, *I'm right behind you, but I don't know enough. Speak for me.*

I nodded.

'I offer parley under terms of truce,' Kitty said.

Well, that was the grabbing option blown out of the water. It would be dishonourable to attack her when she'd offered parley and waved a theoretical white flag.

'Speak your mind,' I said, using the formal words to close the deal.

She relaxed slightly and turned to pace in front of us. 'You've vowed never to hurt a human, Emma. But you've agreed to give me to them. Would you betray your own kind and give a human to the demons?'

'You forfeited all claim to humanity when you harmed innocent children to prolong your own life,' I said.

'I think that makes me particularly human,' she said with humour. 'Ask your Mr Chen here, he'll tell you.'

'Demons are often stunned by the depths of atrocity that humans are capable of,' John said without emotion. 'In the ways of cruelty, they often seek to learn from you.'

'I'm one hundred per cent human,' Kitty said. 'Ask him, he'll tell you. You can't do anything to me, Emma. You can't give me to them — that goes against everything both of you stand for. You keep humans safe from demons; you don't hand them over for the demons to play with.'

I was silent at that. She was right. I pulled myself together. 'Name your terms.'

'You've agreed to give me to the King. He's already paid for me. But if he's destroyed, you don't need to pay the price.'

'The last thing we need right now is a civil war in Hell,' I said. 'He may be a two-faced bastard, but at least he doesn't create demons that are self-aware, think they're human and are programmed to turn — like the ones your friend the Death Mother is making. Such things are cruel beyond belief.'

'Not my doing,' Kitty said. 'I'm only after Immortality; I don't want to destroy anybody. I've never hurt your students. I've stayed quietly in my corner doing my stuff. It's not my fault that I scare the living shit out of the King.'

'You're nice and humble now your little posse's gone,' I said.

'Destroy the King and I'll set up a replacement. I have one ready to go; he's intelligent, powerful and does what I tell him. Do this for me and I'll put a King on the throne who will never bother you again. You'll no longer have the forces of Hell breathing down your neck, killing your Celestials and harming your little human students.'

'You want to set a puppet on the throne of Hell?' I said.

She gestured with impatience. 'I don't want to rule Hell. I just want to be left alone to succeed with my Immortality and then live my life in peace! I've never wanted any of you dead; I just want to be left alone.'

'Gloria Ho,' I said. 'Andy Ho. The Death Mother. Before that, Six, and the Geek, and Simon Wong. Don't tell me you won't try to kill us, Kitty; you and your friends haven't stopped trying. You've been the leader of this all along, so don't play the innocent. You want to put a puppet on the throne of Hell and then try to take over the Earthly Plane as well.'

She raised her arms to the side. 'This is a waste of time. Get me out.'

The two bodyguards transformed into humanoid demons with black scales and tusks. All three of them disappeared.

'Whoa!' Simone said. 'They were demons? I saw them as human.'

'Me too,' Leo said, and Michael nodded agreement.

'Did you see them as demons or human, John?'

I said, turning to see him, but he'd disappeared. 'Is he all right, Simone?'

'Daddy went back to the Grotto,' Simone said. 'He seemed totally confused by the whole thing.'

'It was strange my sword didn't come to me,' I said. 'Kitty must have been blocking it somehow, which is very disturbing.' I raised my hand and summoned the sword and it still didn't come. 'Are you having the same problem?'

Simone raised her hand and Dark Heavens appeared in it. She dismissed it. 'I have no trouble calling my sword.'

'You haven't called the Murasame since you lost your demon essence,' Leo said.

'You're right,' I said. 'Maybe it doesn't serve me any more. Maybe it went back to the King?'

'After this, we'll head back to the Mountain and ask Miss Chen,' Simone said. She ran her hands through her hair and fluffed it out over her shoulders. 'Let's go upstairs and raise some money for these poor kids.'

CHAPTER 5

We made our way back up in the lift to the floor above. The speeches had started, and we slipped in at the back to watch. Michael nodded to Leo, then went to the side table and grabbed a tray of drinks for us.

About halfway through David's welcoming speech, a deep vibration thrummed through the floor beneath us. Water hissed for a couple of seconds, then stopped. There was silence from the crowd, then a few giggles and confused conversation. Nothing else happened so David continued his speech.

Oh my God, Emma, look out the window, Simone said.

I glanced left and stared. The sky and the other side of the harbour had gone. There was just a wall of blackness next to us, as high as the fifteen-metre windows. Its slightly curved vertical surface shifted like liquid in the reflected light of the Convention Centre.

David continued his speech, but people next to the window began moving away. More people noticed, and the chatter became louder and gained a frightened edge.

'Don't worry, it's just an optical illusion,' David said, frantically waving me towards the podium. 'It happens sometimes when there's an inversion layer over the water, because of the change in seasons. It's an atmospheric anomaly, that's all. Don't bother taking photos; you won't capture anything because it's not really there — it's something like a mirage.'

'What is it?' I asked Simone, waving back to David to indicate that I'd be there in a minute.

'It's just water,' Simone said. 'A wall of water. Not an optical illusion.'

'Your dad?'

'No. Only water. It might be elementals playing around, but I can't sense any.' She moved closer to the glass and concentrated. 'No intelligence behind it.' She cocked her head. 'Why is it doing that?'

I walked towards the podium to reassure David, and some of the people nearby reacted loudly. A lump two metres across had emerged from the wall and was following me. I took a couple more steps towards David and the ball paced me. I continued and a snake's head, at least a metre across, shot out of the water and slammed its snout into the window glass with a wet crack. People screamed and scurried away from the glass.

I stopped and turned to face the snake. Something in its eyes called to me and I raised one hand, desperately wishing I could touch it. It pushed its head more slowly towards me and came through the glass as if it wasn't there. It touched its snout to my hand and time stopped. We hung suspended in the moment, touching snake to snake. The world spiralled away from me and the water rose up to meet me, its darkness filled with the immeasurable cold intelligence of the Serpent. It pulled its head back, nodded to me, and spun to disappear back into the wall of water.

The water collapsed, sending a black surge against the glass and then subsiding.

I jogged up to the podium to speak in David's ear. 'Pretend that was part of the show, courtesy of Chencorp, please. Nobody's in danger.'

David raised his hands and spoke loudly over the PA system. 'Ladies and gentlemen, a round of applause for the special three-dimensional installation courtesy of Chencorp, one of the patrons for this evening. That was a one-off display of the installation before it is dismantled for a world tour, a demonstration of some of today's most advanced holographic technology.' He dropped his voice. 'How's that?'

'Absolutely perfect. I owe you.'

There was scattered applause through the room, then people surged forward and applauded me loudly, discussing the snake and water. I patted David on the shoulder and turned to go back down.

'Wait,' he said. 'What if something like that happens again?'

'Just say it's an encore,' I said.

He shrugged. 'Turnout will be double next time we have a charity opening.'

'All good for the kids,' I said, and went back down to Simone and the men.

Before the auction we wandered around the paintings. Simone showed me a Western-style oil painting of a group of running horses, one of them palomino.

'I like this one. Do you think it would look good in my room?'

'Which room — on the Peak or at home?' I said.

'At home. It's too big for the Peak, it's a metre across. It would look good in the living room in my apartment on the Mountain.'

Leo studied the painting. 'This isn't terribly well done, you know. You only want to buy it because it looks like Freddo.'

She nodded a reply.

'He should pay for it to compensate you for destroying

the carpet and making you move out while it was replaced,' Michael said.

'Pay with what?' Simone said.

'A promise not to pee on the carpet in future would be a good start,' Leo said.

'Oh geez,' Simone said softly, looking behind me, then quickly went to another painting, Michael and Leo trailing her.

I turned to see what had spooked them and nearly sighed with dismay. It was George Wilson, taipan of one of the big shipping companies. He was a good head taller than me and nearly the same around, carrying a large glass of scotch leaning against his stomach and a predatory grin above his double chins.

'Here's the girl in charge,' he said too loudly, surrounding me in a cloud of alcohol. 'Running the business by yourself, real executive woman. You can be in charge of me any day, honey.' He moved closer and I backed away. He leaned into me and his breath made my eyes water. 'I bet you just love showing your good-looking bodyguards how you're in charge.'

Simone stormed to us and glared at him. 'You're drunk, George, and you're making inappropriate comments to my stepmother.'

He grinned at her. 'Look at Missy being the boss. I bet your Michael-boy likes you being the boss.' His grin grew into a leer. 'You're growing up fast, honey.'

'This is sexual harassment!' Simone said.

'Oh, Simone, really,' he said, spreading his arms and spilling his drink on the carpet. 'I'm just having a bit of fun — don't go all feminazi on me. Don't take offence when I'm just joking around. I haven't even touched you.'

'Touch me and I'll break your arm,' she said, and walked stiffly back to Michael and Leo.

'You need to teach her, Emma, or she'll end up one of these radical feminists who think they know better than men; ugly and bossy and no man'll be interested in her,' George said. He sidled closer to me. 'So do you have a new man in your life yet? Peter Tong keeps boasting he's dating you, but I don't believe it.'

'I'm not looking, thanks, George,' I said.

'No such thing as a woman who isn't looking. Tell you what.' He moved so we were side by side facing the art. 'My wife's gone to South Africa for a couple of weeks. Why don't you come over? I have some fantastic art at my place.' He turned to me and grinned broadly. 'Why don't you pop over, have a drink, maybe lunch ... or dinner ... take a look?'

I shook my head. 'I'm not really that interested in art. I think I'll go catch up with Simone. Later, George.'

He waved his drink at me. 'Don't be a stranger, darling. Has to be hard running that big company without any help.'

I rejoined Simone, Leo and Michael, who were forcedly discussing a garish abstract canvas.

'Why are you so polite to him?' Simone said. 'Why don't you just tell him where to go?'

Leo bent to speak softly to me. 'You should, Emma. He'll only respect you if you tell him to his face. Being polite is only giving him ammunition.'

'Being rude would give him even more ammunition,' I said. 'There's really no way of dealing with a man like that. I didn't agree to go to his house to see his "art" while his wife's away, so he's probably labelled me already.'

'He invited you to his house?' Michael said, aghast.

'You should tell his wife!' Simone said.

'She knows all about it,' I said. 'She just puts up with it because that's the way he is. She went to South Africa to get away from him for a while.'

We watched as George joined another group, one that held his personal assistant. He placed his hand around her waist then casually drifted it lower. She stiffened, obviously uncomfortable, but didn't move away.

Simone shivered. 'She should sue him for sexual harassment.'

'This is the Earthly Plane, Simone. If she did that, he'd make sure she never worked anywhere again. She'd get a bad reputation and be unemployable. These women stay in the job for a year, he gives them a glowing reference, and they go on to something well-paid and worthwhile.'

'That is so wrong,' Simone said. 'All those other people are standing around talking as if it isn't happening.'

'Go to the lectures at CH about power and dominance,' Michael said. 'They're fascinating.'

'I stayed away because I'm not interested in either,' Simone said. 'But I think I will now.'

David Hawkes approached us again and towered over me. 'Emma, do you mind if I have a quiet word?'

I nodded and we went to the side together. He gestured towards a seat placed facing the windows and we sat.

'George Wilson is telling everybody that you're a lesbian,' David said with humour. 'Just thought you'd like to know.'

I shrugged. 'I'm not surprised. I turned him down.'

'I wanted to ask you about Taoist philosophy. If all that stuff is real, then it's worth pursuing.' He gestured with his chin towards Leo. 'Taoist Immortal. Who would have believed it? Everybody's asking who his plastic surgeon is.'

'Leo didn't attain the Tao, though, he was Raised by the Jade Emperor.'

David let his breath out in a long gasp. 'Damn. The Jade Emperor. And I thought meeting the President of the United States was cool. So tell me about pine nuts and spring water.'

'You've been doing some research?'

'There isn't much in English. You have the word straight from the source — so, how do you do it?'

I shrugged. 'I haven't done it so I don't know.'

'Is there anyone I can ask?'

'Do what?' Bridget said from where she'd approached behind us.

David turned and smiled at her. 'Emma's an expert on Taoist philosophy. I was asking her about it.'

She studied him carefully, her expression severe, then relaxed, and I did too.

'I noticed you've been reading up on Taoism — you bought a lot of books,' she said. 'Are you thinking of converting?'

'You don't convert to Taoism, it's not really a religion ...' I began, then changed tack. 'It's not an exclusive religion, anyway. Many Taoists are also Buddhists; it's more like a spiritual philosophy than a religion. Taoists want to achieve Immortality, but once they've done that, they'll go on to try to attain Enlightenment and become a Buddha. They don't have a god as such ...' I changed direction again. 'Or a single, all-powerful jealous god that doesn't like you worshipping anyone else. It's more about finding yourself and where you fit in the universe. Because when you know who you are, and where you are, and what you are, the rest of Reality just slots into place and you find yourself attuned to it — able to see it and affect it as much as it affects you.'

'I have good reason to believe that what Taoists teach — about achieving Immortality — is true,' David said to Bridget.

She studied him for a long moment. 'As long as it doesn't interfere with anything else, I suppose.'

'I take it that means I'm not allowed to go to the top of a mountain and exist on pine nuts and spring water any time soon,' he said with a grin.

She tapped him on the shoulder. 'Don't you dare. I need help taking the boys to soccer on the weekend.'

David rose. 'I'll ask you more about it later, Emma.'

'It's traditional for a Taoist to fulfil his or her duty, then pursue the Tao,' I said. 'Raise a family, see to their wellbeing, then take themselves off, as you said, to the top of a mountain.'

'I was thinking Spain for our retirement, actually,' Bridget said. 'I don't think there are any mountains there.'

'Pyrenees darling, best skiing on the Continent,' he said. 'You can retire to caring for our visiting grandchildren, and I'll study Taoist philosophy.'

She grimaced theatrically. 'Grandchildren? Don't wish that on me yet, Phillip's only fourteen.' She gestured towards the podium. 'The bidding starts soon, honey, better get up there and do your stuff.'

David nodded to me and straightened his suit. 'Duty calls, Emma, let's see some money raised for these kids.' He held his hand out and I shook it.

Bridget smiled. 'Go do your thing, Mr Hawkes, and Ms Donahoe and I will discuss the best places to retire.'

He bent and kissed her on the cheek. 'Don't bother asking her, I don't think she'll share hers.' He winked at me and strode away.

'Please don't set him on a path that will ruin his family,' Bridget said mildly without looking away from David, who was loping up onto the dais. 'I need him.'

'Don't worry, Bridget, I have too much respect for you to do anything like that,' I said, also watching David as he introduced the auctioneer. 'I'll give him the information he asks for, but I know that his family needs him.'

She turned, quickly hugged me and kissed my cheek. 'Thanks, Emma.'

The auctioneer moved up to the lectern and David returned to the floor to sit in front of the bidders.

'We're up,' I said to Bridget. 'Time to spend some money.'

When the auction was over, most of the guests hung around chatting, but Simone had spent a long day in school and we decided to head home to the Peak. We'd return to the Mountain in the morning after she'd rested. We paid for the parking at the shroff office under the Convention Centre and made our way to the car. Our footsteps echoed eerily in the car park; there weren't many other people around.

A loud bang reverberated around the concrete walls. There was a horrible wet splat sound and Michael staggered. Someone was shooting at us.

I quickly raised my arms and summoned chi armour, which snapped into existence around me. Then I grabbed Michael and headed for the car. Leo threw himself out of the wheelchair, wrapped himself around Simone and pushed her towards the car as well.

'Get low and run alongside the wall!' Leo shouted.

A bullet hit my chi armour in the middle of my back and I staggered at the impact. There was a metallic ping as the bullet hit the concrete, its energy spent. Another bullet hit the floor behind us and shards of concrete sprayed across the back of my legs.

I half-pushed, half-dragged Michael towards the car, squeezing between the backs of parked cars and the wall. When we got there, I dragged him to the side and propped him against the concrete. My chi armour disintegrated; it would only hold for a minute at most and I'd done well to keep it around me that long.

'Come on, Simone!' Leo said, his voice full of urgency. 'Disable that thing.'

'What?' Simone said.

'Someone's shooting at us,' Michael said through his teeth. 'I'm hit, I can't ... I'm sorry.'

He slid down the wall of the car park to sit, pulling me down with him. I pulled his jacket away and wrenched open his dress shirt; he'd been hit in the abdomen just below his ribs. Leo took off his tuxedo jacket and held it out to me. I wadded it into a rough pad and shoved it into Michael's shirt.

'Oh, shit, I didn't realise,' Simone said. 'Give me a second ...' She hissed a long breath. 'There are four enormous Snake Mothers out there, and they're headed straight for us.'

'Stop talking and disable that gun!' Leo said.

'I can't see it,' Simone said. 'Michael ...' She knelt next to us and peered into his face. 'How bad is it?'

'I can't heal it,' Michael said, gasping. 'There's a lot of damage.'

One of the Mothers called from the centre of the car park lane: 'Come out and play, little humans. We want to see what you can do.'

'You take Emma, I'll take Michael,' Leo told Simone. 'Let's get them out of here.'

Simone put her hand on my arm and concentrated again. 'Blocked,' she said. She moved her head from side to side. 'I think one of Six's stones is in here somewhere.'

David Hawkes's voice called out from the edge of the car park. 'Emma, are you here? Emma, they say there's a gas leak —'

The gun went off again and Bridget shrieked. I crawled towards the end of the car to see: David was lying on the ground, and he looked dead. Bridget stood over him, mouth open, frozen and screaming. Then they shot her too and she fell next to him, whimpering with pain.

'They killed humans,' Leo said.

'What do you want?' I called. 'Don't kill anybody. Let's do a deal.'

'They're fine, they're alive,' one of the Mothers said, her voice hissing. 'We're not One Two Two, we're honourable demons. We just want you, Emma. Come on out and we'll let the others go.'

Simone's head shot up and her eyes unfocused. She shook her head violently, grimacing with distaste, then appeared to give in.

'What?' I said. 'Who's talking to you?'

'Your stone,' she said. 'Through your touch. Michael, Emma, hold still, this is worth a try.'

She reached towards Michael, slipped her hand inside his shirt, then pulled it out covered in blood. She quickly turned to me and swiped her hand across my face. I put my hand up to stop her, but too late.

'What the hell, Simone?' I started, then I tasted it. Michael's blood tasted of Shen: warmth, sunshine and fresh air full of an icy fizz and mown grass. It poured into me and something dark and strong grew. I rose to stand and the power sang inside me with a deep bass rolling surge.

I pulled Leo up with one hand so he was standing next to me. 'You and me, Lion, let's go get them. When you have a good view of them, try your new shen energy.' I glanced at him. 'You've been abstaining, right?'

'What happened to you, Emma?' Simone said.

'I have no idea,' I said, the power growing and roaring, making me bigger, wider, darker and much, much meaner. 'But it worked.'

Leo stared at me. 'Yeah, I've been abstaining. What have you been doing?'

'Tasting the blood of a child of Shen,' I said, my voice deeper than it normally was. 'Call your sword, it's time for some reckoning. David and Bridget didn't deserve that.'

I put my hand out and demanded that the Murasame obey me. It appeared in my hand, then grew slightly to fit me.

'Am I in some sort of Celestial Form?' I said.

'No, you're just … taller,' Simone said.

'Stay here. Stay back.'

Leo called his sword, the Black Lion, and flanked me on my left shoulder. I walked around the front of the car into the centre of the lane. I smelled the demons before I saw them. The earthy rich scent of human blood from David and Bridget was a nagging distraction on the edge of my senses, but these demons needed to die.

They shot at me, but I saw the bullet slide slowly towards me and easily evaded it. The four Mothers stood in front of a van in human form: tall, sleek, beautiful women. One of them had a modern assault rifle, but I didn't recognise the type; time to ask the Mountain staff about firearms training so I knew what I was up against. She shot at me again, and again I easily evaded it; obviously not an automatic weapon.

The range of effects I could accomplish with my black chi scrolled inside my head. It was an incredibly useful tool and I could achieve so much with it. I hoped I'd remember the list when I came down off this insane blood high.

I moved into a long defensive stance, held the Murasame horizontally above my head with the point towards the demons, put some black chi into it and shot it at the demon with the gun. She exploded. The other three Mothers backed up, intimidated.

'Who's the boss?' I said. 'I see you all as about the same size.'

73

One of them summoned a slender Chinese sword and rushed us. Leo hit her with a ball of shen energy sixty centimetres across and she exploded.

'Nice,' I said.

'Thanks.'

The two Mothers remaining changed to True Form and summoned weapons. The one on the left took a polearm; the one on the right, a two-handed battleaxe.

'Stay back,' I said. 'These ones are mine.'

I ran to them and swung the Murasame in a wide circular stroke towards the one on the left, dodged easily under her weapon and cut her in half. Ordinarily a swing like that was an invitation for a skewering, but I moved so fast she didn't have a chance. I turned to the last one, pulled some demon essence out of her into the ecstatically vibrating Murasame and bound her.

'Right,' I said, as casually as I could. 'Who sent you?'

She relaxed and concentrated, and something to the left of me in a corner of the car park pinged loudly.

I raised my left hand and pulled it towards me: it was a pebble, one of Six's stones. This was what was blocking teleportation and telepathy inside the car park. It flew into my hand and I crushed it; the blocking ceased.

Leo went to David and Bridget and knelt to check them.

'A buttload of big Celestials are on their way,' I said to the demon. 'You can turn if you like; or you can tell me who sent you and why, and I'll spare you. Do neither and I'll suck the life out of you and put you in my demon jar.'

'The Death Mother sent me,' she said urgently. 'She wants you dead. She knows you've made a pact with the King to take Kitty Kwok to him. It's only a matter of time before you know where she is, and she won't have Kitty's protection any more.'

'You're here because she's scared,' I said. 'Good. She has reason to be. Where's her base?'

She shook her head, mute.

I put my left hand around her throat and lifted her. A small part of me whistled with admiration at me doing this to a level eighty-three Mother.

'Holy shit, Emma,' Leo said softly from behind me.

The Mother's eyes bugged out and I enjoyed the show as I throttled her. 'Where's. Her. Base?'

'I don't know!' she gasped. 'One of the other Mothers organised this — I don't know where Forty-Four's base is. That's the truth, you can see it!'

It was the truth. I released her slightly.

'I told you who sent me; you vowed to spare me.'

'That I did,' I said, my hand still around her throat. 'The only one who'll be able to change you back is the Demon King himself. Good luck going to see him; he may not be as merciful as I am.' I sent some black chi into my hand, pumped it into her and changed her into a cat. I stroked the top of her head and released her. 'Go find a rat to eat.'

I sighed. I shouldn't have destroyed all of the Mothers; the last one hadn't given me any information that I didn't already know. I heard footsteps behind me: Simone, with Michael leaning heavily on her. I turned and smiled at their shocked expressions.

'We have people on their way,' Simone said. 'Are you okay?'

'Just fine,' I said, going to David and Leo.

Leo had loosened David's shirt collar and was checking him for injuries. 'He's been hit in the abdomen. Bridget's been shot in the leg.'

Bridget was lying panting on the ground, her eyes wide and glazed.

'Simone, get me a pad to put on David's bleeding,' Leo said.

'I can't, I'm flat out telling them where we are,' Simone said.

'Bridget,' I said, and she focused on me. 'Tell me your home phone number and your domestic helper's name. We'll take you to hospital, but we need to tell your boys that you're all right and you'll be late home.'

'We need to call an ambulance,' Bridget said. She howled with pain. 'God, it hurts!'

'Help is coming but we need to fix up your boys,' I said.

She reeled off a mobile phone number. 'Rosalinda's our helper. She's at home with them right now.'

'Stone, can you relay through someone?' I said.

'We're underground, Emma,' Simone said. 'I'm in touch with Gold and he's sending the message.'

Bridget groaned and lay back on the floor. I moved to hold her head in my lap and her hand in mine while Leo looked after David, who was still unconscious.

'God, hurry with the ambulance, any pain relief, please,' Bridget said.

I used the contact I had with her hand and worked through her meridians, easing the pain.

She panted again and turned her head to see me. 'What did you do?'

'Magic,' I said, but the buzz was leaving me and I was beginning to feel weak. I could barely hold myself upright where I sat.

I turned to Simone. 'Are they close?'

Meredith and Liu appeared behind her.

'Do you want us to drop them at a human hospital or take them with us?' Meredith said.

'Take them with us,' I said. 'David knows all about it; Bridget doesn't. But they were shot by demons so we'll have to check the wounds and make sure they weren't contaminated with essence.'

Meredith pulled Michael's shirt open and examined

him. 'Let's get all of these people to the infirmary.' She leaned towards me. 'Are you all right? You look terribly drained.'

'I changed, went bigger,' I said. 'I'm coming down off it now.'

'I see,' Meredith said. She looked up at Liu. 'Let's get them home.'

'Leo, human male; Meredith, human female,' Liu said. 'I'll take Michael; Simone take Emma.'

The car park disappeared.

We arrived at the infirmary and the staff rushed to help us. I leaned against the nearest wall, but it was moving behind me.

'Something's wrong with Emma,' Simone said loudly as Michael, Bridget and David were put onto gurneys. 'She changed down there — she did her powerful thing — and now she's white as a ghost.'

I completely lost my balance and Simone caught me. 'Someone help Emma!'

'Bring her in,' Edwin called from inside, and Simone picked me up and carried me into the ward. I didn't really understand what was happening as Simone placed me onto one of the four beds. People were rushing from bed to bed, but it was all a blur.

'Is everybody all right?' I said, but Simone had gone. I moved my head with difficulty to see where she was and relaxed. She was at Michael's bedside.

The noise and light faded in and out, and I hoped with detachment that it was just exhaustion and nothing more serious.

Meredith's face swam into view above me and she put her hands on either side of my face. Her exploratory energy moved through me. 'Emma's fine, just exhaustion,' she said.

I grabbed her hand to stop her before she left me. 'Is everybody okay?' I said. 'They shot David and Bridget because they were with us. Are they all right?'

She smiled and squeezed my hand to reassure me. 'They're fine; everybody will be okay. Close your eyes and rest.'

'Do you need my snake?'

'Not while you're half-dead like this,' she said. 'So close your eyes, go down deep, rebuild your energy, and when you're back you can help. Either way they'll be fine; the injuries aren't life-threatening.'

'Good,' I said, and let go.

CHAPTER 6

I came around in my own bed in the servants' quarters. As soon as I sat up, Meredith and Simone appeared next to me.

'How do you feel?' Simone said.

'Great. Full of energy. How are the others?'

'They're in the infirmary, they're fine,' Meredith said. 'We've done some energy healing. With a few hours' rest they'll be up and around again.'

'Any permanent damage?'

'No,' Simone said. 'But we need to talk about Michael later. I honestly think he's out of his league guarding you; he keeps getting injured.'

Meredith leaned in to study me carefully. 'That's right, talk later. Right now, tell me: do you crave Shen blood? Do you want to taste it again?'

I thought about it for a moment, then shook my head. 'No. Not like I did when I had the demon essence in me. I have to admit that it tasted great, but I don't feel like an addict.'

'It tasted great?' Simone said, incredulous.

'It doesn't taste like blood at all,' I said. 'Remember that drink at Nu Wa's palace?'

'That was awesome.'

'That's what Michael's blood tasted like. Better than that, if possible.'

Simone hesitated. 'I wonder if it tastes like that to me too.'

I was wearing my pyjamas. 'How long have I been out?'

'Only a couple of hours,' Simone said.

'So it's what ... 2 am? Why aren't you in bed?'

'I wanted to make sure you were okay. I don't have school tomorrow anyway.'

I found my tatty purple chenille robe in a pile of clothes next to the bed and pulled it around me. 'Go to bed.'

'Where are you going?' Meredith said.

'I'm going to check on the others.'

'They're asleep, leave them,' Meredith said. 'Leo's there watching them. They're fine.'

'It's so cute: Clarissa's asleep at Michael's bedside,' Simone said.

'I still need to check something out. You two go to bed.'

'Check what out?' Simone said suspiciously. 'It's the middle of the night.'

'I want to see if the Murasame came back,' I said. 'It won't come when I call. It only came when I did my strong thing.'

'You haven't recovered enough to do any sword work,' Meredith said. 'When did you call it?'

'This evening, when the Mothers cornered us. I just want to pop down to the Armoury and see if it's there. If it isn't, then I'll need to get myself a new one, because it's probably at the bottom of the sea somewhere, or back in Hell.'

'Go straight back to bed after you've checked it,' Meredith said, and disappeared.

'I'm coming too,' Simone said. 'I won't sleep unless I know. That sword is kind of like a bad-tempered guard dog for you.'

'Careful, you'll upset the stone,' I said.

We headed down the hill and around the peaks to the Armoury. Mist had gathered in the gorges and we walked carefully across an arched bridge, the scent of the pine trees filling the air around us. The sky had the clarity of late autumn, and the stars blazed bigger and brighter than any on the Earthly. The seven stars of the Big Dipper shone in the centre of the sky: the symbol of the Dark Lord's power. I shivered in my robe; the early autumn breeze was chilly. First snow soon.

'I must have some eucalypts planted here,' I said. 'I miss the smell.'

'Can you see okay?' Simone said, gesturing towards the ball of light she'd summoned for me.

'Just fine.'

We wound past the forge to the Armoury building, which dwarfed its much smaller neighbour, its roof soaring twenty metres above the ground. The back of the Armoury was flush with the stone mountainside, and it had black walls and a black-tiled roof, making it more difficult to spot from the air. We went to the front of the building. The black stone doors stood silent, each one fifteen metres high and four wide, carved with images of the combined Xuan Wu, the snake and turtle heads facing each other with their mouths open as if in conflict.

'Open,' I said, and the doors slid smoothly apart.

We stepped into its dark interior, the black roof tiles visible high above us. The building didn't have an internal ceiling, making it bitterly cold in the middle of winter. The huge open space stretched for fifty metres away from us, and a rustling sound came from the high beams above.

An unadorned ebony screen, three metres tall, stood just inside the entrance, and in front of that stood a metre-tall bronze urn, filled with sand, to hold incense.

I moved to the side of the urn and opened the cupboard next to it.

'Move the light closer, I can't see,' I said, and Simone obliged.

The cabinet contained open canisters of incense sticks, their wooden ends protruding so they could be easily removed. I rifled through the canisters, checking the sticks: some were dyed red, others were plain wood. Eventually I found the one I was looking for: it had a tiny dot of black on the very end of the stick. I pulled it out, lit it from the candle burning below the urn, then shook it until the flame went out. Blowing out the flame was an insult to the wind spirits. I stuck the incense into the sand and waited a moment for the fragrance to waft through the hall and into the ceiling.

'I can smell it, we can go,' Simone said, and we moved into the main part of the hall.

Racks of weapons stood on either side of us, resembling the shelves in a library. Those closest to the door held the standard training weapons used by students; the Celestial weapons were further back.

The rustling above us changed to flapping, and one of the flying demons that resided in the roof flew down to us. Simone readied herself to destroy it, obviously concerned that I'd chosen the wrong incense. The demon was black and a metre long with four legs and wings; it looked something like a flying lizard but much uglier. It clacked its grotesquely toothed beak at me and strutted up and down, blocking my way, then turned to speak. It sounded like a parrot.

'Dark Lady.'

'Hello, little one,' I said.

'It's the middle of the night, Lady, why do you disturb us?'

'I apologise for disturbing you. I wanted to check my weapon. Is it in there?'

The flyer hissed and took a few steps back, shaking its wings. 'I don't want to know anything about that thing.' It took off again, spiralling up into the rafters.

We walked past the shelves to the back wall of the building, which was the Mountain itself.

'Open,' I said, and the wall disappeared, revealing a room full of brass that shone in Simone's light.

The ceiling in the Celestial Weapons Archive was much lower, and carved with twining snakes and turtles. The walls were smooth polished stone, and the pillars and beams holding up the roof were clad with brass, again embossed with the symbols of snakes and turtles. Soft voices sounded just at the edge of hearing: some of the weapons were talking in their sleep.

The far end of the room, from one side to the other, was partitioned off with iron bars clad in gold. I stopped and took a few deep breaths: this was the hard part. I preferred not to do it, but it was the only way.

'It's in there, Emma, don't worry about it,' Simone said.

'That's beside the point,' I said. 'I need to go in there and have a little chat with it about why it's not coming when I call it.'

'It's not worth the risk.'

'No risk. I can do it.'

'I'll bring it out for you.'

'It's not talking to me so I can't tell it not to hurt you. Still want to try?'

Simone was silent at that. She'd touched the sword before and knew how much it hurt.

I took some more deep breaths and concentrated, then closed my eyes. I took three steps forward and opened them again. I was inside.

Simone did the same thing, and stood beside me.

Seven Stars stood vertically on a solid silver stand in the centre of the room, its presence dwarfing the auras of the other weapons. I went around it, but Simone stopped to run her finger over the well-worn hilt.

The Murasame sat in the corner, laid horizontally Japanese-style on a stand of carved bone. Its darkness provided an eerie counterpoint to the brittle whiteness of its stand. I went to it and took its handle, then hissed with pain and pulled my hand away.

'It hurt you?' Simone said.

'It doesn't recognise me,' I said.

'This is the first time since you've recovered,' she said.

'I know,' I said. 'It hasn't seen me without the demon essence.'

'Want some blood?' she said.

I turned to her and glared. 'Don't you even think about it.'

She shrugged. 'Worth a try.'

I put my hand out towards the sword. 'I'll just have to tell it who's the master.'

'Well, that's what you're good at,' she said, and moved away.

'Is that you, Simone?' Miss Chen, the Weapons Master, called from the main room.

'It's just us, Lucy,' I said.

She walked through the bars with her eyes closed and approached us. 'What are you doing here at this time of night?'

She was wearing a hot pink bathrobe pulled around her portly form, over old-fashioned flannel pyjamas decorated with tiny pink flowers. Simone stared at her for a moment, then grinned.

Miss Chen peered at Simone through her thick glasses. 'What's so funny?'

Simone smothered the grin and turned away. 'Nothing, nothing.'

Miss Chen straightened the curlers in her hair. 'You'll get as old as me one day, young lady, and it'll be just as much hard work.' She turned to me. 'Now what are you doing here in the Celestial Armoury in your pyjamas? Seems a strange place for a sleepover.'

'The Murasame won't come when I call it,' I said.

She came to stand next to me and studied the sword without touching it. 'This is the first time you've called it since the demon essence was burnt from you?'

I nodded.

She frowned for a moment as she thought about it. 'I guess the reason you're not touching it is because it doesn't recognise you as its master any more and it's hurting you?'

I nodded again.

She rubbed her chin. 'But it's still here, so it hasn't reverted to anyone else's ownership. Basically what you have to do is tell it who's the boss.'

'Which is what she's good at,' Simone repeated with humour.

'Can you wrap something around your hand and try?' Miss Chen said.

'The pain isn't from the contact itself,' I said. 'It's more like spiritual damage from the proximity.'

'Go to bed and come back tomorrow,' Miss Chen said. 'The sword's not going anywhere. It's nearly 3 am and both of you are tired, making it a bad time to be messing around with one of the most powerful destructive forces on the planet. Do it tomorrow, and I'll come help you.'

'She's right, Emma,' Simone said.

I tapped the sword with frustration and it burned my finger. 'All right.'

The next morning I headed straight for the infirmary. Bridget, David and Michael were sitting in the courtyard under the peach trees in the sunshine. All three of them were wearing plain black Mountain uniforms, and

Bridget had a pair of crutches leaning on the bench next to her. Michael rose, fell to one knee and saluted me, to David's and Bridget's obvious amusement.

'No need, Michael,' I said as he rose and painfully sat on the bench again. 'How are you all feeling?'

'Remarkably good, all things considered,' David said. 'Thanks so much for looking after us.'

'Don't thank me. You took a bullet because we were there,' I said. 'Bridget, do you mind giving me your hand? I'd like to check you.'

She hesitated a moment and looked at David. He nodded confirmation, so she held her hand out. I took it, holding her wrist at the pulse point. She gasped as I entered her energy stream to check the wound in her leg.

'Does it hurt?' David said.

'No,' Bridget said. 'It just feels … strange.'

I moved my energy to the wound in her knee. The bullet had lodged itself in her kneecap, but someone had removed it and done a rough job of half-healing it. The energy healers would have been stretched fixing all three of them, particularly as Michael's and David's injuries had been severe. I completed the job, moving my energy over the shattered bone, knitting its structure together and fixing the tendon damage. Bridget shivered as I withdrew my consciousness.

'All fixed,' I said. 'Try standing up.'

She leaned heavily on the bench and gingerly put weight on the leg. Her surprise was obvious as she stood with more confidence and took a few steps around the courtyard. 'This is amazing.'

'It's not a hundred per cent yet,' I said. 'Don't do any strenuous exercise on it for a week or so; the bone hasn't completely healed.' I turned to David. 'Hand, please, let me look at you.'

'What about young Michael?' David said without giving me his hand. 'He was hurt more than I was.'

'I'm Emma's bodyguard, it's my job,' Michael said. 'You were innocent bystanders and definitely come first, and I know it.'

David shrugged and held his hand out.

'You are slightly more difficult, Mr Hawkes,' I said as I entered his energy stream. 'This is more than a simple bone and muscle injury, there are multiple layers involved here.' I boosted the healing process as much as I could, and snapped back.

'Wow, it does feel very strange,' he said.

'Same for you: take it easy for a week or so, and no heavy lifting,' I said. 'Have you called home?'

'Yes, one of your staff gave us a mobile phone,' Bridget said. 'We need to get home as soon as we can, the boys need us. Emma ...' Her voice trailed off.

'Hmm?' I took Michael's hand. His was the worst injury of all; the bullet had clipped his liver and spleen, and he'd require more than a couple of days to recuperate. I didn't have enough energy left to help him out. He'd have to wait a day or so before he could be completely healed.

'Are we really in Heaven?' Bridget said. 'Your staff tell us we're definitely not dead and we can go home, but ... really? Heaven? And John is a god?'

'Really,' I said. 'Chinese Heaven doesn't work like Western mythology. It's a higher plane of existence.'

'Is that why you were asking her about Taoist philosophy?' Bridget asked David.

'Absolutely,' David said. He spread his hands. 'Wouldn't you want this?'

Bridget took a deep breath. 'It's wonderful.'

'Come and take a walk with me, I'll show you around,' I said, releasing Michael. 'Not you, Michael. You stay put, and don't move around too much for forty-eight hours.'

'I have three classes this afternoon!' Michael said, protesting.

'No teleporting, no heavy lifting, no energy work, no martial arts for forty-eight hours,' I said. 'That's an order.'

He grinned ruefully and saluted me, shaking his hands in front of his face. 'Yes, ma'am.'

'Teleporting?' David said, looking from Michael to me.

'No teleporting, flying, changing shape except to tiger, and no manipulating metal,' I said, counting them off on my fingers. 'And you have to stay home from school.'

'But, Mooom ...' Michael whined, then winced as he realised what he'd said.

I patted him on the shoulder, then turned to Bridget and David. 'Come on. Let me show you around Celestial Wudangshan.'

'You often hear about buildings being evacuated because of the smell of gas, then the authorities finding nothing there,' Bridget said as we headed along the path towards the centre of the complex. 'Is that what happened to us?'

'Yes, it's a tool the demons use to clear an area,' I said. 'It's a damn nuisance.'

'The police think it's mass hysteria,' David said, linking his arm in Bridget's and looking around with delight as we passed through the gardens.

'The effect is very similar: everybody gets an awful feeling of horror and foreboding and takes off,' I said. 'It's the best option, actually, as you can see.'

'The best option for what?' Bridget said.

'Emma fights those monsters. She doesn't want people like us around to get hurt when she does,' David said.

'And you knew all about this and didn't tell me?' Bridget said.

'Guess what Emma Donahoe told me today?' David said. 'You know John Chen? He's a god. And Emma lives in Heaven, and her huge black friend Leo is a Taoist Immortal.'

Bridget shook her head, smiling. 'I see your point.'

We'd arrived at the forecourt of Yuzhengong, in front of Dragon Tiger and Purple Mist halls.

'This reminds me of somewhere,' Bridget said, studying the layout. She pointed at Golden Temple. 'I've seen that before.'

'You've been to Earthly Wudang then,' I said.

Her mouth fell open as she realised. 'But this is three times bigger, and not nearly as run-down.'

I nodded. 'Thank you.'

'Master present!' someone yelled, and a group of students who had come up behind us saluted me, then waited.

It was a senior weapons class, led by Miss Chen herself. I moved Bridget and David to one side so that the students could go through to the forecourt. Miss Chen saluted me as they passed and I nodded back.

'When are you going to talk to your sword?' she said.

'When I've sent these two home.'

'Don't start without me, I don't trust that bastard blade,' she said. 'Let me know when you're going in.' She turned to the students. 'Take positions.'

I went to stand next to Bridget and David and we watched the students move into position on the forecourt.

'Is that the teacher?' Bridget said.

'That's the Weapons Master,' I said. 'The only one better than her with weapons is John himself.'

'Is she an Immortal too?' David said with interest.

I nodded. 'She's over seven hundred years old.'

Bridget raised one hand towards Miss Chen, who began to lead the spear set with elegance and grace despite her short and portly form. 'Why does she look so ordinary?'

'You're stuck in the form you were when you were Raised to be Immortal,' I said. 'They can change their form, but it takes effort. And frankly, I think she likes being underestimated.'

The students changed position to work in pairs, and Miss Chen moved between them, supervising.

'That looks very dangerous,' Bridget said. 'They're going to take each other's eyes out.'

'Leo will be furious,' I said. 'He loves spear, and never misses a chance to join in. How are you both feeling? You can probably go home now.'

They shared a look, then turned back to me.

'That would be for the best. We need to reassure the boys, and there's probably been at least three disasters back at the office,' David said.

'I'll arrange for someone to take you back down,' I said, and guided them towards my office. 'I'm so sorry this happened.'

'I'm not, I got to see what I'm aiming for,' David said. 'And I could share it with Bridget.'

'Yes, I think I may look into this Taoism business a little more myself,' Bridget said.

CHAPTER 7

Later I went into the Celestial Armoury to try again with the Murasame. Meredith, Simone and Miss Chen were all waiting for me inside, leaving little room for the weapons themselves.

'This is not a circus sideshow,' I said.

'You sure you can't block the pain, Meredith?' Simone said.

'It's spiritual damage, not physical,' Meredith said. 'She just has to bear it for as long as she can until one of them submits.'

Simone came to me and put her hand on my arm. 'We can always have another weapon made for you. You're still weak. Don't hurt yourself, it's not worth it, okay?' She leaned her cheek on my shoulder. 'I need you.'

'I'll listen to Meredith —' I began.

'Now there's a first,' Meredith said with humour.

'I'll listen to Meredith, and if she tells me to drop it, I will.'

'Are you just going to hold it until it concedes?' Meredith said.

'She's going to feed it,' Miss Chen said grimly.

'That is a very bad idea in your current state, Emma.'

'So watch me carefully. Now move back and give me room. I'll have to take it out of its scabbard to feed it.'

91

I stood in front of the sword and felt its brooding malevolence. Its corner seemed to be darker than the rest of the room; the sword sucked the light out of the air. I took some slow, deep breaths and moved my chi in time with my breathing, clearing my thoughts and quietly revelling in the absence of the demon essence. I planted my feet on the earth and raised my head to the sky and touched the nature of the Celestial: purer, cleaner and more alive than the Earthly.

I relaxed into it, then made my spirit a well of motionless tranquillity and reached towards the sword. The energy calming didn't help; the sword's burn ripped through my hand the minute I touched it. I bit my lip with the effort and took short, gasping breaths to increase my oxygen in the vain hope that it would lessen the pain. I raised the sword off its stand and pulled the black lacquer scabbard off the blade, feeling its bite on my left hand as I let it clatter to the floor.

I rotated the blade in my right hand, keeping it horizontal so that the sharp side faced up, and moved my left wrist above it, ready to slice the back of my hand.

John's voice sounded in my head. *What is hurting you, Emma?*

I fought to retain my concentration. *The Murasame; it doesn't recognise me any more.*

I didn't see John appear in human form next to me, but I felt his presence against my back. He reached around and put his right hand on mine where I held the hilt of the sword. The Murasame leapt beneath our hands, its spirit singing with joy at his presence, its dark essence rising to salute his. The pain stopped.

'It acknowledges you as master,' I said.

'All weapons acknowledge me as master,' he said, his voice a low rumble against my back. 'I am the master of all weapons.'

'Hello, Daddy,' Simone said.

'We will not talk, we are going to concentrate,' John said, his hand still on mine holding the quivering sword. 'If Emma messes this up, the Murasame could eat her alive. Everybody stay quiet.'

Simone squeaked softly with distress.

John guided my left hand so that the palm was up, and released it. 'Lower it gently onto the blade. Don't stop breathing.'

I did as he said and lowered my wrist carefully onto the blade. If I dropped my hand even slightly too hard, the sword would take it off with relish. I felt the sting and quickly raised my hand again as the blood spiralled into the sword.

'I'm letting it go. Talk to it,' John said, and released my hands.

The contact burned again and I touched consciousness with the sword.

I am your master.

The sword laughed, a ringing sound of steel.

I strengthened my will and made my internal voice stronger.

Acknowledge me, Destroyer, I am your master! We have shared blood and death and destroyed together, and you are mine!

The sword was silent and the pain lessened.

I healed the wound, stopping the feed, and the sword made a metallic squeal inside my head at the withdrawal of the blood. The pain didn't ease further.

I. Am. Your. Master. Obey me!

The sword seemed to think about it for a moment, then the pain ceased. The sword saluted me, the scabbard flew back onto its blade, and it drifted out of my hand and returned to its rack.

'The sword is tamed,' John said. He leaned over my shoulder to smile into my eyes. 'Well done.'

I slipped my hand around the back of his head and kissed him, and he pulled me closer, side-on to me.

'Oh come on, you two! Do you have to be so yucky all the time?' Simone said. 'I want to talk to you about my horse, Daddy, and what's been happening, and my grades at school, and everything!'

He released me to gaze into my eyes, then shrugged and grinned. He turned to Simone. 'Let's walk around the gardens and you can tell me. I want to see the rebuilt Mountain.'

'Come on, Emma,' Simone said, gesturing with her head as I hesitated. 'Come and have a walk and talk Daddy's ears off.' She linked her arm in his. 'Are you here for good? Please say you are.'

'No,' he said. 'Not yet. I remember being nearby though?'

'You've been at the bottom of the lake for nearly a whole day now,' I said.

'No wonder I feel so good, that's like plugging me into a battery charger.' He walked without difficulty through the bars, then closed his eyes and concentrated for a moment. 'My Serpent is here!' He turned back to us, grinning broadly, then his face fell. 'I'm sure I sensed it right here.'

'Can you rejoin now? If we find it?' Simone said.

He waved the others through the bars. 'Come on, Lucy, Meredith, you can talk to me too, I'm sure you all have a lot to share.' He turned back to Simone. 'If we find the Serpent, I can rejoin with it and be more powerful than either of you have ever seen me.' He shook out his shoulders. 'Looking forward to that. The demon horde won't know what hit it. Now.' He put one arm around each of our shoulders. 'Come and show me my Mountain. Why aren't you at the Peak any more? I went there looking for you and the flat was empty. It ripped my heart out.'

'We still use the flat,' I said, 'but we had to move out for a while because Simone's horse piddled on the carpet in her room and we had to take all the carpet out.'

He glared at her. 'Simone! You should know better.'

She hung her head. 'Sorry, Daddy.'

He pulled her in and squeezed her. 'Are you based here now?'

'We use the Peak as an Earthly base, but spend most of our time here,' she said.

He stopped and turned to face us, holding one of our hands in each of his. 'Do you like being here? Living here? We don't have to live here if you don't want it.'

'I love it,' I said. 'I don't want to live anywhere else.'

'Let me decide when I've graduated,' Simone said, thoughtful. 'I may choose the Palace in the Northern Heavens. I don't think I want to go back to the Earthly — humans can be a real pain to deal with sometimes. Right now though, I want to be here with you and Emma and Leo.'

We went out of the Armoury. John held our hands as we walked through the breezeway towards the central plaza. We passed a small courtyard where a group of students were sitting under the pavilion beneath the trees, working on some academic notes. They stared at us, and a few of them asked each other if that was really John.

'Salute your Master!' Miss Chen barked, and they all dropped to one knee.

John turned and grinned at her. 'Don't scare them like that. It will take them a while to become accustomed to having me back.'

After we'd passed, the students rose and took off running, obviously to tell their friends and bring them to see.

'We'll be mobbed,' Miss Chen said.

'If we are, I'll demote you,' John said.

'If we are, I'll deserve it.'

We'd arrived at the central area, and the path widened to lead the fifty-metre distance to the terrace in front of True Way. John's face was alight with joy and he released our hands and turned on the spot, taking it all in.

'Go up and take a look from above,' Simone said.

He took her hand and raised it. 'Can you come up with me?'

She nodded.

He turned to me. 'Can you?'

'I can't fly, John, I'm just an ordinary human.'

He touched me on the cheek with his free hand. 'Absolutely nothing ordinary about you.' He took my hand as well and we shot fifty metres straight up, then hovered above the complex.

Simone released his hand and turned in the air, her hair floating in the Celestial breeze. 'That way's the Northern Heavens; Emma's knocked down the Serpent Concubine Pavilion and built a new Hall of Serene Meditation. The barracks are over there, and the training halls are on this side, there.' She turned towards the higher peaks and pointed. 'Golden Temple's all fixed up.'

John released my hand to turn and see, and I concentrated to slow my fall, but I didn't move. He was still holding me up.

'It looks wonderful,' he said.

He took my hand and kissed it, and we drifted back down to land on the forecourt at the bottom of the stairs up to Purple Mist.

He raised my hand and we walked up the stairs to the hall together, Simone on his other side. We went in, and he released my hand, took three sticks of incense from the stand, lit them, and placed them in the urn in front of the Buddha statue. He knelt on a black cushion in front of the statue, bowed three times with his hands clasped in supplication, then rose and studied the statue.

I joined him and did the same thing on the cushion next to him, and we stood contemplating the Buddha together. Simone took some incense and added it, and joined us in studying the serene visage of the Buddha.

John turned back towards the door and sat on the cushion. His hair tie fell out and his hair spread over his shoulders. 'I'm losing it already. I don't think I'll make it to the Three Purities.'

'They wouldn't care anyway,' I said.

'Go back into the lake,' Simone said.

'One more thing to do,' he said, grabbing both of our hands and rising with renewed energy. He retied his ponytail, then led us briskly down the stairs and onto the forecourt where Meredith and Miss Chen waited for us.

A group of students had gathered, and approached us at the bottom of the stairs. They fell to one knee and saluted us.

'Up you get,' I said. 'Say hello to the boss man.'

They grinned shyly, some of them obviously intimidated.

'Lucy,' John said, and waved Miss Chen towards us.

She came and fell to one knee as well.

'Spread out and face True Way, everybody,' John said. He spread his arms and turned to face Yuzhengong, the Hall of the True Way, and we all moved as he directed. 'Now. Eighty-eight form Yang-style Tai Chi Chuan.'

'We have to move into ranks,' one of the students said urgently. 'We can't just be scattered like this.'

A few students were still arriving and trotted to join the group.

John turned back to face them. 'Scattered is what you want. Order is good, but chaos is the force that rules the universe, and you must learn to accept it and embrace it, and bend rather than break when it strikes. Yes, when your Masters say to be in ordered ranks, there is purpose. But right here, right now, there will be power in the chaos.' He waved a few straggling students closer. 'Not too close to the Western edge, give yourselves room to complete the set.'

He looked around, then spoke silently. *Anyone arriving late join the back of the group.* He turned and shifted his feet so that he was in position, and we fell into silence as we joined him.

'Touch the Earth. Touch the sky. Breathe the purity of the chi. Commence,' John said.

As we performed the first twenty moves of the set, more students arrived, quietly joining the group and catching up with us. They stopped arriving at about the twenty-fifth move, but I didn't notice; I lost my awareness into the graceful beauty of the set and the joy of completing it with John and Simone together.

Shortly after my awareness disconnected from reality and I lost myself into the set, the air around us began to vibrate with each move we made. The Immortals had generated shen energy and were carrying it on their hands. I kept my chi inside, holding it close to preserve my strength. With each move we made, the air sang: a musical note that rose and fell with our movements, clear and full of the warmth of the chi and shen.

Some exclamations of astonishment came from the students behind us, but as more of them joined the trance state, the singing became louder, filling the court with musical tones that turned the moving meditation of the Tai Chi into a symphony of perfect sounds.

As we completed the set and released the energy, the sounds faded and the air seemed to have become even clearer. John turned, grabbed Simone and me and pulled us into a hug so fierce I thought he would kill us.

The Masters who had joined the set quietly shepherded the students back to their classes, leaving the three of us alone in the forecourt that still resonated with energy.

'Did that happen because you're here, Daddy?' Simone said.

'Many things will happen when I am fully returned,' he said. 'I don't have much longer.' He bent to kiss me, then pulled back and gazed into my eyes. 'My Emma.' He turned and embraced Simone again, and kissed the top of her head. 'My little girl, my Simone.'

'Daddy,' she said, crushed into his chest, and then he was gone.

Simone wiped her eyes and sighed. 'I always thought Tai Chi was kind of boring. I think I'll do it more often now.'

'Don't let him hear you say that,' I said. 'He'll say he's failed as a Master.'

She leaned into me and smiled. 'He's back at the bottom of the lake. It won't be long now, Emma. And then we have to arrange a big fancy wedding.' She ran away giggling.

I rested on a bench next to a bridge over one of the gorges on the way back to the administrative complex. I was still too weak to handle long distances. The mists had cleared, but the bottom of the gorge wasn't visible; the Masters often teased the students by claiming, while they were floating over them, that the gorges were bottomless. Chanting from one of the temples, accompanied by a wooden drum, drifted in and out of earshot, adding to the warm buzz of sound that was the Mountain.

I wished I could conjure some tea and retire to one of the pagodas sitting high on the cliffs. Instead, I clumsily pulled myself to my feet and headed towards the offices.

The administrative buildings were terraced into the hillside on the eastern side of the complex, and small by necessity because of the steepness. The larger residential and training buildings were closer to the centre, where there was more available flat land. The buildings were joined together with breezeways that meandered through them, containing stairs that joined the levels. Each breezeway had red columns holding up the traditional bracketed roof, which had scenes of birds and flowers painted on the panels just below it. My office stood on the southern side of the cluster, hard against the side of the mountain. It had been designed as the office for John's second-in-command and I'd appropriated it as the most suitable place for me — right next to him when he came back.

An ancient cypress tree, twisted with age, stood guard in front of the doorway. I touched its trunk as I passed and it shifted its branches slightly in response. It wasn't a Shen or sentient as such, but it was aware of the comings and goings around it and seemed to enjoy the times when I performed a Tai Chi set in the small clearing beneath it.

Yi Hao nodded to me as I went past her desk. I stopped when I saw who was in my waiting room.

One of the Tiger's Horsemen stood against the wall, guarding two of my young nephews. Mark, slender, dark-haired and dark-eyed, was Amanda's son. Jennifer's son, Andrew, had an unruly thatch of sandy hair and bright blue eyes similar to my own. They were both fourteen years old, but Andrew was ten centimetres taller than Mark. His father, Leonard, was tall. They both rose as I came in and gave me quick hugs.

'Both of you here for a visit at the same time? What's the occasion?' I said.

They shared a quick look, then Mark said, 'Can we talk to you, Aunty Emma?'

'Sure,' I said, gesturing towards the office. 'Come on in.' I nodded again to Yi Hao. 'Anything urgent?'

'Nothing urgent, ma'am,' she said.

'Good.' I took the boys into my office, closed the door and leaned on the desk. 'Is there a problem, guys? It's not like you to be up here on the Celestial Plane, Mark. You know your mother prefers you to stay on the Earthly.'

Both of them fell to one knee and saluted me Chinese-style.

I jumped up. 'None of that, you're family, get up off your knees right now.'

They didn't rise. 'Please permit us to join the Dark Disciples, ma'am,' Mark said. 'We want to learn the Arts.'

'I'm not listening to anything you have to say until you're back on your feet where you belong,' I said. 'There's absolutely no need to kowtow to me.'

'We want to,' Andrew said, but they rose anyway. 'We want to acknowledge you as Master, learn the Arts, and do some of the stuff your Disciples can do.'

I went around the desk and flopped into my chair, then waved for them to sit. 'They're not my Disciples, they're Xuan Wu's. And I don't think this is a good idea.'

'We want to learn,' Andrew said, stubborn. He glanced at Mark. 'Both of us.'

'Your mothers would kill me. They'd chop me into very small pieces with my own sword.'

'We want different names,' Mark said. 'Our names are so boring compared to the Disciples — Cold Wind, Black Tree, Triumphant Dragon. We want to be part of Wudang.'

Andrew put his elbows on his knees and leaned forward. 'It's just so cool.'

'I can't, guys,' I said. 'It's not cool. It's joining the army. Are you ready for military service? Boot camp?'

They both grinned broadly. 'Yes!'

'Even if you did want this, even if you were talented enough to be accepted, I can't do this to your mothers,' I said. 'I can't guarantee any Disciple's safety, guys. You'd be in danger. We all know the risk, and I can't do that to them.'

'What if they gave their permission?' Mark said eagerly.

'They won't do that in a million years,' I said. 'Guys, you won't be safe.'

'We won't leave until you let us come here,' Andrew said.

I rose and leaned on the desk. 'And I'm saying that we won't take you. You might as well go now, because it's not going to happen.'

I went to the door and opened it, then nodded to the Horseman. 'Take them home, please. We're done here.' I turned back to the boys. 'I'll see you guys on the weekend.'

The Horseman came in and saluted me. 'Ma'am.'

'At least say you'll think about it!' Andrew said.

'I'll talk to your mothers about it. If they say it's okay, then I'll take you,' I said.

Mark punched the air. 'Yes!'

The Horseman touched each of the boys and they all disappeared.

I returned to my desk and called my mother.

'Hello, darling, anything happen?' she said. 'You only call me when there's an emergency.'

'Mark and Andrew were just in here, wanting to join Wudang,' I said.

'Oh, that's nice. Did you let them?'

'I can't let them!' I said. 'They wouldn't be safe.'

'They'd be safe there with you, wouldn't they? I mean, that Mountain place is called the Stronghold of Heaven. It's supposed to be the safest place anywhere.'

'Not until John is back, Mum. And remember what happened eleven years ago? The Demon King broke in here and burned the place to the ground.'

'But that was just property damage, wasn't it? None of his students were killed or anything?'

I sighed with feeling. 'Three hundred human Disciples died. It was covered up. Not one of Heaven's greatest triumphs.'

She was silent on the other end of the line.

'We can't guarantee anyone's safety, not even with John here,' I said. 'Accidents happen. And I won't put the boys at risk.'

'I'll talk to Amanda and Jen,' she said. 'I think you should too.'

'Don't worry, I will. I just wanted to check with you first, find out where they are.'

'Jen's on a shopping trip down on the Earthly, and Amanda's at home,' my mother said. 'She's going to be so cross when she finds out Mark went up to visit you! They're supposed to be living normal lives.'

'She's doubly going to kill him then.'

'I think you're right.'

Mid-afternoon Yi Hao came into my office with a cup of fresh coffee for me. She put the mug on my desk and stood on the other side of it, fidgeting.

'What?' I said.

'That man is here again.'

'Show him in!'

She opened the door and stood next to it without speaking.

'Come on in,' I called to Er Lang, who was waiting outside.

As soon as Er Lang was in my office, Yi Hao made a snorting sound of disgust, went out and slammed the door behind her.

Er Lang fell to one knee. 'My Lady First Heavenly General.'

'My Lord Er Lang. Please rise.'

He remained on one knee, head bowed.

'Oh no, here we go again,' I moaned, and took a sip of the coffee. 'The answer is no. The answer will always be no. Now get the hell up off the floor and you'd better have something worthwhile to bother me about.'

He didn't get up, he just stayed on one knee. 'This humble servant respectfully requests of you, most Honoured One, that he be permitted to take his own life and spend a protracted time in the Hell of Trees Full of Swords.'

I made my voice more brisk. 'Up off the floor now, and get into one of these chairs and talk to me.'

He rose sheepishly and sat, carefully keeping his eyes down in a show of humility.

'All right, be like that,' I said. 'For the last time: no, you can't go off and kill yourself. I need you to help me out in the Celestial Palace.'

He shook his hands in front of his face. 'I deserve to suffer.'

I rose and walked around the desk. 'Stone, are any of the pagodas free?'

'All of them are free.'

I gestured impatiently to Er Lang. 'Come with me.'

I went out of the office and told Yi Hao: 'I'm taking Er Lang up to one of the pagodas for a talk. If anyone needs me, tell them to talk to the stone.'

'Ma'am,' Yi Hao said, glaring at Er Lang.

Outside the office, I put my hand out. 'You'll have to carry me. I'll show you the way.'

He lifted me without a word and, as we flew, I guided him to one of the pagodas that sat just below the top of the highest peaks on Wudang Mountain. We landed gently at the edge of the steep drop and sat at the table inside.

'Tea, my Lady?' he said, and I nodded. A pot of Sow Mei appeared with a pair of cups.

I turned to view the Wudang complex spread a hundred metres below us. Its black roofs shone in the Celestial sunlight, and the black wall around the entire complex was clearly visible. The central area, with its huge paved court, was a mass of movement: a class was being held there. The halls on either side were visible higher on the mountainside, as well as the glowing Golden Temple above. The rest of the buildings clung in the folds between the peaks. The sound of drums and the shouts of the disciples echoed through the mountain tops.

I turned back to Er Lang. His young-looking face was full of misery.

'Please allow me to be punished in the Hell of Trees Full of Swords,' he said.

'For the last time, no.'

'Why not?'

'It wouldn't achieve anything!' I snapped, and he jumped.

'Don't you want to have your vengeance on me?'

'No!' I poured the tea, sloshing it into my cup. 'Revenge is the most pointless thing ever. I don't want to see you suffer. What I want is to work alongside you to protect the Celestial Plane.'

'You are too merciful.'

'No, I'm not.' I raised my teacup and waved it at him. 'You want to go to Hell and suffer horribly because that will make you feel a whole lot better — like you've atoned. Well, I won't let you. You stay here, and you help me out. I don't want to see you hurt, Er Lang, I just want to work with you. Let's get past this and move on already!'

'The Jade Emperor refuses to punish me as well,' he said, miserable.

'You know as well as I do that something's coming. There's a threat hanging over our heads, and the Dark Lord is still incapacitated. We need to be at full strength to face this — and I need you to liaise with the Celestial. Now for fuck's sake will you get the hell over yourself, stop feeling sorry for yourself — which is priceless since I'm the one that got barbecued — and do your goddamn job?'

He sat for a while, looking at his teacup, then looked back up at me. 'I've been a complete ass, haven't I?'

'Yes!'

He sighed and put his cup down. 'I just wish the Celestial would demote me. I'm not fit for this. Look at you — ordinary human, female, not even Immortal, and you're running rings around me. First a monkey, now a woman —'

'You sexist bastard.' I slammed my teacup on the table. 'One on one, down on the forecourt. You, me, staves.' I glared at him. 'Come on, show me what you've got.'

He hesitated for a moment, watching me, then shot to his feet and held his hand out. I grabbed it and we were on the forecourt in front of Dragon Tiger.

Liu was teaching a group of advanced students Shaolin long sword; they all stopped.

'Clear the area, bring us two suitable staves, and stand back,' I called to Liu without looking away from Er Lang. I grinned. 'No holds barred. No mercy, no quarter, no rules except that you're not allowed to kill me. Got it?'

Er Lang saluted me with a grim smile.

Liu threw a staff to me and one to Er Lang. The students moved back, discussing the match under their breath.

'Silence!' Liu barked, and they went quiet.

I saluted Er Lang, holding my staff, and he saluted back. We moved into position. I held my staff in front of

106

me, guarding, just as I had when I'd kicked Leo's ass all that time ago. This time, however, my opponent was going to give me a lesson I wouldn't forget, and I knew it.

We remained motionless for nearly twenty seconds. As the challenger, I had to make a move after that time or the match would be forfeit.

I swung the staff above me in a move that was more show than substance and kept it rotating as a strike towards Er Lang's head. He blocked it easily, swung it down in the direction it was already moving and locked it onto the ground. He held it there without effort; I was stuck already.

I pulled the staff straight along its length and it slid out. I swung it and tried to take his feet out with the other end; he blocked me. He jammed my staff against the ground again; he was being purely defensive without attacking. I pulled the staff out of the lock and swung it directly up at his face, hoping to hit him under the chin, and he blocked me again, pushed my staff sideways, and used the other end to tap me on the ankle. He hit me right on the nerve point at the protruding bone and I yelped and hopped back, then lifted the foot as the pain eased. A couple of students squeaked with me, feeling my pain.

He followed the advantage, swinging at my staff so fast that I was barely able to block it. He continued to press me back, hitting my staff relentlessly. The worst part was that he wasn't hitting it very hard, just tapping it, but he was so fast I had trouble keeping up. He raised the speed and I couldn't stop him: his blow passed my staff and hit me on the abdomen. He finished it with a flick to take my feet out from under me and I hit the ground hard, my muscles soft after so many months of enforced rest.

I lay on my back, trying to get my breath back, and he stood over me.

'I yield,' I managed to wheeze out. 'You've beaten me fairly.'

He held his hand out to me and I took it. He pulled me easily to my feet and we stood with our hands clasped for a long moment while he gazed into my eyes.

'You were holding back,' he said. 'You're much better than that, I know it.'

'That was the best I can do at the moment,' I said. 'I didn't hold back.'

He released my hand but continued to examine me. 'But I've heard stories about you. You took down some huge Mothers. You turned one into a cat. You fought off One Two Two single-handed. You defeated the Demon King in single combat.'

'Really?' I couldn't help myself: I grinned like an idiot. 'Who's spreading these ridiculous stories, and where can I sign them up to write my memoirs? Most of that's pure fabrication.'

'Is it?'

'Hell, yeah. I may have taken down a couple of medium-sized Mothers and done the cat thing, but that was probably when I was possessed by the Xuan Wu's Serpent. Without any supernatural help I'm about as good as a really good human.'

He studied me with his face rigid.

'Do it. Go ahead,' I said, and braced for the impact.

He snapped his Third Eye open in the middle of his forehead. His intense gaze swept right through me like a blast of brilliant light, burning my flesh from my bones and shredding my essence. The light blinked out and I bent over, gasping.

You should have warned me before you let him do that, Emma. You could have damaged me, the stone said.

I don't think anything can damage you, I said. *You're surrounded by an impenetrable field of your own superiority.*

'I have misjudged you, ma'am,' Er Lang said. He held his hand out again. 'My Earthly name is Robert. People call me Rob when they work with me in English.'

I straightened and shook his hand. 'And I'd prefer to be called Emma, really. Hey, I know where Liu's secret boutique beer stash is, and where his vintage wines are. He's occupied with the students right now — want to come and raid it?'

'What?' Liu said from the side.

'I'd love to, Emma,' Er Lang said. He waved cheerily to Liu. 'Meet up with us later, we might have some alcohol left over for you.'

This play-acting is extremely tedious, the stone said. *Why don't you just be yourself? Drinking alcohol indeed. You can't stand the stuff.*

The safety of all the Celestial is at stake, I said. *It's worth a little play-acting.*

And you could have done better against him.

Uh, no, I gave it all I have. He's just straight-up better than me.

I completely disagree.

CHAPTER 8

I sat with Mum and Dad on the back terrace of their house, talking as the sun set over the Western Plains. I took a deep breath: they'd planted a few wattle trees in the yard and the powdery fragrance spread over us. I was fiddling with my still-full plate of salad when my sister Jen knocked on the door and the demon maid let her in. She came out to the terrace and sat next to me, giving me a quick hug.

'Emma, you should have told me that Andrew's visiting the Mountain. I didn't know he was heading over there. I only just got it out of Colin when I came home from work.'

My stomach fell out. 'Andrew never made it home?'

Her eyes widened. 'Isn't he staying at your Academy?'

I shook my head. 'I sent him home with the Horseman and Mark. I told them I wouldn't take them, it's too dangerous.'

She sagged with relief. 'Thank you.'

'But he never came home?'

'No,' Jennifer said, her voice weak.

'Call him, see if he answers,' I said, and pulled out my own phone. I dialled Amanda's number and she answered. 'Amanda, it's me. Did Mark come back from Wudang?'

'I don't know — he's not home. He went to Wudang? He knows we're trying to live a normal life down here and he was specifically told not to harass you about joining Wudang. He did it anyway?'

I dropped the phone into my lap, my mind racing. I put it back to my ear. 'Amanda, I'm going to hang up now. I want you to call around and try to find Mark. He was with Andrew, but he's not home either. Get your opal to help.'

'Oh my God,' she said.

'Hang up, and start looking for him. I want to make sure both boys are okay.'

She hung up and I turned to Jen, who was holding her phone to her ear. She shook her head and snapped it shut. 'Voicemail.'

'They've taken them,' Simone said.

'We can't be sure of that. They may have tried to find another way into Wudang,' I said. 'They were determined.'

Jen thumped the table, then rose and paced the terrace. 'You are non-stop trouble, you know that, Emma Donahoe? You cause nothing but difficulty for this family.'

'That's not fair, Jen,' my mother said.

I raised a hand to stop her. 'She's right, Mum. I've caused the family nothing but strife since I met John.'

Simone made a small gasping sound of pain and disappeared.

'Where'd she go?' my father said.

'Probably to look for the boys. She'll feel as responsible as I do.' I tapped the stone. 'Wake up.'

'I'm awake, I'm hooked into the network,' the stone said. 'Opal says that Amanda's son isn't answering his phone. Hold.'

My father leaned on the table to speak to me, the burning steaks behind him forgotten. 'Who's taken them?'

I shook my head.

'Tell us,' Jennifer said. 'Don't try to keep it a secret from us.'

'There's a chance the Death Mother may have abducted them,' I said. 'She knows we're after her and she wants to stop us before we get there. She tried to assassinate us last night; Michael and a couple of our human friends were shot.'

My father thumped the table. 'Someone tried to *kill* you and you didn't bother to tell us?'

'There's always someone trying to kill me.'

My mother put her hand over her mouth and turned away.

'Where's John?' my father said. 'Can't he protect you?'

'He's a turtle in the heart of Wudang Mountain, and no,' I said. 'He may come to defend me if my life's in danger, but then again he may not.'

Simone reappeared. 'I have no idea where they are.'

'Opal's looking, also has no idea,' the stone said. 'They seem to have just disappeared.'

'What about the Horseman who was looking after them?' I said. 'Ask the Tiger.'

The Tiger knocked on the door and came in without being invited. 'They ditched the guard, they were very clever about it. He's close on committing suicide over it. Don't worry, we'll find them. This is an insult to the House of the West — not being able to defend our own. It will not go unavenged.'

Jen leaned on the table, holding her stomach. The Tiger went to her and guided her to a chair. 'Take it easy. You're in no condition to be under stress. Don't worry, we'll find them.'

'What condition?' I said, alarmed.

'I'm pregnant,' Jennifer said.

'Congratulations,' I said.

112

'You and my son must marry, it's the honourable thing to do,' the Tiger said.

'Not while my son is missing.' Jennifer glanced at me. 'We have to tell Leonard; he has a right to know as well.'

'Stone?'

'Done,' the stone said. 'Leonard requests entry to the Western Heavens to join the search.'

'There isn't much he can do here,' the Tiger said.

'Let him come. It'll be better than him staying at home worrying,' Jennifer said. She leaned her forehead on her hand.

'You okay to see him?' I said.

She nodded into her hand. 'It's been a few years since the divorce now, Emma. We're still friends.'

'Tiger?' I said.

The Tiger nodded. 'Ma'am.' He took a deep breath. 'Now what? We have absolutely no leads on where they went.'

Jennifer's phone rang and she jumped, then answered it. 'Hello?' She listened for a while, then burst into tears. 'You have no idea how worried we were. Where were you?' She didn't wait for a reply. 'I don't care what you were doing, you get yourself home now! Then you're grounded for a month, young man. We thought you'd been taken by ... by ...' She took a deep breath and shook her head. 'Is Mark with you? He went home too? I'll be there shortly. Don't you go anywhere, I want to have a serious talk with you.'

She snapped the phone shut and grabbed some napkins from the table to wipe her face. 'They're home. They're all home. He says he wanted to show Mark the Celestial Plane since Mark isn't allowed up here.' She wiped her eyes and blew her nose. 'They're okay.' She rose. 'I have to go see him. And give him a big hug.'

I got up too and embraced her. 'Go tell him what an idiot he is for giving all of us such a scare, and never to do it again. And congratulations again on the little one.'

She nodded and left.

The Tiger's face was grim. 'I have to go talk to their guard. I have no idea what the fuck that idiot was thinking.' He disappeared.

My father sighed loudly and tipped the burnt meat into the garbage. 'I'll find something else to cook. Won't be a minute.' He left the plate on the table and went inside.

My mother buttered a slice of bread and pushed the plate across to share it with Simone. 'The Tiger gave us some giraffe steaks once. Your father popped them on the barbecue and they were absolutely horrible. We're sticking to good old beef and lamb now.'

Simone wrinkled her nose. 'Lamb is too strong.'

I gave her a friendly push. 'You're such a Chinese kid sometimes.'

She shrugged. 'Lamb is yuck.'

My father returned with a plate of sausages. 'This is it, I'm afraid.'

'Whatever,' Simone said. 'I'm starving.'

Michael and Clarissa came and visited me the next morning, and I waved them into my office. Since returning to the Celestial, Michael had gained muscle mass from spending time practising the Arts, and he'd grown his hair out into a short ponytail. Clarissa looked much the same as she always had: a slender Chinese girl with a sweet smile and shoulder-length hair cut to frame her face.

'The Mountain is very beautiful,' she said. 'Michael told me about the attack, but you'd hardly know it ever happened.'

'Thank you,' I said. 'We've worked hard to bring it

back to what it was.' I turned to Michael. 'I hear you've been promoted. Congratulations.'

Michael shook his head. 'I've been given a lower number, that's all. He had to move fifty of us up because of the fifty that died when the elementals attacked the ski lodge. It doesn't mean much, particularly when everybody calls me by name anyway.'

'Apparently it's a huge honour,' Clarissa said, glancing sideways at him with obvious pride. 'He's not even thirty years old and already lower than two hundred. It's unheard of. Some say he'll be given a double-digit number even before he attains Immortality.'

Michael gestured dismissively. 'Means nothing. I am here because of the promotion, though. I want to ask you something.'

'Ask away,' I said.

'Dad's offered us space in the barracks in the West, as is fitting for a high-ranking son. But what I'd really like to do, if I'm going to full-time it on the Celestial, is to be here ...' His voice petered out.

'We want to move here and join the Wudang staff, if that's okay,' Clarissa finished for him, and he looked relieved at her assistance.

'How do you feel about it, Clarissa?' I asked.

'About moving to the Celestial or moving here?'

'Both.'

'Moving to the Celestial ...' She smiled slightly. 'It's a chance that's too good to refuse. I'll be able to learn what to do to attain Immortality, and who wouldn't want that? Even if I don't attain it, I'll live extra long and illness free. I'd have to be completely crazy to turn down an opportunity like this.'

'And the Mountain?'

'Doesn't matter where we live, as long as Michael's happy,' she said. 'Both places are beautiful in different ways, and we'll spend time in the Western Heavens anyway.' She leaned towards me. 'But ... would you have something like a job for me to do? I'd die of boredom being a housewife for Michael. I'd rather stay on the Earthly Plane if I can't work.'

'We'll definitely have something for you to do, and it won't be mundane, I can guarantee it,' I said. 'We have extensive investments on the Earthly that need to be managed, and frankly, if you could take over the management of the shares and properties down there it would be a boon for both me and Jade.'

'A portfolio?' she said.

'Several hundred million Hong Kong dollars worth,' I said.

'A really big portfolio all to myself? That's a dream come true,' Clarissa said with enthusiasm.

'As for me, I want to take up duty full-time as your personal bodyguard again, ma'am,' Michael said. 'If you'll have me, that is. I want to permanently join the staff of Wudang, as opposed to the Western Heavens.'

Clarissa turned to glare at him. 'What are you talking about? I never agreed to that. You said you were just coming on staff to teach, there wasn't anything about being her bodyguard again.' She glanced from me to Michael. 'You just took a bullet for her the other night, you haven't even recovered from that and you want to put yourself back in the firing line again?'

'It's all right, Clarissa, I won't let him do it anyway,' I said. 'Michael's been injured too many times protecting me, and we've decided it'll be best if I'm only guarded by Immortals.'

She exhaled loudly. 'Well, that's a relief.'

'You decided, did you? Without consulting me? You can't give the job to anyone else — I won't let you!' Michael said.

'Not even Leo?'

Michael swiped his hand through the air. 'Leo's in a wheelchair.'

'You say that in front of him and he'll call you out,' I said.

'And own my ass,' he said wryly. He sagged. 'I concede if it's Leo.' His expression grew stern. 'But nobody else; and if I get good enough or attain Immortality, the job is mine, right?'

'Deal,' I said.

I put my hand out over the table and he shook it.

'Good,' he said. 'So, can I come?'

I pulled a blank scroll off a stack sitting to one side, pushed it open, scribbled the directions to give Michael a staff position and residence on the Mountain, then signed it. I pulled my black jade chop — square and three centimetres to a side — closer, flipped open the modern Japanese stamp pad, inked the chop well and stamped it over my signature. I rolled the scroll back up and handed it to Michael. 'Orders. Give them to Gold.'

He took the scroll with both hands. 'Ma'am.'

'That seal is beautiful. What's that on top of it? Is it a dragon?' Clarissa said, curious.

I passed the chop to her and she admired it, carefully avoiding the remaining red ink on the bottom. 'Oh, it's a snake.' She turned it in her hands, then glanced up at me. 'Is that what you look like?'

I nodded.

'Is it big?'

'Huge,' Michael said. 'Smallest is about three metres long, and I've seen her up to ten metres when she's really big.'

Clarissa appeared thoughtful as she handed the seal back. 'To look at you, no one would ever think you're something so completely scary.'

'What you're seeing now is the scariest Emma ever,' Michael said. 'The snake is nothing.'

'Give me that scroll back and go home to your father,' I said. 'I don't want you.'

He saluted me with it. 'I'll be back when I'm done moving in, and we can talk about what you want me to do.'

'I've told Gold to give you Persimmon Tree Pavilion; it's a nice one, and nobody's living there right now.'

He fell to one knee and saluted me. Clarissa smiled and they went out together.

A couple of hours later my mobile rang.

'Miss Donahoe, is Citrus. We have major problem in Wellington Street. Can you come over visit now? We need you.'

'I'm on my way,' I said, then called Leo. 'I have to go down to Wellington Street — Citrus sounded really upset. Can you take me?'

'On my way.'

I thought for a moment, then tapped the stone in my ring.

'Yes? I was asleep.'

'Of course you were. I need to go down to Wellington Street. Ask Zara if Clarissa would like to come along.'

The stone was silent for a moment, then said, 'Clarissa's on her way. Zara says she's eager to take up her duties. Do we have to continue calling it Zara? It should take its stone name back.'

'Zara says she likes being female and she likes being called something that means "star", so deal.'

'Humph.'

Leo wheeled himself into my office. 'What happened?'

'Citrus wouldn't say. Can you carry me and Clarissa?'

Clarissa came in behind him, obviously excited. 'Looks like I have things to manage before I've even

118

signed the contract with you. Do you guys even work with contracts? How much do you pay? What are my hours?'

'Whatever you like, on both counts,' I said.

'She's tiny. I can carry both of you,' Leo said.

'So, how about ten million a year and four hours a day?' she said, grinning with mischief.

'Oh, I like this one,' Leo said.

'Done,' I said. 'Whatever it takes to get the job done and free me and Jade up.'

She saluted me Western style, hand to forehead. 'Ma'am. Let's go down to Wellington Street and see the paperwork. How old is the building?'

'About thirty years old.'

'Okay. I want to start by ensuring that you're making enough rent, and that the property's being maintained to a satisfactory standard. Some of those older buildings in Central are falling down. Let's go down and check.'

'I really like this one,' Leo said.

Clarissa touched his arm where it rested on his wheelchair. 'That means a lot to me, Leo. Michael's told me about you — how you saved him and helped make him into what he is today.'

Leo dropped his head.

'He's blushing,' I said. 'Shame you can't see it.'

Leo waved me forward. 'Get over here and let's see what the big emergency is.'

We landed outside the Celestial Arena door at the end of Wo On Lane where it connected with Wellington Street — a small, narrow, well-hidden spot. The hoardings had gone from the building across from us and the new grey granite wall was polished to a mirror-like finish. Leo led us down the alley towards Wellington Street, then stopped and checked the traffic.

Wellington Street was only a couple of streets inland from Des Voeux Road, the main thoroughfare through

Central, but it was perilously narrow, only just wide enough to allow two taxis to pass. It was also so steep that the footpaths on either side had been concreted into steps in some parts, meaning that Leo had to wheel himself on the road.

He swung out onto the road and a taxi blared its horn at him as it passed. Leo stopped the chair, waited a moment as the taxi headed a little more up the hill, then, when it was fifty metres away, he concentrated and one of its tyres blew out. The taxi stopped and the passenger and driver got out and stood on the road, arguing loudly about what they were going to do.

'Karma's a bitch, eh?' he said in their general direction.

We headed up the hill towards the Wellington Street building, passing a couple of noodle shops and a temporary clearance store with piles of socks and underwear tossed into laundry baskets with prices stuck on the front.

Leo stopped first and whistled as he looked up at the building. I looked up too and took a step back.

'Holy shit,' Clarissa said quietly.

The entire side of the building, all eleven storeys, was covered in a black spray painted depiction of a snake striking. A circle with a flame rising from it — the fire wheel — was painted in at the bottom right corner.

I pointed at the fire wheel. 'Na Zha did this. I will take his head off.'

'Who's Na Zha?' Clarissa said.

'Demigod,' I said. 'Spirit of youth. Looks and acts like a teen. He used to be good friends with Michael, but I think Michael outgrew him and they stopped hanging out.' I stomped to the entrance of the building. 'And a royal pain in the ass.'

We took the lift up to the first floor.

'Needs refurbishing,' Clarissa said.

'Go right ahead. Ask Jade for the list of preferred contractors,' I said. The lift doors opened and we went out. I dropped my voice so those inside the lift behind us couldn't hear. 'We mostly deal with Earth-based Shen, helping them to keep their cover and make a living here.'

'There are Shen who live on the Earthly? Why would anyone want to do that?' Clarissa said as we went down the corridor towards the management office.

'Some have committed crimes and are in hiding from Celestial justice — we generally don't deal with them. Others are in hiding from other Shen who have a vendetta against them because of a romantic entanglement. Others are keeping a very low profile because they've pissed off a senior Celestial. There's any number of reasons.'

'I thought the Celestial Plane was supposed to be perfect, filled with wise and enlightened spirits living in loving harmony,' she said.

'That's the Second Platform,' I said.

'You're not supposed to talk about that,' Leo said.

I pressed the button to request that the glass office door be unlocked. 'Yes, sir, Mr Shen, sir, I won't talk about it at all.' I smiled at Clarissa as I opened the door. 'The Second Platform is the higher level of Heaven where the Buddhas live. The Heaven of Perfection and Enlightenment. Our Celestial Plane, where the Immortals and Shen live, is nearly as prone to bad behaviour as the Earthly is.'

'Is there a book or something about this?' she said, moving out of the way so Leo could wheel himself into the cramped management office.

'I'll see what I can find for you,' I said. 'But the answer to your question is: not really.'

'Stop it,' Leo said.

'Sorry,' I said.

'Stop what?' Clarissa said.

'Sounding like John,' I said. I leaned on the reception desk to talk to Citrus. 'Hi, Citrus. I saw the graffiti. This is Clarissa, she'll be doing the property management and can arrange for it to be removed.'

'Already arranging,' Citrus said, glaring at Clarissa. 'Police are here to talk to you, Emma.'

I straightened. 'What?'

She gestured with her head towards the tiny meeting room. 'Policeman in there, wants to talk to you about the snake painting.'

'Oh, I see,' I said. 'They probably want to know if we have a security video of it being done. Clarissa, introduce yourself to Citrus and Feena and get them to show you the files.' I touched Citrus's arm. 'Clarissa's very good, Citrus, she's Michael MacLaren's girlfriend and part of the family.'

'Michael's girlfriend?' Citrus said.

'That's right,' Clarissa said.

Citrus moved closer to Clarissa and spoke softly. 'You're lucky.' Her expression softened to a smile. 'Let me show you the files.'

'I'll hang around out here,' Leo said.

'Okay,' I said, and went into the meeting room. I felt a jolt of dismay when I saw who the policeman was, and tapped the stone in my ring, then held my hand out for the policeman to shake. 'Hello, Lieutenant Cheung.'

'Miss Donahoe.' He gestured towards the other seat at the meeting table and sat himself. 'Please sit and tell me what happened.'

'I have no idea,' I said. 'I just saw this myself.'

He flipped open a file containing photographs of graffiti from all over town. 'There is a suggestion that this may be a Triad territorial mark.' He snapped the folder shut. 'Tell me, Miss Donahoe, why would the Triads be marking your building in such a large and obvious manner? And why didn't anyone notice it being done?'

Think quickly, Emma. 'I don't think it's a Triad mark, Lieutenant. I actually have a pretty good idea who did it — his tag is on the bottom. It's a kid called ...' I furiously tried to think of a name. 'A kid called Neil; he used to be a friend of the family, and he's been in trouble a few times.'

'Neil who?'

'Uh ... Neil Zhou. He —'

He didn't let me finish. 'Address?'

'I have no idea.'

'But you say he was a friend of the family? You don't know where he lives? How about a phone number?'

'We stopped being friends with him about four years ago, mostly because he was so much trouble,' I said.

'If you give me a previous address or phone number, we can find him and you can press charges. We take defacement of property seriously, ma'am, and this is particularly bad. We'd very much like to talk to him, and I'm sure you want to help. This will be expensive to remove, and you don't want it to happen again.'

'I'm sure it won't happen again,' I said.

'And why is that? Have you spoken to someone? How do you know for sure it won't happen again?'

I wiped my forehead. I was sweating, even though this wasn't something I needed to worry about. I had much more pressing business on the Celestial Plane and didn't really have time to deal with this.

'I know this kid and he's a one-off prankster,' I said.

'Do you have a security camera?'

'Yes, but it's facing outwards in the lobby.'

'It may show him walking past.'

I deliberately made myself look happier. 'Yes, it may! What a good idea. How about I get my staff to go through the tapes and see if there's any of him last night?'

'*Your* staff?'

I made my voice deliberately mechanical. 'Staff employed by the Chen Corporation acting in trust for Miss Simone Chen. It's easier to just say "my".'

He glanced down at his folder. 'You have a really bad attitude, you know that?'

I nearly exploded but bit my tongue. 'I'll have the staff go through the tapes, and if we see any video of the young man who did it, I will be in touch. I'll also go through my records and try to find anything on Neil that we have, an old address or phone number. Michael might know.'

'Who is Michael?'

I nearly thumped the table with frustration, annoyed at myself. The last thing Michael needed was the police digging up his old Triad involvement.

'Another friend of the family. One of Simone's friends from when she was at school. I'll go through her old school records.' I rose. 'Is there anything else I can help you with, sir?' I didn't wait for him to reply. 'Leo, come show the gentleman out, please.'

Leo wheeled himself into the doorway. 'If you'll come with me, sir.'

Cheung hesitated for a moment, his face rigid, then followed Leo out the door.

I waited until I saw him safely in the lift through the office's glass doors before I spoke to Citrus and Clarissa again. 'Don't worry about having the graffiti cleaned off. I'm getting the person who did it to clean it for us.'

'Can you do that?' Clarissa said.

'Just watch me,' I growled, and opened the office door. 'I'm going up to the roof to see how we can arrange this. Stay down here, Clarissa, but call me if anything happens.'

'I'll start checking the files,' Clarissa said.

I waited until we were out in the corridor with the

office door shut behind us before I spoke to Leo. 'Can you talk to Liu?'

Leo's eyes turned inwards for a moment, then he nodded.

'Tell Liu that I summon the Third Prince, and he has to get his ass to the top of 15 Wellington Street, Central, in less than five minutes. And that's an order, as First Heavenly General.'

Leo relayed the message as we walked to the lift.

'I added that you were on the warpath,' Leo said.

'Won't make any difference to that little asshole,' I said.

'Then he's unique,' Leo said.

We took the lift up to the top floor, then I unlocked the stairway to the roof. The rooftop was bare concrete stained with mould, the lift mechanism and the large concrete water tank the only features.

Leo looked around. 'Not even a window-cleaning cradle.'

Na Zha appeared, flying towards us, clouds of mist forming and disappearing around him as he broke the sound barrier. He halted three metres away from the roof, standing on his fire wheels over the road. He was wearing a pair of black skinny jeans and a black tank top, and didn't even salute me.

I pointed towards the ground. 'Clean that off. Now.'

'What?'

I jabbed my finger. 'That. Get rid of it. The police were here, accusing me of being a Triad member because they thought that was a Triad mark.'

He leaned over to see and grinned broadly. 'Really? Cool. I wish I'd done it.'

'They're on my case constantly because of this bullshit. They may even look Michael up now because I mentioned him. If they go after him, Na Zha, it's your fault.'

He shrugged. 'Not my fault, I didn't do it.'

I stomped to the edge of the roof. 'I'm giving you an order as First Heavenly General, asshole. Make that go away.'

He grew irate. 'I didn't do it — don't blame me!' he said, then his face went blank with shock.

Leo shouted, 'Watch out!'

I was struck from behind and propelled over the edge of the roof. My legs hit the waist-high concrete wall as I went over with a shock of pain in my shins. I tried to concentrate on the energy centres as I fell, my shins screaming with pain. I slowed my fall, but it wasn't enough: I was going to land on a car going up Wellington Street.

Na Zha caught me with a blow that knocked the wind out of me. He carried me back up to the rooftop, hoisted me over the edge and dropped me next to Leo's empty wheelchair. I lay helpless for a few long moments, trying to get my breath back.

Na Zha landed and immediately joined Leo in fighting the demons that had attacked us. There were three of them: big red humanoids carrying swords. I checked them and they were at least level eighty: really big ones. A challenge for Leo but Na Zha shouldn't have a problem.

I hauled myself to my feet, my shins still sharp with pain. One felt like a fracture and was already starting to swell. I did my best to stand on it but when the adrenaline wore off I'd be in trouble. My vision blurred, and I took deep breaths and dropped my head. The last thing I needed was to pass out.

I leaned against the wall and watched. The two Shen had changed to Celestial Form: Leo in his larger form, wearing the Mountain uniform; Na Zha in his more adult form, wearing pale blue Tang robes. Na Zha had no difficulty with the two demons he was facing, and Leo was more than a match for his. I sat down on the concrete with the wall at my back, still trying to suck in air.

Na Zha seemed to be enjoying himself, blocking the blows from weapons on both sides with his whip and wheel without doing any damage to the demons in return. Leo wasn't wasting energy, though; as I watched, he broke through the demon's guard and sliced it from midriff to shoulder and out, making it dissipate. He turned and took the head off one of the demons fighting Na Zha, then dismissed his sword and came to check on me. He knelt in front of me and put his hands on my head, feeling for lumps, then pulled my eyelids open, checking my pupils.

'I'm okay,' I said. 'Just winded.'

'Did you hit your head?'

'No.'

'Lion!' Na Zha yelled, and Leo turned, then jumped back up and recalled his sword.

Na Zha had finished the humanoid he was facing and had taken a couple of steps back. A flock of flyers approached us, more than twenty of them.

'These are really big ones,' Na Zha said. He glanced back at me. 'Run, Emma. Take off over the rooftops and wait for us.'

I shook my head; I wouldn't leave them.

'A stray could get through us with this many,' Na Zha said. 'We'll keep them busy; just move so we don't have to worry about you.'

The flyers landed on the roof between us and the stairs. I couldn't go back inside now.

Leo patted me on the shoulder, then helped me up. 'He's right. Head along a few roofs to the end of the street and wait for us there.'

'Let me help you,' I said. 'Let me fight.' I summoned the Murasame and it came to me without difficulty. I raised it. 'I can do it.'

Na Zha backed up slightly as the flyers moved menacingly towards him. 'Remind me to get you to sign a waiver next time I see you, so that black bastard doesn't blame me if something happens to you.'

Leo stood in front of me and faced them. 'I won't blame you, because nothing will happen to her.'

'I didn't mean you.'

'Call Simone,' I said to the stone.

'I'm blocked,' it said.

'Absolutely bloody useless in a crisis,' I grumbled.

'Stay behind us,' Leo said, and moved next to Na Zha.

'They're scared of you,' I said, watching the flyers hesitate. None of them wanted to be first to attack. I gathered the energy within me, generated a ball of chi and blew up a couple of them that were trying to ease their way around Na Zha and Leo to me. The energy return bolstered me and I stood straighter and stronger.

That was enough to set them off. The demons attacked.

Leo and Na Zha had no difficulty with them, the flyers never made it through their guard. Leo worked with elegant precision, close on the skill he'd had before he'd gone to Hell all that time ago. It wouldn't be long before he exceeded any human warrior.

A flyer leapt over Na Zha's head and he missed it on the way through. I destroyed it with chi and enjoyed the sensation of its energy returning to me — it'd been a long time since I'd felt that rush.

A couple more made it round Na Zha, and I destroyed them with the Murasame before they even hit me.

I scanned around, watching for anything bigger that could possibly ambush us. These were too easy; there had to be something else.

The rooftop door opened and Clarissa appeared

behind the flyers. She looked around and her face filled with fear.

I took a huge leap over the top of the flyers to Clarissa and pushed her behind me into the top of the stairwell. The demons turned to face me, and Leo and Na Zha took advantage of their distraction to hit them from behind.

'Stay there, don't move,' I said to Clarissa, and stepped forward.

The stairwell was in the corner of the roof and only a couple of them could try for me at a time. They were slower than me and, although bigger and stronger, also clumsy. The one in front of me swiped with its front leg and I stepped back to avoid it. It swung its head to grab me in its mouth, and I rolled under its chin and shoved my sword into its belly.

'That is very bad technique!' Leo shouted as I ducked to avoid the spray of demon essence then jumped back.

'You can talk!' I shouted back as I used my backwards momentum to avoid another flyer's foreleg, bounced off the wall of the stairwell and sliced its head off, somersaulting over it.

I stuck my sword into the forehead of the next one, turned sideways to avoid the attack behind me, and sliced off the head of the one behind. I continued the stroke to take both the front legs off the one to the right of me, and ducked to avoid the head of the one to the left. I rolled backwards and righted myself, leaning against the wall of the stairwell.

Leo's face went rigid and he sent a blast of chi from his sword into one of the three remaining demons. He stepped forward and took the head off another; and Na Zha's ring weapon sliced the third into two pieces.

The three of us stood there panting. Now that the adrenaline and chi rush had worn off I felt like I'd run a marathon, and that shin really did feel cracked.

I caught my breath then checked on Clarissa. She was huddled in a corner of the stairs with her arm over her eyes. I knelt next to her and put my arms around her. She let go into my shoulder, her whole body shaking with sobs.

'Humans,' Na Zha said with distaste. 'Always making a fuss.'

I spoke to him over Clarissa's head. 'Get rid of that goddamn graffiti before I haul you before the Courts of the Northern Heavens. And never do that to any of the Dark Lord's property again.'

He shrugged and turned his back on me.

'Leo,' I said, and he came to sit with Clarissa for me.

I limped to Na Zha and spoke to his back. 'I am ordering you as First Heavenly General, asshole. Get rid of it and never do it again.'

Na Zha jumped a metre off the roof and his fire wheels materialised beneath his feet. 'It's already gone.' He spun on his wheels to face me. 'I don't appreciate being called an asshole, madam. Particularly for something I didn't do. Next time you're attacked, I won't be there. Hey!' He shouted to Clarissa. 'Human!'

Clarissa looked up at him from the floor, her face swollen and terrified.

Na Zha took full True Form; his head had four faces, one in each direction. He sprouted six more arms, stretching his torso to fit them. He leaned towards Clarissa, still on his fire wheels, and she cringed into Leo.

'You made a bad decision working for the North, human, because without the Dark Lord around, you're gonna get yourself killed. These amateurs have no idea how to deal with a real threat.'

His wheels slowly rose with a sound like a jet engine, roared into flames with a blast of heat that drove me back, and he flew away.

I went back to Clarissa and sat next to her on the concrete. I put my arm around her shoulders. 'Are you okay?'

She shook her head into Leo's chest.

'Take a moment to catch your breath, then we'll go downstairs and have a cup of tea in the office,' I said. 'Stone.'

'Michael's on his way,' the stone said.

'Thank you. Zara?'

'I'm not sure what to do,' Clarissa's stone said in her soft female voice. 'I don't know what to do.'

'Next time, call Michael,' I said. 'He can protect her.'

'Can her stone talk direct to others?' Leo said. 'Yours can't.'

'It can. Mine's useless, it's too old to communicate directly,' I said.

'Not my fault I'm old,' the stone said.

CHAPTER 9

We went back down to the office and I guided Clarissa into the meeting room, then sat to check my leg. Citrus and Feena saw how distraught Clarissa was and came in.

'What happened?' Citrus said.

'Just a scare: a man came and yelled at us,' I said. 'Can you put the hot water on? We'll make some tea for her.'

Citrus nodded and went out to the shared tearoom in the corridor outside the office. Feena put her hand on Clarissa's shoulder, trying to comfort her.

'I know I'm safe,' Clarissa said. 'I shouldn't be worried while I'm with you. I should be enjoying all this action movie stuff. Why can't I stop crying?'

'Your stress index is probably through the roof,' I said, rolling my jeans up to examine my throbbing shin. 'You've just agreed to move house — and moving up to Wudang will be as good as moving countries. Of course you'll have a strong reaction to anything else that's thrown on top of it. I think uncontrollable crying is a perfectly understandable response to having your life threatened, particularly when you saw what was threatening you.'

'I just want to stop crying,' Clarissa said, pulling another tissue out of the box. Leo patted her back and she leaned into him.

My shin hadn't started to bruise yet, but it was hugely swollen over the bone, tight and painful. I knew better than to try and rub it.

'Michael will be here soon, he'll look after you,' I said. 'Take some time away from everything.' I glanced up from my leg. 'Actually, you could get the Wudang staff to do the move for you, and go spend some time together in Malaysia or Thailand. What do you say?'

'I'd rather get the house on the Mountain all set up.'

'Just don't overdo it, okay?' I glanced up at Feena. 'Is there any ice in the fridge in the tearoom, Feena? I fell down and hurt my leg.'

She bobbed her head. 'I'll look, ma'am.'

'Thanks.'

Leo peered over the table with his hand on Clarissa's back. 'How bad is it?'

'I think it's cracked. I'm too weak to use my Inner Eye at the moment. Can you see?'

His eyes unfocused and his face went slack. 'Whoa,' he said. 'This beats X-rays every time. The bone is definitely cracked. It's not too severe, more like a stress fracture, but it's definitely broken.' He straightened in the wheelchair. 'Would energy healing work on it?'

'Yes, but again I'm too drained to do anything,' I said.

Leo gave Clarissa a parting pat on the back and wheeled himself around the table to me. 'Show me what to do.'

'You didn't look that weak on the rooftop,' Clarissa said, taking deep breaths and controlling the tears. 'You kicked ass.'

'Thanks, but that was pure adrenaline,' I said, taking Leo's hand and linking up to him. 'I'm turning into an adrenaline junkie. Soon I'll start putting myself in harm's way just for the rush.'

Clarissa gasped. 'Michael ...?'

'Maybe, Clarissa.'

'Shut up, woman, and show me how to do this,' Leo growled. 'Deal with Michael's mental problems later.'

'He's not that mental,' I said. 'Look at her.'

'Shut up.'

'Focus your energy on the damage,' I said, showing him where to place the chi. 'Wrap it around a small section of the fracture — not too much chi, that's too hot — that's perfect. Cover that small part of the fracture with the energy, and leave it there until the bone has knitted together.'

'This is like watching a clinical video of the healing happening in fast-motion,' Leo said. 'That's about four weeks' worth of healing right there, and it cost me next to nothing.'

'He's mending a broken bone?' Clarissa said, fascinated.

'And doing a fine job of it,' I said. 'Move to the next section. If it costs too much chi, just leave it.'

Citrus came back with a thermos jug full of hot water and put it on the table. She pulled some ceramic mugs, tea bags and sugar out of the cupboard in the meeting room.

'Any coffee in there?' Leo said. 'But not for Clarissa, caffeine's a bad idea for someone suffering from shock.'

'We have yin-yang,' Citrus said.

'What's that?' Clarissa said.

'Half-tea, half-coffee, vilest concoction on the face of the planet,' Leo said.

'Ew,' Clarissa said. 'Tea, please.'

Feena came back with a jug. 'No ice, Emma, would cold water do?'

'No, it's fine,' I said. 'Leo's doing some Reiki on it, it's very small.'

She nodded and went back out again, unperturbed.

'We're fine, Citrus. We'll let Clarissa get her breath

back then take her home,' I said. 'The graffiti will be cleaned off, no more problems.'

'Okay, Emma,' Citrus said. She gave Clarissa a friendly pat on the back and went out.

Clarissa put three big teaspoons of sugar into a cup of tea. 'Reiki, eh?'

'Perfectly normal, humdrum Reiki,' I said.

Michael stormed in and sat next to Clarissa, peering into her eyes. 'Are you all right? What happened?' He glanced around the room. 'Is everything okay?'

'Everything's fine,' I said. 'A few flyers, a couple of humanoids, nothing major.'

'Emma broke her leg, though,' Clarissa said with relish.

'You should have told me — I would have been down here straightaway to help out,' Michael said.

'What took you so long?' Leo said.

'I apologise,' Zara said. 'I didn't know what to do.'

'Next time this happens, you let me know right away,' Michael said fiercely to Zara. He put his arm around Clarissa and held her so hard she spilled her tea. 'Next time I'm not letting you go out by yourself.'

Clarissa snorted and pushed him away, then grabbed some tissues to wipe up the tea. 'That's all I need, you following me around all the time.'

'I just want to make sure you're safe,' he said.

'It was my own stupid fault. If I'd stayed down here like they told me, I wouldn't have been in any danger at all.' She elbowed him in the ribs. 'You don't need to follow me around — next time I won't give in to any stupid urges to check out what's happening.'

'Done,' Leo said, withdrawing the energy from my leg.

I flexed the knee; the pain had eased and most of the swelling was gone. 'Thanks.'

'You still need to take it easy for a couple of days,' Leo said. 'No brisk weapon work, no running. Soft, slow Tai Chi only.'

I saluted him Western style, the same way Clarissa had saluted me. 'Yes, sir, Lord Leo, sir!'

'Oh, cut it out,' Leo said. 'Let's go back to the Mountain, it'll heal up three times faster there.'

'If I came down here by myself to manage the properties, how much danger would I be in?' Clarissa said.

'I can come down with you if you're worried,' Michael said.

'You're an untrained ordinary human, absolutely not a target,' I said. 'If you don't mind bringing Michael with you, he could guard you as part of his Mountain duties. Then you'd be in no danger at all; he's one of the finest talents among the non-Immortals.'

She wagged her finger at him. 'Only if you promise not to smother me.'

He raised his hands. 'Cross my heart.'

'Then do you have time to stay with me while I look over the files?' Clarissa said.

'I'll help you with them,' he said.

'No, this is my job,' she said. 'If you want to do it for me, you can go back up and someone else can guard me.'

He grinned with delight. 'I'll just sit in here and drink coffee and be a good little driver, then. Do you want me to bring the car around when you're done, ma'am?'

'Good idea. We can grab the stuff out of the flat when I'm done here and take it up to the Mountain,' she said.

He saluted her Chinese-style. 'Ma'am.'

'If you need me for anything, call me on my mobile, or get Zara to contact my stone through the network,' I said, and raised my hand for Leo to take it.

'Out through the front door, the staff are human,' Leo said, slapping my hand away. 'And slowly on that leg.'

I pulled myself up with difficulty; it still felt stiff and all the fluid hadn't drained completely. 'Yes, sir.'

'See you later, Emma,' Clarissa said, and I waved to her as I went out.

'Want the wheelchair?' Leo said as I opened the office door for him.

'That would look really good,' I said. 'You go in disabled and come out healed, and I come out disabled. People will flock to the office looking for the miraculous remedy.'

'Everything about us is miraculous,' Leo said as he pushed the button to call the lift.

'Damn straight,' I said.

The lift doors opened; the lift was empty. We went in and, after the doors had closed, we linked hands and went back to the Mountain.

I managed to stay upright when we landed, tottered a few paces, then stopped. 'Is it eleven yet?'

'Close enough,' the stone said.

I bent to hug Leo. 'Meditation time. See you at lunch.'

'I'm having lunch with Martin,' he said.

I patted him on the shoulder. 'Awesome, have fun. See you later then.'

'Energy work at three, don't forget.'

'Don't worry, I have my iPhone with all the appointments in it. Don't I, stone?'

The stone made some squeaking noises at that but didn't say anything.

I walked to the western side of the Mountain, towards the student residences. An ancient, clay-brick temple stood on the edge of the area, with a paved garden all around it. Wizened pine trees stood in patches of open ground, and there were large bonsai trees — some as tall as a metre — in pots. Bamboo lattices marked the pathways, adding the final touch to the traditional Chinese look.

I went into the temple, removing my shoes at the entrance. The ceiling was thick with enormous incense coils, up to sixty centimetres around and as many high, suspended from the rafters and filling the air with fragrant smoke. The monks and nuns had already seated themselves on mats. I took one at the back, furthest from the altar where two of the clergy were ready to tap the drum and gong. Nobody paid any attention to me.

They all went quiet and very still. I sat cross-legged, closed my eyes, and the chanting began. The low intonation of the Scriptures was marked by the tapping of the fish-shaped wooden drum and the tiny bell-like gong. I let myself drift away into the rhythm of the chant, the Heart Sutra, and became disconnected.

Reality is emptiness; emptiness is reality. Emptiness is not different to reality; reality is not different to emptiness. In the same way, emotions, ideas, logic, and consciousness are emptiness.

Therefore all experience is emptiness. It is not defined. It is not created or destroyed, impure or free from impurity, not incomplete or complete.

Therefore in emptiness, there is no reality, no emotion, no ideas, no logic, no consciousness; no eye, no ear, no nose, no tongue, no body, no mind, no form, no sound, no smell, no taste, no touch; no vision up to no mind leading to no consciousness; no ignorance, no end of ignorance leading to no old age and death, no end of old age and death; no suffering, no origin, no end, no path; no clear awareness, no attainment, and no non-attainment.

Therefore, for Bodhisattvas, there is no attainment; they abide, trusting the perfection of wisdom. With nothing clouding their minds, they have no fear. They leave delusion behind and come to the emptiness of Nirvana.

As I drifted away it felt like I was on the Second Platform, the Heaven of Perfection and Enlightenment, where the Buddhas lived. The feeling of purity resonated amongst all present, filling the air around us with perfect harmony and love for all living things. Time meant nothing as the sound of the sutra filled the air, the gentle rhythm clearing my thoughts and filling me with the peace of emptiness.

It seemed like only a couple of minutes before the echoes of the sutra faded away, leaving me with a feeling of perfect contentment. I took deep breaths, moving my chi, and felt the tiny roiling centre of darkness within me stilled and controlled. Even without the demon essence, something dark and powerful and bloodthirsty sat inside me that would never allow me to reach the perfection that these humans sought.

I went to the head monk and greeted him Buddhist-style, hands clasped as if in prayer. He greeted me back and waved for me to sit on the mat near the altar.

'Your energy is progressing well,' he said, sitting cross-legged in front of me. 'Now that the demon essence has been cleared, the path is open.'

'Thank you for coming to the Mountain. We all appreciate your time.'

'Time means nothing. Spending time sharing the Teachings, however, means a great deal to us.'

'Can you help me with something that's bothering me?' I said.

'Probably not, but fire away.'

'I'm having visions of the future. When the session finished just then, it came even more clearly. It's a horrible feeling of foreboding. Something terrible is going to happen.'

'You are not the first,' he said.

'You should all leave,' I said.

'Why? To protect our lives? Life is an illusion.'

'To protect those who would lose access to your wisdom if you were to be pulled into our conflict. Wudang is a centre of turmoil. You are centres of peace. Please leave.'

'We will go when we must.'

'Then you'll stay much longer than the three months you promised.'

He leaned forward and clasped my hands in his. 'We will not. But when we do leave, it will be without warning. And when we do, arm yourself, Lady Emma, because the Teachings are the Truth, but the Dark Lord keeps all of humanity safe.'

He released my hands and rose, then leaned to help me up. 'Don't you have something productive to do? You shouldn't waste your time sitting around in here all day with us navel-gazers.'

'Absolutely,' I said, and sighed. Back to work.

Later that afternoon I waited for Leo in Fragrant Lotus Pavilion. He didn't show. I tapped the stone.

'What?'

'Where's Leo? Is he okay? We're supposed to have an energy work session. Is he still doing the demon taming with Gold?'

'Hold,' the stone said, and was quiet for a moment, then came back. 'Gold says he never turned up to taming, and he couldn't find him so he gave up and went back to work. He's concerned.'

'Call him on the PA, please.'

The PA was the stone network sitting over the Mountain; the announcement filled my head immediately. *Lord Leo to Fragrant Lotus, please.*

He's here, ma'am, a voice said.

'Who's that?' I said.

'One of the fish,' the stone said. 'Just a sec.'

He's here in the Grotto with us.

'Oh.'

I climbed down the Grotto stairs to the bottom. I only had a small ball of chi and the light reached about a metre ahead of me. The glowing fish were shadowy shapes in the dark water.

'Leo?'

'Over here, Emma.'

I turned the light towards him. He was sitting in his wheelchair near the rocks at the edge of the platform, his elbows on his knees.

I sat on the rocks next to him. 'What happened?'

'He's down there,' Leo said. 'I can see him.'

'You're progressing faster than anyone could have expected, Leo.'

'I can see him.' He sighed and leaned forward. 'Why won't he come up?'

'He said it's like being plugged into a power socket.'

'You need him back. You both need him back.'

I put my hand on his. 'We need you too, mate.'

'I should never have let you talk me into accepting Immortality. Now the only way I can be free is if he drains me. Even the other Shen can't do it — only him.'

'You have so many people who love you.'

He turned to me and his eyes glowed in the darkness. 'What about me? Don't I get a say in the matter? You promised me, Emma. Don't go back on your word.'

'I will do my damnedest to get him to drain you, if that's what you want.'

He looked down at his lap. 'That's all I want.'

I tapped his knee. 'Now come on up into the sunshine and be with the people who love you.'

'There's something big coming, Emma.' His eyes unfocused. 'Can't you sense it?'

'Yes,' I said. 'Probably not as well as you can, though.'

'You'll need him; your survival will depend on it. Everybody who's not Immortal. All of Wudang. Something awful's going to happen and you'll need him, and he'll be down here, still weak.' He gripped my hand where it sat on his leg. 'Someone will have to feed him to bring him completely back. The Generals think they'll be able to do it if they get together, but they can't. Feeding him will kill all of them, and they'll be needed too. Someone needs to be sacrificed; not just killed but completely destroyed. It'd be best if it was me.'

I stood and turned to go. 'Let's cross that bridge when we come to it.'

'Promise me, Emma: if it comes to that, you'll let me do it.'

I didn't look back at him. 'I already did, mate. You have my word. I'll do my best.'

'That's all I can ask for.' He wheeled himself so that he was next to me. 'What were we supposed to be doing? Taming or energy?'

'You missed taming with Gold. You have energy with me now.'

'Do me a favour and reschedule me? I think I need to go do something seriously physical for a while.'

'How about we meet up in front of Dragon Tiger and do a Wu set?'

He nodded. 'Sounds like a plan. See you there.' He disappeared.

CHAPTER 10

As Leo and I worked through the Wu set, students gathered to watch, sitting on the steps below Dragon Tiger. We both put chi into our hands, moving it with our focus as we completed the set, and it vibrated in harmony.

We were about two-thirds done with the set when Martin appeared in front of us and saluted. 'Forgive my intrusion, Lady Emma, there is something you should know.'

I froze in place, and Leo stopped as well.

'What?' I said.

'The Generals — the Marshals — Lady, all thirty-six of them have gathered at the Gates of Heaven, at Guan Yu's abode. Are you aware of this?'

I dropped my hands. 'All thirty-six?'

He nodded a reply.

'A coup?' Leo said behind me.

'Not possible,' I said, but I wasn't sure. I turned to Leo, who'd pulled his wheelchair closer to sit in it. 'Can you take me to the Gates?'

'I've never been. I have Divine Mandate and don't need to go through them,' Leo said. 'So I have no idea where they are.'

'I know,' Martin said, and raised his hands to us. 'I should come as well; you may need support.'

We arrived in front of the Gates of Heaven, where those without Divine Mandate were appraised before being given permission to enter. The gates were actually a five-storey tall, windowless building built of brick and carved with the Four Winds, painted in red and enhanced with gold. The Phoenix was above the main door; the Dragon to the left; the Tiger to the right; and the Xuan Wu along the bottom painted across the wood of the doors. Chinese always put North at the bottom of the map. The left and right doors were painted with images of the Door Gods; and the massive central door was inscribed with a simplified image of the Jade Emperor himself. The roof was traditional tiles, but they were covered with gold as well, making the whole building shine in the sun. The gate building was fifty metres thick, and a wall stretched from either side of it, red with a gold roof, all the way around the Celestial.

I went through the right gate, as was my entitlement, and the demons on either side of the gate saluted me, fist to chest. I opened the door on the side of the corridor that led through the building, and Leo floated to follow me up the five flights of stairs to the top where Guan Yu's quarters occupied the entire top floor.

Two doors led off the lobby: one to Guan Yu's apartment, and the other to his meeting room. I went to the door of the meeting room and stood quietly for a moment, listening.

General Ma was speaking. 'So we can remove the eleven thunder gods and the three tiger gods straight away. Of the twenty-two remaining, seven have a very close association with demonic forces: too much of a risk they'd bring out the Dark Lord's demonic side.'

'I could feed him. I'm not that demonic!' someone said, protesting.

'Looked in a mirror lately?' a deep voice growled.

'That leaves fifteen. Dang is too small, the Zhu sisters are girls ...'

I went into the room and they stopped. The room was decked with triangular banners down the side, displaying Guan Yu's Heavenly Guard allegiances, and held a U-shaped table around which all thirty-six of the Generals sat. They were all in human form, wearing armour over their robes, even those who were usually non-combatants in the battles against demonkind. It was definitely a council of war.

'Oh shit,' one of them said softly.

Ma rose and strode around the back of the table to me. 'Lady Emma. I can explain ...'

'Leo will be the one to feed the Dark Lord, not one of you,' I said.

'Thanks, Emma,' Leo said behind me.

Marshal Zhao rose, his dark face fierce under the skinned tiger's head he wore into battle. 'With all due respect, ma'am, the Black Lion simply isn't big enough to bring the Dark Lord back.'

Ma gestured towards the table. 'Since you're here, you might as well contribute. Just don't order us not to do this, because it has to be done if mortal lives are to be saved.'

I went around the table and Zhu Bo Niang moved down a seat to give me room. Leo wheeled his chair to sit behind me and Martin stayed near the door. I looked down at the table in front of me: they'd made a list of all the Generals with their elemental or demonic natures, and had been crossing themselves off it.

I glanced up at Ma, who'd taken a seat next to me. 'First, tell me how much you can see. Leo and I were just talking about this; all of us can see it. I only have a very nasty sense of powerful foreboding but nothing specific. Lives will be lost, some of them close and precious.' I tried to control my voice. 'And Simone is mortal.'

'So are you, ma'am,' Ma said. 'Nobody has details. All we know is that it's big, it's soon, and lives will be lost.' He put his hand on the list. 'Some of us simply aren't qualified to feed the Dark Lord to complete health. He can't be fed by one who is too small or too elementally opposing —'

I cut him off. 'I know all that. Who do you have left?'

'Fifteen. Less Dang, who is too small, and the Zhu girls —'

'We're not little girls!' Zhu Bo Niang said.

'You're female. That's enough,' Ma said. 'Twelve.'

Bo Niang took the list in front of me, crossed the three names off with a modern ballpoint, and placed the list so that both of us could see it.

'I'm too fire-related,' Ma continued. 'Zhou's too wind-based. Ten.'

'Guan Yu can't be spared, he guards this Gate,' Marshal Zhou said.

'Conceded,' Ma said. 'Nine.'

'I'm probably too fire-related as well,' Marshal Tie said. 'And so is Xie Shi Rong.'

'Yes,' Ma said. 'Seven.'

'The Pure Ones, who've never taken a life, or are pursuing the Teachings,' Bo Niang said. 'Xun and Kang Xi the Humane Sage. They'd destroy him with their type of energy.'

'You sure?' Marshal Kang said.

'Yeah, she's right,' Liang Tian said. 'He's still way too dark to receive that sort of light.'

'Five,' Ma said. He lifted the paper. 'The two biggest of those who could easily fill the Dark Lord to full strength are Gao Yuan the Heavenly Star, and Xiao Lei Qiong the Grand Marshal of the Hours.'

'You can't sacrifice time!' Liang Tian said. 'You can't use Xiao!'

'Time goes on without me,' Xiao said. 'Not as reliably, but it will.'

146

'Not worth the risk,' Ma said. 'That leaves four: Gao Yuan, Marshal Meng of the City of Hell, Yang Biao the Earth spirit, and Wang Zhong of the Yellow River Delta.'

'And me,' Leo said.

'Wang's needed to control the river,' Zhou said.

'The humans should try living without his moderation of the floods and see the devastation that their stripping of the forests has caused,' Liang Tian said with venom.

'The humans in the lower reaches of the delta have no control over what happens in the mountains,' Wang said. 'They need to be alive and scared and raising their voices if change is to happen. If they're dead, they have no voice.'

'If the demon horde invade, they'll have no voice anyway,' Bo Niang said, leaning her chin on her hand. 'We need the Dark Lord back.'

'We need Meng to guard the Gates of Hell as well,' Ma said. 'We don't know the extent of what they're planning, except that it's something big.'

'I will guard the Gates,' Meng said.

'That leaves only two who are both available and qualified to feed the Dark Lord in case of emergency.' He looked pointedly at Leo. 'And are big enough to fill him. Gao Yuan and Yang Biao.'

'Is Yang Biao big enough?' Zhou said.

'I was big enough to imprison all of you in the Earth when I Fell,' Yang said, speaking for the first time. 'Took the Dark Lord himself to take the form of a water dragon to subdue me. That was a grand battle.'

'He's perfect for the job,' Liang Tian said. 'Thick, useless and powerful.'

'Just be glad you're not on ground level where my power rules,' Yang said.

'Would Leo and myself be enough, if both of us were to feed him?' I said.

'No way,' Leo said. 'Don't even think about it.'

'Frankly, ma'am, although you're bigger than many humans, compared to us you're tiny,' Ma said. 'You'd be a drop in the ocean, lost for no purpose.' He nodded to Leo. 'With all due respect, sir, you are too small and too new and would share a similar fate.'

'You promised,' Leo said to me.

'I'll make it happen. Even if they bring him back using someone else, I'll ask him when he is back.'

Leo was silent for a moment, then said, 'Okay.'

'What about if all of you got together and fed him?' I said.

Ma nodded. 'All of us could join forces and feed him close to all our energy without being destroyed, and that would bring him back at full health. But it would kill us all.'

'And then you'd all be stuck in Court Ten while this hurricane occurs,' I said. 'I see.'

'You could tell Judge Pao to let them out straight away,' Leo said.

I snorted with laughter. 'Even if the world was on the edge of destruction and the Jade Emperor himself gave Pao a direct order, he wouldn't let them out straight away because that's not the procedure. The shortest time anybody's been held in Court Ten is twelve hours.'

'Twelve hours is too long with what we can see coming,' Ma said.

'Anyone have any idea how long we have until this storm breaks?' Leo said.

'Not really,' Zhou said. 'But we called this meeting because of a very disturbing development.'

'What's that?' I said. 'And why didn't you tell me?'

'You know already, ma'am, and I'm surprised you haven't put it together,' Ma said.

'She's still very weak,' Bo Niang said. 'It's understandable.'

'Not really,' I said. 'What?'

'When was the last time you identified a demon copy?' Zhou said.

I inhaled sharply. 'Weeks. We haven't seen one in weeks.' I rose and strode to the side of the room, next to the banners. 'We haven't seen one in *weeks*, and I never noticed.' I slapped my forehead. 'The Demon King burned out my intelligence with that demon essence.'

'For the first time in more than ten years, you've had a new batch of students with no demon copies at all,' Ma said. 'None of your existing testing methods worked.'

'Well, that's good, isn't it?' Leo said. 'It's possible there are no copies and they gave up making them.'

'The Death Mother is still out there, and she's been making copies for ten years. Do you think she would suddenly give up?' Zhou said.

'I need to go back right now and call Ronnie Wong in to see if he can identify them,' I said, and returned to sit at the table. 'Everybody else, I suggest you return to your posts, because our dominion is undefended while you are all here. Ma, Gao Yuan, Yiang Biao, Guan Yu: remain. Everybody else, dismissed, and you don't need to tell me; I know.'

'My Lord,' the Generals said, and disappeared.

'Know what?' Martin said as he came into the room to join us.

'She sounds like him,' Leo said.

'Exactly like him,' Ma said. 'Have you been sitting down in the Grotto next to the water?'

'Maybe,' I said. 'Leo's not the only one who likes hanging out down there.'

Guan Yu raised one hand and the meeting room shrank, the table becoming smaller until it was a round ten-seater. Ma conjured tea for us.

'Now,' I said. 'Gao Yuan. Yang Biao. Each of you give me one good reason why I should let you sacrifice yourself to bring him back.'

Gao Yuan let his breath out in a long gasp. 'You are his Serpent. You have to be.'

I tapped the stone.

'What are we doing here?' it said. 'You're supposed to be doing energy work with Leo in Fragrant Lotus.'

'Am I John's Serpent?' I said.

The stone didn't reply.

'That would solve the problem. I feed him, we rejoin, you have him back, no sacrifice necessary,' I said.

'Your sacrifice,' Ma said.

'Not if I'm his Serpent.'

'The stone said you're powerful but not all the time,' Leo said. 'Could you be his Serpent just some of the time?'

'Yes,' I said, 'it's possessing me. When Simone or I are in terrible danger, it takes me over, makes me more powerful, and helps me take the danger out.'

'That's what happened at the Convention Centre!' Leo said.

'No, that was all me, I didn't black out. But the Serpent's definitely been possessing me when I can't do something by myself. Please don't mention it to Simone; she hasn't worked it out yet. If John's Serpent possesses me and then rejoins with the Turtle, I'll probably be taken as part of the equation. If that happens, Simone may never forgive him.'

'Neither would he,' Ma said.

'We don't want to have to put up with the aftermath of him losing you,' Guan Yu said with grim humour. 'It was bad enough after Michelle died. Losing you or Simone as well would push him totally over the edge. He could turn away from the Celestial.'

'If he changes sides, it's all over,' Ma said.

'Would Heaven fall?' I said.

'We may be able to hold Heaven, but the Earthly would fall. The Celestial Plane would be under siege, and I don't know how long we could defend it.'

'You wanted an extremely good reason for letting one of us make the sacrifice,' Gao Yuan said. 'There it is.'

'Conceded,' I said. 'Neither of you has family, those who need you?'

Leo rose out of his wheelchair and walked to the windows. He leaned on the window ledge. The meeting room looked over the interior of the Celestial dominion, and Guan Yu's demon troops were doing weapons training on the grassy hillside below.

'I have chosen to be without family,' Gao Yuan said. 'And I've had enough of this sentient life. I would prefer to end it now after three thousand years of being alone.'

'My nature is Stone,' Yang Biao said. 'I'm more of an Earth God, though, aligned with the soil rather than rock. The Dark Lord is weak to my elemental alignment regardless, and I would be the ideal candidate to fill him.'

'My special nature means that I would not be destroyed. I would just lose my sentience and revert,' Gao Yuan said.

'You really are a star?'

'I really am.'

'I would return to become one with the Earth in a similar way,' Yang Biao said.

'So neither of you would be completely destroyed; you would just become non-sentient nature spirits?' I said.

'That is correct,' Gao said. 'We are not strong enough to ever return; we would be gone.'

'I see.' I turned to Ma. 'And you wasted all this time cutting down the list?'

He shrugged. 'I was already at this point, but everybody wanted to do the stupid noble thing and make the sacrifice. I had to get them all together and let them all see exactly why these two are the only choices.'

'It's not like the Generals to be that obtuse,' I said.

'When it comes to being all noble and selfless, they can be a royal pain,' Guan Yu said.

'I see your point. All right.' I leaned back. 'Gao and Yang, when the time comes, you have to be ready to do it. Ideally he'll be back before then and we won't need to do this, but if we have to, you need to be alive.'

'So that means keeping yourselves safe, no throwing yourself suicidally at stupid targets,' Ma said.

Leo turned and yelled at us. 'I don't know how you can all discuss this so calmly. You're talking about killing these two wonderful men, and you don't even seem to care! Do you love him so much that you're willing to sacrifice anybody to see him back?'

'Do you love him that much?' I said.

He swiped one hand in front of him. 'No!'

'Then I don't think you love him enough to sacrifice yourself to bring him back.'

His face screwed up. 'Don't play word games with me. I know how I feel.'

'Okay, I'll put it straight then. If you have a choice of sacrificing the entire mortal world or the intelligence of one of these noble gentlemen, which do you choose?'

'Neither.'

'That may not be an option.' I rose. 'I think we're done here. We all know what we have to do.'

Leo went to his wheelchair, fell to sit in it, and disappeared.

'And it looks like I'll need someone to give me a lift back to Wudang,' I said.

'I'll take you, then I'll try to find him,' Martin said.

'Thanks, Martin, but don't try to find him. When he's ready he'll come back.'

Martin disappeared the minute we arrived at the Mountain, probably to go look for Leo anyway. I pulled out my mobile and stormed towards the admin section.

'Wong.'

'Ronnie, it's Emma. I need you here right now if you could. We're not detecting them.'

He inhaled sharply. 'When did this happen?'

I stopped walking and turned on the spot, frustrated at my own stupidity. 'We had our latest intake two weeks ago and there were no copies. I never noticed. How soon can you be up here?'

He was silent for a moment, then said, 'Let me close up shop and I'll be right there. Can you provide an escort for me at your gates?'

'Done,' I said, and snapped the phone shut. 'Stone, get a Celestial to meet him.'

LK Pak and Meredith appeared in front of me and I nearly walked into them.

'Wudang Mountain wins first prize in a stupidity contest,' I said. 'Have you ordered a sweep?'

'We've been sweeping regularly, Emma, the last one was this morning,' Meredith said. 'Ma asked me not to tip you off. He was concerned you'd order them not to make the sacrifice.'

'LK, Ronnie's on his way, can you meet him at the gates, please? Meredith, with me,' I said, and headed towards the admin centre.

'Stop spending time in the Grotto,' Meredith said.

'Would spending time down there make it easier for him to possess me?' I said.

She stopped walking and I bent to catch my breath, panting at the effort.

'How long have you known that's what it is?' she said.

'I'm going to formally reprimand every single Celestial who's been keeping stuff from me,' I said, and moved off again. 'Call Simone back from school. She might be able to see the copies.'

'Good idea,' she said, and unfocused as she walked beside me.

CHAPTER 11

LK brought Ronnie up to my office and we closed the door.

'Let me see the list of the latest recruits,' Ronnie said, sitting across the desk from me. LK parked himself next to the wall and watched.

I pulled up the student database, then rotated the screen so Ronnie could see. 'Last intake was two weeks ago. No demons were identified.' I pulled up the timetable. 'They're having a basic hand-to-hand class right now.'

Ronnie pulled himself to his feet. 'Let's go.'

'How do you want to do this?' I said as the three of us walked towards the junior training rooms.

'Simone has arrived,' the stone said. 'She'll meet you there.'

'Enthusiastic weird parent,' Ronnie said, and changed his form so that he appeared as an older Chinese man with a dreadful comb-over and a poorly fitting navy polyester suit.

'Warn Simone,' I said.

'Done,' the stone said. 'She's going to wait out of sight to see if Ronnie can identify any among the students. If he doesn't spot any, she'll go through them herself.'

We arrived at the training room and Ronnie started talking loudly with a thick Cantonese accent. 'But then he told me, I am learning from a god, and I said, is that better than doctor or lawyer, and he said, yes! He said it is what he wants to do. So.'

We stopped at the doorway, and the class halted and saluted.

'I'm good father,' Ronnie said loudly to everybody present. 'I say, even if it's not doctor or lawyer, you be happy, I be happy. Just study hard, be good student, marry good girl and have lots of grandsons for me.'

Some of the students sniggered at his rampant Hong Kong parent stereotype.

Ronnie spread his arms expansively and spoke even louder. 'These are his colleagues? So fine and strong!' He turned to me and spoke in a stage whisper loud enough for everybody to hear. 'So many pretty girls!'

A couple of the girls turned away, covering their grins.

'This is Peter's father. He would only give Peter permission to come if he saw what it was like here,' I said.

A few of the students looked confused, trying to work out who Peter was. Thankfully, nobody showed any recognition. I was almost positive there wasn't a Peter in their year but I wasn't completely sure.

Ronnie raced to the students and shook their hands with enthusiasm, even grabbing the girls' hands when they shyly didn't put them out. 'I'm Peter's father, he tells me so much about you! He loves being here, he is so happy, so I say, okay, stay, but I must see what it is like.'

'Have you seen enough?' I said. 'We can move on to Peter's dorm.'

Ronnie spread his arms and turned on the spot, grinning like an idiot. 'I am in Heaven where my son is learning from gods.' He nodded to me, his grin still wide. 'I have seen enough pretty girls. Now to see if his room is clean.'

'This way then, sir,' I said.

The students burst into laughter and scornful chatter after we'd left.

We walked about twenty metres and Ronnie took his normal mid-thirties human form. He removed the glasses and wiped them on the hem of his shirt. 'One of them is strange. I can't put my finger on it. She's completely human, but somehow she looks ... different. The tamed demon is obvious: the Fire Essence Pill glows like a beacon inside her; she's not a problem. But that one ...' He turned back to the training room and put his glasses back on. 'That one feels weird.' He faced me again. 'Do you take blood from them when they come in?'

'No. Haven't needed to.'

'Well, you do now, and make sure you do it under controlled conditions, because if they see demon essence in the syringe they'll probably self-destruct,' Ronnie said. 'Pull this one out and do a blood test now.'

'Which student was it?' the stone said. 'Send me an image. I'll have her sent up to the infirmary.'

Ronnie focused on the stone for a moment, then snapped back.

'The students will finish in ten minutes,' the stone said. 'Head to the infirmary and I'll have her sent to you.'

The student arrived at the infirmary ten minutes later. Her face filled with shock when she saw all of us there.

I ignored her and spoke loudly to Edwin. 'Just order some more, I'll have the budget extended. I understand that with more students you're going to need more supplies. Just give me a rough idea and I'll fix it up.' I touched Simone on the arm. 'Come on, you can get the ingredients for the assignment off him when the supplies come in.'

Simone picked up on it straightaway. 'But it's due Tuesday,' she whined. 'The supplies won't be here in time and I'll fail.'

'I'll see if I can find some iodine for you in one of the first-aid kits,' Edwin said, playing along.

Simone hugged him. 'Thanks, Edwin, you're the best.'

Edwin turned to Ronnie and LK. 'Can you wait until after I've seen this student, Master Pak? It won't take a second.'

'Of course,' LK said. He sat on one of the chairs and gestured for Ronnie to sit next to him.

Simone and I went out, walked about ten metres, and watched proceedings with our Inner Eyes, light enough to not be detected.

'You didn't provide a blood sample, Ellie,' Edwin said, opening a folder. 'We need your blood type, just in case. Do you mind giving one now before you go back to class?'

'Sure,' Ellie said, unfazed. She sat on the couch and held her arm out. 'I haven't had one of these in forever. When I was little, my father had us tested for bird flu, and then a couple of years later when the SARS went through. Since then I haven't needed it.' She smiled up at Edwin as he fixed the tourniquet on her upper arm. 'I think the martial arts help you to stay healthy. And, of course, being on the Mountain ... it's great, isn't it?'

'Truly wonderful,' Edwin said, raising the syringe. He pushed it into her arm and she winced, then relaxed.

Ronnie shot to his feet and yelled, 'Everybody out! Edwin, out!' He grabbed Edwin and threw him out the door.

Edwin landed on his back a good five metres away. LK ran out, grabbed him and ran with him towards me and Simone.

Ronnie appeared in the doorway just as Ellie exploded. He was thrown towards us by the blast. I ducked and protected my head as all the glass blew out of the infirmary windows. All I could hear then was dull thumping.

I ran to Ronnie. He was lying on his stomach so I turned him over onto his back and looked him up and down, unsure. I wasn't even confident that he had a pulse. LK pushed me away and ran his hands down Ronnie's face and neck. He said something, but his voice was muffled by the thumping.

'I'm deafened by the blast,' I said, but even my own voice sounded strange in my head.

Someone grabbed me, pulled me up and turned me around. Edwin was in my face, checking my eyes.

'I'm not injured, just deafened,' I said.

He nodded and said something in return that appeared to be, 'I am too.'

You need to go somewhere quiet and get over this, both of you, the stone said, its voice clear in my head. *The deafness may be permanent; you will need to be examined.*

'How's Ronnie?' I shouted.

Ronnie pushed LK away, pulled himself to his feet and staggered slightly, his hand on his face. He said something, his unusually deep voice throbbing in the background noise.

He says he'll live, the stone said. *Remember, demons are much tougher than humans. Now he, Simone and LK have a job to do. You and Edwin go up to your office, close the door and stay put.*

Please do as the stone says, Simone said.

'Come on, Edwin,' I said. From his expression, he didn't get a word of it.

Meredith appeared next to us and shooed us to the office.

The sound of Ronnie and Simone entering my office jerked me awake and I drowsily raised my head off my desk. Meredith was still healing Edwin's ears, one hand on either side of his head.

Simone came to me and put her hand on my back. 'How do you feel?'

'She'll be fine,' Meredith said. 'She'll have some residual ringing in her ears and she probably has the headache from hell right now. Emma, you're still weak. You need to slow down.'

'How many demons did you find?' I asked Simone.

'Only three. The first one exploded the minute Ronnie singled it out, and the blast killed two of the students in its class.' Simone's expression was rigid with restraint. 'We were more careful taking out the other two; they never knew what hit them.'

I dropped my head on my desk again. 'Which students?'

'Died or demon?'

'Both.'

She was silent a moment, then said, her voice soft, 'I don't know their names, Emma.'

'That's understandable. They've only been here two weeks and you've hardly seen them,' I said.

'I'm responsible here while Daddy's incapacitated,' she said.

'No, you aren't,' I said. 'I am. Your responsibility is to go to school and gather all the skills and training you need to decide what you want to do with your life.'

She sighed loudly and leaned on the desk. 'You know, I was supposed to go shopping with a couple of friends from school this afternoon.'

'Then go.'

'All I want to do is curl up in a corner with a DVD that's just mindless fun. Disney even. Something really cute and harmless and safe.'

'Sounds like the perfect prescription to me,' Meredith said.

'Come on,' I said, and rose. I staggered slightly and Simone took my arm to make sure I didn't fall over. 'Let's go watch *The Lion King*.'

She released me and brushed her hand through her honey-coloured hair. 'Right now *The Lion King* sounds a bit too grim.'

'We'll find something suitably silly for you then,' I said. I put my arm around her waist. 'Let's go eat some chocolate and watch *Toy Story*.'

'Actually ...' Meredith said, releasing Edwin's head, 'can I join you? That sounds like the best use of an afternoon I've heard in a while.'

'Is this for women only?' Edwin said.

I pointed at him and glared. 'You come, you bring extra chocolate.'

He grinned wryly. 'I'll have to pop down to the Earthly to get some. Will you wait?'

'No,' I said. 'We'll send a demon or one of the senior Celestial Masters. It's about time they were used for something worthwhile.'

'It'll have to be Swiss chocolate to do this properly,' Meredith said. 'I'll be right back. Don't start the video without me.'

The next morning I still had the headache from hell, even with painkillers. I was trying to do some paperwork, with limited success, when Yi Hao tapped on the door.

'There's a horse here to see you, ma'am.'

I looked up at her, unsure of what I'd heard through the ringing in my ears. 'A what?'

She opened the door wider. 'A man and a horse. You have to come out, ma'am, they won't fit in your office.'

I went out to find Simone's demon horse, Freddo, standing under the tree outside the office, a man beside him. Freddo was eight months old now and turning into a fine young stallion. His hide was a bright, rich gold and his immaculately groomed white mane and tail hung long over his neck and hind legs. He appeared full-grown, only his slightly too-big head and gangly legs indicating that he still had some growing to do before he could carry a rider. He was tall as well: the top of his shoulder was level with the top of my head, and his ears were well above me.

He lowered himself on one foreleg and the man saluted me. I nodded back.

'Can I help you, guys?'

Freddo took a step forward and spoke, his voice sounding like that of a strong young man. 'This is Ah Cheung, my mafoo at Lord Bai Hu's stables. He looks after me, does my feed and whatnot. He helped me come here so I could talk to you.'

'What's the problem?'

He looked back at Ah Cheung. 'Can we walk, Lady Emma? This is kind of personal.'

'I will wait here, ma'am,' the groom said.

I gestured towards the path and Freddo fell into step beside me. His head bobbed as he walked; he was holding it low as a sign of respect.

'I really want to be everything that Simone wants in a horse, Lady Emma. I can't wait until I can carry her and be the best steed possible for her.' He glanced at me. 'I love her so much.'

I put my hand on the solid crest of his neck. 'I'm glad to hear it. She loves you too.'

He looked away, his expression pained. 'I haven't seen her in ages. She doesn't like me any more.'

'She's been awfully busy, Freddo, she doesn't have a lot of time to spend with you —' I began.

He cut me off and moved out of reach. 'No, it's not that. I'm embarrassing her.' He lowered his head slightly. 'I'm embarrassing myself.'

I stopped at the edge of a gorge and we stood together facing the spectacular view of the heavenly mountains below. 'What's happening?'

He reached to put his nose on my hand. 'I asked my mafoo about it, and he talked to the Lord Bai Hu about it, and he came and talked to me about it, and they talked to Simone about it. They can fix me, but she won't let them.'

'It's not that bad, is it? I mean, you don't attack her, do you?'

He dropped his head so his nose was nearly on the ground, his voice soft with misery. 'I tried to mount her.'

'I didn't know. She's never mentioned it.'

'She was so embarrassed, she cried and ran away. I didn't know what I'd done wrong.'

'You've had all that explained, though?'

'Yes, the Tiger came and talked to me after it happened.' His voice broke. 'I made her cry.' He shook his head. 'I never want to make her cry!'

'So it won't happen again, right?'

'No, I would never dream of hurting her like that again.' His voice became softer. 'Emma, I love her so much — I get a huge erection every time I see her. And I'm a horse. Not the sort of thing you can hide.'

'That would embarrass her. No wonder she's staying away.'

He tossed his head. 'I have no control over it! It's so stupid! There's another thing too. If Simone's with me and someone approaches — anyone — I'll attack them before I have time to think. Sometimes my mafoo will come into the stall and I'll try to bite him before I even know what I'm doing. He's scared of me, and I don't blame him.'

'Have they tried anything to help you with this?' I said. 'Have you talked to anyone about it?'

'The Lord Bai Hu suggested a few things, stuff they use to control natural stallions. Nothing works. Apparently I'm ... what's the term? Very hormonal. Very horsy.' He laughed in his throat, a cross between a human laugh and a nicker. 'I have aggressive urges, and

I'm extremely territorial, and I have absolutely no control over any of it.' He looked into my eyes, his own brown eyes full of desperation. 'Please talk Simone into letting me be castrated. I'd be a much better companion for her as a gelding.'

I put my hand on his shoulder. 'That's a huge decision to make, Freddo.'

'No, it isn't. There's only one thing I want from life and that's to be Simone's horse. Lord Bai Hu explained everything: because I'm half demon, I'll never sire anything anyway. It's the best course all around.'

'What about chemical castration?'

He dropped his head. 'They tried that. For three marvellous weeks, I was everything that Simone would want from me. Lord Bai Hu said that when I was sane, I was the most talented horse he'd ever seen, demon or natural. I memorised and completed a medium-level dressage test by myself; Lord Bai Hu said he'd never seen any horse do that before, that I was unique. It was wonderful.'

'But?'

'But it wore off. And then they had to raise the dose to keep it working. Over the long term it would have killed me.' He gazed out over the mountains. 'I would love to be that horse again, ma'am. To be able to concentrate and see the world clearly without the haze of hormones making my brain a mess of stupidity.' He looked at me. 'A tiny operation, under local anaesthetic, and I'll be everything that I want to be. But she won't let them do it.'

'You don't seem to be any trouble right now, Freddo. How do you know that with the right training and concentration techniques you won't grow out of it? You're still very young.'

'Ma'am, horses become more hormonal as they grow older. In a year or so, I may be so out of control that I'll be insane.'

'I know many stallions who are perfectly calm, sensible rides.'

'And you also know of racing stallions who are so dangerous they have to be controlled with devices that can only be classed as torture. Even with handling by talented, experienced humans who know what they're doing, a hormonal stallion is a dangerous thing. And that's me.'

'You're different.'

'No, I'm not. I'm just like them — an uncontrollable animal.'

I stroked his shoulder. 'You have something that none of those horses has: intelligence. And from the way you talk, intelligence equal to that of an extremely smart human. Use it.'

'Freddo,' Simone said from his other side. 'I'm sorry, I didn't know.'

'Oh God,' Freddo moaned, a low sound of pain. 'Let them cut me, please. I want to be with you.'

She stood in front of him. He leaned into her and she cradled his head. 'I don't want to do that to you. It would make you different from what you are, and I love you just like this.'

'But you stay away from me.'

'I won't any more.' She leaned down to see into his eyes. 'You don't have an erection right now, see? You can learn to control it.'

'Spoke too soon,' he said, lowering his head.

She giggled, and he laughed as well.

'Stone, is the Tiger free?' I said.

'No,' the stone said. 'But I can relay.'

'Tiger, Freddo's extremely intelligent. Could he use human meditation and concentration techniques to control these impulses?'

The stone spoke with the Tiger's voice. 'Just cut the little bastard and be done with it. Best solution all around.'

'I won't let you!' Simone said.

'Oh,' the Tiger said. 'Sorry, little one, didn't know you were there. It is the best thing to do.'

'How about we get them working with a behavioural therapist for a few months and see if they can't work this out?' I said. 'Don't treat him like an animal, treat him like a person.'

'If that doesn't work, what then?' Freddo said.

'Then Simone has to let you have the operation,' I said.

Simone stroked his forelock and rested her forehead on his. 'I don't want to.'

'I do,' he said.

'Compromise,' I said. 'Say six months. In six months you'll be old enough to begin your training, Freddo; that will be moment-of-truth time. I won't let you carry Simone if you can't control yourself. Okay?'

'Sounds like a plan,' the Tiger said, 'but you're paying for the therapist.'

'Deal,' I said.

'Okay,' Freddo said.

'You have to try your hardest,' Simone said. 'Don't play up just so you have to be cut. There are a lot of advantages to staying entire, Freddy-frog, you know that?'

'You'll be bigger and stronger entire,' I said.

'And it's cool to ride a stallion,' Simone said. 'Prestigious. It's like being a heroine in a fairytale.'

Freddo raised his head, nearly hitting Simone on the nose. 'There's prestige in riding a stallion? The Tiger makes it sound like only idiots use stallions as riding horses.'

'That's because it's true,' the Tiger said. 'Stallions are fucking useless as a saddle horse: totally unable to concentrate, particularly when there's a mare in heat around. You want spirit, ride a mare; you want reliable, ride a gelding; you want to die, ride a stallion.' His voice became rueful again. 'Sorry, Simone.'

'That will be the test then,' I said to Freddo. 'In six months, let's see you do a dressage test with a mare in heat in the next paddock.'

'Can't be done,' the Tiger said.

'We can do it, right, Freddo?' Simone said.

'Wanna bet?' the Tiger said.

'Yes!' she said.

'What do you bet?'

'My testicles,' Freddo said with amusement.

'All right,' the Tiger said. 'You do a test with a mare nearby, you keep your balls. Now, if you'll excuse me, I was just about to supervise one of my own stallions.'

'You two go and talk about stuff,' I said to Simone and Freddo. 'I have work to do. Go and watch a video together.'

Freddo tossed his head at me. 'Don't treat me like a human, Emma, I'm a horse. I don't watch videos.'

'Olympic showjumping?' Simone said.

'Ooh,' Freddo said, eyes wide. 'They have videos of showjumping? What about the dressage?'

'And the cross-country.' She slapped him on the neck. 'Come on!'

He pranced, flicking his tail. 'Cool!'

They ran off together towards Simone's apartment.

'And if you need to wee, do it outside!' I shouted after them.

CHAPTER 12

Clarissa and Michael held their engagement party in a function room at one of the Tiger's hotels. Most of the guests were their young friends, human and Shen; they played mah-jongg and sang at the karaoke screen in the corner of the room.

Michael met us at the door and guided us to the red-clothed table for VIPs. He gestured towards a Chinese couple sitting with Clarissa. 'These are Clarissa's parents, Kevin and Christine Huang. This is Emma Donahoe, my boss, and Simone Chen, and Leo Alexander.' He sat next to Clarissa and put his arm protectively around her.

'Mr and Mrs Huang, pleased to meet you,' I said, shaking both their hands.

Mr Huang was slim and relaxed, wearing a tailored grey silk business suit. His wife was small and round, with a kind, shy smile and an unflattering skirt suit. I sat at the table after I'd moved a chair out for Leo to wheel himself in, and Simone sat next to me.

Kevin Huang beamed. 'We are so proud of Clarissa. We thought she couldn't do better than working for such a prestigious company, and then we hear she's engaged to a prince.' He spread his hands and grinned at his wife, obviously embarrassing Clarissa. 'She deserves the finest!'

I glanced at Michael and he grimaced. *Dad pulled the Arab sheik thing*, he said.

The Tiger, wearing Arab robes, came over to us and grinned at me. 'Lady Emma, good to see you.' He glanced around. 'Great party, eh?'

'Hi, Barry,' I said.

'Ah, just the man I wanted to see,' Kevin said, and gestured for the Tiger to sit. 'I need to ask you some questions about wedding preparations.'

'Such as, who pays?' the Tiger said, the grin not shifting. 'Chinese: the father of the groom pays; Western: the father of the bride pays. You're probably wondering how we do it where I come from?'

Kevin thumped the table and shouted, 'Exactly!'

The Tiger spread his arms, nearly knocking over a water glass with his robes, and matched Kevin's volume. 'How about we split the difference?'

Kevin laughed loudly and artificially. 'Works for me!' He turned to me and pointed at the Tiger. 'This guy is great. I thought that Clarissa would have to cover herself up, but he's terrific.'

'I know!' the Tiger said expansively.

'Wait,' Kevin said. 'Lady Emma? More royalty?'

'No, no, no,' I said. 'It's just a joke amongst them. They say I'm so bossy that they have to call me that.'

He started theatrically and glared at me. 'Bossy woman no good.'

'She's my boss, she's allowed to be bossy,' Clarissa said.

Kevin made a show of being taken aback. 'You are boss of Chencorp?'

I nodded. 'Simone owns the company. I run it for her until she's old enough to take control herself.'

Kevin turned his attention to Simone. 'I have a son who would love to meet you.'

'Oh, Dad,' Clarissa said, reaching past her mother to tap him on the arm. 'Cut it out.'

'You have a brother, Clarissa?' I said.

'Yeah. He's in Canada studying, he's eighteen. He didn't come, he has exams, but he's promised to come to the wedding.'

The Tiger stood again. 'Come and play a round with me, Kevin. Winnings can go towards the wedding, and you can tell me about business in Canada.'

Kevin rose, and tapped the table next to his wife. 'Get me some more tea.'

Christine nodded silently. When they were gone, she smiled at me. 'What sort of business are you involved in? Kevin just said it was big.'

'We're mostly a holding firm for a large portfolio of investments, but we do have some sidelines,' I said. 'It's complicated. When Clarissa and Michael are married, we'll explain in more detail for you.'

'And both of them are working for you? Last time Clarissa talked to me, she and Michael were working for a big American bank.' She turned to Clarissa. 'This only happened a few weeks ago?'

'Michael's known Simone's family for a long time,' Clarissa said. 'They helped him out when he was younger; Simone's father is like Michael's uncle. Michael had an offer from his father's firm in the Middle East, but he decided he'd rather work for Emma instead. I joined as well. She's given me a big portfolio to manage by myself.'

'Clarissa's very smart and talented, Mrs Huang, you should be proud,' I said.

Christine nodded and her smile grew wider. 'I know.'

'So what do you do, Mrs Huang? Michael told me your husband was in plastics. Are you in the same business?'

'I run the engineering part of the company, Kevin runs the rest,' Christine said. 'He's the boss; I just manage the machines.'

'Don't sell yourself short, Christine,' Michael said. 'Without you the company wouldn't run at all.'

Christine shrugged.

'Mom owns three patents for plastic extrusion processes,' Clarissa said. 'She's a leader in the field.'

'Doesn't mean much here in China,' Christine said. 'Other factories have already stolen our technology. But it doesn't matter provided we make a good turnover for our children.'

'Your factories are in China?' I said.

'Yes. We manufacture here, and ship to Canada and the US. I spend about half my time running into Shenzhen to fix things, and Kevin runs things back home.'

'It's exhausting for them,' Clarissa said.

'Worth every second,' Christine said. 'Building a future for you.'

'I hope you're not boring everybody with stories about plastic,' Kevin said as he and the Tiger returned to the table. He put one arm around Clarissa's shoulders and squeezed her. 'Your fiancé's father just lost enough to pay for the wedding anyway.'

The Tiger waved one hand at Kevin, grinning broadly. 'He cleaned me out.'

'We were just talking about how living in Hong Kong has changed you,' Kevin said to Clarissa, still holding her. 'How it's made you more confident.'

'Hasn't changed me at all,' she said, extricating herself from his grasp and taking his hand to hold it. 'I'm just the same.'

'No, darling, he's right,' Christine said. 'You seem so much more confident and sure of what you're doing — it's great to see.'

'See? Even your mother noticed,' Kevin said.

'I don't feel any different,' Clarissa said.

'Oh, shit, here's trouble,' the Tiger said softly.

There was a bemused murmur through the crowd as Martin came into the room. He was wearing traditional robes and armour, with his long hair in a topknot and the Silver Serpent in its scabbard in his right hand. He staggered slightly when he stopped in front of us, then fell to one knee and nearly toppled over. Leo jumped out of his wheelchair to catch him.

Up close it was apparent that Martin was injured: his armour was hanging off him and dark with blood. The Tiger's sons who were present quickly came to the table and stood around us.

Martin was breathless, barely getting the words out. 'Attack on the Gates of Heaven. Guan Yu needs reinforcements.' He tried to salute me and failed, dropping his sword and leaning on Leo. He clutched Leo's arm. 'We have Disciples heading that way but the Princess and some Horsemen are sorely needed.'

The Tiger rose and concentrated. 'Why are we blocked in here?' He looked around. 'What the fuck?'

'You are unreachable here,' Martin said. 'My Lords, my Ladies ... help them.' His breath left him in a long gasp and he collapsed into Leo's arms.

'Still alive, unconscious,' Leo said, and glanced up at the Horsemen. 'Someone take him to the lake in the Northern Heavens; he needs to be a turtle in the water.'

One of the Horsemen nodded, reached for Martin, and they both disappeared.

I rose. 'Michael, grab a couple of your brothers as guards and stay here with the humans. Simone, take me to the Gates. Tiger, round up your Horsemen and get yourself out there too. Stone.'

'What's going on?' Kevin said weakly.

'Heaven's under attack, and it won't make any difference to you because in an hour you won't remember anything about it,' Michael said grimly.

'Yes, Emma?' the stone said.

'I want you to stay here and find the cause of that blockage. See if there's been a Six-type stone planted here, and then find out where it came from. Michael, help it. As soon as we're clear of the blockage, I'll have Gold come down to assist. Let's go, Simone.'

The stone floated out of my ring and changed to human form. Simone took my hand and everything disappeared.

We landed on top of the Gates, with the battle raging below us. An army of about a thousand demons — mostly humanoids, with flyers sweeping overhead, and a few nasty lizard things — had engaged the gate guards. Pennants held on pikes showed where the Generals fought, and the battle was particularly thick around them. It was hard to tell our own troops because they were blackened with demon essence from those they'd destroyed.

'Stay up here and relay what's going on,' Simone said.

'Ah geez, I can't,' I said. 'I don't have the stupid stone.'

The stone appeared in front of me with an audible pop. 'Zara's handling things there, I thought you'd need me.' It flew into the setting on my ring. 'I was right.'

Simone took Celestial Form and summoned Seven Stars. She filled the sword with energy, then dived off the edge of the gate, somersaulting a couple of times with her dark blue robes flying around her before landing in a thick cluster of demons at the back of the formation. She used shen energy and Seven Stars to cut through them and the air around her became black with demon essence. The gate guards saw her and cheered, fighting with new energy.

I didn't have the strength to jump off the Gates myself. I summoned the Murasame and fidgeted with frustration at not being able to join the battle below.

'How many Horsemen is the Tiger bringing?' I asked the stone.

'Two hundred.'

'Bah, that's not many. Tell him to bring them in at seven o'clock from where Simone is. They'll form the third point of the triangle, and the joint forces can crush them.'

The Tiger appeared at the back of the demon army in huge True Form; he must have been at least ten metres long from his whiskers to his tail. His Horsemen appeared around him, all mounted and with spears, but nowhere near where I'd said to go. They threw themselves at the demons.

Liu appeared next to me.

'How many do we have ready?' I said.

'Two hundred Disciples.'

I inhaled sharply. 'I don't want to see mortals pulled into this!'

A group of Wudang archers appeared on the roof around me, moved into position, and used energy arrows to take out the flyers.

'Lives will be lost this day, Lady Emma, we have all foreseen it,' Liu said. 'That is what the Disciples are here for. It is what they live for, and hopefully we will see one or two Raised.'

He used his staff as a pole and vaulted over the edge of the roof. The Disciples appeared in two groups as he landed: half to shore up the guards in front of the huge gate doors; the other half as the third point of the triangle around the demons.

The Disciples, Guards and Horsemen now had the demons enclosed from three sides and proceeded to cut them to pieces.

Freddo appeared next to me. 'I heard Simone's in trouble.' He arched his neck and gazed over the edge of the roof. 'Simone's in trouble!'

'Wait,' I said, but he had already leapt over the edge of the roof.

He landed lightly next to her, twenty metres below, reared and lashed out, then turned and protected her back as she destroyed the demons in front of her. She lifted herself onto his back and he ran her in circles as she swept Seven Stars, killing demons around them.

'He's still too young to be ridden,' I said.

'A short time like this won't hurt him,' the stone said. 'He appears to be enjoying himself.'

'Both of them are,' I said.

Simone swung the sword, her face a fierce grimace of battle fury. Freddo reared and lashed out behind him, grinding demons beneath his hooves, his mouth open with matching ferocity. He roared, sounding like a huge monstrous creature rather than a horse, and the sound vibrated through the ground.

'She just gained a whole new level of scariness,' the stone said. 'The two of them together are like a killing machine.'

'She's getting a big rush from the violence. That's bloodlust,' I said softly.

'That's her father emerging in her nature,' the stone said. 'It was inevitable. Remember what you said about being an adrenaline junkie?'

I leaned on the battlements and sighed. The battle was done, they had started to mop up. The archers nearby were cheering and high-fiving each other, comparing the number of kills.

'It will take her days to come down off this,' I said.

'Do I detect a hint of jealousy?' the stone said.

'Maybe I should take some time off and let myself heal completely after all,' I said. 'I'm sick to death of being this weak. That's the last time I sit it out and do the strategy-type thing.'

'I was right,' the stone said. 'You two are as bloodthirsty as each other.'

'Demon essence, not blood.'

'The violence is the same,' the stone said.

A male voice spoke behind me. 'Yes, it is, and delicious.'

I turned to see the Demon King standing on top of the wall in his Celestial Form. He towered over me. The nearby archers froze, suspended in time.

'Call someone,' I said.

'No need,' the stone said. 'He's not there.'

The Demon King shrugged. 'Just a projection. Thought I'd say hello while they clean up.'

I gripped the stone wall behind me. 'Hi, George.'

He bowed slightly. 'Dark Lady.'

I waited silently, but he just stood watching me with a gentle smile on his face.

I caved first. 'So what do you want?'

'Just looking, if you don't mind.'

'What do you see in me anyway? I'm small and human and nothing special.'

'He thinks you are.'

'Even if he lost me, as long as Simone is alive he won't turn.'

'Ah, but if he lost her, what would happen?' His expression filled with bliss. 'He would turn, and I would love to see it.'

'Why? You'd be dead. He'd kill you and take your place as King. You'd be destroyed.'

He swept his hand to encompass the Celestial around us. 'And this would be destroyed with me. I have built a formidable army, Emma, and with him at the head of it, all the Celestial would fall.' He leaned towards me and his grin grew malicious. 'All of you would be destroyed.'

'I thought you wanted me?'

175

'Oh, I do, believe me,' he said.

'So why this little sortie today? You must have known you had no chance.'

He shrugged again, and his grin didn't shift. 'Hello, Emma.'

'Humph.'

'That's all I wanted. To say hello, give you a scare, see how lovely you are when you realise exactly how much the fate of the Planes resides with you. Care for yourself well, madam, and take no risks, because if we break through and grab you, it is all over.' He disappeared.

'That's what he wants. For me to lock myself up and wrap myself in cotton wool, and be much less of a problem for him.'

'So of course you're going to rush out and put yourself in harm's way just to prove a point — and make yourself an easier target,' the stone said.

I turned and slapped the stone wall. 'I trust Leo to defend me.'

'Yeah, he's done such a great job up until now,' the stone said. 'Just ask Michelle's family.'

'That was uncalled for!'

'But it was the truth.'

We gathered in Guan Yu's meeting room after the battle was done. Somehow the Celestials had managed to clean their armour and they appeared as fresh as if they'd never fought.

'Thank you all for your assistance,' Guan Yu said.

'Not a problem, Lord Guan,' I said. 'How many lost altogether?'

'Five,' Liu said. 'Fifteen injured.'

'That wasn't it,' I said.

They shook their heads.

'That was a thousand, and that wasn't it.'

'The massed armies of Hell are twenty times that,'

Guan Yu said. 'I will step up patrols and ensure lines of communication are open.'

'Has anyone had anything from the agents planted there?' the Tiger said.

'Our agents last less than forty-eight hours before they're found and destroyed,' I said. 'Feel free to develop something that they won't detect; we've given up. I hate doing it to them, even if they volunteer.'

The next morning, Yi Hao tapped on my office door and opened it. 'It's Master Liu and Edwin, ma'am.'

'Show them in.'

Meredith and Edwin entered, their expressions grim.

'What happened?' I said.

'It's more than six months since you had the demon essence burnt out of you, Emma,' Meredith said. 'Healing was only supposed to take three months, and you're still too weak to engage in battle.'

I shuffled the papers. 'I know, I know, I need to take some time off and rest and let myself heal.'

Edwin fingered the papers in his lap. 'Actually, ma'am, that won't help. This is the result of your latest blood test, taken after the Convention Centre attack.'

I leaned over the desk to see the results, but the numbers were too small to be legible. 'So what's the problem? Is there lingering demon essence or something? If there is, we're off the hook with the Demon King.'

Neither of them replied, their expressions even grimmer.

I began to be concerned. 'What? What's wrong with me?'

'Sometime after the essence was burnt out of you, you became HIV positive,' Edwin said. He shook his head. 'I'm sorry, Emma. The virus is active. We'll have to start you on treatment immediately.'

That knocked the wind out of me. 'No way. It's more than ten years since I drank Leo's blood. I've been a goddamn snake for half that time. It just isn't possible.'

'Being on the Celestial will slow the progression of the disease, but not forever,' Meredith said.

'John will come back and heal me,' I said with conviction.

'He's still in two pieces, ma'am, and the Serpent part of him *possesses* you,' Edwin said.

Meredith raised one hand. 'We thought that if it possessed you again, it would clear the virus. He possessed you the other night, and it didn't. So we need him back, and we need him whole, if you're to be cured.'

'You waited before telling me because you wanted to see if being possessed would fix it?'

Meredith smiled slightly. 'It was worth a shot.'

'I wasn't possessed the other night. That was all me.'

'What makes you think that?'

'Because when I'm possessed by John, I black out. When it's just me, I remember what happened.'

'Please come with me to the temporary infirmary and I'll show you the pills you have to take,' Edwin said.

I pushed myself away from the desk. 'I thought I was clear!'

'So did I,' Edwin said.

'Go through the infection-control procedures at the same time, Edwin,' Meredith said. 'And, Emma, I'm sorry, but no more energy work until this is sorted.'

I stopped halfway up then fell to sit again. 'What?'

'Same as when Leo was positive. Even in Heaven. I'll take your classes. Head up to the infirmary now.'

I didn't rise from my chair. 'One more thing before we go.'

'What?' Meredith said.

'Neither of you is to tell Leo. Nobody is to tell Leo. This is to be kept strictly confidential, need-to-know only. For God's sake, guys, whatever you do, *don't tell Leo.*'

I went to the door and opened it, to find Leo sitting in his wheelchair in front of Yi Hao's desk. 'Tell me what?'

I stormed past him. 'That you're a rainbow fairy queen and I bought you a pink sequinned tutu for your birthday.'

'I hope it has tulle wings, it's not complete without the wings. And the wand,' Leo said. 'But seriously — what? Tell me.'

I walked out of the office and headed towards the infirmary, and he chased me, the chair moving by itself.

'You stop right there, Miss Emma keeping-secrets Donahoe, and tell me right now!' Leo shouted behind me. 'So much for everything being open and honest, eh? When it suits you, you're as tight with information as they are!'

I stopped at that, then took a deep breath, turned on my heel and returned to the office.

'Don't, Emma,' Meredith said.

'Edwin, I'll see you at the infirmary. Meredith dismissed,' I said.

'Don't do this to yourselves,' Meredith said. She turned to Leo. 'Believe me, Leo, it's better if you don't know. Don't make her tell you. Please.'

Leo stopped in his chair and stared at her. 'What has she done? What have I done?'

'Nothing. Nobody's done anything. There are no serious consequences for now. Leave it.'

'Emma?'

I took another deep breath. 'It would be best for everybody if you didn't know what this is about.'

'Okay then. I'm here to talk to you about some of the first years,' he said. 'The demons don't want the other students to see when they have their blood tests.'

'The demons don't need to be tested. If we can see the Fire Essence Pill they're definitely not copies,' I said.

'That's even worse, singling them out. It makes it obvious that they're demons.'

'I need to go see Edwin. I'll ask him to mock it up for them.'

Leo nodded. 'Good idea.' He grimaced. 'Whatever this is, it had better be damn good. And you'd better have a damn good reason for not telling me.'

'It's inconsequential. And I do.'

'I guess I have to trust you then.'

I went to him and put my hand on his shoulder. 'Your trust means a lot to me, Leo. Thank you.'

He pulled me down to sit in his lap and hugged me. I rested my head on his shoulder and sighed deeply.

'I changed my mind, I prefer blue to pink,' he said softly into my ear. 'And really don't forget the tulle wings.'

'I'll sew the sequins on myself.'

CHAPTER 13

'And it hit the middle of the target,' Martin said, 'and I won!'

Simone hid her smile behind one hand and held her other hand out to me under the table. I slipped a Hong Kong ten dollar note into it.

'We've heard that story a million times now, Di Di,' Yue Gui said patiently.

'Only half a million!' he said, protesting. 'And every time I tell it, Simone wins ten dollars.'

Simone nearly spat out her tea.

'Emma,' Martin said, more serious, 'I would like to take you for a tour of the new meditation pavilion.' He bowed towards Simone and Yue Gui. 'Do you mind?'

'We'll stay here and catch up,' Yue Gui said.

Martin nodded. He and I rose, then he escorted me out of his residence and towards the far north end of the Celestial Palace complex.

'Leo has asked me to request that you tell me what it is that he is not to know,' Martin said. 'And then for me to decide whether he should be told.'

'He said he trusted me,' I said.

We walked over a white marble bridge that hung suspended over a pond of transparent water filled with glowing purple lotus blossoms, each sixty centimetres across with dark blue glowing pollen drifting up from the flowers. Black koi carp, with a lilac glow on the edges of their fins and tails, hovered sleepily under the surface.

'He does. He isn't so trusting of your judgement.'

I snorted with laughter. 'That I believe.'

We arrived at the new pavilion that had replaced Serpent Concubine. The roof was held up with ebony pillars and the walls were open, with screens that could be pulled down from the ceiling in inclement weather. The pavilion was the same size as the old Serpent Concubine Pavilion, but was one large rectangular room.

We sat together on the tatami mats in front of the Buddha statue, and Martin lit a stick of incense and placed it in the brazier.

'So tell me what it is that has happened,' he said.

'The first time you and I met was in Borneo, many years ago,' I said. 'We'd flown out there when your father was nearly lost to us.'

'I remember.'

'On the way there, we were attacked. The pilot was a demon. He killed the co-pilot and attempted to take us. Simon Wong — One Two Two, the demon after us — appeared on the plane, with Kitty Kwok.'

He glanced sharply at me. 'I didn't know that.'

'Kitty thought she could control me because of what they'd done to me. I went along with it, hoping to have a chance to get to the Demon King's phone and hand myself over in return for Simone's safety.'

'I follow you. What happened? Obviously you somehow defeated them and didn't need to use the phone.'

'I changed into a snake. The taste of blood turned me into a snake.'

'Whose blood?'

'One Two Two crushed Leo's throat, then took a big

182

mouthful of his blood and kissed me. It was a test to see if I was controlled, so I drank it.'

'The taste of Leo's blood turned you into a snake and then you defended everybody. I see. What does that have to do with this though? Are you craving blood?'

'No. It was *Leo's* blood. A good cupful of it. And at the time, he was HIV positive. He was unconscious; he doesn't know the details of what happened.'

'HIV positive? What is that?'

'The disease, Martin. AIDS. The blood-borne disease that they have no cure for. I was infected.'

'But that was ten years ago! Surely it would have shown by ... Wait.' His voice went weak. 'No cure?'

'There is no cure for AIDS. There is treatment that slows its progression, and the virus can take a long time to become active, but there's no cure. Burning the demon essence out of me activated the virus, and it's killing me.'

'But Celestial healing —'

'Doesn't work. It's like cancer in that regard.'

'How long do you have?'

'Probably a couple of years.'

He sat straighter. 'Father will be well and truly back by then and able to cure you. His Serpent can cure anything.'

'I know. I'm sure he will be. So there's no need to tell Leo.'

Martin nodded, and his voice grew firm. 'He doesn't know you drank his blood. He doesn't know you have the virus. He carries enough guilt as it is. He would immediately blame himself if he was to find out, even though it isn't his fault.'

'That's why we don't want to tell him.'

'The curiosity is killing him.'

'I know.'

'Is this the disease that struck the gay community hard during the 1980s? I seem to recall something about it.'

'That's the one. Leo caught it before the establishment provided information on how to stop the spread. It still gets around though.'

'I remember now. Divine retribution for our deviant lifestyle.' He dropped his head and shook it. 'I have had divine retribution enough, thank you. My father is a god and he has punished me for six hundred years.'

'Not for being gay, Martin.'

'No, for a real crime. For being a liar, hurting innocents, and abusing my family's trust.'

I was silent at that, because he was right.

My phone rang and I took it out of my pocket and flipped it open. 'Emma.'

'Hi, Emma!' It was David Hawkes, sounding cheerful. 'I need a hand down here. Think you could pop down and help us mere mortals?'

'What happened, David?'

'Five nights ago, Bridget and I disappeared from the car park of the Convention Centre, leaving a pool of blood. They identified the blood as our type — apparently DNA tests take months, but they worked out the blood types in a few hours. Anyway ...' He took a deep breath. 'The blood was ours, obviously. And the last person we were seen with was you, and we were gone until lunchtime the next day and reappeared without a cover story.' His voice changed to sheepish. 'The police were giving us a hell of a time, Emma, so I just told them the truth. I mean, damn, it's so much fun, the whole business! Now they want to take us to the mental ward at the hospital. Any chance of some help?'

I choked the words out. 'You told them the truth?'

He sounded even more sheepish. 'All of it.'

'That is absolutely the worst thing you could have done.'

'I realise that now.'

184

'You're supposed to be the genius business grand master, David, the saviour who's going to lead Hong Kong out of the recession, and you told the police the *truth*? I despair for humanity.'

'I'm just too honest for my own good, I suppose. I was expecting a different sort of reaction.'

'How many police are involved?'

'Just the two.'

I hesitated, weighing up the options, then decided. To hell with the Jade Emperor's little rules, this was major. 'Where are you right now?'

'In my office. They've given me five minutes to get my stuff together, then we're off to hospital to see if we haven't had a bump on the head.'

'Is Bridget with you?'

'Yes. She came to back me up.'

Bridget called out in the background, her voice sounding tinny. 'Bring a weapon of some sort to use on him, Emma!'

'Tell her I will. I'll be there in five minutes. Have your staff expect us and let us straight up.'

He breathed a loud sigh of relief. 'Thanks, Emma.'

I tapped the stone. 'Hey, stone, wake up.'

'I wasn't asleep, I was playing solitaire on my desktop. What?'

'Did you hear that phone call while you were cheating?'

'No. What? Accessing.' The stone was silent for a moment. 'He's supposed to be smart!'

'I need someone powerful enough to blank out the cops' minds. Who's free?'

'Me,' Martin said.

'Are you skilled enough to do it without damaging them?'

'Yes,' he said.

'Can you take me down there?'

185

'Yes.'

I held my hand out and he took it. 'That's what I like about you, Martin, you're an extremely agreeable young man.'

'Yes. But not young.'

We landed outside the old Star Ferry terminal building. The autumn breeze from the harbour was still warm and damp even this late in the evening.

David's office was in a large, silver-plated tower that had round windows, each two metres across, instead of the usual glass walls — a sensible precaution next to the harbour. When typhoon winds became very strong, standard plate glass could blow out, as had happened to a new tower in Wan Chai.

'Change your clothes,' I said, looking around for more police.

'Sorry,' Martin said, and his green robe slipped almost imperceptibly into a dark green pinstripe suit with a brown shirt and green tie. He left his hair long and in a topknot.

I looked him up and down. 'You look like a gangster. If you and your father ever get together in business suits, the police will arrest you on sight.'

'It seems to be a twentieth-century thing — they check my ID whenever I pass them,' he said.

'Twenty-first century now,' the stone said. 'And that explains his skill with the mind-blast.'

We headed towards the round-windowed building.

'Stop calling it a mind-blast, that's ridiculous,' Martin said. 'For a stone you are overly prone to exaggeration.'

'It's a troll, it does it for the attention,' I said.

Martin stopped, then shook his head, smiled slightly, and caught up with me.

We had to pass a security guard to get to the top floor; it was the middle of the evening and all the offices were closed. I signed the guest book and the guard unlocked the lift.

'Just blank out what David said and fill the cops' heads with something more believable,' I said in the lift on the way up.

'Understood.'

On the top floor, a receptionist sat at a huge mahogany desk in a wood-panelled entrance lobby, a metre-tall company crest on the wall behind her. She showed us to David's office: a corner office, ten by five metres, with a view over the harbour to Kowloon on the other side.

I stopped when I saw Lieutenant Cheung. 'Oh shit, not you.'

Cheung drew a gun and pointed it at me. 'Just the woman we wanted to see. Good. Now we have you all together, we can work out what happened here. I think I'll have you accompany me to the station where we can talk about this kidnapping.'

I raised my hand to stop Martin. 'You can't do this one. He's had his mind blanked two or three times, and last time was by the Tiger.'

Martin went to Cheung and put his hands on either side of his face. The other policeman, a man I'd never seen before, stood silent and frozen.

'Oh dear. I wish the Tiger would sheathe his claws when he does things like this,' Martin said.

He released Cheung and stepped back. Cheung dropped his gun and collapsed into a chair.

'You're right,' Martin said to me. 'This one can't be blanked without permanent damage. It's already been done too many times, and the Tiger has the finesse of a big stupid elephant. What will you do?'

'Second-best option: take him to see Tian Guai. At least then I won't have to deal with him any more.' I turned to David and Bridget and waved one hand without enthusiasm. 'Hi, guys.'

'Hi, Emma,' David said, his shame making him look smaller than his usual height. 'Sorry about this.' He nodded to Martin. 'I don't think we've met.'

Martin held his hand out to David, who shook it. 'My name's Martin, I'm Xuan Wu's — John Chen's son. Madam.' Martin nodded to Bridget, who put her hand on her cheek then tidied her hair.

'I saw that,' David said out the corner of his mouth.

'Don't be concerned, David. Right now Martin's dating Leo,' I said.

'That's okay with them up there?' David asked Martin. 'You being ... you know?'

Martin shrugged. 'I am what I am, and that is the essence of the Tao. Besides, the Jade Emperor gave up on us reptiles a very long time ago.'

'They're more relaxed than we are,' Bridget said with amusement.

'More like what Martin said — they gave up,' I said. 'You really don't want to know what those damn reptiles get up to.'

'Wait — you're a reptile?' David said.

Martin nodded. 'I'm a Turtle, like my father.'

'Oh, very good, you just insulted yourself and your father in a single breath,' Leo said from where he'd appeared on the other side of the room.

'What can I say? It's a gift.'

Leo looked around and spoke more briskly. 'So what idiocy have you people been up to? I hear Emma's in trouble with the police again and we need to bail her out.'

I pointed at Cheung, sitting in the chair. Martin had frozen him too. 'Cheung again. We can't wipe his memory because it's been done too many times already. David told him the truth about us, so we need to do it James Bond-style and take him to see the head of the Secret Service.'

'Give me a moment,' Leo said, and concentrated. 'You're lucky: Tian Guai's working late. I'll get the car, meet me downstairs.' He disappeared.

'Who's Tian Guai?' David said, fascinated.

'Second-in-command of the PLA stationed here in Hong Kong,' I said.

His mouth fell open. 'The second-in-command is one of yours?'

'No,' I said. 'The commander is one of mine. The second-in-command is his writing brush.'

David stared at me, then realised his mouth was still open and closed it with a snap. 'You almost sound like you mean it,' he said.

'Absolutely. Celestial objects can gain sentience and awareness after being around an Immortal for enough time. Tian Guai is Major General Xin Jiang's brush that has gained a life of its own.'

'And it's second-in-command at the PLA barracks,' David said. His face lit up. 'You have to let me come too. I've met him before; I have to hear this from his own lips.'

'We won't all fit in the car,' I said.

Bridget put her hands on her hips. 'I'm not coming. It's late and the boys are at home with the amah.'

'You go in your car, darling,' David said. 'I'll come in my own car. I need to be in on this so that I can explain further to Cheung when we're done.'

'He has a point,' Martin said. 'Bring him with us.'

David raised one hand, mock-serious. 'Let us therefore travel in state from the House of a Thousand Assholes to the Upside-down Gin Bottle.'

I choked with laughter. 'You know this building's called that?'

'With these round windows...' He gestured towards the view, framed by the two-metre circular opening. 'Could it be called anything else?' He opened the door and spoke conspiratorially to me. 'Besides, have you met some of the other executives? I think it's a very fitting epithet.'

'I'll tell Tony you said that,' Bridget said.

'He's the one who first told me about it when I arrived here,' David said. 'Kiss the boys for me; I'll be there as soon as I can.'

She reached up to peck him on the cheek. 'Don't do anything silly, okay? We need you.'

He smiled down at her. 'Don't worry, I know.'

The guards opened the gates for us and we swept through into the PLA barracks next to the harbour between Wan Chai and Central. The old Prince of Wales Building, which had housed the British before the handover, really did look like an upside-down gin bottle: the rectangular building was perched on top of a pillar about half its width, with an upside-down pyramid shape supporting the building above the pillar. It had been designed this way to make it near impregnable to a climbing attack, and it sat next to the water in a vast open space that gave a clear view all around it.

A young woman in a khaki PLA uniform, complete with peaked cap, was waiting for us at the entrance. She saluted me Western style. I nodded back to her and she opened the doors for us to go in.

Cheung came out of his trance about halfway to the visitors book. He stopped and stared at the armed guards on either side of the lift doors, and then back at the entrance. He went rigid, obviously confused about what to do.

David put his hand on Cheung's arm. 'I apologise if you're disoriented, sir. But the medication only just wore off when we entered the building.'

'I'm in the PLA building?' Cheung said.

'That's right, and I apologise as well,' I said. 'I'm taking you to see my boss. He can tell you the whole story.'

'You work for the PLA?' he said, aghast. 'But you're not Chinese! How could they let you ... Wait, you work for the mainland government?'

'That's right,' I said. 'I owe my allegiance to China. I want to help the Chinese people, and the glorious army of liberation is giving me an opportunity to show my loyalty.'

Lay it on with a spatula, why don't you? Leo said.

Why not? They do in the propaganda, I said.

The lift doors opened and I gestured for Cheung and the other policeman to go in. Once inside, I pressed the button for the top floor and the doors closed.

'You work for them as well?' Cheung asked David.

'No, no,' David said. 'I help out, that's all. That business in the car park was the closest I've gotten to any of it.'

I forgot about that. Can we give Tian Guai a good cover story to explain the blood and disappearances to the policemen? I asked the stone.

Way ahead of you; just nod and smile, the stone said.

We reached the top floor, the bell rang, and the doors opened.

Tian Guai in his khaki PLA uniform was waiting for us in the lobby. He was tall and strongly built with a huge welcoming smile. He shook my hand in both of his, grinning broadly, and spoke Putonghua to me. 'Miss Donahoe. So good to see you, but don't make a habit of this, all right? We don't want people seeing you come in and out.'

'Brigadier Tian,' I said, nodding with deference and replying fluently in the same language with Martin's assistance. 'Thank you so much for helping me on such short notice.'

Tian turned to Cheung and switched to Cantonese. 'Lieutenant Cheung. I believe you have been following your civic duty and pursuing Miss Donahoe's activities. You are to be commended.' He gestured with one hand. 'But it is entirely unnecessary. Please come into my office and I will explain everything.'

About half an hour later, I slipped out of the office with David, leaving Cheung and the other policeman, who'd turned out to be called Chan, with Tian Guai. Leo and Martin were waiting in the lobby.

'All sorted?' Leo said.

'Tian wants to recruit Cheung,' David said. 'Said he's going to bring him into the Chinese Secret Service because he's so dedicated.'

'Can he do that?' Martin said.

'Yeah, they have a lot of pull in the Territory,' I said. 'It'll keep Cheung out of my hair, so I'm not complaining.'

'Then he threw us out because I don't have enough clearance to hear what they're saying,' David said.

'Suits me,' I said. 'The rest was boring.'

'You don't think one of you could do a magical lift home for me and my car, do you?' David said as we went back down in the lift. 'It's nearly bedtime for the boys. If I drive all the way back to Shek O I'll miss them altogether.'

'Leo? Martin?' I said.

'I'll take our car back to the car park, then take Emma home,' Leo said. 'Martin, can you carry Mr Hawkes and his car?'

Martin nodded. 'Done.'

David shook Leo's hand, then bent and kissed me on the cheek. 'Thanks, Emma, you make my life way more fun. And now I get to spend another evening telling stories to Bridget.'

'Let's try not to make a habit of this, okay?' I said,

and waved as he and Martin got into his car and Martin drove it away.

'He forgot to put his hands on the steering wheel,' Leo said, watching them go. He opened the rear passenger door of our car. 'Ma'am, if you'll permit me to escort you home.'

'Where's Simone?' I said as I settled into the back of the car.

'Waiting for us back at the Mountain; she made her own way home,' Leo said as he pulled himself into the driver's seat. He glanced at me in the rear-view mirror. 'You're even paler than usual, Emma, are you all right? You look unwell.'

I rubbed my hands over my face. 'Just tired. Too much all at once, and I haven't fully recovered. I just need to go home and rest.'

'Take some vitamin C,' Leo said as he pulled out of the PLA compound and headed towards our private car park under the Landmark shopping centre. 'Meredith said it would only take three months, but you're still not back to even half of what you were. You should talk to them about it.'

'I did. They said I'm doing too much and I need to rest,' I said, leaning back on the seat and closing my eyes.

He didn't reply and I opened my eyes. He was watching me in the mirror and I glanced away.

CHAPTER 14

'This will be the first night in a while it'll be just us three for dinner,' I said over breakfast the next morning.

'Curse our frantic social life,' Leo said.

'Uh, actually ... I was planning to go out tonight. Is that okay?' Simone said.

'Where to?' Leo said sharply.

'Just ... out,' Simone said, obviously cringing.

'Where ... to?' Leo said slowly and with force.

'The movies with a friend.'

'You have another date with that dragon?' I said.

Simone opened and closed her mouth a few times, then looked down at her congee. 'Maybe.' She glanced back up at me. 'How do you know about this? You're stalking me.'

'He's one of Qing Long's. I was concerned about the ... family aspect of it,' I said. 'So I asked Qing Long.'

'Yeah,' Leo said, rounding on Simone. 'Qing Long is like a brother to your father. Dating one of his kids is like dating your own cousin.' He leaned back and spoke with satisfaction. 'You can't date any of the Four Winds' children, so there.'

'Well, if you asked Qing Long then you know there isn't any family aspect about it at all,' Simone said, defiant. 'The kids aren't blood-related, they're not even real family, and they get together all the time.'

Leo glanced from Simone to me. 'Really? I would have thought they were like cousins.'

'Like Simone said, not blood relatives; there's no restriction on them getting together,' I said, then turned to her. 'You have school tomorrow so don't be home too late.'

'He'd better not be anything like his father,' Leo growled.

'He's a lovely kid,' I said. 'I've met him. He's in Simone's poisons and demon classes at CH.'

'You're too young to be dating anybody,' Leo said.

'I'm seventeen!' Simone said.

'Only just seventeen, young lady. Way too young. This kid'll turn out like his father and treat you like rubbish.'

'Leo, I've only ever been out with him once, and that was with some other friends. This is the first time for the two of us alone.'

'I don't like it.'

'I don't believe you're actually sulking about this,' Simone said. 'I thought Emma would be the one giving me trouble, and here you are acting like my over-protective auntie.'

'Demons could come after you, and you'd have no bodyguard —'

'Leo!' Simone and I both exclaimed at the same time.

I finished the point for both of us. 'She's the second most powerful thing on any Plane, Leo Alexander, and you know it. About the only thing that could take her down is a demon army, and even then they'd have trouble. She can call for help any time; and she has access to Seven Stars and knows how to use it.' I turned to Simone and winked at her. 'Frankly, I think this young man should be the one who's worried.'

Leo sat lower in his seat and crossed his arms over his chest. 'I just don't like it.'

'What you don't like,' I said, pouring him some more coffee, 'is the idea of our little girl growing up.'

He glared at her over his crossed arms. 'I won't let you.'

'What, grow up?' she said.

He settled even lower and recrossed his arms protectively. 'No.'

'Oh, and I'll be a bit late home from school, Freddo and me are having another session with the therapist.'

'How's that working for you?'

She grimaced. 'The therapist gave me this ... electric thing. It's like a taser but doesn't shoot. Every time he gets ... embarrassing, I have to give him an electric shock.' She shuddered. 'He cries. It's awful.'

'Poor little guy.'

'It's worse — I have to shock him where it hurts.'

Leo quickly sat upright and shifted uncomfortably.

'He must hate it,' I said.

'He doesn't care, he wants me to do it. He wants it to work.'

'Good luck with that,' Leo said.

'Aversion therapy,' I said. 'It should be effective.'

'That's what the therapist said.' Simone pushed her congee bowl away and rose. 'Oh, and you wanted to go to Macau today or tomorrow?'

'I want to check on Ben and Tom,' I said. 'They're with the Rats, and I haven't been to that village in a while. Can you carry me from Hong Kong?'

'I have an assignment coming up,' Simone said. 'Get Michael or something.'

'Yi Hao can arrange it,' I said. 'I'll just go down and be right back.'

I ran across the helipad on the roof of the Macau Ferry Terminal in Hong Kong, unable to resist the urge to duck under the blades, which seemed to be whizzing at neck height. I crawled into the chopper's cabin, Leo wrestled with stowing his wheelchair, and we were in. The technician on the pad checked the doors, rapped the cabin twice, and we were up and heading towards Macau.

Hong Kong Island and Kowloon were a mass of grey high rises, their tops drifting in and out of the low clouds. We passed over the greenery of Lantau, still below the cloud cover, then the helicopter ascended and we were in the middle of the clouds. The chopper was buffeted by turbulence; I held onto the frame of the door next to me, and we were above it. Leo yelled something but I shook my head; I couldn't hear him over the noise and his intercom wasn't working.

He switched to silent speech. *We should buy a new boat to go over to Macau. This helicopter business is too damn uncomfortable.*

Tell him it wouldn't be an issue if he swallowed his pride and learned to ride a cloud, I said to the stone, but it didn't reply — probably asleep.

The clouds moved under us, gaps between them giving us quick views of the wakes of boats on the water.

It was a thirty minute ride to Macau, and the water became more brown as we approached. Macau's harbour wasn't as deep and sheltered as Hong Kong's, making it a less attractive port for the opium traders all that time ago and leading to Macau becoming a poorer colony. It had overcome its limitations by legalising gambling, and every hotel on the ex-Portuguese enclave had a casino. The place had a faded European charm that still managed to delight despite the crass trashiness of the gambling attractions, brightly lit to appeal to the visiting Hong Kong punters.

We put down on the roof of the ferry terminal in Macau just as a jetfoil roared into life, lifted out of the water on its wings, and thundered out of the bay to start its one-hour journey back to Hong Kong. Four of these ferries left every hour carrying a vast number of Hong Kong visitors. Even more visitors came from the Mainland to visit the casinos every day, filling Macau with easy money.

The terminal had minimal disabled facilities, so Leo shrugged, pulled himself out of his wheelchair and carried it. Master Long, the headman of Rat Village, met us at the bottom of the ferry terminal, shook our hands as though we were visiting businesspeople, and escorted us to his van. Leo put the chair into the back of the van and sat in the front next to Long.

'How are our visitors?' I asked Long as he drove us over the huge bridge to the next island.

'They are managing. Their possessions are in storage, and they're in one of our guesthouses.'

'Have you uncovered anything about Tom?'

Long glanced back at me, his eyes full of amusement. 'Demon boy. He's fascinating, but we haven't been able to gain any useful information. We're not even sure what level he is by our standards. He seems to be totally unrelated to anything we've ever seen.'

'How many Western demons have you seen before?' Leo said.

'None at all, sir. We must send some hunting trips over there,' Long said. 'Up until now we thought that the Centre business kept us safe — demons from other Centres wouldn't move between regions. It looks like our enemies have found a way around it.'

'By breeding new hybrids from more than one region,' I said.

'Precisely. That's what Tom appears to be.'

'I'm something like that as well. You'll have to take a look at me when we're at the village.'

'If you like. I doubt if we'll find anything, ma'am. You're the chosen of the Dark Lord, and he wouldn't be hooking up — if you don't mind the expression — with any sort of demon. If there's one thing we can rely on, it's his ability to pick them.'

'I know.'

We arrived at the village: a collection of three-storey apartment blocks around a central grassy area, a long way from the bright lights and casinos. A few children played in the playground, watched by a small group of gossiping Filipina domestic helpers. Long led us into the village hall, which was actually more like a shared clubhouse for the village. It had been decorated in European style, with a marble floor and wood inlay on the walls. A small gym took up one room, and a karaoke machine occupied another. The main area was full of chairs and tables, moved to form a horseshoe-shaped conference table. The leaders of the village stood around chatting with Ben and Tom as they waited for us.

They nodded when Leo and I entered, and we all sat at the table.

Long pulled a piece of paper in front of him and put on some reading glasses. 'We have a report and a few recommendations for you, sir, ma'am.'

'Go right ahead,' I said.

'First the report. Tom.' He peered at Tom over his glasses. 'Definitely an East-West hybrid; his mother was probably just that — a Mother. Ben tells us she went home for a few weeks every year, back to Hong Kong, so that's how she was able to survive for so long in the West.' He tapped the paper with his pen. 'We aren't sure, but we guess he's about level eighty-five, even though he's half human. He could probably sire spawn on a Mother if he wished.'

'No wonder they want him back,' I said.

'Ben is the interesting one, though,' Long said, and Ben shifted uncomfortably.

'Tom is all that, and *Ben* is the interesting one?' I said.

Long nodded, tapping the paper again. 'Ben is something we've never seen before ... No, I take that back. We've only seen something like him once before.'

'Me.'

'Yes, ma'am. We don't know how to study him; every demon identification technique we use on him fails. We scan him as completely human, but there's something deep down inside, something dark and monstrous that wants to destroy the whole world.' He took his glasses off to study me. 'Frankly, he's more than a little scary.'

'Just like you,' said Long's wife, Camilla.

'I understand,' I said. 'So what next?'

'We want to send both of them to the Tiger's lab in the West,' Long said. 'We've already arranged it; we just need the go-ahead from you.'

'And what do you say to this?' I asked Ben and Tom.

'We're a threat,' Tom said. 'Take us to the lab.'

'They may want to experiment extensively on you, gentlemen,' I said. 'Make sure you don't give them permission to do anything you're not comfortable with.'

'As long as we're together and safe, nothing else matters,' Tom said.

'Very well,' I said. 'Let's arrange someone to carry them to the West.'

'We'd like to make a stop at the Mountain and see how Vincent's going, if you don't mind,' Tom said.

'Then we need to organise someone to take them up there first,' I said to Long.

'Already done. All you need to do is give the go-ahead and we'll move them first thing tomorrow,' Long said.

'Go right ahead. I'll meet you on the Mountain tomorrow morning,' I said.

'Will you stay here this evening?' Long said. 'We can

show you our latest projects. The Blue Dragon's people have been working with us on high-tech espionage equipment; we've a lot to show you.'

'I can't stay tonight, I have to leave after dinner,' I said. 'But I'll be happy to stay until then.' I turned to Leo. 'Do you want to stay here or go back to the Mountain? Do you have a class to teach?'

'By your leave, ma'am, I'd like to scout the territory, see what people are saying around town,' Leo said.

I sighed with exasperation. 'Is Gold meeting you at the track?'

He spoke with forced dignity. 'I have no idea what you're talking about.'

'Go, have fun, and be back here after the last race so we can go back to the Mountain,' I said. 'Amy'll shred Gold when she finds out.'

'I am not a gambling man,' Leo said, still intensely dignified, and wheeled himself out.

After breakfast the next morning, I went into the temple to share a meditation session with the visiting monks. The incense coils in the ceiling filled the temple with smoke, but apart from that it was empty. I went to the office behind the shrine; that was deserted as well.

'Stone,' I said.

'I'm checking,' the stone said. 'They were here half an hour ago.'

'Are they in the mess?'

'No.'

'Double-check. Are they anywhere on the Mountain?'

'Give me a moment, I'll hook into the network. Processing ... No.'

I fell to kneel on one of the mats, then changed my mind and went out of the temple. Preparing for war wasn't a suitable activity in that place.

'Put the word out, stone. We've run out of time. See if any of the Five are available for a meeting in the War Room.'

Meredith appeared next to me as I walked back from the temple across the bridge to the administrative centre and the War Room: a rectangular building, twenty by ten metres, with a modular divider system that allowed it to be made into one large training room or smaller meeting rooms. The demons were already dividing it into a quarter-sized meeting room for us, and rolled a wooden tabletop from the back of the building to place it on top of an ordinary six-seater, making it big enough to fit all of us. They threw a black silk cloth decorated with warriors on horseback over the table.

'Liu's on his way,' Meredith said. 'LK Pak is in the middle of examining a demon and will be along shortly. Ma was on patrol, but likewise will be here soon, and Ming Gui is also on his way.'

I sat at the table. 'Stone, get Yi Hao to bring me some notepaper.'

'Ma'am,' the stone said.

Meredith sat next to me. 'Must be serious if the stone's being polite to you.'

LK and Liu came in, saluted me, then sat at the table.

'All the temple clergy have gone,' I said.

They were silent for a moment.

'LK, when was the last sweep of the students?' Liu said.

'This morning. We're doing them daily and finding nothing. All of them have had blood tests and have been cleared. We have to presume this will be an outside attack.'

Ma came into the room, saluted me, and sat as well. 'Meredith told me.'

'Recommendations?' I said.

'Move all the juniors out,' Ma said.

'No,' Meredith said. 'We don't know how long we have yet; I won't stop their training to wait for it. We prepare as much as we can, and continue as usual.'

'This is an army, defence is what we do,' Liu said. 'I'm with Meredith.'

Martin came in, saluted around the table, and sat. 'The stone told me. Can any of the Thirty-Six come in on this?'

Ma considered for a moment. 'The twenty-eighth and thirty-first battalions are under utilised at the moment. I'll put them on standby and have them patrol the periphery of the Mountain.'

'Any other suggestions?' I said.

'Yes,' Ma said. 'Bring him back now. For good.'

'How will you do that?' Meredith said.

'Kill a General and feed him to John,' I said.

'That is unacceptable,' Liu said.

'Nevertheless, it's the plan. But we won't sacrifice a useful General to buy a Xuan Wu of indeterminate power and sentience. The price is too high.'

'What if the Mountain is attacked?' Ma said.

'We see how we go,' I said. 'Anything further to add?'

'Does anybody have any time frame in their vision of the future?' Ma said.

They all looked around the table, then shook their heads.

'Emma?' Ma said.

'I have no idea. "Soon" could be anything from a week to a couple of months.'

'That's the way I see it too,' Martin said.

'So we stay on alert, patrol our borders, and be ready for the storm that's building,' I said. 'And come through it with as few deaths as possible.'

'No deaths at all would be the best option,' Meredith said.

'And we all know it's an option that isn't available,' I said. 'Dismissed.'

Later that morning I met Ben and Tom and their escort on the western side of the Mountain Palace, on one of the small courts between the mess hall and the residential buildings. The junior students didn't know the situation, but all the seniors and Masters were edgy and the atmosphere on the Mountain was tense.

'Stone, please call Vincent,' I said.

'He's on his way.'

Vincent came out of the mess hall and brightened when he saw Ben and Tom. He went to them and shook their hands.

'How did it go? Can you come here permanently?' he asked them.

'We're going to a laboratory to be examined and experimented on,' Tom said.

Vincent took a step back. 'They can't do that to you!' He turned to me, horrified. 'I'll fight you if you try to experiment on them.'

Ben took Vincent by the arm. 'It's all right, mate, we're volunteering.'

'They won't hurt us. Much,' Tom said.

'Don't do this to yourselves,' Vincent said. 'You're good men.'

'Turns out both of us are something strange,' Ben said wryly. 'We're dangerous, and if they can find out exactly what we are, they may be able to fix us. Right, Emma?'

'I sincerely hope a cure can be found for both of you,' I said. 'Because then I can be fully human myself.'

'What are you doing on my Mountain?' John said sharply behind me.

Vincent, Ben and Tom all blanched and took a step back. I turned to see and took a step back myself. John was in full Celestial Form, the first time I'd seen it in years. He was nearly three metres tall, dark and ugly, with a thin black beard. He wore black silk Tang-style robes embossed with silver turtles, and his long hair moved around his head as if it was in water.

'Hello, Emma,' he said. 'Why are there untamed demons on my Mountain?'

I gestured towards Ben and Tom. 'They're all right; we're about to take them to the West to be studied.'

'I don't mean this one,' John said. 'It is very interesting, though. Stand still, let me look at you.'

Tom quailed as John strode to him and put his hands on either side of Tom's face, concentrating. Tom jumped and screamed, a long drawn-out sound of agony that abruptly stopped. He stood panting, hanging from John's hands and staring into his eyes.

'John, let him go,' I said. 'He's not a threat.'

'Are you sure?' John said. He dropped his head and concentrated on Tom, and Tom screamed again.

Vincent grabbed John's arm but John ignored him completely, his attention fixed on Tom.

'Yes, I'm sure!' I said.

'Stop hurting him!' Ben said, putting his hand on John's arm as well. He dropped his voice. 'Please don't hurt him.' He turned back to me. 'He's hurting him! Is he from the West?'

John released Tom and the boy crumpled to sit on the ground, gasping. Ben knelt next to him and pulled him into a rough embrace.

John spun and took me by the upper arms, speaking urgently. 'There are untamed demons on my Mountain. They are close to undetectable. What are they doing here?'

'These two won't hurt anybody, John; they're heading to the West to be studied.'

He shook his head with impatience. 'I don't mean these! There are close on a hundred extremely well-hidden demons among the students. What are they doing here?' His expression cleared. 'You don't know they're there.'

'Oh dear Lord, this is it,' I said. 'You're right, we can't detect them.'

John released me and stepped back. 'I see. This is very bad.'

'What's going on?' Ben said.

'I will not tolerate untamed demons on my Mountain.' John held out one robed arm and Seven Stars appeared in his hand. He raised it towards Ben and Tom.

Vincent and I moved in front of them, protecting them.

'I don't know who you are, but I won't let you hurt them,' Vincent said.

John raised his free hand towards Vincent and hit him with the full force of his dark Celestial gaze. 'No child of mine stands in my way.' He turned his hand over and waved Vincent away.

Vincent's expression went blank and he stepped aside.

'They aren't a threat,' I said, standing my ground between John and the two men. 'We know what they are. We need you to identify the ones we don't know about.'

'Out of the way, Emma.'

'No. Let these two go somewhere safe. It's more important to identify the hidden ones.'

He lowered his head and his dark eyes burned into me.

'We're wasting time!' I said. 'We need to give the unidentified threat priority. We've been compromised, and these two are the least of our problems!'

John spoke to Ben and Tom without looking away from me. 'Go into the mess hall and stay quiet about this, or I will remove your heads myself.'

They appeared frozen, staring up at him.

I didn't look away from John. 'Ben and Tom, go to the mess hall with Vincent right now. Don't ask questions, don't talk to anyone, just go.'

'Go!' John said, and they raced towards the mess hall.

'John, summon the Lius and LK,' I said. 'We need to get these demons away from the rest of the students.'

The Immortals appeared next to us and fell to one knee to John. John nodded back to them and shrank to normal human size.

'There are about a hundred untamed demons out there, very high level, well hidden,' he said. 'They are all disguised as humans.'

'Oh, shit,' Liu said softly. 'My Lord, you must point them out and quickly. We've been infiltrated.'

'Come over to the offices,' I said. 'I have some spray paint you can use to identify them. The Masters can follow you and take them out.'

'No,' John said. 'At this stage, it would be best if you quietly withdraw them from what they're doing. If they realise they've been exposed, they'll probably attack, and they're all through the Mountain.'

'Stone, you awake?' I said.

'I'm here.'

'John, tell us what and where they are, and we'll take it from there.'

He nodded, and we headed towards his office, the Lius following.

'I'm weaker than I expected,' John said. 'What's wrong with me?' He raised his hand. 'Never mind. Let's get these demons identified and neutralised. First: large training room, east of Purple Mist; the demon has taken the form of a young human female. In a meditation room beside the deity hall next to Dragon Tiger: one in the form of a young black male.' He took a deep breath.

'That's one of mine. I never picked him,' I said with wonder.

'Third … Let me see.' John stopped and rubbed his hand over his forehead. 'This is hard.' He started walking again, but slower. 'Third: there's a human teaching … Get Gold here immediately. I thought we'd fixed this issue of disguised demons being promoted to teaching here … Obviously a junior Master, teaching a basic energy-work class.'

'That's Roderick,' I said. 'He's a demon? No way. He generates chi like a pro.'

'The nature of these demons is extremely complex and disturbing. I've never seen anything like them before. They seem to be not of this region.' John stopped to put his head in his hands, then brushed his hands through his long tangle of hair, mirroring one of Simone's gestures. 'Fourth: extremely junior student in the form of a small human girl, in a very basic hand-to-hand class over near True Way. I like what you've done with the buildings, Emma, the fung shui is even more auspicious, if that is possible.' He sat on a low wall and bent forward. 'This is very hard.'

Meredith crouched in front of him. 'Let me feed you some energy. We need to know them all.'

He nodded, and took some deep breaths. They linked hands and both of them glowed with shen energy, a luminous silver halo that shimmered around them. Meredith's face filled with horror, and Liu took a few long strides to them, grabbed Meredith and pulled her away from John. John disappeared.

Liu stroked Meredith's hair. 'Nearly did it.'

'He nearly drained you?' I said. 'I thought he'd stopped doing that.'

'He was right,' Meredith said. 'Identifying those demons was draining the life out of him. He's still very weak, and it will take him a while to fully return. I'm actually surprised he can manage human form for such a long duration.'

'We need to withdraw and hold those students, and move them away from the rest of the Academy without attracting attention,' I said.

'One of them is a Master, as well,' Meredith said.

'If any of the copies realises we know about them, they'll probably all explode,' I said. 'We have to keep things as normal as possible until we can deal with them.'

'Taoist meditation retreat. I'll identify them as candidates and take them to one of the distant mountaintops,' Liu said.

'Take some non-demons as well, so they're not singled out,' I said. 'While you have them, we'll have to get all the Celestials to try to identify what makes them different. Stone, quietly summon Gold, please.'

Gold appeared in front of me wearing red silk boxers with white hearts on them and a matching red silk robe, his sandy hair sticking straight up. He quickly changed to his normal tan polo shirt and slacks, and ran his hands through his hair. 'Babies gave us a bad night, but Dad says something's up.' His face went blank, then grim as the stone filled him in. 'I'll go through the records and identify all students who've never been vetted by the Dark Lord. Unfortunately, that's a good three-quarters of them. I'll have the list for you in ten minutes.' He disappeared.

'The very junior student sounds like Emily,' I said. 'Emily Fang from Malaysia. Let's do something special with her; let's send her home, put a tail on her and see where she goes. If she's a demon, she'll head to the nest.'

'Good idea,' Liu said. 'I'll drop Meredith off in our quarters and meet you in the office in ten minutes.'

Before going to my office, I went to my quarters to find the pearl to summon Kwan Yin, but she was already there. I fell to one knee and saluted her, and she pulled me up into a hug.

She released me and smiled her sad smile. 'Yes. You may use my Garden to talk to the Winds.' She handed me three sets of Buddhist prayer beads. 'Give these to each of them and tell them to recite the Lotus Sutra, and they will be in the Garden. When they are there, I will take you and yours there too.'

'Can you identify the demons for me, Lady?'

'They may be demons, but they have within them the potential to be divine. I cannot betray my nature and identify them for you to destroy.'

'Is that why you walk the Halls assisting the Snake Mothers to produce more like themselves?'

'Such an accusation is beneath you, Emma. You have seen the Second and know of our nature. All demons have within them the power to be divine, no matter what they are. If I do not aid the lowest of the low and the cruellest of the cruel to find the right path, then who will? All you practise on the Third is destruction.'

I knelt before her again. 'Truly your nature is Mercy, Lady.'

'Heaven's greatest champion was once the cruellest of the cruel, little one. Destruction is sometimes a necessary path that must be taken, but it is far better to teach understanding, serenity and enlightenment.'

I rose. 'What of me?' I said, taking advantage of her unusual openness.

'You are another example, nearly as great as his, of overcoming your nature and seeking enlightenment.'

'What is my nature?'

'Send out your agents, and hurry. You must meet quickly and tell the Winds of this infiltration,' she said, and disappeared.

CHAPTER 15

Liu, Meredith and Gold were already in the conference room near my office when I arrived.

I went to Gold and held out the beads to him. 'Send three stones out to the other three Winds, tell them to recite the Lotus Sutra over these beads right away. Tell them that's an order.'

Gold took the beads and raised them in front of his face. 'Are they all the same?'

'Yes,' I said. 'Hurry.'

'What do they do?'

'You're wasting time,' I said. 'Just do it. It is important that these sutras are said immediately; and you don't question Kwan Yin.'

He saluted me with the beads in his hand and disappeared.

'In the meantime,' I said, 'it's time to share a special secret with one of our high-ranking students. Let's get Roderick and take him down to the Grotto and show him the lake. As an initiation.'

Liu picked up my intent immediately. He rose and pushed his chair back, saying for the benefit of anyone eavesdropping: 'I'll go get him. It's an important part of the retreat preparation.'

Liu and Roderick were already standing on the ledge next to the water when I arrived in the Grotto.

Roderick gestured towards what I was carrying. 'What's that? Is it part of the initiation?'

'Sort of,' I said.

'It looks like a dish for dog food.'

'Cat,' I said, and placed the dish on the ground. I peeled open a can of pilchards and tipped them into the bowl, then slid it to the edge of the water.

Nothing happened, so I took a small amount out of the bowl and threw it into the water, wincing at the slimy feeling.

What's going on? the fish said.

'Don't eat it, it's not for you,' I said.

Wouldn't eat that disgusting stuff anyway, we're not cannibals, the fish said with dignity.

The Turtle surfaced and raised its head slightly above the water, peering at me. It slid gracefully to the edge, then hauled itself out of the water and took a few steps. It was around two metres long, significantly bigger than when Simone had first brought it down to the Grotto. It buried its beak in the cat food, then raised its snout and half-closed its eyes with bliss, eating with loud smacking sounds.

'Do you feel anything special here?' Liu asked Roderick.

'Nothing,' Roderick said. 'Is that the Dark Lord's Turtle?'

I nodded. 'Come and touch its head and receive its blessing for your retreat. Hopefully you will attain greater understanding in your search for the Tao.'

'I am blessed already to be on Wudang,' Roderick said. He walked quietly to the Turtle, crouched and touched its head. The Turtle paid no attention to him, concentrating on the cat food. 'It's all animal right now, isn't it?'

Liu, standing behind Roderick, scowled with frustration.

'Yes, it's terribly drained by all that's happened recently,' I said. 'But he comes and goes, and is with us for longer periods all the time.'

Roderick rose again and saluted the Turtle. 'I feel blessed. To have touched the Dark Lord, even when he is beast, is truly wonderful.'

'Won't be long before you'll be taught by him,' Liu said, composing his expression again. He gestured towards the stairs. 'Let's go back up. I'm sure you still have some packing to do.'

'Why didn't you bring the others who are coming to the retreat down here?' Roderick said. 'Why just me?'

'You've been teaching; they're still just students,' I said. 'It's part of the transition from student to Master.'

'I see.' Roderick took a few steps towards the stairs then turned back. 'Is it very difficult to come down here?'

'Yes,' I said. 'You have to be attuned to the gate, otherwise it will just be rock to you. It's something we teach the more senior Masters when there's a need for it. Most of the time, though, there isn't.'

Roderick bobbed his head. 'I should like to learn so I can help with the care of the Turtle.' He smiled slightly. 'I used to have a cat; it would bring back fond memories.'

Liu shot me a concerned glance behind Roderick's back.

I nodded to Roderick. 'We'll see what happens when you come back from retreat.'

Roderick saluted me and proceeded up the stairs. Liu and I followed.

Gold met me back at my office. 'We gave them the beads and received the usual shit from them — sorry for the expression but that's what it was. They'll do it immediately.'

'Good. Be ready for transport,' I said, and the world around us disappeared.

We arrived on a pavilion in the middle of a lake so huge that its edges weren't visible. The water was flat and black — frozen. Scattered snowflakes floated through the air, but the temperature was brisk without being cold. Mountains surrounded the lake, dark grey in the distance.

The pavilion was fifty metres to a side, with no walls and a gold-tiled roof held up by red pillars and beams. The roof rose in three tiers, and each tier had windows beneath the roof line. The three Winds sat at a large table that held steaming tea and bamboo baskets of small white buns.

Gold, Liu and Meredith materialised next to me.

The Dragon waved us impatiently towards them. 'Come and tell us what's so important that you had to drag us all the way here.'

We entered the pavilion and sat at the table. As the most junior Immortal there, Meredith reached for the teapot and poured for all of us, the Winds nodding their thanks without tapping the table.

'Now what's all this about?' the Tiger said, pulling out a bun and breaking it open. He grimaced and put it back when he saw it had vegetarian stuffing.

The Phoenix glared at him, took the bun he'd discarded, delicately pulled the bread from the filling and popped it into her mouth. She passed the filling to the Dragon and he ate it without a word.

I gestured for Liu to explain.

'Wudang has been infiltrated by a hundred demons that are such good copies they are undetectable by anybody except the Dark Lord himself,' Liu said. 'He took human form for a brief moment, identified four of them, then returned to animal in the lake at the core of the Mountain. We have no way of knowing who the others are. He said the copies all appeared as human, but not Immortal or Shen. Every human is suspect.'

'We need to see these copies,' the Tiger said.

'As soon as we are done here, we'll show them to you. They don't know we're onto them; we've separated three of them out for a Taoist meditation retreat.'

'Good,' the Phoenix said. 'The second they know you're onto them, all hundred will attack.'

'Explode, actually,' I said with resignation, and they became even more concerned.

'What about the fourth?' the Dragon said.

'We sent her home with a tail on her,' Liu said. 'Reports so far are that she has returned to her home town in Sarawak, Malaysian Borneo.'

'We need an excuse for visiting the retreat,' the Phoenix said to Liu.

'Go and yell at him about something,' I said. 'That way they won't suspect you're working together.'

'All three of us?' the Tiger said. He leaned his elbow on the table and his chin in his hand. 'What could we possibly have to yell at Old Liu about?'

'I taught your kids something wrong?' Liu said. He shook his head. 'That wouldn't work.'

'Drag races,' I said.

Liu leaned back and glared at me. 'Nobody was supposed to know about that.'

I stared at him. 'You have been drag racing with their kids?'

Liu's face fell. 'Uh-oh.'

Gold spluttered with amusement.

'Where is this retreat?' the Phoenix said, suddenly stern.

'Blue Star Peak,' Liu said, wincing.

'I will be there in thirty minutes. Be ready,' she said, and disappeared in a swirl of red.

Liu spread his hands. 'It's perfectly safe, I swear, and all of them have their licences ...'

'I want a list when I get there,' the Tiger growled, and disappeared as well.

'I don't care what they're up to, but if they've used one of *my* cars there will be hell to pay,' the Dragon said. 'I'm checking the odometers now, and if any of them shows unusual mileage your ass is mine.' He rose, saluted me, and disappeared.

Liu's misery deepened. 'The Dragon has a splendid collection of supercars. Loves them more than he loves his children.'

'Wow, you are in serious trouble,' Gold said.

'Good,' I said. 'They won't be acting.'

Liu reported back to me later that morning. 'The other Winds can't find anything different about them,' he said. 'Emily is with her family in Malaysia; one of our stone Shen is keeping watch on her.'

'She wasn't suspicious about being sent home?'

'It isn't that unusual to be sent home for a while,' he said. 'She has been struggling with the energy work, so I told her to take a break and see her family.'

'Maybe we should isolate the other juniors who are having trouble with energy.'

'That's most of them, Emma. You know how hard it is.'

'We should send them all home.'

'You know how well that works out.' He rubbed his hands over his face. 'We need him back right now, dammit.'

'Keep Leo away from the Turtle,' I said.

'All the energy from Leo wouldn't be nearly enough to bring him back fully.'

'Just make sure he doesn't try to make the sacrifice.'

'Any sign of the Serpent?'

'No.'

Liu's head shot up and he unfocused, listening. 'Emily has disappeared. The tail lost her. They have no idea where she is.'

I was waiting for Simone in her living room, reading a book, when she arrived home from school in the middle of the afternoon.

'You're not stalking me?' she said, incredulous.

I held up a piece of paper. It said: *Don't ask any questions. Don't say anything. Just take me down to the Peak right now.*

At the same time, I said, 'No, I just needed to be sure that you'd be home on time. Now let's go down to the Peak and pick up your books.'

She looked from the paper to me, opened her mouth to speak, then thought better of it. She came to me and held out her hand and took me down to the Peak.

We landed in the living room, which had been returned to its original configuration, except with a darker shade of cream for the carpet.

Simone put her hands on her hips. 'What's this about?'

I sat on one of the sofas and gestured for her to join me. 'Your dad came around, took human form and told us there are a hundred demon copies on the Mountain right now. He didn't have time to identify them all before he lost it.'

'So why aren't we up there destroying them?' she said.

'Because we don't know which ones they are, and the minute we start taking them down, they'll all activate and either explode or attack the students.'

She opened and closed her mouth a few times. 'I didn't know.'

'He told us while you were with Freddo. We can't do anything even slightly different, because that will tip them off. We have to keep everything absolutely as normal as possible until John comes back and identifies them.' I sighed. 'Either way, you have to stay down here, where it's safe, until this whole business is sorted.'

'Did he identify any of them?'

'Yes. Four. Three of them are on retreat at Blue Star Peak with Liu —'

She disappeared.

I threw myself back in the chair. 'Great. There goes my ride.'

'Do you want to wait for her to return or head back up now?' the stone asked.

'I'll wait for her.'

I turned on the television. Although we had cable in the Peak apartment, there was only one English channel, which targeted the Middle Eastern market and cycled a constant stream of *Baywatch* reruns. I turned it off again and headed to the training room to do sword katas until Simone returned.

John appeared after I'd been practising for about half an hour. 'Why are you here alone and unguarded?'

'It's a long story.'

'I have all of eternity.'

'I don't.'

He smiled slightly. 'Yes, you do.'

He summoned Dark Heavens and pointed at the floor in front of him. I didn't move.

'We need you back,' I said. 'A hundred demons on the Mountain.'

'I remember.' He raised one hand, dismissed the sword, and his eyes unfocused. 'They really are very well hidden. I can't see them from here; I have to be on the Mountain.'

I went to him and put my hand on his arm, relishing the ability to touch him without hesitation. 'I put a couple of boxes of brightly coloured spray paint in your office on the Mountain. If the demons attack, grab the paint and mark the demons so we can identify them.'

'I should do it right now,' he said.

I gripped his arm tighter. 'No. We're not ready. All the students are there, and these copies could explode when they know we're onto them.'

'I see. Where's Simone?'

'Blue Star Peak.'

He disappeared. A minute later, Leo appeared on the other side of the room in his wheelchair. He glanced around, appearing surprised, then saw me.

'What am I doing here?' he said.

'I think John just dropped you here to guard me.'

'Lovely. Don't I get a say in the matter?'

'Yes,' I said. 'You can choose not to be my personal guard.'

He grunted and pulled himself out of the chair to stand, then summoned the Black Lion. 'You're not getting rid of me that easy, lady.'

I sighed, summoned the Murasame, and saluted him with it. 'It was worth a try.'

He saluted me back and we readied ourselves. He started with a broad horizontal sweep towards my neck; more style than substance. I parried it with the Murasame, pushing his blade down. He moved with it, yielding, then swept his sword back up and swung it in another arc towards my right shoulder. I twisted my blade in my hands and blocked him, and again pushed him down.

'Martin says I should trust you,' he said, and stopped yielding to my movement. He held my blade as I tried to force it down.

'Thank you,' I said.

It became a test of strength. I tried to force his sword down; he held it. We were evenly matched until he exhaled, softened his stance and effortlessly swept my blade back up again. I let him push it completely away and up over my shoulder, leaving my centre line unguarded, but he didn't press home the advantage.

'I concede,' I said.

'How about energy?' he said. 'You were always better. I'd like to match you now that I'm Immortal.'

'Meredith says no energy for a while. I have to conserve my chi and get better,' I said.

He nodded and lowered his sword. 'Makes sense.' He looked around. 'It's not the same here without the weapons museum on the wall.' He grinned at me. 'We had some good times, though, eh?'

'More will come,' John said from the other side of the room where he'd appeared with Simone. He gestured towards Leo. 'Let me see.'

Leo went to John, fell to one knee in front of him and held out his sword horizontally.

John took it and held it vertically, eyeing the blade with interest. 'After the fifteenth fold it just becomes academic; it's more for show and boasting rights than anything. They've done a fine job.'

He held the sword out horizontally to Leo and Leo took it back, his head bowed.

'Up,' John said.

Leo rose, summoned the scabbard and put the sword away.

'Meeting, dining room,' John said. He stopped and glanced at me. 'Is this area secure?'

'Yes,' I said.

He nodded and led us out of the training room into the dining room, where we sat at the table.

'Where's Monica?' John said.

'John, Monica's in her mid-fifties now. She married one of the Tiger's sons from a Filipina wife, and asked to retire so they could return to the Philippines to be with their respective families.'

'Is she provided for?'

'Generously.'

'Do you visit?' he asked Simone.

'As much as I can, Daddy, but school takes up a lot of my time.'

'Ah Yat?' he said.

'She Ascended.'

He slammed one palm on the table. 'Excellent. Now that the important business is taken care of, we have to deal with these demons. Not even Simone can identify them; I'm the only one. You said you had some spray paint?'

'Yes, in the Mountain office. But I'm concerned that once they realise we're onto them, they'll all explode.'

He leaned back, his face rigid with restraint. 'The current King does not permit the creation of such demons.'

'He didn't create them.'

He grimaced. 'Civil war in Hell just as I return. This is very bad. What do you suggest we do about the demons?'

'Go up to the Mountain, go to your office, seal it from anyone listening, and tell a stone which are the demons. We'll do our very best to quietly remove them from classes and destroy them before they can explode.'

He rose and nodded. 'Good. Let's go.' He concentrated a moment. 'Some of the Celestial Masters will meet us there.'

'John.' I stood in front of him. 'Do me a favour? Do something for me that you've never done?' I held out my hand and my voice thickened through my control. 'Take me to the Mountain?'

'Oh,' Simone said, and disappeared.

He pulled me into a fierce hug and held me tight as he spoke into my ear. 'Serpent, Turtle, Mountain. All of me is yours.' He took a deep breath, moving his chest into me, and we were on the Mountain.

He stepped back slightly, still holding my hands, and gazed into my eyes. 'Lady Emma. Welcome to my Mountain, the seat of my power and my home. Will you share it with me?'

'I would be honoured, Lord Xuan Wu.'

He grinned. 'Good. Now let's sort these demons out.'

'Emma and Simone should go back down, they're both mortal,' Leo said.

'Don't even think about,' I said, but John had stopped.

'No!' Simone said. 'You send me down and I'll be right back up here.'

'Ditto; I'll just order Leo to take me,' I said. 'If things go pear-shaped, we'll head out. But if we do this right, they'll never know we're onto them.'

'We could use your brains as well, Serpent Lady,' John said. 'The minute we've dealt with this, I am finding the other half of me.'

'Oh God, Daddy, tell me you're back for good,' Simone said.

'This time I think I am,' he said, full of delight. 'Now let's go to the office, summon Gold, and see if we can tidy this up very quietly.'

CHAPTER 16

Meredith, Liu and Gold were waiting for us in John's office.

'Why do you have all this spray paint here anyway?' John said as I pulled the box out of the cupboard.

'Because I saw this coming,' I said. 'They've been harder and harder to identify. I thought that eventually only Immortals would be able to do it, and we'd have to mark them. Hopefully we can pull them out quietly without having to use it.'

'You are extremely scary sometimes,' John said.

'Thank you, Dark Lord. Now tell us where the students are.'

'First: in the mess hall; there are two eating together. Chinese girl and white girl, southwest corner.'

'Got it,' Meredith said. 'Sending someone now.'

There was an explosion and everybody jumped.

'They're onto us!' I said. 'Gold, announce the spread procedure. Meredith, get Edwin down there; we'll have injured students.'

All students into demon-defence spread formation immediately. We are under attack, Gold broadcasted. *All students into demon-defence spread formation immediately. We are under attack.*

I handed some spray paint to John. 'Go and identify them.'

There was another explosion, closer this time, and the ground shook.

John grabbed a few more cans of paint. 'Stay here.' He raced out the door, followed by Meredith and Liu.

Gold changed to his battle form.

'Continue the broadcast,' I said.

'Sorry,' he said. 'Just checking the babies.' He restarted the announcement, then stopped and his eyes unfocused. 'Done. The students and Masters are now so far apart across the Mountain that each explosion will only kill two or three of them.'

As if to punctuate his sentence, another blast went off.

'Oh God, no,' I said. 'How's John doing?'

'He is moving through them quickly ...' He stopped for a moment. 'They've given up on exploding, it doesn't do enough damage. They're attacking the students with physical ... Oh no.'

'What?'

He let his breath out in a long gasp. 'The Dark Lord lost it again and returned to the Grotto.'

I jumped to my feet. 'Gold with me. Leo and Simone — don't argue, guys, just head down to the Earthly and I'll let you know the minute you can come back up.'

'You should go down too,' Leo said, reaching for me.

I moved away. 'No! We have to bring him back, and I'll be needed.' I scrabbled through the cupboard and found the cat food and bowl. 'Now head down, and this time we're bringing him back for good.'

'Don't do it, Emma,' Simone said.

I stopped and looked into her eyes. 'We don't have a choice. Now go.'

'Come on, sweetheart, she's right,' Leo said gruffly, and Simone didn't protest.

'Gold, see if we're the only Bastion under attack.'

'We are.'

'Summon Ma and Yang Biao and Gao Yuan. It's time to pay the price.'

'Done, ma'am. They're on their way.'

'Is the way to the Grotto clear?'

'No.'

'We'll have to fight our way through then. Ready?'

'Ma'am.'

I opened the door of the office and looked out. A few students were moving through the courtyard, taking their positions in the spread formation, which kept them a good five metres apart.

'Stay put,' I said to the terrified students standing in the spread formation. 'We're handling this. Whatever you do, don't group together. The minute you do, you'll be a bomb target. Understood?'

They nodded, but their faces were full of fear. One of the girls, Rachel, from my junior energy-work class was hugging herself desperately and crying uncontrollably. She fell to sit on the ground, rocking and weeping.

A boy nearby strode towards her and raised his hand to slap her out of it. I ran to catch up with him and blocked him.

'Don't even think about it,' I said.

'But she's hysterical!' he said, trying to pull his arm away.

'Is she more talented than you?'

'No ...'

'Did she attack you?'

'That's beside the point.'

I pushed him away. 'You would strike someone weaker than you who has made no move towards you? I don't care what the situation is, that's completely without honour. See me later. It's obvious you haven't understood the lecture about the power rush from dominating someone weaker than you. Now move back to your place.'

His face reddened, but he said 'Ma'am', and returned to position.

'Time's moving,' Gold said.

I bent to speak to Rachel. 'I know you're scared and you can't control the crying. But I need you to stand up and be brave. Keep crying if you can't do anything about it, but stand up and be ready to run if you need to. All right?'

She sat for a moment, still sobbing, then nodded. I reached down and pulled her to her feet and then into a hug.

'Be brave, Rachel. I'm bringing Lord Xuan back and we'll make sure our Mountain is safe. Okay?'

She nodded into my shoulder, then pushed me away and stood proud and brave and still gasping with huge sobs.

Stay in the allocated spaces, Liu said to everybody. *Do not group together.*

'Let's go,' I said to Gold.

As we ran through the Mountain gardens towards the Grotto, we heard the occasional explosion and sounds of battle. We passed through the administrative complex towards the Armoury, where we encountered two girls fighting in one of the small paved courtyards between the buildings. One had a dagger, and they were circling each other with menace.

'Disengage,' I said.

'I can't, ma'am,' said the girl with the dagger, Melissa. 'She attacked me.'

'She attacked me! I'm just defending myself,' the other girl, Lydia, said.

They continued to circle one another.

'Disengage!' I said. 'Let us handle it.'

A boy strode out of one of the breezeways. 'Lydia, honey, come and stand with me; I'll defend you. She has a knife and you don't.'

Lydia didn't look away from the other girl. 'The minute I take my attention off her, she'll try to kill me again. She's armed and way stronger than me — she'll kill me for sure.'

'Drop your weapon, Melissa,' I said.

The boy, Steven, took a couple of steps towards them and Melissa took advantage of the distraction to slash at Lydia. Lydia dodged the attack, spun and performed an almost perfect roundhouse kick into Melissa's head. Melissa fell hard and limp, her neck obviously broken. The knife dropped to the ground. Lydia picked it up and stared at it.

Steven rushed to Lydia and held her. 'Are you okay? You're not injured?' His expression filled with shock. 'Why? What?'

He grunted and fell — she'd stabbed him. She turned towards us and her face went bright red in the seconds before she exploded.

Gold spread himself to shield me from the blast, then returned to his battle form. 'Are you all right, Emma?'

'I'm fine. Some essence on me, but not injured.' I knelt to check the students.

'They're all dead,' Gold said. 'Let's get down there and bring the Dark Lord back.'

I stood and looked down at myself. I was covered in slimy demon essence, but it was a dark rich red colour instead of black, and looked unpleasantly like coagulating blood. I focused on what needed to be done. This could wait. 'What's the damage so far?'

'Twelve have exploded. Another fifty-odd are fighting. It appears that the rest are biding their time and haven't been activated yet.'

'Not the demons! How many students have we lost?'

'More than forty already.'

That hit me like a physical blow. I took a deep breath and grabbed that thought again; focus on what needed to be done. We continued towards the Grotto, passing terrified students, all still standing rigid in the spread formation. Some of them saw me and their faces filled with even more horror.

'No chance of doing something about the state I'm in?' I asked Gold. 'It's starting to burn.'

'Sorry, ma'am, not a dragon,' he said without stopping.

I changed to snake, quickly changed back again, and sighed with relief. The gore was gone.

Ma, Gao Yuan in brown robes and Yang Biao gently glowing in his silver robes were waiting at the entrance for us, with the two platoons of demon soldiers. We all ducked when another explosion rocked the Mountain, and the soldiers moved into a defensive formation around us.

'Send the soldiers out and put them on guard,' I said. 'Destroy anyone who attacks without provocation. If there are students already fighting, they're to do their best to separate them without hurting them. We don't know which is which.'

The demon soldiers moved off to spread out among the students.

I put my hand out and opened the Grotto. We raced down the stairs.

'How do we make the Turtle come up?' Gold said, standing at the edge of the water.

'Dammit, I lost the cat bowl and food when I changed to snake.' I sighed with resignation. 'Call Simone. She can carry him up here.'

Martin appeared next to us. 'No need. Give me a moment.'

He ran towards the water and dived in.

'Rock, paper, scissors?' Yang Biao said.

Gao Yuan and Yang Biao faced each other.

'Ma, call it,' Gao said.

'On three. One, two, three,' Ma said.

Gao won, and Yang turned away, frustrated. He turned back. 'Best of three?'

'Nope, I'm the one who cuts the chains of the Wheel,' Gao said. 'If you want it that bad, ask him later.'

'I believe I will,' Yang said. 'I was completely ready.'

Martin surfaced, holding John's Turtle by the front of its shell. It must have been four metres long, too big for him to carry in his arms. He floated to the ledge and lowered the Turtle gently onto it.

The Turtle spun to return to the water, moving with unnatural speed, and Martin stopped it. His expression filled with effort and he fell to one knee, holding the Turtle's shell with both hands. Another explosion went off and the ground shook.

'I can't hold it for long, it's extremely strong,' Martin said. 'Do what you were planning to do.'

Leo charged down the stairs in black lion form, stopped halfway and took a huge leap towards the Turtle.

Gao grabbed him in midair with one hand and slammed him into the ground. 'No, you don't, this is my job.'

Leo changed back to human form, jumped up and pushed Gao away. 'Let me do it!'

'With all due respect, sir,' Gao said, 'I have the power of a burning star and even that will not bring him to one-tenth of his full strength — but it will bring him back. What you have to give is nothing compared to that.'

Leo tried to shove past him. Gao reached towards Leo and touched him in the middle of the forehead with his index finger. Leo stopped, staring at Gao, and Gao effortlessly pushed him down onto his knees.

'Stay there,' Gao said, and Leo knelt unmoving, his eyes wide.

'Hurry,' Martin said, his voice strained with effort.

'Shut your eyes, ma'am,' Gao said, and exploded in a searing flash of brilliant light that sent everything around us into black and white relief. He became a glowing white-hot sun a metre across with arcs of burning fluorescence shooting from him. I reeled back, shading my eyes; the heat coming off him was immense.

He moved towards the Turtle and it turned to stare at him, transfixed.

'Can John refuse the energy?' I said.

'No,' Gao said, his voice crackling from the interior of the star. 'Say hello to him for me — and goodbye.'

He shot into John's shell and the Turtle lit up from within. There was another brilliant flash and John stood on the ledge in front of us in female human form, dazed and naked. She staggered back then regained her balance. A tiny ball of light, ten centimetres across, appeared from her abdomen and floated at waist height. It hovered for a moment, then shot straight up through the roof of the cavern and disappeared.

'Oh my God,' I said softly.

'This is new,' Ma said.

If John had a sister, this was how she would look: very tall, with a strong, muscular build, small breasts and generous hips, her long black hair floating in a tangle around her.

John concentrated for a moment and conjured a black Mountain uniform. 'That was totally unnecessary and the needless sacrifice of a good man!' she shouted.

'Definitely still him,' Gold said softly.

'Yell at us about it later,' I said. 'Right now, there are demons exploding on the Mountain above us and you're the only one who can identify them.'

'Right, I remember,' she said. She came to me and quickly bent to kiss me. 'I'll grab those spray cans and start marking them.' She looked around. 'Ma, with me.

Grab a platoon of demons and help take them out as I identify them. Gold, go up and coordinate. Emma.' She smiled into my eyes. 'Stay beautiful, and stay here where it's safe. I'll be right back when this has all been handled.'

She trotted gracefully up the stairs barefoot and disappeared into the darkness.

'Oh, my,' Ma said. 'He doesn't know.'

'He'll retake male form as soon as he realises. Don't worry, Emma,' Gold said.

'I'm sure he will.'

He glanced at me. 'You don't seem to care that much.'

I shrugged. 'What's important is that he's back and our students are protected.'

'She, now,' he said.

'Just get up there and make the damn announcements,' I said.

He inhaled sharply. 'Kitty Kwok and the Death Mother just landed on the forecourt outside Dragon Tiger.'

We have Michael's woman, and we'll kill her if you don't come to us right now, the Death Mother said.

I didn't say anything, I just ran.

When we reached the top of the stairs another explosion went off nearby, making the ground shake. I staggered and Gold caught me.

'Lord Xuan's taking them down one at a time,' he said.

Keep them busy until I finish up here, John said, her voice male in my head.

I ran at full pelt towards the main court. I stopped when I saw Kitty and the Death Mother standing at the northern end, holding a terrified Clarissa between them.

'Do what we say and the girl is yours,' Kitty said.

'We just want to make a trade,' the Death Mother said.

I walked up to them and Clarissa shrieked.

'That's close enough,' Kitty said. 'Any closer and the little girl gets cut.'

Nearly done, keep them talking, John said.

Another explosion went off.

Michael appeared next to me. 'Are you okay, Clarissa?'

'Just a bit scared,' Clarissa said. 'I'm glad you're here, Michael.'

'Try anything and she'll be more than scared,' Kitty said.

'Don't try to intimidate me, Kitty,' Michael said. 'I've known you far too long for that.' He summoned his sword and strode towards them.

The Death Mother raised her hands and slammed Michael with a blast of black energy. He was knocked off his feet and skidded three metres, hitting me and nearly knocking me over. I helped him up; neither of us had taken any damage.

The Death Mother raised her hand and summoned a pale blue aura of crackling energy around it. 'Try that again and it'll be a lethal blow.'

'Tell me what you want,' I said.

'Anything you want, you can have it,' Michael said. 'Just for God's sake don't hurt her. Don't worry, Clarissa, we'll sort this out.'

'Emma, come with me and she's all yours,' Kitty said. 'A fair swap: Emma for this one.'

'Not going to happen,' I said.

Clarissa shrieked and struggled in Kitty's grasp. Kitty grabbed the back of her head by her hair and pulled it so far back, Clarissa's neck was in danger of snapping.

'Don't hurt her!' I shouted. 'I'll come with you. Just let me say goodbye to Simone and we can trade. Me for her.'

'Good. You have two minutes,' Kitty said.

'Where's the Dark Lord?' Michael said under his breath.

The Death Mother grinned with malice. 'No turtles to help you right now.'

John appeared next to us, still in female form. 'Really?'

'You aren't supposed to be back yet,' Kitty said.

'We killed a star and fed it to her,' I said.

Michael stared at John. 'Emma ...'

'This is Lord Xuan.'

'Okay.' Michael turned his attention back to Clarissa. 'We'll sort this out now, honey, don't worry.'

'Things must be really bad if you're calling me pet names,' Clarissa said through her teeth, her head still pulled painfully back.

'Who is this?' John said.

'Kitty Kwok,' I said. 'You remember?'

'I know that one. Human woman. Hurts children. Who are the other two?'

'The Mother is Number Forty-Four, the Death Mother. The one that's been making the demon copies.'

'And the other demon?'

'That's not a demon,' Michael said. 'That's my fiancée.'

'Dammit, you said they wouldn't be able to detect her!' Kitty shouted with rage at the Death Mother. 'You said even the Third Prince didn't know! Leave it and get us out of here. This has all been for nothing!'

They pushed Clarissa towards us and disappeared.

'Clarissa's not a demon,' Michael said, moving towards Clarissa, who had fallen to the ground.

'Hold, Michael,' John said. 'That's not human.'

Clarissa pulled herself to her feet. 'I don't know what you're talking about. Michael, can we go home now?'

233

Michael stopped and studied Clarissa. 'I think you must be confused, my Lord. That's Clarissa, and she's an ordinary human. Her stone will vouch for her.'

'Ordinary human, my Lord,' Zara said.

'See?' Michael said. He went to her and held her. 'I'm so glad you're all right.'

'I can't bind her,' John said. 'I'm too weak!'

I tried to run to Michael but John held me back. 'Michael,' I yelled, 'she's a — ' But it was too late.

'That's right,' Clarissa said. She smiled up at Michael, her face went bright red and she exploded.

The force of the blast knocked me off my feet, then I was blinded by shen energy. I staggered upright again to see Michael floating above the ground in a cloud of brilliant white light. He glowed from within and his face was full of serenity.

John fell to one knee and lowered her head.

'What's happening?' Michael said. 'Clarissa?' Then he shot up into the air and disappeared.

John pulled herself to her feet. 'Raised. One of the youngest I've ever seen.'

I desperately needed a hug from John, but I couldn't bring myself to feel happy at her return after so much loss. I rubbed my eyes; they were full of tears.

John turned to study me. 'I know this is a shock for you,' she said. 'I don't seem able to make the form male at the moment.' She stood in front of me, hesitant, her dark eyes full of doubt. 'It is me, though, Emma, and I will be male for you as soon as I can.'

I threw myself into her arms and spoke into her shoulder. 'It's not that, John. So many of our students died today. Michael lost the love of his life and now he's down in Hell being judged. It breaks my heart.'

'Mine too,' she said.

I pulled back and wiped my eyes again. 'We have a big and unpleasant job to do now. How many have we lost?'

'Gold will know.' She put her arm around my shoulders and I leaned into her as we headed back to the administrative centre. 'You've been doing far too much, Emma, you're terribly weak. I would never have put you in charge if I'd known it would be so draining for you.'

'It's not that,' I said. 'Look closer.'

She stopped and turned to study me, her ice-cold consciousness searing through me. 'How did this happen?'

'I drank Leo's blood and caught the virus from him a long time ago. When the demon essence was burnt out of me, the virus was activated.'

She put her arm around me again. 'I see. I definitely need to find my Serpent then.'

I put my arm around her waist and we walked on together. 'I'm just so damn glad to have you back, Xuan Wu.'

'I'm glad to be back,' she said, squeezing me around the shoulders. 'They're holding off to give us room to talk. Even Simone is waiting for us to sort this out.'

'Nothing to sort out,' I said. 'You're back. That's all that matters.'

'I feel the same way.'

CHAPTER 17

*M*eet in the Throne Room, John said in broadcast mode. *Four; Gold; Simone; Leo.*

'Five now, not four,' I said. 'Martin redeemed himself. He gave himself to the Demon King as a hostage in return for Simone's safety, and he's been my liaison with the Northern Heavens since he was released.'

'That was courageous of him,' John said without stopping. 'The Demon King could have given him to the Mothers.'

'He did.'

'I see.' She broadcast again. *Five; Gold; Simone; Leo.*

The Throne Room was actually the living room in the Emperor's Residence, and there wasn't a throne there at all. It was furnished with modern black leather couches, carved rosewood coffee tables and an ebony entertainment unit holding a flat-screen TV. I'd had it carpeted in heavy-duty coffee-coloured wool; the original black slate floor was miserably cold in the middle of winter. The rest of the decoration was Michelle's, and I'd left it because she'd had three times more style than I ever would.

The Five — Meredith, Liu, Martin, Ma and LK Pak — together with Gold, Simone and Leo were waiting for us as we entered. All of them stood uncomfortably, their faces a mixture of grief and concern.

Simone ran to John and threw herself into her arms. 'I don't care, you're still my daddy.'

'Don't worry, Simone, it will be all right,' John said.

She pulled back and choked out the words. 'Is Michael dead? Please tell me he's not dead.'

'Michael's been taken to be Judged.'

'He's Raised? He'll be back? He has to come back.' Her voice became more desperate. 'He has to come back!'

'That's up to Judge Pao.'

Her face filled with determination. 'I'll go down there and tell Judge Stupid Pao to let him out right now. I ... *We* need him back!'

John's head shot up and I felt the summons at the same time. We shared a look: we'd both been summoned, and from the others' expressions they hadn't.

'We've just been ordered to Court Ten to bear witness at Michael's hearing,' I said. 'We have about an hour before we have to go, so let's sit and work out the plan for dealing with the aftermath of this attack.' I took John's hand and led her to the couches. 'Come on, we don't have long.'

'Casualty numbers. Give me a short summary, Gold,' John said as we sat together.

Gold projected the names above the coffee table. 'Forty-seven first years; nearly all the first years were completely wiped out. Nineteen second years; seven third years. Twenty-five injured; three critical, one probably won't make it. One Master died protecting them. This includes the ten students at Blue Star Peak who were killed when the demons with them exploded all at the same time for no discernible reason. No Immortals were lost; the demons didn't target them.

They went for the weakest. Including the hundred and three students that were replaced by demon copies: overall loss to the Mountain is one hundred and seventy-seven Disciples.'

'A high cost for the victory, but they are all destroyed,' John said.

I checked the list of names: Rachel hadn't made it, and neither had the boy who'd wanted to slap her.

'Are there enough remains for us to do anything with the dead?' I said.

'Some, yes. Not those who were close by when any of the demons exploded.'

'God,' Leo said quietly.

'Who's on clean-up?' John said.

'Edwin's coordinating the Celestials who are experienced in dealing with death. The students are in their dorms being counselled by non-Immortal Masters and seniors,' Liu said.

'Clear out Purple Mist and Dragon Tiger, move the statues into True Way, and put the photographs and offerings in there,' John said. 'Arrange for at least a hundred thousand Earthly dollars worth of effigies from Ronnie Wong for each of the dead. Find eight Buddhist monks and nuns to do the sutras for three full days. Did I miss anything?'

'Students of other faiths won't need that, and we have to arrange Earthly funerals,' I said. 'Gold, find out which was which, then do as the Dark Lord ... Lady —'

'I'm the Dark Lord, that's who I am,' John said. 'You're the Dark Lady and always will be.'

'Do as John directed for the Taoist and Buddhist students,' I went on. 'For the other students we'll arrange funerals of the relevant type. When I come back from Court Ten we'll discuss the funerals and Earthly ceremonies. We also need to inform their families.'

Gold winced.

'You won't have to do that, Gold, I'll do it myself,' I said. 'It's part of my responsibility.'

'We'll do it together,' John said. 'Our responsibility.'

I took John's hand. 'Sorry. It'll take me a while to get used to having you back and in charge.'

'You've always been the one in charge,' she said, her dark eyes full of amusement.

'Ain't that the truth,' Leo said.

'Oh, give it a rest, both of you.' I leaned back on the couch and a wave of dizziness made the room around me wobble.

John raised my hand and fed me energy. It wasn't her usual cold consciousness; this was pure and golden chi energy, enhanced with the warmth of her love for me. The air around me glowed and tasted of the freshness of the ocean, then the energy ceased.

'You are still too weak to be doing that, my Lord,' Meredith said.

'Emma's too weak to be doing anything,' John said, still holding my hand. 'I'll take her to rest until we visit Court Ten, then I'll come back and we can start the arrangements with the Temple staff, and analyse those demons.'

She put her arms under me and lifted me easily. I relaxed as she carried me through the living room and upstairs into the Emperor's bedroom. John was back and I could rest and let her handle things for a while.

'I don't sleep in here,' I said. 'I sleep in the servants' quarters.'

'Not on my watch, madam,' she said, and laid me on her bed. She pulled the covers back and slipped them around me. 'Do you think you can sleep for an hour or so until we have to go to Court Ten?'

'I'll need twenty minutes to tidy myself up before I go down there,' I said. 'My clothes are a mess and my hair is a disaster.'

She moved closer to gaze into my eyes. 'That makes us a matched set.'

I closed the gap between us, pressing my mouth onto hers. She stopped in surprise, then responded, wrapping her strong arms around me and pulling me into her.

I slipped my hands inside her jacket and felt her cool skin, but she took them in hers and gently moved them out again. I allowed her to guide my hands out of her clothes and stifled my disappointment. She really was female. But she would be male again soon. She had to become male again soon.

'You need to rest,' she said.

'I just want to touch you. It's been so long.'

She pushed me gently to lie down. 'Rest. I'm too weak at the moment to fully keep your virus at bay; I need to rest myself. Let me talk to them and then we'll head to Court Ten.'

I wanted to reply but she brushed her hand over my forehead and I was asleep.

I was woken by her hand gently touching my face. 'Er Lang is here with a damnable red box. It's for both of us. Sorry to wake you, love.'

'How long have I been out?' I said, pulling myself upright and swaying slightly as the bed moved beneath me.

She steadied me. 'Nearly an hour. We have ten minutes before we have to go down. Here.' She sat next to me on the bed, took my hair out of its tie, smoothed it and retied it. 'Perfect. That's all you need. Now let's go and listen to Rob the Rambler tell us all about our most painful duties.'

I gestured towards the tea table, always set with a pot of tea and four cups upside down on a tray. 'I need a drink first.'

'You should eat something as well, but we don't have

time.' John poured tea into three cups for me, and handed them to me one by one as I drained them. 'Enough?'

I nodded, and she took my hand and helped me out of the bed. 'I have been back less than an hour, we've lost more than a hundred students, and already the Celestial is throwing our duties at us. Is there no mercy?'

'Unfortunately in the last ten years I've learnt the answer to that question,' I said.

She stopped. 'Ten years?'

I pulled her arm to keep her moving. 'That's it.'

She didn't move. 'That's too short. I should not be back yet. Wait.' She unfocused. 'I'm definitely back for good, but why? It's too soon.'

'We fed Gao Yuan to you, John. You absorbed the power of a star, and you're still weak.'

'No, that doesn't explain it.' She shook her head and moved off again. 'Most strange.'

'Are Simone and Leo okay?' I said.

'Simone and I had an argument for a good ten minutes about why she can't go to Hell for Michael's hearing,' John said. 'I didn't know she felt so strongly about him. Perhaps you were right.'

'She wasn't aware she felt like that,' I said. 'Part of her reaction is because she didn't know how much she cared.'

'That much?'

'It's been obvious to everybody for a while now.'

'Even Michael? While he was engaged to Clarissa?'

'Except Michael. He had absolutely no clue.'

'Wonderful.'

Er Lang was waiting for us in the Throne Room; everybody else had left. He knelt before us, holding the red box.

'Lady Xuan Wu. Lady Emma Donahoe. I bear an Edict from the Celestial One himself, may he live ten thousand times ten thousand years.'

John and I both knelt and repeated the mantra. 'Ten thousand times ten thousand years.'

We all rose and Er Lang handed the box to John.

'Your worst nightmare, eh, Rob?' I said.

'I'm not Lady Xuan Wu, I'm the Dark Lord still,' John said. 'And as soon as I am able to take some time away from my duties to rest,' her voice became more pointed, 'I will be returning to male form.'

John passed the box to me and I took it to the coffee table and thumbed it open. I turned back; John and Er Lang were staring at each other. After what seemed like forever, Er Lang held his hand out.

'It's mightily good to have you returned, Ah Wu.'

John grabbed Er Lang's hand, held it clasped, and moved closer to hug him stiffly and thump him on the back as a comrade-in-arms. Er Lang thumped John on the back as well.

'It's good to be back, old friend,' John said.

I turned back to the Edict and rolled it open. John came up behind me and put her arm around my waist.

I read the scroll out. 'Bullshit bullshit, present yourself three days hence, blah blah blah, return to duties, bring Emma and Simone, formal transfer of title and position, more blahs, more formal bullshit, love the JE.'

'Emma,' John said mildly, 'please show proper respect. You'll break poor Er Lang's brain.'

'The Dark Lady,' Er Lang said, 'has already broken, shattered and destroyed my poor brain, and I completely deserved it.'

'Ah, you've learnt how to deal with him then,' John said.

The reminder call hit us both.

'We're late,' John said. She turned to Er Lang. 'We've been summoned to Court Ten to bear witness at a hearing. Is there anything major that I need to deal with right at this moment?'

'I saw what happened with those demons,' Er Lang said. 'Expect the rest of the Celestial on your doorstep in the next twenty-four hours demanding that you check for copies in their domains. Apart from that, things seem to be relatively quiet.'

'Damn,' John said. 'Very well. I'll catch up with you in a day or so and we can go through the current status.'

Er Lang saluted John. 'As you will, my Lord. And please, do hurry and get your head back.'

John roared with laughter as Er Lang disappeared.

'Your head?' I said as she controlled herself and reached to take my hand.

'My turtle head.' She saw my confusion and pointed at her crotch. 'That.'

We landed outside Court Ten in the centre of the wheel of Hell, next to the lake that divided the Celestial side from the demonic.

'Change to a more intimidating form,' I said. 'At least one of us should do this right.'

She frowned. 'I've half a mind to stay like this, and make myself shorter to match you, just to prove a point. We're not required for this and have much more important things to deal with right now.'

'Just do it,' I said. 'Michael's life is in the balance.'

'Being returned to the Wheel isn't death … No, it is worse than death, actually. He has a chance to Ascend, and you're right, we need to do our best.'

She concentrated and grew to two metres tall. Her skin became darker, her face squarer, and her hair longer and more tangled. Her black Tang robes floated around her in a Celestial breeze that wasn't there. She raised one hand, summoned Seven Stars in its scabbard, and slung it over her shoulder.

I shook out my shoulders. 'You should have woken me sooner; I would have put my armour on.'

'Visualise your armour. Think hard about what it looks like,' she said.

She raised one hand towards me and her eyes glowed with darkness. My clothes changed to my armour over my black silk robe; she even pinned up my hair and put it into a spike.

I summoned the Murasame and held it by its scabbard in my right hand. I nodded to John and we approached the court building together.

I will need to sleep for a week when we get back home, she said, and it was strange to hear her speaking in her male voice.

We walked side by side into the courtroom: John, huge and Celestial with her sword on her back; me, smaller in my armour and holding the Destroyer in my right hand. Judge Pao sat at his desk on his dais, his near-black face fierce as he gazed at us. Michael knelt on the stone floor in front of the dais, wearing the white cotton pants and shirt of a convict being tried.

'My Lord Xuan Wu. Miss Donahoe. You have delayed these proceedings,' Pao said.

'My Lord Pao. Too bad,' John said, not missing the lack of honorific towards me.

There was a whisper of soft conversation around the courtroom and Judge Pao silenced it with a glare.

I knelt and saluted the judge as a warrior with the sword in my hand. 'Your esteemed Honour. We attend at your summons.'

John silently stood her ground, waiting. I pulled myself to my feet and stood on her left to wait with her.

Judge Pao was obviously enraged by our blatant disregard for protocol. He waved one hand at Michael.

'This young son of the Tiger may be Worthy. Will you witness?'

John gestured for me to step forward without looking away from Pao. They were staring each other down.

'Prince Michael has distinguished himself with honour and valour in the service of the House of the North,' I said. 'He has acted with courage and protected the lives of both myself and Princess Simone, often to the cost of his own suffering. He is mightily Worthy.'

'He is close on the balance of Worthiness with regard to his intentions and deeds,' Judge Pao said. 'However, he was only beginning to pursue the Way; he was young and impetuous and prone to poor judgement.' He studied Michael, who didn't look up from the floor. 'He had attained no detachment, and was still bound by Earthly struggles.'

'He shows wisdom beyond his years and courage beyond his limitations,' John said. 'He truly belongs on the Third Platform, with the opportunity to attain the Second.'

Judge Pao studied Michael for a long time. 'Raising one so young is unheard of. You both witness most favourably, but by all accounts he should be reattached to the Wheel.' He raised his voice. 'Prince Michael, son of the White Tiger, stand.'

Michael rose, but he didn't stand straight; he seemed defeated.

'Give me one good reason why you should be Raised, sir,' Judge Pao said.

Michael stared at the judge for a long time, then put his hand on his hip and glared arrogantly at him. 'I'm the best warrior Heaven's ever seen. I'm the mightiest fighter on any Plane. I'm so damn good that you'd be doing yourself a favour to Raise me. Hurry up and do it so I can take my place in Heaven and show you what a real Immortal looks like.'

Everybody present seemed to take a breath at the same time, and the courtroom went completely silent. John made a soft sound next to me. I glanced at her but her face remained impassive.

'Your lies are painfully transparent, young man,' the judge said. 'It is obvious you do not wish to be Raised.'

Michael gestured angrily towards Pao. 'Don't be ridiculous, of course I want to be Raised, you stupid old fuck! I'd heard you were thick, but this is ridiculous.'

Judge Pao scribbled on the scroll in front of him. 'I pass judgement. You have been judged Worthy, Lord Michael. Take your place among the Celestial, and rejoice.' He banged his woodblock on the desk and rolled up the papers. 'Next case.'

Michael raised his arms and stared down at himself as his convict clothes changed into a Tang robe embroidered with a huge gold and white tiger that spread from the back to the front.

He glared up at Judge Pao. 'What about my mother?'

Judge Pao didn't look up from the paperwork. 'Who?'

'My mother, Rhonda MacLaren. Dammit, she was Empress of the West when she died! What happened to her? She was judged Worthy. Why hasn't she been given Immortality as well?'

'Leave it, lad,' John said. 'We'll discuss it later.'

'I remember that case,' Judge Pao said. 'There was some consternation as to the nature of her demise.' He glared at Michael. 'She was never judged Worthy; the White Tiger, in his folly, decided to Raise her himself. Such an act is within his rights as Emperor of the West, but it was a separate case when she arrived here. She was judged unworthy and reattached to the Wheel.'

'She was mightily Worthy!' I said.

'You have no jurisdiction here, madam,' Judge Pao said.

'She was my friend.'

'As I said. I will not repeat myself.'

'So that's it?' Michael said, suddenly looking small and abandoned in the centre of the courtroom. 'My fiancée's dead, my mother's back on the Wheel, and I'm Immortal now, and alone?'

'No Celestial is ever alone,' Judge Pao said. 'Rejoice, and return to your family.'

'My family are dead!'

'I'm highly tempted to revoke your status,' Judge Pao said.

'You can't,' Michael said. 'I know how it works. Great.' He turned to John and me. 'Wonderful. Well, I achieved Immortality, Emma, looks like I can be your bodyguard now. Now, if you'll forgive me, I need to find a quiet mountaintop where I can mourn my mother and the love of my life.' He disappeared.

'I really think you should have Raised Rhonda, she was such a fine, strong, smart woman,' I said to Pao.

'She had not made any attempt at all to find the Way,' Judge Pao said. 'I stand by my judgement. If I found all fine, strong, smart people Worthy, Heaven would collapse under the weight of them.'

'What about me?' I said.

His expression softened slightly. 'We shall see when it is time for you to be Judged.'

'I hope I never am.'

'Madam,' he said, pushing the papers aside, 'so do I.'

Simone came charging through the courtroom doors, dragging with her the demon guards, who were attempting to stop her, one on each arm. She threw one hard to the ground so it landed on its back, and slammed the other into the wall, stunning it. She stormed up to Judge Pao and raised the jade stone the Jade Emperor had given her.

'I have the Jade Emperor's personal endorsement,' she said. 'You have to Raise Michael.' She looked

247

around. 'Where is he?' She turned back to Pao. 'Is he down at the Room of Forgetting already? Stop him!'

'Prince Michael has been found Worthy and Raised to the Celestial. And you will leave my courtroom,' Judge Pao said. He glared at John. 'Control your child.'

'Where is he?' Simone said, her voice echoing in the chamber.

'He's been Raised, but he's gone to meditate for a while. Rhonda's never coming back, and Clarissa's dead,' I said.

Simone disappeared.

'Next case,' Judge Pao said. 'Lord Xuan Wu, Lady Emma, clear the court so that the next defendant may stand.'

'Come on, Emma, let's go,' John said, and took my hand.

Back home on the Mountain, she fell to sit on the couch and returned to human form. 'Simone's looking for Michael, but I doubt she'll find him.' She sighed with feeling. 'I would love to be a turtle in the heart of the Mountain and sleep for a week.' She saw my face. 'Don't worry, I'm not going anywhere. I'm staying here and in human form until this all blows over.'

The stone interrupted. 'Turtle, she hasn't had anything to eat since breakfast, and it's nearly dinnertime. Take her and feed her before she passes out; it's extremely annoying when she does that.'

'Ho fan?' John said.

'I'm not hungry,' I said.

'You will be once you eat something. The stone is right: you need to eat.'

I followed her into the dining room. 'I usually eat in the mess,' I said as I pulled off my armour and yanked the spike out of my hair.

'So do I,' she said. 'But you need some quiet time.'

She looked around. 'How many household staff do you have here?'

I hesitated, then said, 'None. I use the general support staff to keep the place clean, but I sleep in the servants' quarters, eat in the mess and work in my office.'

'But this is your house as much as mine, and it's criminal that it has no staff,' she said. 'You might as well have been living in a tent!'

'John, I didn't want to be in here at all without you, but they wouldn't let me live anywhere else. Even Simone took apartments nearby so she wouldn't have to be in the Emperor's Residence without you.'

She leaned back. 'Oh.' She took my hand. 'That will change, Dark Lady.'

She concentrated for a moment and a demon entered and set the table. Another came in with a steaming tureen of vegetarian dumpling ho fan with bright green baby bok choy floating in it.

'You eat too,' I said. 'I think the last thing you ate was a bowl of cat food this morning.'

She eyed the noodles with interest. 'I think I just may.'

The demon served the noodles into the bowls and passed them to us. It made us tikuanyin tea and then left us to it.

'You are taking this remarkably well,' she said.

'I know. I'm surprising myself. The pain of the loss is made less by your return, I think.' I leaned into her. 'I'm just so damn glad you're back.'

Her head shot up. 'Doorbell.' She snapped back. 'Ming and Yue wish to pay their respects. I'll tell them to wait —'

'Don't make them wait, let them in.'

Both of us stood to accept them as they entered. They fell to one knee in front of John.

Martin spoke first. 'My Lord, this small Shen welcomes you.'

'Welcome back, my Lord,' Yue Gui said.

They rose again and Martin hugged John. 'Welcome back, Mother,' he said softly.

Yue Gui gasped. Martin and John shared a horrified look, then all three of them quickly looked at me and just as quickly looked away.

Realisation hit me between the eyes. 'Wait. Stop. Wait! No *way*.'

They shared a guilt-filled look and all three sat at the table. John ignored her noodles and concentrated on me.

I pointed my finger at Martin. 'You disgraced yourself six hundred years ago, but I don't know how old you are. Ming Gui, exactly how old are you?'

Martin shot a glance at John, and John nodded slightly. Martin turned back to me. 'I am close on four thousand years old.'

I dropped my finger. 'That's before he joined. Oh, dear Lord, the Turtle's your mother.'

Martin sat watching me placidly as if this was perfectly normal dinnertime conversation. 'That is correct. The Xuan Wu Turtle is my mother.'

John made a very small sigh of relief and relaxed slightly.

'And the Serpent's your father, isn't it?'

'Shit,' John said softly.

I stared at John. 'You're both his parents.'

She nodded once, her expression grim.

I stood up and moved to the other side of the room. 'I'm used to you being strange, John, but this ... this is unbelievable. You've fathered a child on yourself.' I turned to see her; her face was full of misery. 'Wait here. I need to go for a walk.'

I left without saying another word and walked all the way around the Mountain on the training track.

At the track's highest point it had a stunning view of the Mountain complex, from the domiciles and villas on the western side, through to the Yuzhengong central complex, to the administrative and support buildings on the eastern side, all nestled against the flanks of the Seven Peaks. The students weren't out practising as they normally would be; they were still recovering from the aftermath of the attack. I could see small groups of people dealing with the corpses, and collecting as much as they could of the remains of the demon copies for further study.

John appeared next to me and leaned on the railing, also studying the Mountain complex.

'You kept that a secret from me,' I said. 'You were worried it would freak me out.'

'It did,' she said, without looking away from the view.

'I asked Martin about his mother once and he dodged the question.'

'It is his information to do with as he wishes. He generally prefers not to share it. A long time ago he was accused of being the issue of an incestuous relationship.'

'The Turtle's female.'

'The Turtle is an Essence. It is either gender, and normally I don't even bother about it. It just happens. In the last thirty years or so, it has been male.'

I turned to see her. 'What pisses me off the most is that both of you decided not to tell me.'

She smiled slightly. 'And you hate it when anybody keeps a secret from you.'

'Anyone I love.'

'The information has no bearing on our relationship as it is right now. Martin prefers not to divulge it. We did the right thing.' She turned to face me, still leaning on the railing. 'I was once two separate creatures. These two mated and produced issue. Then they joined and

251

became one creature, one mind, one sentience. That creature gained a human form and was Raised to the Celestial. That joined creature, in human form, is me.'

'That creature was demonic.'

'It was, yes.'

'The stone won that bet, by the way. You lost. You owe us your shell.'

'It is already yours.'

I leaned on the rail and put my head in my hands. 'God, you're weird, John.'

She put her hand on my back; a light touch. 'I think you like it.'

'I'm exhausted. What a hell of a day.'

'Ming and Yue have returned to the North, but they have asked for our presence tomorrow for a handover in the Northern Heavens. You don't have to go if you don't want to.'

I nearly opted out, but duty came first. 'I need to be there. How complicated will it be?'

'They were planning a celebration when I returned, but under the circumstances they've downgraded it to a simple ceremony. Afterwards we'll have dinner in the Palace, family only.'

'Sounds good.'

She moved closer and put her arm around me. 'Am I forgiven?'

'You know you always are. But ...' I stopped.

'But what?'

I shook my head.

'Tell me. You've just learnt something embarrassing and stupid about me. Now tell me whatever embarrassing and stupid thought you had. What was it?'

The sun dipped below the horizon in a blaze of red, lighting up the clouds from behind.

'How much will you change when you regain your Serpent?' I said.

She was silent for a moment, her arm around me, then she squeezed me gently. 'I honestly don't know.'

'I see.'

'This is a problem?'

I nodded without speaking.

'Then I must find it in a hurry so that it ceases to be one. In the meantime, your noodles are getting cold and it's nearly dinnertime. How about we bring Leo and Simone in and share the meal together?'

'Pass on to Martin and Yue that I'll keep his secret,' I said. 'You're right: nobody needs to know.' I turned to face John. 'And there's a secret about me that you need to know.'

'And that is?' Her voice was sharp with concern.

'Not that serious. I haven't told Leo that I have AIDS from drinking his blood. When you regain your Serpent, the issue is academic anyway, so there's no need for him to know and beat himself up over it. I've told everybody that I'm weak from having the demon essence burnt out of me and I need to take some time out and rest.'

She was silent for a moment, then said, 'See? Sometimes there is a very good reason for keeping a secret.'

'Oh, shut up,' I said, turning away.

She kept her arm around my shoulders, I put mine around her waist, and we walked together back to the Imperial Residence.

CHAPTER 18

I excused myself shortly after dinner and left them to chat, heading straight to bed. John planned to gather the Celestial Masters in the War Room and have a strategy meeting while the rest of the Mountain slept. Sleep was a luxury for the Celestials, not a necessity.

I hesitated outside the Emperor's room and then decided against it; John was female and may not want to find me in her bed. I went into my little room in the servants' quarters, took a shower, then slid into my single bed and smiled at the scroll on the wall with the character *si* on it that he'd given to me for my birthday so long ago. More memories to make now.

I turned over and was asleep before I knew it.

'Emma.' She touched me on the cheek and I woke. She was sitting on my bed wearing nothing but a pair of black pyjama pants. 'What are you doing here?'

I sat up. 'John, you're a girl now. You need to cover the top half too.'

She looked down at herself and smiled ruefully. 'Oh yes, you're right.' She concentrated and winced. 'I have no energy left to summon anything; I closed the meeting because I need to sleep. Do you have something that would fit me?'

'Nothing of mine would fit you, John. Even female you're way bigger than me.'

I went to the tiny closet and searched through its mess, eventually handing her a T-shirt that had once belonged to her.

'You kept one of mine?' she said, pulling it on.

'It smelled of you,' I said.

She put her hand on my face. 'I understand.'

I put my own hand over hers.

'Why are you in here?' she asked again.

'I wasn't sure if you wanted me in your room,' I said. 'But it really feels good to sleep here knowing that you're finally back in your own room.'

'It would be better with you in there with me,' she said.

'Was the human form originally female?'

'I don't know, Emma. It was thousands of years ago. I hardly remember anything more than about three thousand years ago.'

'How long until you can be male?' I said.

'I have no idea. Will you come and join me anyway?'

I moved close and looked her right in the eyes. 'There is nothing I would rather do more.'

She took my hand and we padded through the empty dining room and past the central garden, up the stairs and to the back of the courtyard house and the Imperial bedroom. John had made a fire in the fireplace and it cast a warm glow over the room and filled it with the comforting scent of burning wood.

I stopped at the bed. 'Which side do you prefer? We've known each other years and you've never told me.'

'You go in first, next to the wall; I will take the outside.'

'You'll regret that when I'm human and need to use the bathroom in the middle of the night.'

'I would regret it more if the Demon King raided and I was not between him and you.'

I pulled the covers back and sat on the side next to the wall.

She gracefully lowered herself onto the bed and pulled me down beside her. I cuddled into her and she wrapped her arms around me. I leaned on her shoulder and she kissed the top of my head. Both of us heaved a huge sigh of bliss.

The lights dimmed and the room filled with the warm glow of the fireplace. Crickets chirped outside the window and the autumn breeze sang through the pines.

'I have returned,' she whispered. 'We have waited so long, and I have returned, and I am something that you cannot love.'

'I love you whatever shape you take,' I said. 'But I understand if what you want is different now.'

She shifted so that she could see into my eyes, her own lit by the fire's glow. 'You.' She put her hand on the side of my face. 'I just want you. Do you still want me?'

I touched my mouth to hers, then pushed the kiss deeper and lost myself in her as she responded. Our hands roamed each other, and eventually we pulled the intrusive clothes off and stretched side by side, skin to skin.

She ran her fingertips down the side of my face. 'Ever made love with a woman before, Emma?'

'No,' I said, sliding my hand over her thigh and watching her reaction. 'Ever made love to a woman as a woman, Xuan Wu?'

'No,' she said, her touch gliding down my shoulder.

I slid my hand up the back of her leg and traced her curves. 'Let me show you the good parts.'

'Oh, a lesson,' she said, her dark eyes glittering. Her voice softened. 'Do I need it?'

'Meet me after class and we'll discuss it,' I said, pushing her onto her back and lowering my mouth onto her.

* * *

'Emma,' she said softly, a long time later.

'Hmm?'

'When I've regained the male form ...'

'Yeah?'

She was silent.

'Sure, John. I don't mind at all.'

'Just now and then. Occasionally.'

'Sure. Occasionally.'

She lowered her voice to a whisper. 'Just don't tell the Tiger.'

'Wouldn't dream of it,' I said, nuzzling into her. 'Now go to sleep.'

She rolled over so that she was facing me, threw her arm over me and held me closer. We cuddled down under the warm silk quilt; the fire had died down and the autumn night was cool.

'Oh, there's something I've been meaning to say for a long time but couldn't,' she said.

'What's that?' I mumbled, half-asleep.

'I love you, Emma Donahoe.'

That woke me. I pulled myself up so that I was face to face with her. 'I love you too, Xuan Wu.'

'And as soon as I can stay male and find my other half, we're making an honest woman of you.'

'Far too late for that,' I said. 'Now shut up and go to sleep. We have a lot to do tomorrow.'

She nuzzled into my hair. 'You won't be going anywhere tomorrow,' she said, her voice warm and low. 'All the classes will be right here.'

'Oh, will they?' I said. 'Well then, I'd better go into my room later and find my instructional aids.'

'Definitely.'

I woke before dawn the next morning, thirsty and needing the bathroom. I rolled over and felt a jolt of shock at the huge black lump beside me, then realised what I was seeing. John was asleep next to me as a sixty-centimetre-long turtle. Its nose rested on the covers with its eyes closed and its beak half-open. I tried to creep around it to go out but it woke and saw me.

'Emma?' it said, its voice male.

I brushed the back of its shell. 'It's all right. Go back to sleep. I need to use the bathroom.'

It nodded its head, then grinned its turtle grin. 'Sorry.'

'Nothing to be sorry about,' I said, and kissed the end of its nose.

'Remind me to give you a gold coin tomorrow morning,' it said.

'Everybody stopped doing that; Simone kept making gagging noises.' I peered around at its back end. 'Are you a boy or a girl right now? You sound male.'

It raised its head and half-closed its eyes, then focused on me. 'The answer to that question is: you do not want to know.'

'Boy then,' I said, and rolled out of the bed to head for the bathroom.

She was human and female when I returned to bed.

'You're looking much better this morning,' Simone said to me over the breakfast table. 'You were completely out of it last night.'

'I don't remember too much,' I said. 'It's all a blur.'

'Has anyone heard from Michael?' John said.

'Nothing,' Simone said. 'He's alive, he has to be, he's just … gone.'

'You won't want to be around the Academy today, Simone,' I said. 'Go to school.'

'No,' she said. 'I want to spend time with Daddy, and I'll help sort things out. Is it okay if I move into one of the upstairs bedrooms in the Residence?'

'Of course, this is the family home. Leo, would you like the other one?' John said.

'I think I'll stay where I am over at the Celestial Residences.'

'This is the family home now, Leo, we really should —' John began, but I kicked her under the table and she understood. 'No, that's fine, stay where you have more privacy. Just remember: ceremony at the Northern Celestial Palace tonight.'

'Can I bring Justin along?' Simone said.

'Who's Justin?' John said sharply.

Simone looked silently at her for a long moment, then said, 'My boyfriend. He's a really nice dragon, one of Qing Long's lesser sons.'

John glanced at me and I shrugged. 'He's a good kid.'

'Then he is welcome,' John said.

'Don't you dare give him the third degree, Daddy. We've only been out once and there's no need to go all hyper-parent on me, okay?'

'I wonder how he'll react when she calls this woman Daddy,' Leo said, almost to himself.

John unfocused and snapped back. 'The other Three Winds are on their way to pay their respects. They'll be here in about half an hour, when we're finished eating. They want to see me before tonight to bring me up to speed. The Generals will be here after lunch.'

'I'm out,' Simone said. 'I'll start moving the stuff out of my quarters.'

'Me too,' Leo said. 'I'll catch you later, I have some kids to sort out.'

'I'll come with you,' I said. 'Wait for me.'

'Emma, they can run, but I'm afraid that as my partner you still have to put up with the Winds,' John said. 'Besides, I want someone to share my misery with.'

'It's just the Dragon who annoys me,' I said, sitting back down and finishing my toast as Leo and Simone tried to race casually out the door.

The Tiger appeared, sitting at the table with us. He saw John and his mouth flopped open. 'Whoa. Holy shit.'

'Bai Hu,' John said, 'you are not supposed to be here for another half-hour, and you are to wait for me in the Throne Room.'

'I had to see for myself,' the Tiger said. 'Am I correct in assuming that you didn't find your Serpent?'

John nodded.

The Tiger looked from John to me. He pointed to us, first one and then the other. 'Have you two ... you two ...' He saw our faces and his eyes widened. '*Hot damn!*' He took the form of a tall, slim, boyish European woman with short platinum-blonde hair. 'Can I play too? No, wait,' he said. 'Let me get a video camera.'

John gestured casually towards the Tiger and he disappeared. She grimaced. 'I should not have done that; he's extremely fat.'

'Where'd you put him?' I said.

'There is a new large construction in orbit on the Earthly. I put him on top of it.'

'That's the International Space Station.'

'He's clinging to the outside. It'll take him at least half an hour to return.'

I nearly choked on my tea. 'What if they see him?'

'One of the people inside is a dragon Shen; he appears to be a Japanese child of the Dragon. He says hello.' Her expression went wry. 'And to please do that more often; something about the Tiger being able to fix a rotating joint on the starboard boom while he's out there.'

My phone rang as I was just about to enter the Throne Room.

'Emma, darling, I hear John's back. They're saying things ... Are they true?'

'It's my mum,' I said, waving John forward. 'You go first, I'll be along in a minute.'

'No, I should say hello to them, pass on my respects,' she said. 'Let me get a stone to patch me into the call.'

I glared at her. 'I am having a private call with my mother. You can talk to her later. Go in and do your stuff, I'm right behind you.'

She bowed to me, amused. 'As you wish, ma'am. I will obey.'

She went into the Throne Room, and I returned to the dining room and sat at the table.

'Yes, he's back,' I said. 'But right now he's a she.'

She was silent for a long moment, then said, 'And how does that affect everything?'

'She'll retake male form as soon as she's able. It won't be long. She's terribly drained after all she's been through.'

My mother made her voice forcibly brighter. 'Well, darling, just remember: we love you no matter what lifestyle you choose, you know that.'

I choked with laughter. 'Don't worry, you won't have to order a wedding cake with two girls on the top. She's still John, and very much him on the inside. I'm sure it won't take long for her to gain her ... bits back. And compared to everything else the Xuan Wu is, being female is minor.'

She sounded suspicious. 'You don't seem to have much trouble talking about your partner as a she.'

'Well, we took a shower together this morning and I can assure you that right now the Dark Lord of the Northern Heavens is one hundred per cent female. The Tiger's thrilled to bits.'

'He would be,' my father said, listening in on the extension.

'Dad!' I said. 'That's very rude.'

'So when is he coming over to say hello to everybody?' my father said, ignoring me.

'Haven't you been invited to tonight's dinner?'

'No. What dinner?' my father said.

'I'll get right on that; you should have received invitations. They're having a welcome back thing at the Northern Heavens tonight. I'd love it if you could come along. Martin probably forgot to send you invitations. He doesn't mean anything by it; he just keeps forgetting that I'm an ordinary human with a family.'

'Can't wait,' my father said with enthusiasm. 'I can have photos taken with my daughter and the hot girl she's engaged to.'

'Brendan, you are impossible,' my mother said.

'Uh, Mum?'

'What, Emma?' she said, hearing the concern in my voice.

'It's quite important that all the family comes: Jen and Mandy too, and their kids — all of them. Can you make sure they turn up?'

'Amanda doesn't like her boys —' my mother began.

I interrupted her. 'I know. She doesn't want them coming up here. But just this once, it's important. Make sure they're there.'

'Is there a problem?'

'I sincerely hope not,' I said with feeling. 'I'd better go. John's lording it over the other three Winds and I want to know what he's telling them.'

'All right. We'll see you tonight then.'

'Cool. And make sure all the boys come.'

I snapped the phone shut and took a deep breath to calm myself. If something had happened to Andrew and Mark, I would never forgive myself. And my family would never forgive me.

I walked into an argument in the Throne Room; the Dragon was shouting at John.

'You must come to our palaces and check for us.

These demon copies were undetectable to anybody but you. I need to be certain!'

'I will scan through your dominions after I have paid my respects to the Celestial,' John said.

'And you must return to male form, my Lord, this is ridiculous. It's a well-known scientific fact that women are more difficult to work for than men; and now I have two women rulers!' The Dragon waved dismissively at me as I sat. 'You must redress this imbalance immediately. It's been ten years since I've had a Sovereign who is easy to deal with, and I deserve some respite.'

'The bastard has a point, Ah Wu,' the Tiger said. 'All fun aside, the Sovereign must be male.'

'I will discuss this with you later,' the Phoenix said to the Dragon with quiet menace.

'Wonderful.' The Dragon spread his hands. 'See? Now you have me in trouble with my major wife. This cannot continue. And *this*.' He jabbed his finger at me. 'You must look inside her; there is definitely something going on here. I heard about those foreigners, that male Snake Mother thing. The Demon King is up to something!'

'There is no need for that,' John said. 'I have vowed; it will be so.'

'But you can't be sure,' the Dragon said. 'Just a quick look, confirm or deny, then all is established and we may move forward. Just listen to the way she speaks; it's become more and more disturbing as time has passed.'

John rose. 'All is established. I will expect you at the Northern Heavens this evening. Dismissed.'

'You are far more trouble than you are worth,' the Dragon said to me, and the Winds disappeared.

'Now I need to talk to the Generals, and they're gathering in the Hall of Martial Strategy,' John said.

We walked from the Imperial Residence over the bridge to the administration area. The Generals were waiting for us in the War Room, sitting around a U-shaped table arrangement, which was draped with a black silk cloth embroidered with images of soldiers in battle on horseback and foot. They stood as one, saluted us, and waited.

'As you were,' John said, and guided me to the central table of the U. We sat and the Generals followed.

'So what needs doing?' John said. 'Anything so major that you couldn't handle it?'

'Not really,' Ma said. 'But Gao Yuan is gone, and we need to find another General to replace him.'

'Any suggestions?' John said.

'Emma?' Bo Niang said.

'Don't be ridiculous,' John said.

'Why not? She was good enough for First Heavenly General,' Bo Niang said. 'Now you're back, she has to fade into the background? Women are sadly under-represented here, we need to redress the balance.'

'I concede your point, but she's not old enough or experienced enough, and she's not a Shen,' John said. 'She was First in name only; Er Lang did all the work. Emma is not qualified.' She turned to see me, obviously concerned at how I'd react.

'John's right: I'm not qualified at all,' I said. 'Find someone who's Immortal.'

'Leo?' Liang Tian said.

'Idiot,' Zhou said.

'Not a complete idiot, but he doesn't really have the brains to do the job terribly well,' John said.

'I meant Liang's an idiot for suggesting the Lion,' Zhou said. 'Leo still has a great deal of growing to do before he has fully expanded into the role of Immortal.'

Ma glared at the Generals. 'Stop suggesting people purely because you think that'll please the Dark Lord. We need to be rational about this.'

They all shared a look, then a communal shrug, and turned back to us.

'Sang Shen?' I said.

'Criminal,' Bo Niang said. 'Attempted murder — and, might I remind you, he tried to murder you.'

'You're all criminals,' I said.

'Not all of us!' she said, protesting.

'To the point: Sang Shen, once again, lacks the brains,' Ma said. He tapped the side of his head. 'Wood from one ear to the other, and when he's flowering he's not even as smart as a block of wood.'

'Martin?' I said.

Liang Tian snorted. 'He has half the brains of Blockhead.'

'Is there anyone who you think is intelligent enough for this job?' I said.

'Off the top of my head, no,' Ma said.

'Either of the Lius?' I said.

'I'm not removing them from the Mountain; they're too vital to its smooth running,' John said.

'Yue Gui?' I said.

There was silence for a moment as they considered it.

'No,' John said. 'She's a fine administrator and an excellent councillor, but she has very little military experience.'

Ma nodded. 'You are correct, my Lord.'

'We'll leave it then, and be the Grand Thirty-Five until something comes up,' John said.

'The Jade Emperor will be extremely displeased at the lack of Harmony with that number,' Ma said.

'He can just put up with it,' John said. 'A General is for nigh on forever, and I refuse to rush into an appointment that will have repercussions for an extremely long time.' She glanced around the table. 'Is there anything further? If there is nothing immediate and urgent, my Lady and I have an important lesson scheduled back in the Residence.'

I had a choking fit and Ma had to slap me on the back. I took a sip of water and nodded that I was okay. John pointedly ignored me.

'We expect your presence in the Northern Heavens for the handover ceremony this evening,' she said. 'Until then, dismissed.'

We lay in each other's arms, silently sharing the moment before we had to go out again.

'I need to keep busy,' I said into her chest. I buried my face between her breasts and she held me close. 'If I don't keep busy, I see their faces.'

'Were you teaching them?'

'Yes. Some of the first years were ready to move up. I've known some of the copies for more than a year.'

'There are no copies left. The remaining students are safe.'

'That doesn't stop me from seeing their faces.'

She held me away slightly to look into my eyes. 'I'm back now, love. This will not happen again. The Heavens are protected.'

'In a way, I'm relieved. I've seen this horrible thing coming for weeks now, and it's finally happened, and it's over, and we can move on.' I snuggled closer. 'But I can't cry for them. Why can't I cry for them?'

'That is a normal reaction. Be ready with tissues at the first funeral, because that is what funerals are for.' She stopped breathing for a moment, then came back. 'Jade is here requesting audience without an appointment. Most unusual.'

'Damn, this is ridiculous,' I said. 'Talk about everybody knowing what we're "up to".'

'There would be much more concern if we weren't up to anything. On the Earthly it's normal for someone to say someone can't come to the phone, "they're in the bathroom"; this is just one step further.'

'So everybody knows?'

'Only those who need to, and then only that we are in the Residence. Those who don't need to know where we are wouldn't bother to check.'

I moved away from her slightly. 'They can't actually see us, can they?'

'No, of course not. What they can see is that we are both in the Imperial Residence, resting together, and have been for about an hour.'

I exhaled with relief. 'That's okay then — you don't need Celestial abilities to know that. I wonder what's so urgent that Jade is interrupting us?'

'My fault, love. I told the servants I would be resting for about an hour and to leave us undisturbed. Our hour is up.'

When the Mountain had moved to Heaven, Jade had stopped dressing in western suits and now wore Tang-style flowing green robes all the time. She gracefully knelt to salute us, then sat with one slender hand on the edge of the sofa, her eyes downcast.

'Are you in trouble, Jade?' I said.

She looked out the window. 'Without your help, I could be.' She turned back to us. 'Welcome back, Lord. I have been waiting for your return to ask you something, but this has come up first and I apologise for taking your time in this difficult hour.'

'What do you wish to ask?' John said.

'First.' She raised her hands and shook her long sleeves down over them. 'I have borne three dragon children while you were away, Lord. Their father is the Blue Dragon of the East.'

'Congratulations. Qing Long did not mention this,' John said.

'He has asked me to marry him. I have refused.'

267

'You might like to get to know him better before you make the decision, Jade,' I said. 'Go spend some time in the Eastern Palace, talk to him …'

'I know enough about him to know that I do not wish this,' she said firmly. She bobbed her head. 'Apologies, but I am sincere.'

'Very well,' John said. 'You have our support.'

'Thank you. He may come to you directly and ask for me to be reassigned.' She shifted uncomfortably on the couch. 'Please don't make me leave here.'

'Oh, Jade, we won't make you go. You're like family,' I said.

'Even when I ask not to work in Accounts any more?' she said, plaintive.

'Where do you want to work?' I said.

She leaned forward and spoke earnestly. 'We have a hundred-odd casualties to handle, with funerals to arrange and families to console. We also have to find a workable cover story for so many deaths. One option is to disseminate the story that an earthquake hit Earthly Wudang and that is the source of the loss of so many students. Earthquakes aren't uncommon throughout China, with large casualty rates. Let's face it, my Lord, my Lady, we need a public relations representative here on the Mountain, and I'd like to put myself up for the post, if I could.'

'What a terrific idea,' I said with awe. 'And you're perfect for it, with so many years of experience on the Earthly.'

'I can arrange the Earthly funerals, liaise with the Earthly media — I'd like to take on that role. My second-in-command in the Finance branch, Flora, is extremely capable of taking over my post as head.' She sat back, seeming surprised at her own fervour. 'With your permission,' she said more softly.

'Why didn't you ask to do this before?' I said. 'You

didn't need to wait until Lord Xuan was back, I would have let you do it.'

'There was a chance the Dark Lord would reposition me in Accounts once he had returned,' Jade said. 'I wanted to be sure that if I made the move to PR, I would be permitted to stay.'

'You have my permission,' John said.

She collapsed with relief.

'If Qing Long gives you any trouble, let us know,' John said. 'Is the relationship between you amicable?'

'Perfectly, my Lord. We share the raising of the children; he has them every second weekend at the Eastern Palace. I'm concerned that if I won't marry him, he will try to arrange for me to be posted in the Eastern Palace so he can have the children full-time.'

'Don't worry,' I said. 'You're our new PR executive. We can't possibly afford to let you go.'

She stood and fell to one knee, her robes flowing around her. 'Thank you. I will start work immediately. There is much that needs to be done.'

'Do you have any assistants in mind?' I said.

'A couple,' she said, standing up. 'Ah Liang in admin, and the little demon Winnie in the accounting section.'

'They're yours.'

She bowed with her hands clasped in front of her. 'Thank you.'

'We are heading to the administrative centre now,' John said. 'Meet us there and we will begin the preparations.'

'My Lord.' Her serene expression dissolved and she grinned broadly. 'And welcome back, my Lord! It is so good to see you again, and I am sincerely looking forward to arranging your wedding.' She sighed with bliss. 'That will be the job of a lifetime.'

'Ah-ha,' I said. 'That's why you're so keen to take on this job.'

She bowed slightly. 'You know how much I love weddings.'

'Except your own,' I said.

'Maybe one day,' she said, the smile not shifting. 'I will see you at the office.' She backed towards the door and went out.

John took my hand. 'Time to do some work, my Lady.'

I leaned into her. 'It's not work when I'm doing it with you.'

She kissed my hand. 'I feel exactly the same way.'

'You two done?' Leo said from the doorway.

'Never,' John said, and waved him in.

Leo wheeled himself into the centre of the room and leaned on one arm of the chair to clamber out of it. He saluted John on one knee, and John stood up to acknowledge it. Leo pulled himself back into the chair with difficulty, and rested his elbows on his knees.

'Has Lady Emma spoken to you about me, my Lord?' he said.

'No.' John looked from Leo to me.

I sighed, running my hands through my hair and then regretting it as strands came out between my fingers.

'How much of the story do you know?' Leo said.

'Probably nothing,' John said. 'Fill me in.'

'I didn't want to be Raised. I failed you far too many times to deserve it. I just want to die,' Leo said.

'You are Worthy, accept it,' John said.

'When my spine was broken and I was dying, you agreed to drain me,' Leo said.

John leaned back and her expression darkened.

'You agreed!' Leo said.

John glanced at me.

'He sat in Hell for nine years refusing the Elixir,' I said. 'He only drank it on the condition that I promise I'd talk you into draining him.'

270

'That's blackmail,' John said.

'It's just what I want,' Leo said.

'That much?' John said.

'More than anything!' Leo's voice was strained with grief. 'I'll never be what I want to you, so make me one with you.' His voice broke. 'Please.'

'I'll think about it,' John said.

'No,' Leo said. 'You already agreed. You have to do it.'

John put one hand over her eyes. 'I cannot express my disappointment with you. Dismissed.'

Leo wheeled himself closer to John. 'Just say you'll do it.'

John nodded once with her hand over her eyes. Leo bowed to her from the chair and wheeled himself out.

CHAPTER 19

Late that afternoon we met up with the Tiger at the guesthouse in the Northern Heavens, about two kilometres from the Palace complex. We all wore black silk Tang-style robes, modified with slits up the sides over the riding trousers beneath, and with armour over the top. The Tiger and his grooms brought us each a black horse: a small, light-boned Arab mare each for me and Simone, and a big, heavyset, warm-blood stallion for John. All of the horses had been saddled and bridled with antique carved leather tack, black and highlighted with silver fittings.

The Tiger held Simone's horse while she mounted. 'If they give you any grief at all, send me a telepathic message,' he said. 'Even the best-trained horses will baulk at some of the rigmarole that's happening at the Palace. The stallion should behave, he's a warhorse, but you never know.'

John stood next to her horse and reached towards the Tiger. 'Lend me a hand, brother.'

The Tiger strode to John, they clasped hands, and both of them dropped their heads slightly. A glowing nimbus of shen energy surrounded them, then disappeared into John.

'Enough?' the Tiger said.

John nodded, and they released hands.

'Fat bastard, you nearly killed me,' the Tiger said.

'I hear the ring joint on the port boom could do with some work as well,' John said.

'Pfft.' The Tiger waved her down. 'Let's see it then.'

'Hold the horse,' John said, and the Tiger took the reins.

John raised her hands slightly out to the side, threw her head back, and the air shimmered around her. She grew and widened and thickened, and took male form. John mounted his horse, took up the reins, and shook out his shoulders with an audible crack. 'That's more like it.'

'Oh, it's about time,' I said.

'This is only temporary,' John said. 'It'll last about two hours. What I really need is to sit at the bottom of the lake for a week or so.'

'Not yet!' I said. 'Jade Emperor tomorrow.'

'Looking forward to that one,' the Tiger said. He gave me a quick leg-up onto my horse, then stepped back and studied us. 'Impressive. You'll make a fine entrance. As I said, if any of them play up, just give me a call.'

'No need,' John said, and turned his horse on the spot. 'I have enough left to keep them in line.'

'See you at the Grand Court then,' the Tiger said, and disappeared.

'Me in the middle, Simone on my left, Emma on my right,' John said. 'And both of you look spectacular.' He sighed with bliss. 'I really am the happiest old Turtle in the whole wide world to have such a family.'

'Your hair's already coming out,' I said, and pushed my horse into a trot, leaving them both behind.

'Damn,' he said. 'Wait!'

The Palace complex glowed in the dusk: the tops of the walls and the roofs of the main buildings in the administrative area had been decked with coloured fairy lights. The horses snorted and flicked their ears as we approached the main gates, but remained steady and didn't flinch.

As we approached the gates, they swung open. All of the residents of the Northern Heavens, the students and Masters of the Mountain, and a variety of other Shen, in both human and True Form, were standing in ranks in the Grand Court, on either side of a pathway leading to a dais that had been erected level with the highest balcony at the entrance of the Hall of Dark Justice. Close on a thousand people must have been waiting for us. They all fell to one knee as we entered, the Shen bowing in True Form, and we rode through their ranks up to the dais.

Three of the Tiger's sons were waiting there to collect the horses and lead them away. We mounted the steps, with John slightly ahead, and at the top we turned to face the crowd.

'Ten thousand years,' everybody said in unison, and rose.

There was complete silence for a long moment and I surreptitiously glanced at John to check he was all right. He appeared to be listening to something. After what seemed forever, he stepped forward to address the crowd. His voice sounded as if he was speaking at normal volume, but he could be heard by everybody.

'I have returned to the Dark Northern Heavens, my dominion and home.'

He spread his hands in front of him and Seven Stars appeared in them, held horizontally. He took the sword from the scabbard and lit it with his internal energy, much faster than Simone could ever do it, the holes in the blade filling in a musical scale. When the sword was completely loaded, a cloud of dark energy floated around it, lit by the different coloured globes in the blade. It produced a sound of pure power, making the ground throb in time with its energy.

John took a huge stride forward to the edge of the dais above the crowd. He held the sword point down and drove it into the dais, falling to one knee at the same time.

'I, Xuan Wu, Dark Lord of the Northern Heavens, swear that I will devote my existence to the preservation, administration and defence of this Heavenly realm. I vow to provide you with a rule that is just; and to serve you with a government that is fair. This I swear as Xuan Tian Shang Di.'

The sword glowed with an expanding field of dark blue-purple energy that spread outwards towards us. It tingled like electricity as it flowed through me, then disappeared.

John removed the sword from the floor and rose to stand in front of the crowd. 'I have returned.'

He removed the energy from his sword, made the scabbard leap into his hand, slid the sword into it and dismissed it.

Everybody applauded.

John raised his hand and they were silent. 'In the last few days the Mountain has suffered a terrible loss: one hundred and seventy-eight students killed by a cowardly demon attack.' His gaze grew solemn. 'It is not fitting that we celebrate my return in such circumstances. After the mourning period is ended we will hold a festival to celebrate the living and mourn the dead. Until then, share time with your families and give thanks for their safety.'

The crowd dispersed; some of them clustering to chat, but many of them simply disappearing.

I went to John and put my hand around his waist; he put his arm around my shoulders.

'A sombre beginning to a new age,' he said.

'So that means things can only get better,' I said.

'I'll go find Justin, you can say hello to him,' Simone said. 'Be right back.' She ran down the steps into the crowd.

'If you don't mind,' my father said loudly from the floor below the dais, 'we'd like to say hello, if we could.'

'Brendan, Barbara.' John spread his hands and went down the stairs to them. He shook my father's hand and kissed my mother on the cheek. 'It is so good to see you. I hope the Tiger's caring for you well.'

My father grinned. 'I knew Emma was joking when she told us you were a girl.' He wagged his finger at me. 'You had everybody else in on the joke too.'

'Oh, but I am,' John said. 'I've taken male form for this ceremony, but by tomorrow morning I'll be female again.' His expression changed to concern. 'I promise it's only temporary, and I will marry your daughter as a male.' He looked from them to me. 'This doesn't affect anything, does it?'

'You have to let me take a photo of you two together as girls,' my father said. 'That'll be one for posterity.'

John hesitated for a moment, watching him, then smiled. 'I'll see what I can do.'

'Where's Amanda and Jen?' I said.

'Jen will be along soon, she sent me a text saying the obstetrician had kept her waiting nearly an hour. Amanda can't make it. They had a parent–teacher night at the boys' school.'

'I said it was very important that she come!' I said.

'You can't just order them around,' my mother said. 'It doesn't work like that.'

'No!' John roared. He summoned Seven Stars and ran towards the gates.

I followed, but he was moving faster than any human. When I caught up, he was standing in front of Jennifer and the Tiger's Number One Son, obviously her new partner, and her sixteen-year-old son, Colin. The three of them were wide-eyed and horrified. There was no sign of Andrew, Jennifer's other son.

Jennifer screamed and fell to the ground. Colin went to her and held her, then jumped up and attacked John. John held him away easily as Colin tried to hit him.

'You killed him! You killed Andrew!' Colin shouted.

'That was a demon,' John said.

'That was my brother!'

'John,' I said, 'my other nephew, Mark — he's been replaced as well. We have to stop the copy before it kills Amanda!'

John turned to me, still holding the furious Colin at arm's length. 'Where are they?'

'Mum! Mum!' I shouted, and my parents caught up with us. 'Where's Amanda? What school?'

'Brisbane Central High,' my mother said, confused. 'What's the problem? Where's Andrew?'

'John,' I said, breathless. 'Are the boys dead?'

'Probably,' John said. 'And if we're not quick, your sister, her husband and her other son will be dead too.'

Jennifer wailed, a long sound of agony.

'Where's Andrew?' my father said. He grabbed John's arm. 'Where is he?'

'He killed him!' Colin shouted. He tried to attack John again and this time I held him back. 'You killed my brother, you bastard!'

'That wasn't Andrew. He was replaced by a demon,' I said. 'And we need to be quick, because Mark's been replaced as well.'

'Emma. Where is the school?' John said. 'Visualise it.'

We concentrated together for a moment, his consciousness touched mine, and I shared the location in Australia with him.

'Stay with them,' he said, and disappeared.

Colin aimed a fist at me and I stopped his hand in front of my face.

'That wasn't Andrew!' I said.

'You killed him.' Colin's voice lowered with menace. 'This is all your fault.'

He went to Jen and helped her up. 'Let's get out of here, Mum, these people are crazy.' He glared at me. 'You will pay for this, Emma. One day, one of us will find you when your back's turned and your precious god isn't looking out for you, and you'll pay.' He looked at Jen's partner. 'You too, Greg. You're one of them. Get us out of here and then you can leave us the fuck alone. We've had enough of you people. Stay away.'

Greg took his hand and all three of them disappeared.

'Andrew's dead?' my mother said, and collapsed into my father. 'He's dead? What about Mark? Is Amanda all right?'

'Trust John,' I said.

'We did trust John,' my father said. He pointed an accusing finger at me. 'We trusted him, and now Mark and Andrew are dead, and Amanda, Allan and David are in danger.' He turned away. 'Let's find the Tiger and get out of here.'

My parents walked away from me without looking back.

'Where's Simone and Leo?' I said.

'They went with the Dark Lord,' the stone said.

Not many people had noticed the small commotion at the gates, and the Grand Court was still full of people socialising.

'It is your duty to host this ceremony in his absence, ma'am,' the stone said.

'I understand completely,' I said.

In a daze, I walked through the middle of the Grand Court, through the internal gate and into the residential part of the Palace. I passed through the gardens and over the bridges without seeing them, and finally ended up in the Emperor's Residence. I took a shower and changed without really being aware of what I was doing. Simone and Leo found me later, curled up against the wall in the living room, staring into space.

Simone pushed her face into mine. 'Emma, Aunty Amanda and Uncle Allan and David are fine. Daddy held down the demon copy and absorbed its explosion.'

'Mark and Andrew are dead,' I said.

Leo sat next to me on the floor. 'There was nothing any of us could do. You sent them home straightaway. It was their choice to lose their guard and stay up here and put themselves in danger.'

I buried my face in my knees. 'If I'd never started all of this, they'd still be alive.'

'None of this is your fault, Emma,' Simone said, sitting on the other side of me. 'Don't blame yourself.'

'It is my fault,' I said. 'I wish the demons would just take me and leave everyone else alone.'

My phone rang and I answered it.

'Emma, it's me! It's Mark. I'm with Andrew — we're okay.'

I sat up straighter. 'Mark! Where are you? Are you sure you're all right? Tell me where you are and I'll come get you —'

Kitty cut me off. 'How much do you want them back, Emma?'

Simone hissed under her breath; she could hear.

'Whatever you want,' I said.

'I want you, my darling,' she said, her voice close to the Demon King's in silkiness. 'Will you swap yourself for the lives of your two relatives here?'

'How do I know they're not copies the Death Mother made?'

'You don't. Want to leave them with me?' Her voice filled with menace. 'I'm sure I can find some use for

279

them. I haven't had a transfusion in a while, and they're such fine, strong, healthy boys.'

'Where and when?'

'My kindergarten in an hour. Can you make it in an hour?'

'I'll be there.' I snapped the phone shut. 'Where's John?'

'He's dead, Emma,' Simone said. 'He's in Court Ten.'

'Contact Court Ten, tell Pao to let him out now.'

'Uh ... I already did.' She dropped her head. 'Apparently you and Daddy were really rude to Judge Pao and he's royally pissed with you, so he's going to hold Daddy up.'

'Tell him the circumstances.'

'I just did. He says, "Too bad".'

'Leo, carry me down, we'll take the car from Central to the kindergarten, and you can drive the boys home.'

'Don't throw yourself away, Emma,' Leo said. 'There's a damn good chance these boys aren't the real ones.'

I looked him in the eye. 'If this was one of your nephews, and there was a chance it was really him, what would you do?'

He held my gaze for a long time, then looked away. 'I'll take you down. Simone, stay here where it's safe. I don't trust that demon bitch at all.'

'Daddy says don't do it,' Simone said.

'Tell Daddy I love him.'

Simone jumped to her feet and ran away.

'And I love you too, Simone.'

Leo wasn't good at landing anywhere on the Earthly except Central, so we arrived at the Star Ferry terminal and collected the car from its park under the Landmark building. I sat silently in the passenger seat, watching the traffic and lights of Hong Kong, as Leo drove.

'We'll come for you,' Leo said eventually, as we sat in the stop-start traffic to enter the Cross-Harbour Tunnel.

'I know you will. I hope these are the real boys.'

We entered the tunnel and went from near standstill to the speed limit. Leo weaved across the lane and the car next to us sounded its horn, making him jump.

'Sorry,' he said. 'Distracted.'

'Is anyone talking to you?'

'No.'

'Leo.' I turned to see him. 'Don't worry. He will find me. He vowed that he would.'

Leo's expression cleared. 'That's right, he did.'

'Even if Heaven and Earth have to be moved for him to achieve it, that oath will be fulfilled. We knew all along that he would have to find me — and for that to happen, I have to be lost.'

He wiped his hand over his face. 'I don't want to lose you.'

'I don't want to lose you either, mate. I hope you're still here when he brings me back.'

He hesitated for a moment, then nodded once. 'I will be. I'll wait until you're back and we can say goodbye properly.'

We shot out of the tunnel on the other side and immediately slowed. The automatic tag on the windscreen beeped as we passed under the gate.

'Sometimes it feels very strange to be back here,' Leo said. 'And sometimes it feels like I've come home.'

'Yeah, the same for me. But when I arrive on the Mountain, it just rings like a bell inside me and I feel: now I'm home.'

'Yeah.'

'Look after Michael,' I said as we travelled down Waterloo Road in the evening traffic towards Kitty's kindergarten in Kowloon Tong. 'Help him. Gaining Immortality wasn't a gift after he's lost so much.'

'He and Simone have a lot in common,' Leo said.

'There'll be some issues when he finds out how she feels. They'll need your guidance; you and John together will have to support them through it.'

'Geez.'

We turned into the street where the kindergarten was located. This older part of Kowloon Tong had originally been a prestigious enclave of two- and three-storey houses close to the old Kai Tak airport back when tall buildings weren't allowed there. Now all the individual houses had been converted into kindergartens and love hotels. There were no cars on the street; the kindergartens were closed for the evening, and the love hotels had private car parks with curtains to hide the numberplates of the customers' cars.

We parked outside Kitty's kindergarten five minutes past the hour she'd given me.

'I want you to do something for me,' I said as Leo turned off the ignition.

He waited without looking at me.

'Give Martin a chance,' I said. 'He really does love you, Leo. He could give you something to live for.'

He pressed the button to open the boot and guided his wheelchair to the front of the car without speaking. I got out of the car to wait for him. He wheeled himself around so he was next to me.

'One other thing.' I looked up at the dark kindergarten building. 'If you see me changed after I've gone to them, do me a favour and end it for me.'

'Don't be ridiculous.'

'Kitty'll use me for a breeding experiment. She'll fill me with demon essence and I don't ever want to face that again. Promise me.' I took his hand. 'I couldn't bear to have it burnt out of me again. John can't do it; and if I'm changed, I can't be Raised. I know he made that vow,

282

but if I'm filled with essence I'd rather be dead. So if you find me, and I'm changed, end it for me.'

'I won't promise you, Emma. But if I do see you again, I'll keep it in mind.'

I bent to hold him close. 'Thanks, mate.'

I pushed away and took a few deep breaths. 'Let's go.'

CHAPTER 20

The kindergarten had a tiny garden with a lawn and bamboo edges. We went along the concrete path to the front door and the light above it lit automatically.

'I'm here,' I said to the door.

It opened to reveal a plain-looking, middle-aged Chinese woman who I didn't recognise. We followed her through the dark office into one of the playrooms, which smelled of waste and disinfectant. The desks were neatly lined up in the room, the tiny chairs on top of them. The walls were covered in educational posters showing the alphabet and the first hundred Chinese characters that children were expected to know for entry into first grade.

I shivered at the memories this place brought back: the children had been lovely, but Kitty's tyranny had been unsettling even back then. The knowledge of what she had done to me here, filling me with demon essence without me even knowing it, made me tremble. I took deep breaths to control it, hoping I wouldn't need to use chi calming.

'We can leave if you change your mind,' Leo said.

I straightened and centred my energy. 'Be ready to run if the boys aren't here.'

'Gotcha.'

The woman waited for us on the other side of the

playroom and we followed her into another, larger room. As we entered, the lights snapped on, blinding me. I put my hand over my eyes and peered into the brilliance.

Figures came into view: Kitty, the Death Mother, a pair of high-level demon guards in human form, and my nephews. The boys stood dully, their eyes wide and unseeing.

'Mark, Andrew, are you all right?' I said.

'They're fine,' Leo said. 'Sedated but okay, from what I can see.' *They look human*, he added silently.

'Emma, walk towards us and we'll send the kids to him,' Kitty said.

'Try anything and Leo will destroy you,' I said.

'He couldn't take both of us in a million years,' the Death Mother said with contempt. 'Gay-lo.'

'Just come over here and let's get this over with,' Kitty said. 'You've caused me way too much trouble over the years, Emma, and it's about time you performed the task you were designed to do.' She waved me forward. 'Come on.'

I stepped forward and she pushed the boys towards me. They moved mechanically, not seeming to notice me as I passed them.

I waited until I was just out of reach of Kitty and the Death Mother before turning to check that Leo had the boys. I saw something out of the corner of my eye, moved to block it, but wasn't quick enough. The Death Mother had shoved a hypodermic into my arm. She quickly pushed the plunger down and ripped it out.

'That was unnecessary, I was coming with you,' I said, holding my arm and glaring at her.

She smiled slightly. 'Just making sure.'

I turned back to Leo. The boys were next to him; he took their hands and they all disappeared.

The Death Mother took advantage of my movement and grabbed my hands, pulling them behind me. She roughly tied them together with raffia packing twine, commonly used to bind boxes and shopping bags in Hong Kong. It would cut my wrists open before I could snap it. She pulled the twine so tight it hurt, then grasped my arm again.

'Let's go,' she said. 'Boat at anchor.'

The building around us disappeared.

We landed on the deck of an old-fashioned Chinese junk floating next to a jungle-covered island just visible in the darkness. I didn't get to see much before they dragged me down the stairs to the front of the boat, but from what I glimpsed we weren't in Hong Kong any more — the water around us was calm and muddy and there were hardly any other boats.

Whatever the Death Mother had given me began to take hold and everything felt heavy. My legs were too massive to lift and I sagged under my own weight.

'Help me,' she said, and one of the demons lifted me by the other arm.

They half-dragged, half-carried me into a stateroom that had been converted into what appeared to be a medical treatment room, with an examination couch and cupboards. When I saw the IV stand next to the couch, I panicked and tried to escape, but both of them held me.

I took deep breaths, trying to clear the drug from me and change to snake, but they'd hit me with a heavy dose. My eyes were closing by themselves and I was a dead weight as they lifted me onto the couch. They pushed me onto my side and unbound my hands, but I couldn't move them even when they were free.

They rolled me back, painfully crushing my left arm, then pulled my right arm out and prepared it for the IV. I tried to yell with fear and pain as they inserted the needle, but all that came out was a heavy, silent gasp.

I tried to stay awake as the black fluid dripped into the tube, but it was too hard.

The pain woke me — the demon essence was being burnt out of me again, but just in my arm. Where was I? My entire right arm was on fire and I wanted to grab at it, but my left arm was bent painfully under me. I tried to roll over to release my left arm but I couldn't move.

If I could have thrashed around, I would have. The demon essence was going in, I couldn't move — someone please kill me now. What had happened, where was I?

Stone?

No reply. The terror burst inside me and I wanted to scream but I couldn't make a sound.

Someone appeared above me next to the couch, their face blurred and their movements in slow motion. They said something, but I didn't understand.

They slapped my face and I didn't react.

What was happening? *John?*

They wrenched the IV out of my arm, stabbed me with a hypodermic, and rolled me over to release my left arm. They did something with my hands — bound me to the couch — and then moved out of sight. I was still paralysed. As I watched the room spin around me, I wondered why I couldn't move. At least the demon essence wasn't going in any more, but my arm was still on fire. *Stone? John?*

Later, the sound of shouting brought me around; my head was clearing. I looked down at my arm: the skin was black and shiny where the essence had gone in; it looked like it was covered in oil. It didn't hurt. I tried to move my left hand to touch it but I was bound to the couch.

I dropped my head back, took some deep breaths and my head cleared even more.

'She didn't die last time, she won't die this time! Just fill her up!' the Death Mother shouted outside the room.

'She will die,' Kitty said, her voice calmer. 'She's somehow caught AIDS. You saw what it did to her arm. If we fill her up, not only will it kill her but I could catch it too. I don't want to even go near her now — she's contagious and that disease is mean.'

'So just kill her and dump her off the boat.'

'We should drop her back in Hong Kong. They'll find her and leave us alone.'

'You'd just let her go?' the Death Mother said, full of spite. 'After all she's done to you? You're weak.'

'Look, you stupid bitch,' Kitty said, 'if we kill her, he'll know. He'll be straight down here and he won't rest until he's torn both of us to tiny pieces. If we throw her out there alive, he'll find her and leave us alone.' Her voice went sly. 'How about we break her head, fill her full of alcohol and dump her in Lan Kwai Fong? She won't know who she is, and the authorities will think she's just another drunk gweipoh who hit her head. Even better, we give her a fake ID, and they'll send her home to Australia thinking she's someone else. Even *she'll* think she's someone else. He'll be busy looking for her for years, and we can find that other one again and breed from him.'

I nearly smiled. *Do it, he'll find me. He vowed he would* ... But I wouldn't remember him.

I concentrated and quietly tried to pull myself free of the bonds that held me on the coach, but they were made of the nylon bands used to hold loads on trucks. They had been ready for me. I tried to change to snake, but the drugs and the demon essence had mixed up my energy and I couldn't.

'Let me do it,' the Death Mother said.

'Oh no, this one's mine,' Kitty said.

They came into the room, both of them looking smug. Kitty leaned over me.

288

'I'll change her name to Donahue,' she said. 'It's about time she spelled it right.'

I was surrounded by noise and confusing light. I was lying on something rough and I ached all over. My head throbbed. People were speaking in a language I didn't understand — all I could see was feet. Someone prodded me and I couldn't do anything. I vomited without moving my head; I couldn't even shift it back out of the way. I tried to lift my head, but I couldn't. Everything was too hard.

I was jostled, then people were speaking softly near me. I opened my eyes — dim light. I looked around: I was in the back of a van. I saw the IV and tried to rip it out, but again I was bound. We swerved and hit a bump — definitely in a van.

'What happened?' I said.

'Going to hospital, stay calm,' someone said with a Cantonese accent.

More Cantonese: they were discussing the quickest route to the hospital in the Saturday-night traffic. Someone made a bawdy comment about gweipohs that I only half-understood, and they all laughed. The radio chattered in Cantonese and I couldn't understand it at all.

Someone shone a light in my eyes and I tried to wince away from it. They held my head and I grabbed their hands. Someone took my wrists and tried to pull them away, so I flipped my hands out to release them, did a one-handed somersault out of the bed, and stood next to it in a long defensive stance.

'Wah,' the doctor said.

I dropped my hands. I was next to a hospital bed, with a doctor and a couple of nurses staring bewildered at me. I bent double as my head thundered with pain, then glanced up at them.

'What happened?' I said.

'You were found drunk and unconscious in Lan Kwai Fong,' one of the nurses said. Her face screwed up with disapproval. 'You hit your head; you have concussion. You could have died of alcohol poisoning.'

I moved out of the stance. 'I can do kung fu.' A wave of weakness swept over me and I leaned on the bed. 'That's a line out of *The Matrix*. I can do kung fu, and I have no idea who I am.' I gripped the bedsheets, wadding them in my hands. 'I have amnesia, I don't know who I am. I can remember lines out of movies, but I don't know who I am!'

'You are ...' The doctor looked down at my chart. 'You are Emily Donahue, you're from Australia. You're a tourist here in Hong Kong, and we're trying to find out which hotel you were staying at. You have an Australian passport and a ticket back to Australia for tomorrow night.' He glanced up at me. 'But I think we'll need to keep you here for a day or so if you don't remember who you are. You had a bad bump on the head. Do you have travel insurance?'

'I don't know.' I sat on the bed; my arm was bleeding. I must have ripped out an IV when I jumped out of it. 'Did I have a phone with me?'

'No.'

'A diary?'

'No.'

'Anything with some contact numbers on it?'

'We'll call the Australian Consulate,' he said, and put my chart back on the clip at the end of the bed. 'You're staying overnight for observation. Put the IV line back into her —'

'No,' I said firmly.

'You need fluids.'

'I don't care, no IVs.'

'Do you have a religious rule?'

'No,' I said. 'I wish I could remember why, but I don't want any IVs.'

The doctor shrugged. 'Drink plenty of water then. Oh. Sit on the bed, there's something I want to ask you.'

I climbed up onto the bed as directed.

He held my right arm out; it was bandaged. 'What happened here? How long have you had this?'

'I don't know. I didn't notice it until now. Is it a cut or something? What happened?'

'We want to ask you.'

The nurses moved closer to watch as the doctor unwound the gauze from my arm.

'Is it poison, or gangrene?' the doctor said. 'Your hand seems to be fine, which is very strange. We're calling in a specialist because we don't know what it is.'

He finished unwinding the gauze and I saw that my skin was black from the middle of my upper arm to close to my wrist. It wasn't the gelatinous black of rotting flesh; it was smooth and shiny. It looked like my arm was coated in black plastic. I touched the surface and it was hard.

I leapt off the bed again, staring at my arm in horror. I backed away from it, but it followed me. I took deep breaths, then moved forward again to stand next to the bed and put my hand around the blackness. The area had the same sensations as regular skin. I clenched my right hand a few times.

'It feels completely normal,' I said with wonder, watching the lights dance across the blackness. I looked up at the doctor. 'And you don't know what it is?'

'The dermatologist will take a look at it tomorrow,' he said. 'Also, you appear to have had recent keyhole surgery in your abdomen. Did you have an ovarian cyst?'

I felt it now that he'd mentioned it: a tight, painful sensation low on my right side. I turned away from them and lifted the hospital gown; I wasn't wearing anything beneath it and I wondered for a moment where my clothes had gone. A piece of self-adhesive gauze was plastered just above my right hip. I lifted the edge of the gauze to find a five-centimetre-long incision closed with stitches. I replaced the gauze and turned back to them. 'I have no idea what that is.'

'It's healing well anyway,' the doctor said. 'Rest now, and we'll let you out as soon as you're better, and the Consulate will find your family in Australia.'

I crawled back into bed and noticed a ring on my left hand. It was on my ring finger, like an engagement ring, but it looked very old, with an old-fashioned setting. The stone, whatever it was, was gone.

The *stone*. Something jolted within me, like a bolt of electricity, from my eyes straight down my spine to my toes, and then it was gone.

'Are you all right?' the doctor said, peering at me.

I nodded. 'I hope you can find my family. Was I with anybody at Lan Kwai Fong?'

'No.'

'I have amnesia,' I said. 'I may get my memory back, or I may never remember. That was a hell of a clout on the head.' I touched the lump; it was exquisitely tender. 'But there's something important I have to do.'

The doctor gave the bandage to one of the nurses and she wound it over my arm again.

'That's probably remembering to take your flight home tomorrow,' the doctor said. 'Don't worry about it. When we contact the Consulate, they will look after you.'

'Okay,' I said, lying back and closing my eyes. I snapped them open again. 'This has happened to me before. I woke up in hospital with a massive headache — but I had family ...' I tried to remember. 'There were people here with me!'

'That's good,' the doctor said. 'We'll find your family, and you'll be just fine.' He patted my foot under the cotton blanket. 'Take it easy, and you'll be out of here in no time.'

'Thanks,' I said. I caught his gaze. 'I appreciate all of you looking after me like this.'

He smiled slightly and I realised he was good-looking and about the same age as me. He had some serious bone structure going on, and a strong chin, with kind eyes and flawless golden skin ... He saw me looking at him and his smile widened, and that same lightning feeling smacked through me again. There was something extremely important that I needed to do; and I had family.

I studied my left hand again. It didn't look like an engagement ring. I slid it off my finger and the impression remained. Whatever it was, I had been wearing it for a very long time: it had worn a groove in my finger. I put it back on and slid my finger over it, feeling for the stone ...

I looked up. The doctor had gone, and the nurse was finishing the bandage on my right arm.

'We tried to take that ring off your hand,' she said. 'But you wouldn't let us.'

She nodded to me and went out, leaving me alone to stare at the curtains around my bed.

I was woken early the next morning by a group of nurses and orderlies loudly discussing something in Cantonese. They gathered around my bed, all in surgical gowns, rubber gloves, masks and goggles. They slid the barriers up around my bed with loud clangs and wheeled me out of the room.

'What's going on?' I said, clutching the side of the bed. 'What happened? Where are you taking me?'

'Move ward,' the nurse at the top of the bed said.

'Why are you all done up like you're going to operate on me?'

She grimaced behind the mask. 'Infection control.'

Panic shot through me. 'I have something infectious? What's wrong with me?'

'You filled in health form when you arrived, you should not have come into Hong Kong,' she said, her voice angry. She added something in Cantonese that I didn't understand and one of the other nurses hushed her.

They took me down three floors in a lift and to a single-occupant room at the very end of the building, in what was obviously the infection-control unit. They wheeled me into the room and one of the nurses stuck a sign onto the wall above me. I peered up to see it. It was a large biohazard sign with 'HIV+' written in marker underneath it. The nurse added a few more signs, in both English and Chinese, giving specific directions on how to deal with me, then glared down at me and left.

'That's not right, is it?' I said. 'I don't have AIDS. I can't have AIDS.'

'Test was positive,' one of the other nurses said. Her expression seemed to soften behind the mask. 'Tested twice. Both times positive. Sorry.'

They went out, closing the door behind them, and I buried my head in the pillow and wept.

At lunchtime, just after they'd cleared away my untouched plates, the doctor came in with two people. One of them was a cranky-looking, middle-aged woman in a Hong Kong Immigration Department uniform; the other was an older Chinese man in an expensive bespoke suit. All three of them pulled on full infection-control coveralls at the doorway.

The man in the suit sat next to the bed. His voice was gentle and he had an Australian accent as strong as mine. 'Miss Donahue, there is a possibility that you are in serious trouble. Your passport isn't genuine, it's a forgery, an extremely good one. We wouldn't have picked it except that one of our staff was very meticulous and checked the microchip page in the middle.'

'Why is that a problem?' I said. 'It's supposed to have a microchip page in the middle.'

'The microchip page has personal details for a woman called April Ho. The passport number matches up with this April Ho, whoever she is. It looks like someone made a fake passport, removed the microchip page out of a real one and put it into the fake. The air ticket wasn't a fake, but we can't find any records of you arriving in Hong Kong. I suggest that you tell us the whole story right now and we'll do our best to help you out. If you can prove your Australian citizenship, we can step in. Otherwise, we'll have to let the police and Immigration take over.'

He thought I was a prostitute with AIDS on a faked passport. I was in serious trouble. I glanced at the Immigration officer; no wonder she was scowling. She was waiting for me to confess so she could lock me up or deport me.

I checked the doctor. His eyes weren't kind any more.

I turned back to the Consular official and did what I always do: I told him the truth. That was what I always did, wasn't it?

'I don't remember anything,' I said. 'I hit my head. The last thing I remember is being dizzy and disoriented in Lan Kwai Fong. I wish I could remember before that, because I really have no idea who I am.'

The Consular officer glanced at the doctor, who nodded confirmation.

'We're trying to track down who you really are,' the official said. 'Is Emily Donahue your real name? Tell me if it isn't — it'll be three times easier on you to be deported back to Australia than it will be to stay here.'

'I'm not sure, but it sounds right. It sounds like me.'

'We'll check it then; track down the Emily Donahues who left Australia.'

'Thanks.' I caught his eye. 'I really have no idea who I am. I swear. Please find someone who knows me so I can go home.'

'Forging passports is a serious offence, Miss Donahue,' he said. 'Miss or Mrs?'

'I have no idea.' I raised my left hand. 'Looks like the diamond fell out, so a Miss on the way to a Mrs, I think.'

He glanced at the doctor again, then back to me. I'd just passed a test.

'Forging a passport is a serious offence,' he said. 'If you can point us in the direction of the people who are making the fake ones, it will make your life very much easier. You may even be able to go home without a custodial sentence.'

That hit hard. They were talking about prison for a crime I couldn't even remember committing.

'I promise,' I said. 'I have no idea — I really do have complete memory loss — but if I remember something I'll be sure to contact you. Can you leave your business card here?'

'No need. The Immigration Department will post a guard on you,' the woman said. 'Just call the officer in.'

I took the Consular official's hand and grasped it. 'Please help me. Find out who I am. I'm sure I'm not a criminal. This all has to be some horrible mistake. Promise you'll help me!'

He squeezed my hand. 'I'll do my best.'

I released his hand and leaned back on the bed. 'Thank you.'

I wasn't really aware of time passing, but I was woken by a young female doctor carrying a kidney dish full of surgical implements. She unwound the bandage on my arm without speaking to me, and raised my arm to inspect it.

'Have you ever seen anything like this before?' I said.

She looked at me as if she was surprised I could speak. Then she pulled herself together. 'It might be some type of allergic reaction.'

'That's a no.'

She raised a hypodermic. 'I'm taking a biopsy. That will help us find out what it is.'

I felt a jolt of panic as she moved the point of the needle next to my arm, and turned away so I couldn't see. There was no pain, so I turned back. She was holding the bent needle up and frowning at it. She left without a word. A minute later she returned with a new needle and a vial of local anaesthetic. She filled the hypo, then attempted to push it into my arm, but it slid off the surface.

'Holy shit, I'm Superman,' I said.

She didn't appreciate the joke and tried to stab the needle into me. It slid off and she became irate and stabbed it particularly hard. The end of the needle broke off and hit the wall behind me with an audible ping.

She glared at me, gathered her equipment and went out.

She came back about twenty minutes later with an older male doctor and another kidney dish. She demonstrated my invulnerability and he tried himself, shaking his head with bemusement. They had a soft conversation in Cantonese, and he pulled a scalpel out of the kidney dish.

'If this hurts, tell me and I'll stop,' he said.

He tried to slice my arm but the blade didn't do anything; he might as well have been trying to cut glass. They had another whispered conversation and went out.

They'd left my arm unwrapped and I prodded it with my other hand. I hadn't felt them trying to stab and cut me, but, weirdly, I could feel the pressure of my fingers perfectly well. I wondered if the heat receptors were working.

How did I know about the existence of heat receptors?

I had no idea what my occupation was; I couldn't remember working at anything. The idea of being a prostitute made me physically ill, but it was possible that I felt ill because I was remembering what it was like. Wonderful.

I wondered if I had children somewhere. I was between thirty and forty by the doctors' reckoning, so it was even possible that I had grown-up children. Maybe they were out there somewhere, worried about me? I decided to ask the doctors if I'd had kids — they should be able to tell. The idea of children generated an aching emptiness inside me — so maybe they were out there. Or maybe the emptiness was because I'd never had any.

The curtains were ripped aside and the nurse who'd been rude about me earlier said something. A man with a camera stepped out from behind her and took a series of shots of me using the flash. I put my hand over my face and turned to find the nurse call button, but the flashes stopped and they closed the curtains again and disappeared.

That was it; I had to get out. I jumped out of bed and checked the tiny locker for my clothes; they weren't there. I went out of the room, looking left and right for the exit, and someone took my arm. I turned to see an Immigration official in full uniform.

'Back inside,' he said, and pushed me back into the room. He stood at the end of the bed while I crawled back into it.

'Someone just took my photo,' I said. 'They didn't have my permission. If it was a journalist, you were supposed to stop them.'

'I didn't see anyone,' the Immigration officer said and went out, closing the door behind him.

The Consulate official visited again later that day. He sat beside the bed and crossed his legs.

'They can't hold you here any more, Miss Donahue,' he said. 'Apart from the amnesia you still claim to have, you've completely recovered. If you don't give us some information soon, you'll be moved to Stanley Prison.'

'I really do have amnesia,' I said. 'I don't remember anything. You have to help me.'

He sat back in the chair. 'No, I don't. You don't have any official confirmation that you're Australian, so this is out of my hands. Unless you give us some information, like your real name and contact details back in Australia, I can't do anything. If you were to provide the Hong Kong police with information on the passport-forging ring, you could be on your way home.'

I put my head in my hands. 'I really don't know anything.'

He rose. 'Then I'm afraid I can't help you, and they'll probably move you to prison for a committal hearing tomorrow morning.'

CHAPTER 21

The next morning the police provided me with prisoner's white T-shirt and shorts, handcuffed me, and led me out of the hospital. As I was about to be put into the car to be taken to prison, a Chinese man in a suit ran up and stopped in front of me.

'It is you,' he said. 'Why didn't you tell anyone?'

My heart leaped and I grabbed his arm with my handcuffed hands. 'Do you know who I am?'

'Of course I do,' he said. 'Just a minute.'

He turned to the policemen and barked some orders in Cantonese. There was some argument, but he seemed to overrule them, showing them a card and some documents.

They unlocked my handcuffs and he gestured to me. 'Come with me. The people in the Agency will be able to fix this up.'

'Who are you? Who am I?'

That stopped him. 'Don't you know?'

'I was hit on the head. I don't remember anything.'

'You're Emma Donahoe, a top agent for the ... I won't say more here. Come with me, the Brigadier will sort this out.'

I hesitated. 'How do I know you're the real thing?'

He stared at me for a moment, thinking, then obviously came to a decision. 'Wei!' he shouted to the other policemen, then yelled something in Cantonese. One of the police officers came over to us.

'Tell her who I am,' he said to the officer.

'This is Lieutenant Cheung, Special Branch,' the policeman said. 'Is there a problem?'

'Show me your ID,' I said to Cheung.

He gave me an ID card that looked legitimate. I glanced at the other policeman and he nodded.

I handed the ID back. 'All right. I hope I'm making the right decision.'

He led me to an unmarked car and opened the passenger door. 'I'll take you to the Agency and we'll sort this out for you.' He closed the door behind me and took the driver's seat. 'You really don't remember anything, Miss Donahoe?'

'It's Donahue, isn't it? And no,' I said.

'Donahoe, Emma Donahoe. You work for the PLA as an undercover agent. I thought you were a criminal for a long time until you finally dragged me in to see Brigadier Tian.' He smiled with satisfaction. 'I work for the Brigadier as well now. I should thank you for giving me the opportunity; it means a great deal to me to be able to serve the Motherland like this.'

'I'm a spy? For China?'

His smile widened.

I leaned back in the car seat. Now things were getting seriously weird; but at least I wasn't a prostitute or working in a passport-forgery ring.

'Do I have a family?' I said. 'Husband? Children?'

'You have a fiancé, and an adopted daughter: John Chen, and Simone Chen. You liaise with an American agent stationed here by the name of Leo Alexander …'

His words smacked me between the eyes, and again the shock ran through me. 'I remember those names. Those names mean a lot to me.'

His phone rang and he picked it up on the car's audio system. I understood about a quarter of the Putonghua conversation: he reported that he had me and was bringing me in. I sincerely hoped that he was what he appeared to be and I wasn't making a huge mistake. The police had handed me over without complaint, so he was probably legitimate. The spy angle would also explain why I knew martial arts.

'Why am I HIV-positive?' I said.

He frowned. 'That I don't know. That may be a mistake, or you may have been infected in the line of duty. The Brigadier will know.'

'I can't wait to meet this Brigadier person.'

As we drove down the hill towards Central, I spotted a thick glossy gossip magazine on the floor next to my feet. I bent to pick it up and stared at the cover, horrified.

'That's how I found you,' he said. 'I saw the name and thought that it couldn't be that much of a coincidence. I checked with the Brigadier and he confirmed you were missing.'

The cover showed a photograph of me in my hospital bed — fortunately my face was pixelated, but my name was clear enough, as was the word 'AIDS', written in English in big letters and three exclamation marks sideways next to my head. The Chinese characters on the cover were red and urgent-looking.

'Does it say "Health warning — foreign prostitutes bringing in deadly disease"?' I said.

'That's it exactly.'

I dropped the magazine in my lap and sighed. 'Wonderful.'

'Particularly funny since the beauty salons just over the border are full of the virus,' he said. He added something in Putonghua.

'I'm sorry, my Putonghua isn't that good,' I said. 'What did you say?'

'Your Putonghua was perfect before,' he said, concerned. 'You've forgotten that too. I said that the police over the border used to warn us which salons not to go to because the girls were infected with all sorts of stuff, but bribed the officials to give them a health certificate anyway.'

'That was generous of them,' I said.

'Extremely. They never asked for anything in return.'

He drove me straight into the PLA barracks in Wan Chai, and the woman at the front door watched with amusement as he led me past her in my prisoner's uniform. We went up to the top floor and he guided me to Brigadier Tian's office. It was a corner office, with floor-to-ceiling windows on one side, facing inland towards the high rises of Admiralty and the Mid-Levels.

The Brigadier was tall, well-built and cheerful. He held his hand out for me to shake. 'Miss Donahoe. So glad Cheung found you. I've contacted Mr Chen and he'll be around shortly to collect you.'

'I don't remember anything,' I said.

The Brigadier's smile disappeared. 'Amnesia?'

'Complete.'

'That should heal quickly once we have you home.' He nodded to Cheung. 'Thank you for fetching her, Cheung. You can leave her with me now and we'll wait for her family.'

'Say hello to Agent Alexander for me,' Cheung said, then he shook my hand and went out.

'Now for the real explaining,' the Brigadier said, gesturing for me to sit across from his desk. 'It will take another five minutes for the Dark Lord to arrive —'

I let my breath out in a long gasp; I felt like I'd been hit in the stomach.

'Ah, that struck a chord,' Tian said. 'Good. Look into my eyes.' He leaned over the desk and gazed into my eyes. 'Xuan Tian Shang Di, Dark Lord of the Northern Heavens, Lord Xuan Wu.' Images flicked over my vision: the Dark Lord, kind eyes, fierce warrior ... 'Wudang Mountain, home of all martial arts. Princess Simone Chen of the Northern Heavens ...' It was like a slide show in fast forward: a child, a young woman, honey-coloured hair and hazel eyes, full of determination.

'And you, Miss Emma Donahoe, Dark Lady, promised of the Dark Lord, Regent of the Northern Heavens, Acting —'

'Stop!' I said, clutching my head. I took deep breaths and centred my chi.

He remained silent and I sat with my eyes closed for a moment, trying to calm my spiralling thoughts.

'Some memories are returning, I hope?'

'I feel like my brain was just put through a blender,' I said. 'It's all a jumble.' I tried to put the thoughts in order. 'Fortunately I didn't need to use energy calming when Kitty took me ...' I looked up at him. 'It's starting to come back. Thank God.'

John, Simone and Leo appeared on the other side of the room. I jumped up so quickly that I knocked my chair over and ran to them. I smothered Simone in a huge hug, nearly lifting her off the floor, then grabbed John and kissed him hard. I turned to Leo, threw my arms around him until he gasped for mercy, then turned back to John and kissed him again.

I stepped back and wiped my eyes. 'I know who you are. I know who you all are.'

John took both my hands and gazed into my eyes. 'What happened?'

'They planned to fill me with demon essence again and use me for breeding experiments, but because I have AIDS the infusion didn't work. So Kitty and the Death Mother broke my head, filled the IV with alcohol, and dropped me in Lan Kwai Fong. They put a fake

304

passport on me; the police and Immigration were ready to imprison me for forging identity documents.'

'Broke her head?' Simone said.

'Let me look inside,' John said. 'Can I look inside?'

'Be my guest,' I said.

He put his hands on either side of my face and trod carefully through my mind, restraining his cold consciousness so it was a gentle brush of snowflakes. He stopped and looked around, prodding at parts of my brain.

He shook his head. 'This feels wrong. I'd prefer never to do this again, Emma. I have too much respect for you to be this invasive to your privacy.'

'You were supposed to let me have a good look at you,' I said. 'I'll take you up on that one day.'

'After we put this back together, you can be my guest.'

'How is she, Daddy?' Simone said.

'Someone took a sledgehammer to the sheet of glass that is her mind. The damage may be irreparable. Great swathes of your memory will be missing, Emma.' I felt his remorse inside my head. 'All of this has happened because of me.'

'When did you get AIDS, Emma?' Simone said, her voice small. 'How did you get it? Did you and Leo ...' Her voice trailed off in disbelief. 'Do I want to know what happened?'

'No, but I do,' I said. 'I have no idea how it happened.'

'I will explain later,' John said.

'Was it from me?' Leo said.

'I will explain when we're home,' John said.

'Avoiding the question. That means yes.'

'Later, Leo. Now is not the time. Let's take Emma home.'

'Were they the real boys?' I said.

'No, they were copies. You threw yourself away for nothing.'

I clutched John harder. 'Damn. Go ahead and tell me how stupid I am.'

John pulled me tighter. 'I would have done the same thing.'

'You're Immortal.'

'That is true. I change my mind. You are very stupid.'

'I know.'

John released me and stepped back. 'Thank you, Tian Guai. You have done well. Reward the human; he has done us a great favour.'

'I will, my Lord,' Tian said.

'Emma.' John dropped his head to see me closely. 'I am going to teleport you about a thousand feet up, and land you on a cloud. Pull your mind together; even this short distance of teleport will strain you. Are you ready?'

I took deep breaths and cleared my mind, filling it full of serenity. I nodded.

Something smacked me between the eyes and I staggered. Strong arms held me up and I didn't fall.

'We're on the cloud. Are you all right?' John said.

I nodded through the nausea. All he needed was me throwing up on his cloud.

'If you have to do it, you have to do it,' he said. 'Remember I can summon water at any time and clean it up. Deep breaths, Emma.'

I nodded again, then straightened and opened my eyes. All of Hong Kong stretched out before me, shimmering against the faded blue-gold of the polluted late-autumn sky.

'I will take you the slow way back to the Mountain,' he said. 'I am changing to Celestial Form to do this; I'm still weak and need to take some time away from my duties. The last two days have been ... hard.'

'Did you have any idea where I was?' I said as he grew to two metres tall with a thin beard and long hair held in a topknot in a spike. His Mountain uniform changed to his black armour over a black silk robe. I eyed him appreciatively. 'You have to take this form more often.'

He pulled me so that my back was against his chest and held both my hands. 'No. I thought I'd lost you. I clung to the knowledge of my oath and the love of my daughter; I think without those two things I would have gone insane.' He wrapped his arms around me and the cloud gently drifted higher. 'Now I have found you, I must Raise you as soon as I can. It is a dreadful feeling to be so terrified at the loss of a mortal I love. Again.'

'John.' I pulled his arms around me. 'I don't remember my family. I know you, and Simone, and Leo. I know there were two boys and I swapped myself for them. Apart from that, I have no idea.'

'Your father is Brendan Donahoe. Your mother is Barbara. You have two sisters: Amanda and Jennifer. Each of them has two sons; and one each of the boys was kidnapped by Kitty and it looks like they're dead.'

'And it's my fault.'

'If it's anyone's fault, it's mine,' he said. 'My stupid oath. My ridiculous inability to restrain myself from falling for you. And my weakness in being unable to defend you and your family.'

'All right, both our faults. Laying blame at this late stage is a complete waste of time anyway.'

He raised my left hand. 'What happened to your stone?'

I looked at the ring. 'I don't know.'

'That's unusual; it should have checked in by now. I wonder where it is.'

'Is it important?'

He chuckled, his chest moving against my back. 'I will have to tell it you said that when it returns.'

'So it's sentient then.'

'Your memory may be gone, but you are still definitely you. It is good to have you back, love.'

'Another hour and I would have been in Stanley Prison waiting for a preliminary hearing,' I said. 'And now everybody knows I have AIDS. How will they react?'

He hesitated for a moment, then said, 'I don't know. For the Celestial, it should make no difference.' He ran his hand over the bandage on my right arm. 'What happened to your arm?'

I unwrapped it and showed it to him, and the cloud stopped. He turned me around, took my arm in his hands and studied it from all angles.

'Have you seen anything like this before?' I said.

'Yes, but not on a live human.' He glanced up at me. 'When we pass through the Gates, I will take it very, very slowly. If the arm begins to burn — even in the slightest — tell me immediately.'

'What gates?'

'The Gates of Heaven.'

I gasped. 'Oh my God, Guan Yu is real and guards the Gates of Heaven.'

'That he is, and a fine, smart comrade as well.'

'Let's go home,' I said, and he moved to stand behind me and steer the cloud again. 'When I lost my memory, I would have given anything for a home and a family. I have found a loving family and a beautiful home; I think I'm the luckiest woman in the world.'

'It is the small things enriching our lives that we should never take for granted,' he said. Clouds appeared around us that hadn't been there a moment ago. 'We are about to enter the Celestial Plane. If your arm burns, tell me.'

An enormous gate emerged from the clouds, and the sky cleared. This was the Heavenly Portal: an analogue to the Gates of Heaven, and a more convenient entry point for those who could fly. It stood alone, with no walls supporting it, making it appear easy to circumvent; but it was impossible for those who did not have the authority of residence in Heaven to enter.

As we approached, my arm tingled, gradually building to a burn.

'It's burning,' I said.

John stopped the cloud. Simone appeared, floating next to us, her hair waving in the breeze. She joined us on the cloud.

'What's that?' she said, looking horrified as she saw my blackened arm.

'It's a result of her being infused with demon essence,' John said. He touched my arm and his fingers were cold. 'Fascinating. I'm drifting the cloud slowly closer to the Gates; if the pain becomes too much to bear, let me know.'

The burning intensified as we approached the Gates, but didn't become so strong that I couldn't tolerate it.

John stopped at the Gates and the cloud hovered. 'How bad is it?'

'Like bad sunburn.'

He hesitated. 'It would be very much easier if you could be on the Celestial. The Jade Emperor will have a fit if I desert my post again to be with my human wife.'

'I want to be on the Celestial,' I said. 'My memory will return faster there.' I tilted my head with confusion. 'How did I know that?'

'Your memories are all there, just in little pieces,' he said. 'Decision time. Rush through the Gates and risk your arm; or hold off and settle you back on the Earthly?'

'Go through very slowly,' I said. 'I'll tell you to stop if I think I'll lose it.'

'Don't risk it,' Simone said. 'Go live in the Peak apartment; you'll be safe there.'

'She will be a hundred times safer inside the walls of Wudang, Simone.'

'If we go through slowly enough I won't be risking anything,' I said. 'Do it, John.'

We glided closer to the Gates, which were embossed in gold with the Four Winds, the Phoenix at the top. A pair of dragon guards in True Form floated on either side of the portal, watching us silently. As we grew closer the burning intensified, but wasn't painful.

John stopped the cloud directly in front of the open Gates. 'Put your hand in,' he said.

I reached and pushed my hand through the Gates. The pain grew stronger as the black part of my arm drew level with the frame.

'God, careful,' Simone said, distraught.

'I am on both counts,' John said. 'I am watching carefully. There, you're inside. How is it?'

I wrenched my arm back and clutched it to my side. 'It hurt like crazy.' I held it out again and studied it. 'But I'm not damaged.' I pushed my arm through the Gates again, and gritted my teeth at the pain; but the arm didn't disintegrate. 'I can do it.'

'Try it as snake,' Simone said.

'You can change to snake?' John said.

'She spent most of the last year or so on the Celestial in Serpent form,' Simone said. 'She couldn't travel to Heaven as a human because of the demon essence.'

He shrugged. 'It's worth a try.'

I concentrated.

'Nothing?' Simone said.

'I think I've forgotten how to do it.'

'Very well, we will try that again later,' John said. 'I can probably bring it out for you, touch it with my own Serpent.'

'That may not be such a good idea.'

310

'Yes, you have a point.' He raised his hand. 'Deep breath, count of three.'

The cloud whizzed through the Gates and I felt a flash of pain in my arm; it flared and was gone.

'Does it still hurt?' John asked urgently.

'No, I'm fine.'

'All right,' he said. The cloud picked up speed. 'Let's take you home.'

'See you there,' Simone said, and shot away, leaving a contrail behind her.

'Impressive,' he said. 'We must have you flying as soon as we find the time.'

'What does my schedule look like for the next few days?' I said. 'I have things I need to do. I don't know what they are, but they need to be done.'

'The schedule looks like — empty,' he said. 'You will not be performing any duties until you can remember that you have them.'

I dropped my voice. 'What about a funeral for my nephews?'

'Your family will not hold one. They live in hope.'

'And the Jade Emperor? What does he have to say?' I paused. 'I suppose it says something about the nature of his authority that I'm well aware of his summons despite everything else being scrambled.'

'That, I am afraid, you must attend. We need to have an official handover from you as Regent to me as Emperor, and that must take place at the Celestial Palace. It was postponed because you were lost, but I expect a red box will be waiting for us at home.'

'Everything you say brings images into my mind,' I said. 'It's so confusing.'

'Do you understand why we need the handover?'

'Of course. I was looking forward to formally offloading all this bullshit onto you ...' My voice trailed off. 'It's like something opens and the memories are

311

sitting there where they've always been. It's a very peculiar feeling.'

'I've just been through something similar myself, so I understand completely,' he said.

The mountains grew taller and steeper and became a darker green as we approached Wudang. The Wudangshan complex came into view and I clutched John's arms where he held me. The Academy's black roofs shone in the sunlight, and black silk banners had been erected at the top of the wall all the way around. Two more huge black banners, each with the motif of the Seven Stars, stood on either side above the gate.

'I have dreamed of this for many years,' he said into my ear. 'Carrying you on a cloud to my home. Now that I have found you, I must arrange for an Elixir of Immortality to be distilled for you as soon as possible.'

The cloud carried us to a courtyard house nestled against the rock spine of the Mountain, and I recognised this as the place I lived even though I didn't have many memories associated with it.

The cloud settled on the ground, but I hesitated, holding John's hand, when I saw how many people were in the garden waiting for me. He guided me off the cloud and walked me to them.

'She may not remember who you are,' he said. 'I don't think she remembers terribly much at all.'

'Should we stay or go?' an older European man said — probably my father.

'Stay. I want to remember you as quickly as I can,' I said. 'Twelve hours ago I wished with all my heart that I had a family, and now I do. I want to remember every single one of you.'

'All of us who are not family will leave then,' a young Chinese man said.

'You're family too, Gold,' Leo said.

'Gold.' I went up to him and touched his face, and

smiled when he blushed. 'I can trust you. That's all I know.'

A small stone shot into the air from behind him and floated at eye level. 'Did they hurt you much, Aunty Emma?'

'No,' I said. 'I can't remember your name.'

'I don't have one,' the stone said.

I turned to a young woman next to Gold. 'I remember you.'

She bowed and saluted ten times more gracefully than I ever could. 'I am Jade, my Lady. Welcome home.'

'You're my friend, aren't you?'

She smiled and gently hugged me. 'I love you like a sister, but I am not your blood family.' She gestured towards the European man and the woman standing with him. 'They should come first.'

Gold saluted John. 'Your orders, my Lord?'

'Immediate family only for now, I think,' John said. 'Simone, Leo, give her some time. Let her reacquaint herself with her parents.' He raised one arm towards the Europeans. 'Brendan, Barbara, come inside. Tea?'

The Chinese people saluted John, and either walked back towards the administrative part of the complex or disappeared.

I went to the European couple. 'Are you my parents?'

'Come on, love,' the woman said. 'Let's go inside and remind you again how silly you are.'

'Mum,' I said. 'You're my mum, and you're my dad.' I looked around. 'Where are my sisters?'

'Neither of them is in much shape to say hello,' my mother said. 'They both just lost a child.'

'I need to say sorry to them.'

John led us through a comfortable, Chinese-furnished living room into a kitchen that sat against the side of the house. He shooed a servant out, sat us at the kitchen table and put the kettle onto the gas.

'No, you don't,' he said. 'None of it was your fault.'

'He's right,' my father said. 'They don't blame you. Hell, you nearly gave your life to try and get the boys back. You are well and truly forgiven.'

'I need to see them,' I said. 'What are their names again?'

'Amanda and Jennifer,' my mother said, gesturing for me to join her at the table. As soon as I sat, she jumped up and helped John with the teapot, hunting through the cupboards for a mismatched set of teacups. 'Give them some time, dear. They've been through a lot and both need time to recover.'

'So does Emma,' John said, pouring the hot water into the pot and joining us at the table.

My father's frown deepened. 'Emma, how did you get AIDS? How long have you had it?'

'Here on the Celestial Plane, and here in my presence, the disease will not progress,' John said firmly. 'You need not fear for her.'

'But how did she get it?' my mother said.

'There was an accident and she was contaminated with Leo's blood,' John said. 'The disease was dormant until she was freed of the demon essence — the extensive burns activated the virus. Don't be concerned. When Emma is made Immortal, it will not be an issue for her.'

'Is that very hard — making someone Immortal? The Heavens aren't full of you Immortals, there must be something to it.'

'Finding the path to Immortality by yourself requires nearly a lifetime of cultivation, but it is easier using the Elixir — which is what I plan to do for Emma. The Elixir can only be requested by the greatest of us, and we must have permission from the Jade Emperor himself.'

'It takes just over a year to distil enough Elixir for

one person,' I said, and stopped, confused. 'How come I knew that and I don't even know my own middle name?'

'You don't have a middle name,' my mother said. 'They're a waste of time.'

'You'd better get started on making this Elixir thing for Emma, then, if it'll cure her,' my father said.

I studied my arm. 'I hope this won't stop it from working.'

'Don't worry about that. We have a year to deal with it,' John said.

'What is that?' my mother said. 'Is it some sort of new high-tech bandage?'

'It's demon essence reacting with the AIDS virus,' I said.

'But you were cleared of demon essence.'

'Kitty Kwok tried to fill me up again. She really is determined to make little half-demon babies from me,' I said. 'There's something else about this, but I can't remember what it is. Something important, something to do with you.'

'The Welsh men, Ben and Tom,' my father said, leaning back. 'I'm tracing their family tree. I don't think they're related to us Donahoes, but it's all leading back to Wales.'

'As soon as all of this is sorted out here, we will go there,' John said.

'How long will that take?' my father said.

'If the Celestial bureaucracy has its way, about a hundred years,' John said with amusement. 'I should be able to make things move faster.' He saw my face. 'Are you all right?'

'Of course she's not all right,' my father said. 'She's been dragged around, hospitalised, threatened with prison, and had her head bashed in. I bet she has the headache from hell.'

'Actually I think I'm going to be sick,' I said.

My mother jumped to her feet and took me around the shoulders. 'Where's the bathroom?' she asked John.

'This way,' he said, and they rushed me in without a minute to spare.

CHAPTER 22

I woke and stared, confused, at the sheer curtains around the bed. I looked left and saw the sofas, the fire, which had burnt down to smouldering coals, and the natural rock wall that formed the third wall of the room. Daylight shone in through the large windows on the other wall.

I went into the bathroom, grabbed a robe from the back of the door, and wandered out.

The courtyard house was made extensively of dark, heavily polished wood, inlaid in some places with mother-of-pearl sea creatures — crabs and shrimps — and engraved in others with snakes and turtles. I went out of the room onto the balcony that circled the central open space and listened. The fountain below splashed into a small pond with three small black tortoises resident in it, and someone was moving below me.

I went around the balcony, checking the other rooms. There were two other bedrooms: one was full of the paraphernalia of a teenage girl; the other had been used but didn't look lived in.

Across the house from the master bedroom was a landing with stairs leading down to the ground level. I wished I had a sword, and one appeared in my hand. I admired its sleek blackness for a moment, then removed the scabbard, quietly put it onto an elegantly

317

carved hall table, and crept down the stairs with the sword in my hand.

The sounds were coming from the back of the house. I went out and leaned against the wall of the courtyard, listening. Someone was moving quietly, without speaking, in a room directly under the bedroom I'd woken in. I used all the skills I'd been trained in and moved silently towards the room. Like the bedroom above, this room had a third wall of unfinished rock, but the floor wasn't carpet, it was modern gymnastic mats, and the walls were covered in a variety of weapons.

A Chinese woman was practising with a large sword. She moved with the elegance of one using a fraction of her true strength, and her movements were absolute perfection. I had no chance of defeating her in any sort of battle, and wondered how I could make the sword in my hand disappear. It went away by itself.

'Do you know where you are?' the woman said without stopping or looking at me.

I didn't reply, unsure whether or not I was trapped.

'There is a cloud of confusion over your head, Emma,' she said. 'Do you remember anything?'

I inched away from her, ready to run.

She stopped working with the sword, looked into my eyes, and spoke. 'I am Xuan Wu,' she said, her voice echoing with power, and the world shattered around me.

I came around lying in John's arms with his concerned face above me and my parents and Simone behind him.

'Do you know who you are?' John said.

'Next time, be in male form when I wake up,' I said. 'I was confused as hell and might have hurt somebody.'

'It's after lunchtime. I'd given up waiting for you and decided to take female form for a while to conserve my energy,' he said.

'It's easier on you?' I said.

'Seems to be.' He raised me so that I was sitting. 'Edwin says the female form is the matrix or something, but I don't really understand. All I know is that it takes slightly less energy.'

'You're my mum and dad,' I said to my parents.

'You're our little girl,' my father said.

'Simone,' I said. 'Are you all right?'

'Typical, Emma,' Simone said. 'All that's happened to you, and you worry about me.'

'How are you feeling?' my mother said.

I rubbed my hand over my forehead. 'Weird. Starving!'

'That's a very good sign,' John said. 'Come into the dining room. Can you walk?'

'I can try,' I said, and they helped me up. I had a wave of dizziness but managed to stand upright, and walked arm in arm with my mother to the dining room at the back corner of the house.

'Edwin is on his way to examine you,' John said. 'He wants to do some tests.'

'I'm not physically damaged …' I began, then understood. 'Brain damage.'

'Possibly.'

'You can see inside me; can't you see any damage?'

'I can see inside, but I don't know what to look for, so he will use me as a scanner.'

A servant came in with a variety of vegetarian dishes, and another with bowls on a tray. They set the table and served the food for us. One of them was a middle-aged woman and I stared at her; she seemed familiar.

'Do I know you?' I said.

'I'm Er Hao, ma'am. The Dark Lord kindly permitted me to take over the management of this residence.' She nodded to him. 'I am honoured.'

'One of your demons runs your office, the other runs your home,' John said. 'I like the symmetry.'

319

'I'm sure I will too when I remember who they are.'

After we'd finished the meal, a young man in a plain business shirt and slacks came to the house — Edwin, the Academy doctor. He took us upstairs to the master bedroom, and had me lie on the bed with John sitting next to me. My parents and Simone stood behind John, hovering with concern.

'Tell me what you want to see and I'll try to show it to you,' John said.

'What would be ideal would be a 3D projection of your observations above her head,' Edwin said. 'Like an MRI.'

'I'd need a stone to help me, I think,' John said, and concentrated.

Gold came in, his child floating at his left shoulder. 'I'll see what I can do. I need to take True Form.' He changed to a stone and floated above my face. 'Link up, my Lord, and let's see what we can achieve.'

John put his hand on Gold and concentrated. There was a loud crack.

'Too cold!' Gold said. 'You'll damage me.'

'Don't hurt Daddy,' the baby stone said, its voice high-pitched with concern.

'Brendan, Barbara, take the stone child out,' John said. 'We need to be able to concentrate, and it may be best if none of you see what we're about to show Edwin. Simone, you too, this could be unpleasant.'

I turned my head to look at them, but John put his other hand on my face to stop me. His touch was like ice-cold metal. 'Keep your head very still. Tell me if it hurts.'

'What's hurting is the cold of your hand,' I said.

'Sorry,' he said, and his hand warmed to slightly less freezing.

'Can you project the image of her brain above her face?' Edwin said. 'The same size, or slightly larger?'

I watched with horror as the image appeared. It was one thing to see an X-ray of a brain; this was *mine*, in lifelike colour, the blood clearly visible moving through the vessels around it.

John felt my distress and a wave of calm travelled from his hand into me. I relaxed.

'Rotate it about its vertical axis,' Edwin said, and the brain spun. 'Now the other axis.' His finger appeared above my face, pointing to an area at the base of my brain, and I watched with detached interest. 'Can you enlarge that area?'

The brain zoomed larger, and hung motionless above me.

'That's fine. Shrink it back to normal size, and, if you could, show her skull around it?'

The brain shrank again and my face appeared, hovering above me. The skin peeled back to reveal just my skull.

'Ew,' Gold said. 'You animals are disgusting. So many layers.'

'Now for the difficult part,' Edwin said. 'Can you show it in slices?'

'Now you ask a great deal,' John said. 'I hope you're not pushing my nature too hard here.'

'If there is the slightest risk, don't try it,' Edwin said.

'Help me, Gold,' John said, and they both went quiet.

The image of my brain separated into two-centimetre slices, each about a centimetre apart.

'Lift them one by one?' Edwin said.

The slices shuffled, each of them lifting in turn, then the whole image disappeared and John collapsed over me, breathing heavily.

'I have to go,' he said. 'I have to go down to the water for a while. But before I go — is she all right?'

'I can't see any damage whatsoever,' Edwin said. 'There's no permanent brain injury. All we have is some memory loss that will probably return over time.'

'Emma,' John said, gasping, 'I have to go into the lake. Our audience with the Jade Emperor is at 3pm tomorrow. Forgive me, love, but I need to go down there until close to the time. Call me up when we have to leave.' He dropped his head on my stomach. 'I am so sorry.'

'Go. Rest. You need it,' I said, but he was already gone.

'Gold, call her family back, and arrange for them to stay here overnight to keep her company,' Edwin said.

'You mean to watch me,' I said.

'That too. I suggest you take it easy. No administrative work, take a short walk, and rest until your audience tomorrow. Heaven will not fall if you both take a day away from your duties.'

'Is it a few miles lower, Gold?' I said.

He stared at me, obviously confused for a moment, then grinned. 'Not a few miles, ma'am. I'd say the most it dropped was a few hundred metres.'

'We did well, then, to manage while he was gone,' I said, leaning my head back and closing my eyes.

'That examination probably tired you out as much as it did us,' Gold said. 'Rest. Spend time with your parents. Tomorrow you have the enviable experience of a top-level audience with the Jade Emperor — something very few of us ever get to witness let alone participate in.'

'Only because you stay the hell away if you're smart enough.'

Edwin rose, and Gold did too. 'I'm glad you're still yourself, ma'am,' Gold said, touching my hand.

I was too exhausted to reply.

* * *

Early the next morning, I sneaked out of the house and walked around the Mountain. I passed over the soaring bridge connecting the section that held the Imperial Residence and Armoury with the administration section. Memories returned to me as I wandered through the campus: students working, battles fought. I studied the slate pathways and low stone walls, looking for bloodstains from the most recent attack, but couldn't find any.

I reached my office, and touched the tree as I passed underneath it, sparking more memories. It would all return to me eventually.

I went into the reception area for my office. Yi Hao sat behind the desk, her face blank. She erupted into life when I neared her, shot to her feet and raced around the desk. She hugged me, pulled back, and hugged me again.

'I thought we'd lost you, ma'am,' she said, and wiped her eyes.

'I'm here. He has an oath to me, remember?' I said. I went around her to go into my office but she moved to block me. 'Oh, come on, Yi Hao, there's probably a zillion emails waiting for me, and the in-tray has to be piled up to the ceiling.'

She screwed her face up with determination. 'There is nothing urgent that the senior members of staff can't handle.' She was obviously reciting from memory. 'You are to rest and not do any work in your office for twenty-four hours.'

'What if I ordered you out of the way?' I said.

Her face fell. 'I would let you in, but the Celestial Masters would be very cross with me.'

I patted her on the shoulder. 'No, they wouldn't. They'd be mad with me.'

'Same thing, ma'am,' she said, miserable.

I leaned to speak conspiratorially to her. 'I just passed the mess. They're putting out the breakfast things, and they just opened a brand new caterer's size jar of really *crunchy* peanut butter.'

She hesitated for a moment, then shook her head. 'Not until I'm sure you won't go into your office.'

I raised my hands. 'All right, you win. I'll go for a walk all the way around the Mountain and be back here tomorrow. And Yi Hao?'

'Ma'am?'

'Find yourself some quarters and try to be more human. Turning yourself off like that behind the desk is wrong, and you deserve better.'

'But it's all I need. And it means I am always here when you need me.'

After doing nearly a full circuit of the six lower peaks, I arrived back at the Imperial Residence, and saw John walking past it towards the Armoury. I was too far away to call out to him so I just followed him, and when I was closer I realised it wasn't John at all, but his son, Martin.

Martin went to the wall of rock next to the Armoury, put his hand out, and opened the entrance to what I remembered now was the Grotto. I followed him, opening the wall myself and heading down the stairs.

'Martin,' I called, and he turned to see me, then created a ball of light so I could see him. 'I'll come too.'

He waited for me to join him, and we proceeded down the stairs together.

'Is he talking?' I said.

'No, that's why I'm down here,' Martin said. 'Oh! Father. Father is talking, yes. He said he prefers to be left alone and is dozing at the bottom of the water.'

'Who's not talking then?' I said, then saw Leo come into view, sitting in his wheelchair next to the water. 'Never mind.'

I told him how you got AIDS, Martin said silently. *He's been down here since.*

Martin raised one hand and a pair of ordinary white PVC outdoor chairs appeared, one on either side of Leo. I sat on Leo's left; Martin sat on his right.

Does Martin think I should talk to Leo about the AIDS? I asked the stone, then remembered that it was gone. It was supposed to be indestructible, but what Prince Six had done with stones was very disturbing, and he'd obviously passed the knowledge on to Kitty Kwok. The more I remembered of the stone's irritating ways, the more I missed it.

I didn't bother asking the question out loud. We sat silently for a while, watching the bioluminescence of the fish smear and shimmer as they played under the surface of the water. Eventually, I took Leo's hand and held it. Leo raised my hand and kissed it without looking away from the water, then dropped it back into his lap and held it with both hands. Martin leaned his head on Leo's shoulder. We stayed there watching the fish for a very long time.

We woke John at 2pm, and he came out of the water and retook human form. We went together up to the Imperial Residence to try to find something suitable to wear for the audience with the Jade Emperor.

'I'll just take full Celestial Form when we're at the Celestial Palace,' John said, eyeing my closet in my servants' quarters. 'You, on the other hand, have to dress up human.' He turned to me, his dark eyes full of amusement. 'Does Qing dynasty work on you?'

'Nothing works on me. I usually just wear a warrior's Tang robe with my armour over the top, like I did at Court Ten.'

'No need for me to summon the outfit for you if it's here already.' He sat on the bed. 'Is it back from the Northern Heavens?'

I pulled the robe and armour out of the closet and showed them to him. The robe particularly was starting to wear around the edges from being worn to so many official functions.

'That robe needs replacing,' he said. 'The armour needs upgrading, with more platinum and something more suitable etched onto the breastplate. That really is much too plain for someone of your station.'

'Your armour's plain,' I said.

'Only the battle suit; the full Celestial armour is much more decorative. I haven't summoned the dress armour in a very long time. I think the last time I wore it was when I told the Jade Emperor to go to hell.' His voice became wistful. 'It's in my apartments in the Celestial Palace, gathering dust.'

I pulled my T-shirt over my head and slipped my jeans off, leaving them on the floor.

'Oh, yes. Even better in daylight,' he said. 'You're still in terrific shape; it's very good to see. But make sure you have some demons move all of this stuff up into the main house. You shouldn't be down here in the servants' quarters.'

I wrapped the robe around me, pulled the armour over my head, and moved closer to him so he could help me with the straps and buckles. 'I've never seen the quarters in the Celestial Palace.'

'I hate to think what state they're in. I hope the staff have at least been oiling the weapons; it would be painful to return to a rusty set.' He pulled the final strap tight. 'There you go.'

I went into the bathroom to stand in front of the mirror, pulled my hair up into a bun and shoved an ebony spike into it. I tidied the remaining wisps of hair with bobby pins, and turned so that he could see me. 'How's that?'

He wasn't paying attention, and I waited for him.

He snapped back. 'Sorry, Simone's ready. We'll meet outside, in front of the house, and travel to the Celestial Palace together.' He unfocused again. 'Everybody is waiting for us there, and apparently most of the residents of the Celestial are in the Grand Audience Hall already.'

'Charming,' I said, and turned to go with him.

When we arrived at the main gates of the Celestial Palace, John raised one hand and the twenty-metre-high doors swung open. We stepped through, me on his right and Simone on his left, and they closed behind us.

The main square of the Palace, with the stream running through the middle, was deserted. There weren't even any fish or dragons playing in the water.

'Change here,' John said, and he and Simone shifted into full Celestial Form.

John was three metres tall, with dark skin and a thin black beard. His hair was a wild, unbound tangle that spread around him down to his waist. His black armour was edged in silver filigree and carved and filled with silver abstract turtle motifs. He wore his name — 'Xuan Wu' — on a shoulder bracer. The Seven Stars of the Big Dipper adorned his breastplate.

Simone matched his majesty: she was more than two metres tall, with her blue-black robes floating around her and her immensely long honey-coloured hair drifting on a Celestial breeze that wasn't there. Her robe was dotted with pinpointed stars, and her gold belt was embossed with black serpents.

John turned to see her, hooked his thumbs into his belt, and his face creased into a smile. 'Very impressive, Simone.'

She bowed slightly to him. 'Thank you, Father.'

'Not scared of me any more?'

She quickly hugged him and leaned up to kiss him on the cheek. He had to bend down so that she could reach him. 'I don't think you're scary any more. I think you're just my silly old dad.'

He put his hands on her shoulders and smiled into her eyes. 'That is exactly right.' He smiled at me over her shoulder. 'Ready, Emma?'

'Feeling thoroughly unimpressive next to you two, but ready as I'll ever be,' I said. 'Just take care you two giants don't tread on me.'

'Wouldn't dream of it,' John said. 'Grand Audience Hall of the Majestic Celestial Eminence.' He took a step forward and disappeared.

Simone and I followed. We arrived at the bottom of the ramp up to the hall doors. The Door Gods, Jade, and Gold were waiting for us at the doorway. Jade and Gold were in their Celestial Retainer forms, both of them close on Simone's height. Gold was in tan robes, with long white hair streaked with gold; Jade wore a brilliant green robe embroidered with golden chrysanthemums, and her dark green hair reached down to her knees.

John strode up and slapped the Door Gods on the back. 'Qin. Wei. Good to see you, gentlemen. We must catch up.'

'Have your people contact our people and we'll do lunch,' Qin said, and winked at me. 'That's the correct Hollywood phraseology, isn't it?'

'Absolutely,' I said.

Er Lang walked around the corner of the building and approached us, with his dog in the form of a black Doberman at his heels. He saluted around to the three of us, and we returned it.

'The Celestial requests a formal handover ceremony,' he said. 'General Donahoe is to take her place at his right hand with her ruyi —'

'I don't have it!'

'I'll get it for you,' Simone said. 'Where is it?'

'Ask Yi Hao.'

'Emma, to the Celestial's right hand; me, on the left,' Er Lang continued. 'Ah Wu, you and the Princess up the centre of the main hall to the dais, where the Dark Lady and you will salute each other to officiate the handover. Then the Dark Lord takes the Celestial's right hand, and the Dark Lady and Princess abase themselves, then move to their positions at the front with their Retainers. Is that suitable?'

'We can,' John said. He glanced around at us. 'All ready?'

My ruyi appeared in Simone's hand. She passed it to me.

'Emma, come with me around the back. We'll take our places behind the Jade Emperor,' Er Lang said. 'When we're in position, I'll signal for Xuan Tian and Simone to enter.'

'Gotcha,' I said. I grinned up at John; my eyes were level with his wide black belt. 'Can't wait to offload this back onto you.'

'Oh, thank you very much,' he said, glaring down at me.

'The Celestial says for us to move our asses,' Er Lang said.

'Whoops, sorry,' I said, and followed him around the outside of the building to the back entrance.

'You'll need your weapon,' he said before we entered. 'You can't summon a weapon inside.'

I put my hand out and summoned the Murasame. I pulled out its telescoping strap and clipped it diagonally to my back. I nodded to Er Lang.

He shook out his shoulders and led me into the rear of the hall. The dais was in the middle, and a clear path led from the rear door to it. Screens sheltered us from the crowd waiting on the other side. We walked to the back of the dais and up the stairs. The Jade Emperor was already present on the throne, and the hall was full of Immortals and Shen, many in True Form, all of them silent. To the left, dressed in black, were the Mountain staff in their uniforms.

Er Lang and I both knelt and saluted the Jade Emperor as warriors. He nodded back, and we took our positions behind him: me on the right and Er Lang on the left. I held my black jade ruyi in the crook of my left arm.

The Jade Emperor appeared to be concentrating for a moment. Images filled my head, like a video on fast-forward. My life scrolled across my eyes. The feeling stopped and I staggered slightly, then righted myself. The Jade Emperor turned his head slightly to nod to me. I straightened and nodded back, hoping that was enough to show my appreciation for what he'd done.

The Jade Emperor turned his attention back to the hall and nodded, and the Door Gods walked into the hall, one on either side of the massive doors.

'Xuan Tian Shang Di has returned,' General Qin said, his voice echoing through the hall.

'He brings his only human daughter, Princess Xuan Si Min,' General Wei said.

John and Simone strode in side by side, and stopped just inside the doors. Jade and Gold were behind them, heads lowered. John caught my eye and smiled, then his face filled with horror. 'Oh shit, I forgot my sword,' he said, loudly enough for everybody to hear, and dashed out again.

The hall echoed with laughter.

'Any chance of you staying on as First, Lady Emma?' the Jade Emperor said without looking at me. 'At least you remembered your weapon.'

'Actually, I didn't, Majesty,' I said, without looking away from the crowd. 'Er Lang had to remind me.'

'And before you ask: no, I do not wish to be

promoted,' Er Lang said. 'Ah Wu can have the job. He deserves it.'

John strode back into the hall, his face composed into a fierce mask. He stopped next to Simone, nodded without looking at her, and the two of them walked down the brilliant yellow carpet through the middle of the crowd of Shen. They stopped at the base of the dais, and both fell to one knee to salute.

'I am Xuan Tian Shang Di, Emperor of the Dark Northern Heavens,' John said, his voice boosted by his size so that it resonated through the hall. 'I have returned to take up my duties as the Celestial directs.'

Simone wasn't senior enough to use first person. 'This small daughter of a Shen greets the Celestial Majesty, and presents herself as first human child of the Xuan Wu.'

The Jade Emperor rose with a rustle of gold silk. He hadn't taken any impressive Celestial Form; he appeared to be an ordinary, slim, elderly gentleman, slightly shorter than me. He raised one hand towards John and Simone.

'Welcome on your return, Dark Lord. Greetings, Princess. You may rise.' He turned to me and nodded. 'You have served me well in the capacity of First, Lady Emma. I now request that you stand down and allow the Dark Lord to return to his duties.'

'With pleasure, Celestial Majesty,' I said. I walked down the stairs to the base of the dais, then turned and saluted him on one knee as a warrior. 'I relinquish my position as First; and trust my services have been satisfactory.' I rose and saluted John, then moved off the carpet to stand at the front of the crowd.

John strode up the steps and stood in front of the Jade Emperor. He pulled Seven Stars out of its scabbard, fell to one knee and rested the sword point-down on the dais. He was so huge that, even kneeling, his head was level with the Emperor's.

'I, Xuan Tian Shang Di, Dark Lord of the Northern Heavens, Celestial Minister of Jade Emptiness, Master of the Glorious Teachings of Primeval Chaos and the Nine Heavens, vow to serve the Celestial and protect both the Heavens and the Earthly from any that would disturb the order of your realm.'

'Take your place as First, Xuan Wu,' the Jade Emperor said.

My mobile phone went off loudly. Unfortunately, I'd thought it cute to set the klaxons from the game show *QI* — loud sirens and ringing bells — as the ring tone. I fumbled through my armour, looking for the pocket in my robe where I'd stowed the phone last time I'd worn it, and couldn't find it.

'Help!' I hissed softly, to the amusement of those around me.

Gold held one hand out towards me and the phone went silent.

'Never in all my reign have I seen a pair so perfectly matched,' the Jade Emperor said. 'You are as disruptive, chaotic and disrespectful as each other.' He gestured to the right side of the dais. 'Take your place, Lord Xuan, and welcome home.'

John moved to stand behind the Jade Emperor at his right. He spared a second to glare down at me, and I shrugged in return, then touched the hilt of the Murasame at my back. He shook his head, smiled slightly, and looked back at the crowd.

'I summon the Northern Heavens to meet with me in my private apartments,' the Jade Emperor said. 'This matter is concluded.'

He turned and left from the back of the dais, with John and Er Lang following.

Gold, Jade and Simone came to me, and the rest of the crowd began to mill around and discuss proceedings.

'I swear I didn't know the phone was there,' I said, then froze as the summons hit me. I looked around. Nobody else had noticed.

'I've been summoned to the Jade Emperor,' I said.

'Do you know where you have to go, ma'am?' Jade said.

'Yes. It's like a map was just slotted straight into my head. He has absolutely no respect for privacy.'

'The map will disappear when you arrive at your destination,' Gold said. 'Good luck.'

The summons hit me again and I jumped.

'He even knows I haven't moved yet!' I said. 'That's not fair.'

'You'd better go,' Jade said. 'After that phone business, he won't want to be kept waiting.'

CHAPTER 23

The Jade Emperor, John and Er Lang were waiting for me in one of the small audience halls at the back of the Palace complex, all in normal human form. I saluted the Emperor on one knee first, then sat next to John on the silk-cushioned couch.

'Welcome, Miss Donahoe,' the Emperor said. 'As I said, all we have achieved to date is that we have managed to contact a few of the other Shen, and they have agreed to meet. Africa and Australia are willing — the Grandmother says she will attend. Europe and North America are silent. South America is prevaricating.'

'Who are your emissaries?' John said.

'My sons, numbers Four and Twelve. They are doing their best, but the Shen appear to be ... non-existent.'

'I will be taking Emma to Europe as soon as she is Raised and we are married,' John said. 'We will be able to assist.' He rose and knelt in front of the Jade Emperor. 'This small Shen requests the use of Lao Zi's Crucible to synthesise the Elixir of Immortality for the human woman he loves.'

'Granted. Get to it so we don't risk losing you again over a mortal, Ah Wu. Oh — this Kwok woman and that Snake Mother. Find them and do something about them — these demon copies are intolerable. Be careful though, Ah Wu; you know my dominion doesn't extend to the demonic side of Hell and there may be more going on than first appears.'

'Nothing would please me more,' John said. He rose and sat next to me, holding my hand. 'They have both harmed my family enough. It is time for them to be neutralised.'

'Have you found a replacement for Gao Yuan?'

'Not yet.'

'I can put the Elite Guard at your disposal: choose one of them. Some of the senior officers in that guard are Heaven's finest, trained by yourself.'

'No need to rush into something as vital as this,' John said.

'No rush, but ensure there is a replacement soon. And one last thing.' The Jade Emperor nodded thanks to the female servant in flowing lilac robes who poured the tea for us. 'I gave you the Jade Girl and the Golden Boy to assist you while you were stuck on the Earthly. What am I going to do with them now you've returned to the Celestial?'

'You have two choices here, Majesty,' I said. 'They've served us well. But the Jade Girl now has three dragon children by Qing Long; if she were to leave our service, he would demand she return to his palace until the children are grown. She may have had children with him, but she doesn't really like him that much and doesn't want to do that.'

'And the Golden Boy?'

'He has married a dragon and they have two human children together. He also has a stone child.'

'Your point, Lady Emma? What are my two choices?'

'Leave them in our service where we allow them a reasonable amount of freedom to care for their families. Or release them from their servitude.'

'I have the feeling that if I release them they will continue to work for the North anyway.'

'That's right. It doesn't make much difference. I recommend you leave them in our service. The population of Heaven will see your strength in continuing to discipline them, and that situation is best to enable them to care for their families, which is the most important thing of all.'

'I must grant them their freedom eventually.'

'If they ever ask for it, I'll let you know.'

John squeezed my hand and I squeezed his back.

'Such a shame the Tiger monopolised the Crucible to make that Elixir for his Empress. It would have been good to have some on hand to Raise you now,' the Emperor said. 'The last two batches have both resulted in the subject exploding — first the Leo copy, then the Western Empress. Pray be sure that will not happen to you.'

I released John's hand to pull the sleeve of my robe further down over my right arm.

'When are the peaches ripe?' Er Lang said. 'That is an alternative.'

'You know, my wife nearly left her retreat and came down from the peach garden to say hello,' the Jade Emperor said. 'Most singular. Not for at least another two thousand years, I'm afraid. The trees are still recovering from the damage that blasted monkey did.'

Er Lang dropped his head.

The Jade Emperor slapped the arm of the couch. 'Oh, come on, Er Lang, get over it already. The combined forces of Heaven couldn't stop him; there was no chance you could. It took the mercy of a holy Bodhisattva to subdue him.'

Er Lang saluted the Jade Emperor without raising his head.

'Now, I believe the Dark Lord has a great deal of catching up to do. Go check your quarters, Ah Wu, I think the fairies …' he glanced up at the young servant in the lilac robe, who bowed slightly, 'have been caring for it suitably. Then keep me up to date on all that's happening in the North — and please have Emma continue to write the monthly reports. She has a vivid, entertaining style, much more amusing than your stuffy rows of numbers.'

'Is the Elite fully staffed?' John said.

The Jade Emperor turned to Er Lang.

'Adequately,' Er Lang said. 'We will need to boost numbers in the next fifty years or so if the candidates for Immortality don't achieve it.'

'Call on the Mountain anytime,' John said. 'One of my priorities is bringing my army back to full strength.'

'That will be good to see,' the Jade Emperor said. 'Are we done? Nothing else?' Nobody replied, and he nodded with satisfaction. 'Good. Dismissed.'

John retook Celestial Form to guide me through the Palace to his apartments. The walls were dark wood around white panels, and the floor was also wood, polished to a silken sheen. Decorative windows spaced along the wall on the left gave glimpses of the formal garden and pond at the centre of the quarters.

He turned right and the doors slid open. We entered his hearing room. It had a cold slate floor, with a raised dais holding a single rosewood desk and chair, with 'Xuan Tian Shang Di' in the Emperor's own hand on a calligraphy plaque above it. A set of the Eighteen Weapons stood against the back wall behind the desk.

John went up to the desk and brushed one finger over the wood. 'Good.'

I walked up to him and turned to study the room. 'You must be horribly forbidding sitting behind this desk in Celestial Form, dealing the discipline that the Jade Emperor is too squeamish to hand out.'

He lifted me and sat me on the desk, moving the ink-brush stand out of the way. 'Am I forbidding now?'

I gazed up at his face, which seemed close to the ceiling from where I sat. 'Yes, you are.'

He shrank to normal human size, wearing his Mountain uniform, and Seven Stars disappeared from his back to reappear on its hooks on the wall below the calligraphy. He smiled gently at me and his eyes crinkled up. 'How about now?'

I didn't reply; I just put my hand around the back of his neck and pulled him down for a kiss. He wrapped his strong arms around me and pushed himself into me. I gasped as my body responded, and his arms tightened.

I wrapped my legs around him and pulled him as close as I could. 'Anywhere we can go?' I said between the kisses.

The doors at the other end of the room slid shut and his hands moved to unbuckle my armour. 'We won't be disturbed here.'

He helped me pull the armour over my head, and I undid the toggles on his jacket, starting at his throat and working my way down over his broad chest. I nearly tore the fabric when I ripped it open, and ran my hands over his chest and onto his back. He quickly shrugged out of the jacket and tossed it onto the desk on one side.

'You could make the clothes disappear,' I said into his ear.

He slipped the belt of my robe undone, then pulled the string that held the other side together, making it fall open over my shoulders. 'Why? This way is much more fun.'

I pulled the robe down and released my arms from the sleeves. His hands went to my breasts, making me jump with response. He slipped them around to my back, and we pressed into each other, our hands running over each other's back.

He slid his hands down to his pants and undid the drawstring. I squeaked with pleasure as he shook them down.

'This is something I've wanted to do for a very long time,' he said into my hair.

My own pants disappeared and I was wrapped around him, skin to skin.

'That's cheating,' I said, breathless.

He went perfectly still for a moment, gazing into my eyes, and we were suspended in time. Then we moved together and everything disappeared.

Afterwards, we sat in plain Mountain uniforms on a rug on the grass in the courtyard of his quarters. The Celestial Palace apartments were smaller than the house on the Mountain: single storey, with two bedrooms and an office, but no training area. The Palace staff provided us with a teapot, cups and some steamed vegetarian buns, and we sat under a tree in the autumn shade.

John lay back on the blanket and put his hands behind his head. 'Family dinner tonight? Michael's back and wants to talk to you.'

I lay down to join him, watching the sun shine through the leaves. 'Which family? It starts as just us four — you, me, Simone, Leo. If we extend it, it includes your kids and Michael, then extends to my parents, my sisters, and then if you go to biggest family it includes the Winds. I hope I remembered everybody.'

'Four? Not five? Leo and Ah Ming aren't a couple?'

'Leo's heart is lost, and Martin knows it.'

'When I saw them sitting together in the Grotto, I hoped that Ah Ming had accepted his true nature and stopped trying to run from it, and Leo had found something worthwhile to live for.'

'Leo was watching you at the bottom of the water. Martin came down to look for him.'

He rolled over to see me. 'I don't want to do it, Emma. They have a chance together. I can't take that away.'

'I don't want to either, but I promised Leo I would do everything in my power to make it happen.'

'It's easy to make that sort of promise when you're not the one who has to kill him.'

'True. But I'll have to watch.'

He rested his hand on my side and stroked me. 'This is as good a time as any to talk about this — about absorbing him. I don't want it to happen to you either.'

'We may not have a choice, Xuan Wu. Your Serpent is powerful and has a mind of its own. It's possessed me at least three times when we were in serious danger. I think it loves me as much as you do.'

'Of course it does; it is me.'

'But with you back, you'll protect us and we won't be in danger. There'll be no need for it to possess me.' I touched his face. 'Do you have any sort of control over it at all?'

'None.' He rolled onto his back again and closed his eyes. 'I still have no idea where it is.'

A great yearning call filled the air and I jumped to my feet. The call wasn't audible, but it made the ground tremble and the air shimmer; the water in the pond vibrated in resonance. My heart felt pulled from my chest with need. I cast around, looking for the source. It was coming from John; and the pull was so strong that I fell to my knees and dropped my head, full of nausea.

The call stopped and I flopped sideways on the grass, panting.

He sat up and stared at me. 'You heard that?'

I nodded without rising from the grass.

'Promise me you'll never take Serpent form again,' he said. 'You've spent too much time as a snake and you've made it easy for me to possess you. Don't risk it.'

'I can't promise you that. My snake form has saved Simone's life more than once.'

He grabbed me and pulled me close, clutching me tight.

We heard the sound of a silver bell being struck and looked up. One of the Palace fairies, in silver robes to match the décor, had appeared in the doorway. She bowed to us, then held out one arm: my black Tang robe was draped across it.

'Yes, you can go ahead and clean it, thank you,' I said.

She bowed again, then approached us and held something out to me. I took it; it was my mobile phone. I had left it in its special pocket in my robe after the ceremony at the Northern Heavens, and had completely forgotten about it until it had gone off during the handover ceremony in the Celestial Palace.

'Thank you,' I said.

She bowed again and floated out of the courtyard.

I flipped the phone open and found twenty-three missed calls. Most of the calls were from Simone, John and from my Mountain office, but a couple were unlisted numbers. I snapped the phone closed and sighed.

'It's 5 pm — time to head home. Oh, the JE gave me most of my memories back.'

'He should have given all of them to you; the only thing stopping him would have been your own weakness. Wait — the JE?'

'His JEness.'

'I like that.'

'He doesn't seem to mind it either.'

'If he sees all three of you standing in the middle of the living room like that,' I said, 'he'll be scared to death and probably run. Just sit down, try to relax, and Simone will show him in.'

John, Leo and Michael sat down on the couches, obviously uncomfortable.

'It just seems wrong,' John said. 'When a junior — particularly a suitor — attends, you stand and do the formalities.'

'It won't hurt you to go without the formalities,' I said. 'It'll make him more at ease, and, let's face it, you're all scary as hell.'

'I'm not scary!' Michael said.

'You keep teaching me to break with tradition like this, Emma,' John said, amused, 'and His JEness will not be pleased.'

'His JEness?' Leo said. 'Not you too.'

'I dunno, I like it,' Michael said.

'Simone's here,' John said.

Simone came in with Justin, saw all of us waiting for her, and rolled her eyes.

Justin was a little older than she was, tall, slim and gangly with some growing to do and the clumsiness of a self-conscious teen. His mother must have been Chinese as he looked fully Chinese himself. He stood transfixed for a moment, staring at the four of us, then jerked as if bitten and fell to one knee, saluting us.

'Xuan Tian Shang Di. Lord Leo. Lady Emma. Lord Michael.'

John nodded to him and all three men rose from the couch.

'Welcome,' John said. 'Up you get, lad, this isn't the Celestial Palace.'

Justin hesitated for a moment, then pulled himself to his feet, carefully not looking any of us in the eyes.

'This isn't like your dad's house,' Simone said. 'We're much more informal.' She grabbed his arm and pulled him towards the dining room. 'Come on.'

John gestured for them to go first, and we followed them into the dining room. Justin held a chair out for Simone, carefully waited until everybody else was seated, then nearly fell over with nervousness as he tried to sit himself.

'I hope you don't mind vegetarian,' I said. 'We're all either vegetarian by choice or it's part of the training right now.'

Justin bobbed his head to me. 'I'm honoured to be included, ma'am.'

'Please don't stand on formality, Justin, this is family-style,' I said. 'Relax.'

Justin looked from me to Leo and Michael, who were both glowering at him, then to John, who was serenely unaware of the awkwardness.

Er Hao and a couple of demon servants brought in the dishes: vegetarian fungi, stir-fried gluten and steamed bean curd. She placed a plate of steamed vegetarian Beijing-style buns triumphantly in front of John.

'Well done,' I said to her, and she blushed and hurried out.

John poured tea for everyone, and Justin watched, horrified. As John filled Justin's cup, Justin pulled himself together and used two fingers to signal his kneeling in thanks. John didn't notice.

'Do you know who everybody is?' I said.

'Yes,' Justin said, gazing around the table with awe. 'Lord Xuan, Lord Leo, Lord Michael. Three of the greatest champions Heaven has ever seen, according to my father.'

Leo and Michael shared a look, then both quietly choked with laughter.

Justin continued. 'You're Lady Emma, Simone's stepmother. I'm honoured to meet you all.'

There was an uncomfortable silence for a moment.

'Tell me about yourself, Justin,' I said, trying to break the ice. 'Do you live in the Eastern Palace?'

'I do, in the students' dorms. I'm on the waiting list for an apartment of my own there,' Justin said.

'Are you trained in the Arts?' John said, suddenly taking an interest.

Justin opened and closed his mouth a few times, then said, 'No, my Lord. I have absolutely no aptitude whatsoever, and my father's weapons master —'

'Ah Yeung,' John cut in. 'One of our best graduates.' Justin didn't reply and John waved one hand at him. 'Go on, go on.'

Justin stuttered then pulled himself together. 'He says that if I continue trying to learn any weapon I'll probably do myself some sort of permanent damage, and it would be best if I continued my studies in other directions.'

'What directions?' Leo said.

'Justin is still at CH with me,' Simone said. 'He'll finish next year and then probably go on to higher study.'

'What are you planning to do?' John said.

'Uh …' Justin shook his head, trying to concentrate. 'I'll probably go down to the Earthly and study at a university; I'm very good with IT.'

He looked to Simone for reassurance, and she smiled at him. She was obviously holding his hand under the table.

'IT?' John said.

'Computers, technology,' I said. 'The Dragon's Eastern Palace is very high tech, from what I hear. Uses all the latest stuff from Japan; he owns significant technology research labs there.'

'Not the undersea one?' Michael said, obviously interested despite himself.

'No, this is the floating Palace of the East,' Justin said, more animated. 'The Tree itself provides the network. It's an extremely fast random neural net; it's sentient — it's amazing. When I graduate I want to work in the AI labs, to try and hook Celestial stones into the network and create some AI of our own.'

'AI?' John said.

'Artificial intelligence,' I said. 'Sounds fascinating. Do you make use of Celestial stone Shen in the network or are all the stones non-sentient?'

Justin spoke with enthusiasm, more relaxed now. 'All non-sentient. The guys in the lab — I work part-time there — are hoping to one day bring a non-Shen stone to full AI sentience. It's very exciting.'

'Gold would find this extremely interesting,' Michael said. 'Have you done any work with him?'

'The Lord Gold? The Golden Boy? We're expanding his original research in Celestial Harmony, but the guys in the lab wouldn't dare contact him about it. He's far too important to be bothered by anything as mundane as this, my Lord.'

'Just Michael, man. I've only been Immortal for a couple of days and I feel no different.'

'I was hoping I could ask you what it felt like,' Justin said.

'Like exploding into a million pieces of shining light, then being put back together again,' Michael said.

'That describes it very well,' Leo said.

John picked up a bun in his chopsticks and pulled the rice paper from the bottom. 'I hate to think that Er Hao's first organised meal may be returned cold to the kitchen. Stop talking and eat.'

Justin quickly picked up some of the fungi in his chopsticks and put them into Simone's bowl, then selected some for himself.

'Good,' John said. 'We'll talk more about your studies later, Justin, but right now we need to schedule. Emma, after dinner the Generals are coming to plan a strategy for the next few months. I'd also like to examine you again.'

'The Thirty-Six?' Justin said, eyes wide. 'All of the Thirty-Six are coming here?'

'We lost one,' I said. 'It's Thirty-Five now.'

'The JE is pissed beyond belief that we haven't replaced Gao Yuan,' John said.

'The JE?' Justin said.

'Ah, my turn. The Jade Emperor,' John said.

Justin stared at him. 'The Celestial One himself ... What's he like?'

'What, the JE?' I said. 'Old.'

'Boring,' Simone said.

'Nearly as boring as me?' John said.

'Not nearly,' Simone said. 'You're by far the most boring thing on any Plane.'

'I can't get over how ... normal you all are,' Justin said. 'You talk about this stuff as if it was every day.'

'Unfortunately, it is,' John said. 'Eat up, or I'll make you sit in on the meeting with the Generals. And believe me, that's a fate worse than death.'

'That it is,' I said.

'Back at the Eastern Palace, if you're invited for dinner with my father, it's a full-on formal banquet,' Justin said. 'They have protocol training beforehand for any of us that are doing it for the first time.'

'Same over in the West,' Michael said. 'And even worse, my dad will have half-a-dozen wives and a bunch of dancing girls there too.'

'Yeah, but your dads are creeps,' Simone said. She saw the way they were looking at her, and protested. 'They are!'

'Back in the East, my father's just there,' Justin said. 'One with the Tree, spirit of the East, and totally unapproachable.' He turned to Simone and obviously squeezed her hand under the table. 'You're very lucky to have such a close father.'

'He's only been close for a few days,' she said. 'This is one of the first meals I've shared with him in ten years.'

'We have a lot of catching up to do,' John said.

'I won't get in the way,' Justin said.

'You're not in the way, mate,' I said. 'It's lovely to have you over. You're welcome anytime.'

He bobbed his head. 'Thanks, ma'am, it's a special feeling to be so welcome.'

After dinner, Simone and Justin went upstairs to play on the consoles on the landing. Michael nabbed me before I went out to the Generals meeting, and we sat in the living room together.

John stopped in front of me before going to the meeting. 'They should have a chaperone up there, Emma.'

'They do. Leo's up there being thoroughly owned at *Speed Drift 2*.'

'I told him he isn't to leave them alone.'

'Well, now tell him that if they decide to go for a walk around the Mountain, he's not to go with them.'

He was silent for a moment, then relented. 'I hope you know what you're doing.'

'Just go start the meeting. I'll be along as soon as I've talked to Michael.'

John saluted me and went out.

'I was all ready to hate this dragon kid,' Michael said. 'But actually, he's not too bad. He's smart and caring and probably a good match for her.'

'I give it no more than two weeks before they decide to be just good friends.'

'Ten yuan.'

'Done.' We shook hands and I leaned back on my couch. 'Are you okay? I haven't had a chance to speak to you since you came back.'

'I'm fine. It took me some time to come to terms with the fact that Clarissa had probably been dead for a while, but ...' He wiped one hand over his eyes. 'I'll get there.'

347

'That's good to hear. So what did you want to ask me?'

'My father's offered me the position of Number One, which is stupid. All the other sons would be after my hide. I would prefer to stay on as Retainer to the North, but I know you have Leo and probably don't need me — so do you have something else I could do?' He leaned his elbows on his knees. 'Does Simone need a full-time minder? Would Leo be willing to share duties with me?'

'We originally put you on as a prospective replacement for Leo when he died, and it looks like that position will be available if you want it. Leo doesn't have long to live.'

'What?'

I dropped my voice. 'He wants to be drained by the Dark Lord, to be one with him.'

Michael's face filled with fury and he shot to his feet. 'We'll see about that.'

I put my hand on his arm to stop him before he could charge upstairs to confront Leo. 'You'd only make it worse. Our big hope is that Martin will convince him that he has something to live for.'

Michael flopped back onto the couch. 'Oh God, poor Martin. I see the way he looks at Leo. They're even talking about sharing a Celestial Residence here — I offered them Persimmon Tree now that Clarissa …' He pulled himself together again. 'Now that I won't be using it.'

'Set yourself up in the room that my parents vacated upstairs. Your position will officially be assistant bodyguard, Retainer to the House of the North.'

'You want me in the Imperial Residence?'

'Yeah, why not? My parents have moved back to the West. I'll give Persimmon Tree to Leo, and hopefully Martin can move in with him and they'll have something happy and harmonious.'

'That would be good to see,' Michael said, wistful.

'The best part of this,' I said, 'is that it'll piss your father off so much we'll hear the yelling from the West.' I waved my phone at him. 'I need to run through my messages to make sure nothing vital was missed. Go play around with the guys upstairs.'

'I don't think …' he started, then changed his mind. 'Yeah, I will. It'll be fun.'

CHAPTER 24

It took me about ten minutes to go through all my messages. The one I'd received during the ceremony with the Jade Emperor stopped me dead.

'Hi, Emma, this is Edwards — Jim Edwards. Call me back on …' He gave a number with an international area code that was familiar to me but not immediately recognisable. 'It's not terribly urgent, but this girl may be in trouble.'

I grabbed some notepaper and a pencil from the sideboard and noted the number down, then immediately called it. Jim answered.

'Emma.'

'Jim, please come home, we'll sort everything out. There's no need for you to stay in hiding.'

'Is her sentence rescinded?'

I was silent at that. The young dragon Hien had been a sex slave in Hong Kong and we'd rescued her. Unfortunately we'd realised too late that she was a drug addict — they'd been feeding her opiates to keep her pliant — and she killed the previous academy doctor in a bout of withdrawal psychosis. There was a standing order on the Celestial to arrest her on sight and her sentence was immediate execution. Jim had taken her and run because she reminded him of his own dead drug-addicted daughter.

'I take it from the silence that the answer is no — you're duty-bound to turn her in for execution. But this seemed quite important so I thought I'd let you know.'

'Go ahead, Jim.'

'Emily, one of the students in my junior class last year — she's from Malaysia, right? Well, I saw her two days ago in Marina shopping centre wandering around alone. I tailed her, and she wandered by herself for hours, looking lost. She's a long way from home and way too young to be in a different country by herself. I was wondering what was going on?'

'She's a demon copy, gone to ground,' I said. 'Is that Marina in Singapore?'

He hesitated for a moment, then said, 'Yes.'

'We'll be there directly. If you sight her again, don't approach; keep her under discreet surveillance and call me straightaway. I'll call you when I've landed at Changi.'

'Don't bother. I'm throwing this phone away the minute we've hung up,' he said.

I ran to the War Room and had to stop when I was inside, panting. I leaned on the desk as my ears filled with the rushing sound of near collapse.

John jumped up from his chair and came to me. He put his hand on my shoulder and fed me chi, clearing my head. He sat me next to him at the head of the table.

'I just got a call from Jim Edwards,' I said. 'The demon copy, Emily — the one we sent out with a tail on her, hoping she'd head back to her nest — she's in Singapore.'

'Where in Singapore?' Ma said.

'He saw her in the Marina shopping centre two days ago.'

'She could be anywhere by now,' John said.

'I doubt it — I think that's where the nest is,' I said. 'We have to go there right away.'

'And stand around Marina shopping centre for days hoping that she walks past? I don't think so,' Ma said. 'Send some people in to stake it out. We'll put people all over Singapore, watching every major thoroughfare, shopping centre, food court and MRT station. The Sixth Brigade is itching for battle; they can go in and learn some patience.'

'As soon as you find the nest, let me know and we will raid it,' John said.

'That is not a good idea, my Lord, you are still weak,' Ma said.

John glowered at him. 'I am the Xuan Wu. Even in this state I am a match for any of them. Do not underestimate me, Ma Hua Guang.'

Ma nodded to John. 'Understood, my Lord, but at least promise that you will take a couple of lieutenants and their demon cohorts.'

'I will. What else is on the agenda?' John said.

'This agreement you made with the Demon King to give him Kitty Kwok,' Ma said. 'May I say, my Lord, with all due respect, now that you are back and sentient, that was a damn stupid thing to do.'

'She's human,' Kang the Humane Sage said. 'You don't give humans to demons. This is unheard of.'

'He has vowed not to harm her,' John said.

'A cage of Celestial Jade,' Zhu Bo Niang said with disdain. 'Could it be any more obvious? If you end up captive in True Form, I will resign my commission. I cannot in conscience work for someone who would do anything that ridiculously idiotic.'

'Done,' John said.

'Destroy the current King and let them sort themselves out,' Bo Niang said. 'That way you don't have to risk being imprisoned.'

'If I destroy the current King, there is a very good chance that Kitty or the Death Mother would take his place,' John said. 'The Death Mother is making these exploding copies who think they're human. Kitty harmed human children. Frankly, I would rather risk being imprisoned in a Celestial Jade cage than having either of those creatures on the throne.'

'I cannot believe you have put yourself into such an impossible position,' Zhu Bei Niang said. 'I'm with my sister. If you let them spring this trap, I'll resign my commission.'

'I will be careful, Ah Bei,' John said.

'You're not strong enough to go down to Hell and face the King,' Guan Yu said. 'There is no time limit on this agreement, my Lord; make sure you are good and ready before you take the risk and go after this Kwok woman.' He looked around the table. 'Even the Demon King himself is scared of her. Take very great care when you do it.'

'Are you all quite finished scolding me?' John said. He raised one hand towards me without looking away from the Generals. 'Don't you dare start taking any sort of blame for this, Emma. It was my decision to make and you are worth it.'

'Damn,' I said.

'Emma's stone, the Jade Building Block,' Ma said. 'The Grandmother herself contacted us, which is without precedent. She received a garbled message from it and was unable to locate the source. The stone is alive — if "alive" applies to it — but it's obviously being held by the demons.'

I let out a huge gasp of relief and sagged in my chair, then wiped my eyes. 'We have to find it.'

'I will have the stones on the Mountain look into it,' John said. 'Oh, I have gained permission for the use of the Crucible. Round up the ingredients, will you? I want this done as soon as possible.'

'With pleasure,' Ma said.

'So: that's the half-yearly strategic plan done, the situation with the copies clarified, and the Jade Emperor's pet UN project shared. Anything else that we need to do?' John said.

'You need to rest,' Zhu Bo Niang said. 'Both of you. Take some time off — down in the Grotto in True Form if it pleases Your Highness. Lady Emma, similar, here on the Mountain. We have guarded it successfully for ten years without you. Let us continue for another week or so while you build your strength.'

'I will, as soon as I've run a sweep for demon copies in the palaces of the other Winds,' John said. 'After that, I will retreat for a few days until the demon copy in Singapore shows up again.'

'Then all is well in the Heavens and Celestial Harmony has been returned to the North,' Ma said with satisfaction.

'Very well. Dismissed,' John said.

As the Generals rose to go, Ma put his arms around John's and my shoulders and walked us to the door. 'Normally I'd suggest we stay and play a few rounds, but frankly both of you look totally wrecked. Go get some sleep and we'll talk later.'

John stopped. 'I'd love to play a round with you.'

Ma slapped him on the back and pushed him out the door. 'Go play around with Emma instead, and both of you get some rest. Oh …' He winked at me. 'Hurry up and make a son for his Highness — he needs a fully human son for the complete set.'

'That won't be happening for a while, Ma,' I said. 'There are a few things that have to be dealt with before we can think about it.'

'Can't be anything too serious holding you back; you're on the Celestial Plane,' he said.

I pulled his arm to lead him into the courtyard outside the hall, then dropped my voice so the other

Generals couldn't hear. 'I have active AIDS, Ah Guang. If I become pregnant, the disease will progress more quickly and could kill me before I give birth. Also there's a chance that the child would be born infected. We have to wait until his Serpent returns and clears it from me.'

'That's the better option anyway,' Ma said, unfazed. 'I'd love to see what sort of child the combined creature would sire on an interesting powerful human like yourself. Or a powerful snake like yourself — now that would be something to see.'

'You're not suggesting that I ... we ...' I looked from Ma to John, who seemed to be considering the concept. 'We're not even sure we know what I *am*, and you want to make me a mother as a *snake*?'

'Your Serpent form *is* incredibly hot,' John said. 'Actually, while we're talking about it ...'

'Not in front of Ma we're not,' I said. I took John's arm and led him away from Ma and towards the Imperial Residence.

'Now we know what he really sees in her,' Ma said loudly, and went back into the War Room.

'You are thoroughly freaking me out here,' I said as we entered the Residence.

'Training room first, there's something I want to do,' he said. 'And I think you're freaked out because secretly you're loving the idea.'

I stopped for a moment, then continued after him. I didn't want to admit it, but he was right. His Serpent attracted my snake nature in ways that I couldn't begin to understand; the Serpent's immense intellect riding on so much raw power made my snake half feel almost predatory.

'I want to be combined and complete and have you in no danger of being possessed and absorbed though,' he said, pulling out the demon jar. 'Also, I want you to be confident that it's what you want. With most shape-changing Shen, it's just part of the relationship: we experiment. With you, it may be different.' He opened the jar. 'This subject had to be broached sooner or later, and the sooner it is, the more time you have to think about it before it becomes an issue.'

'When you're two creatures ...' I hesitated.

'Hm?'

'How do you ... in True Form ... I mean, there's two of you. How do you ...?'

The reptile leaped within his eyes. 'However you want me to. I can provide you with some truly remarkable experiences — human or animal. *Both* of me.'

I gasped. 'Just when I thought I had everything under control.'

He took a bead out of the jar and approached me with it. 'I am yin, the force of chaos. Things always go out of control around me — get used to it.' He held the bead out towards my arm. 'Hold your arm up.'

I did as he asked, and felt a pull towards the demon bead.

'Fascinating,' he said. 'Appears to be made of the same stuff; the demon essence has been compressed into the arm. If I moved it close enough, your arm would probably absorb it.'

He put the bead away and sealed the jar; then waved one hand and it drifted into the corner. 'I need to make some more. I believe there are only about ten still in existence on all Planes.'

'Why are you the only one who can make them?' I said.

'Because I am what I am.'

'When I was full of demon essence, I could do it too.'

'Did the Dragon wet himself?'

'I think he nearly did.'

He took my hand and guided me back towards the stairs. Everybody was still playing games; Martin had joined in and they were laughing at a four-player party game on the Wii.

'We're going to bed,' John said. 'Don't stay up too late.'

'We'll move it over to my house then, so we won't disturb you,' Leo said.

'You really should move in here, Leo,' John said. 'We have another room free, and we can always add another floor.'

'Actually, we're planning for Michael to move in here, and for Leo to take Persimmon Tree Pavilion,' I said.

'You're putting Michael back on here as a Retainer?' John studied Michael. 'Is that what you want? You could be a senior single-digit son if you wanted.'

'Dad offered me Number One,' Michael said.

'Whoa,' Justin said softly.

'I turned it down, too much politics. Emma said I can stay here.'

'Wise choice. So Michael here, and Leo at Persimmon?' John grinned at me. 'The Empress is doing a fine job of managing the domestic household.'

There was a moment of complete silence as everybody looked from John to me, waiting for the explosion.

'He's joking, people, hear the sarcasm,' I said.

He raised his hands. 'I was female myself a couple of days ago, remember?' He held one hand out to me. 'Come on, Emma, come to bed. Don't stay up too late, children, school tomorrow.'

'Yes, Mother,' Martin said, and everybody laughed.

Simone jumped up, ran to John and hugged him. 'Good night, Daddy. Sleep well.' She hugged me too. 'Get some rest, Emma, you look terrible.'

'Thanks very much,' I said, and allowed myself to be guided to the bedroom.

John stopped just inside and eyed my closet. 'Is there enough room in there for your things? Michelle always said it was too small.'

'I think I'll use about a third of that space.'

I went into the bathroom to prepare for bed. When I came out again he was already in bed with only his tangle of hair and dark eyes visible above the covers.

'You cold?' I said.

'Cold-blooded. Come and be a mammal under here and warm me up.'

'Lies,' I said, crawling over him and under the silk quilt. 'You're a mammal yourself right now.'

'Oh yeah?' He slipped one hand under the top of my pyjamas and I yelped when I felt his frozen fingers against my skin. 'I hope you don't mind: I skipped all the human "getting ready for bed" nonsense. Michelle appreciated me making the effort but right now I'm exhausted and frankly I couldn't be damned.'

I wrapped myself around him. He wore a plain pair of black pyjama pants with no top, and the skin of his back and stomach were ice-cold. 'I think we both just need to sleep. A lot.'

He pulled me closer and spoke softly into my hair. 'Sounds like an excellent idea.'

'Are you permanently male now?' I said, holding him tight.

'I spent the time while you were gone mostly in the Grotto, not talking to anyone. I slip out of the form when I'm very tired, but I can hold it most of the time.' He nuzzled my hair. 'And right now I think you should sleep. You've been through a lot.'

'Um,' I said.

'Um?'

'John, I won't be able to sleep unless you raise your

body temperature. It's like being in bed with an ice block. My boobs are going numb here.'

'Well, we can't have that; let me warm up for a couple of minutes,' he said.

He slipped out of bed, changed to Turtle form, and lay on the silk rug in front of the fire, his eyes closed with bliss. I moved to sit next to him, leaning on his shell and feeling it gradually grow comfortably warm as we watched the flames.

I fell asleep over his shell and didn't know when he carried me back to bed.

I left John sleeping the next morning and joined Leo, Simone and Michael for breakfast. All three of them were subdued.

'You look like something terrible happened,' I said.

'It did,' Simone said. 'I broke Justin's arm.'

'What?'

'You know how we never permitted any sort of horseplay, any physical rough-and-tumble?' Leo said. 'With skills like ours, it could lead to —'

'Broken arms,' Simone said. She leaned her chin on her hand. 'Justin got excited when he won, went to tickle me or something, and I guarded, twisted his arm and pushed him away without thinking about it.' She ran her hands through her hair and sighed. 'Broken in three places, and a dislocated shoulder. It hurt so much he screamed. A lot.'

'You should have woken me,' I said. 'I could have healed him.'

'We healed it enough that it stopped hurting and didn't need to go into plaster,' Michael said. 'He'll be fine.'

'The worst part is that he kept apologising,' Simone said, wiping her eyes. 'He yelled at himself for being such an idiot and not realising I could do that. He even

359

apologised for underestimating me; he said of course I'd defend myself, being who I am.'

'He understands, Simone. That's a good thing.'

'And now I have to go to school,' Simone said, her voice breaking. 'Everybody will know.'

'I doubt it,' I said. 'My bet is that he hasn't told anyone. And you need to talk to him and let him know — after you hurt him so much — that it's okay and you forgive him.'

'I want him to forgive me.'

'Then you can meet up before class and forgive each other. Have you spoken since he went home last night?'

'No.'

'When does school start?'

'First lesson's at eleven, but I want to visit Freddo before I go up.'

'Can he meet you at Freddo's stable in the West?'

She winced. 'He can't fly. He can't teleport. He can't do anything terribly special, actually. He has to be carried to CH to go to school. One of his brothers helps him out — but sometimes he forgets and leaves Justin stranded.'

'Not uncommon for a half-dragon to show no talent,' I said. 'He's a smart kid, he'll do well anyway, and it may come out later.'

'He's not half,' Leo said. 'He's full-blood dragon. His mother's a dragon too.'

'Whoa, really?' Michael said. 'That's extremely unusual — is he sure that Qing Long is his ...' He realised what he was saying and closed up.

'Yes, he's sure. His mother's as confused about it as he is. His father's even had tests done to find out why he's like this,' Simone said. 'They can't find anything.'

'God, life in the Eastern Palace must be absolute hell for him,' Michael said.

'It is,' Simone said.

John came in. 'Why doesn't he move out from there?'

'Because he loves the technology, and the Tree is really nice to him.'

John sat at the table and concentrated, and Er Hao brought him a bowl of congee. 'Should we bring him over here and start an IT research establishment of our own?'

'I don't recommend it, Highness,' I said. 'We do the Arts of War. The Tiger researches demonkind. The Dragon handles the technology. The Phoenix's people are materials specialists. Provided we share the information, having the groups centralised works well.'

'Noted and ratified,' John said. 'I'll be visiting the Eastern Palace today. Do you want me to talk to the Dragon about better treatment for the lad?'

'Don't you dare!' Simone said.

He bobbed his head. 'As you wish, Princess.'

'Oh, cut it out, Daddy,' Simone said. 'I get enough of that from the boys at CH.'

'Do you want me to talk to —'

'No!' She glared at him. 'Don't talk to anybody! The last thing I need is you throwing your weight around to get me special treatment. That would make me really popular.'

John sipped his congee, his dark eyes amused over the bowl. 'Forgive me, Simone, it's been a long time since I've been human and it will take me a while to grow accustomed to social niceties again.'

'Well, hurry up and do it, because Hongie will probably call you in to say hello,' Simone said. She rose and hugged her father around his shoulders, kissing him on the top of his head. 'I'm off to see Freddo, then on to CH. I'll see you guys later.'

He patted her back without rising. 'I'll be here when you get home.'

That stopped her, and she smiled. 'That's something I've been wanting to hear for a very long time.'

She disappeared, and John turned to me. 'Do you want to come with me to the other three Bastions while I check their populations for demon copies?'

'Sure,' I said. 'I haven't said hello to the Tree in a long time. But I can't go to the Phoenix's palace, it's too hot.'

'I can leave you with your parents at the West while I do hers.' He turned to Leo. 'It is very strange to have you still here after Simone has gone. I keep having the nagging feeling that she's been left undefended.'

'I have that feeling all the time,' Leo said. 'I still can't get used to it.' His expression darkened. 'Michael, if you're done, could you go find something to do?'

'I can see I'm not wanted,' Michael said, and disappeared.

'What, Leo?' I said.

'Give me a date and time so I can put my affairs in order.'

'Let me build up some energy first,' John said. 'If I were to attempt this now it is possible I would drain anybody within a twenty li radius.'

'Then do it somewhere away from people.'

'I won't take that risk.'

'Don't you dare make excuses for putting this off!'

John opened his mouth to say something, then closed it again and smiled wryly. 'Very well, Lion. After I have spent a few days in the core of the Mountain, we will arrange something.'

Leo saluted John and disappeared.

I pulled Leo's newspaper closer to my tea and toast and opened it.

'There was an explosion at Town Hall MRT station in Singapore last night!' I said. 'That has to have been Emily. Why haven't the Thirty-Six been in contact with us about this?'

'They have. I keep forgetting you don't have your stone to relay messages for you,' John said. 'They told me a while ago. They're searching the area for the nest entrance and will update us when they have more.'

I closed the paper and leaned on it. 'We need to go. Right now.'

'No, we don't,' he said, placidly stirring his congee. 'Trust the Generals; they can be relied upon. We have more pressing issues.'

'Make sure they let us know when they find the nest. I want in on that action.'

'That may not be such a good idea, Emma.'

'I don't care if it's the stupidest idea in the world. I want to be there when they pin that Mother down.'

'I will let you know the minute they find something.'

'Even if you're busy in one of the other Bastions?'

'Of course.'

I flipped through the rest of the paper. Much of it was shrill journalistic wittering about the 'terrorist threat that had finally come to Asia'. They had no idea.

'The Lius wish to speak to us before we head out,' John said.

'Okay,' I said, and we finished our breakfast together in companionable silence, both thinking the same thing: it is the smallest times together that bring the greatest joy.

We met the Lius and LK in John's office. The Imperial office sat at the far southeast corner of the complex: a five-by-five-metre building separate from the other buildings in the administrative centre. Two sides of the office were flush with the corner of the wall, and John could walk through French doors onto the top of the wall whenever he wished. From behind his desk he could look out over the wall to the mountains beyond.

I stopped at the entrance. 'How many days have you been back?'

'Five. No, six,' he said, sitting behind his massive ebony desk and checking his email.

I waved one hand at the pile of papers in danger of spilling onto the floor. 'I do not believe this.'

'He won't suffer a secretary either,' Liu said, sitting at the small conference table. 'Talk to him, please.'

John glared over the desk at Liu. 'I've had secretaries in the past. I can never find anything. No more.' He picked up his diary and pen — green and gold with the Xuan Wu animal on it: a special limited edition made by a Japanese pen company — and joined us at the table. 'Is everything under control?'

'We still have funerals to hold down on the Earthly,' Liu said. 'We need to restart classes to keep the students busy.'

'Thanks for notifying the families while I was out of action,' I said, feeling guilty.

'We Immortals are better suited for such tasks anyway,' Meredith said.

'Don't worry, Emma, we can handle things like this. Delegate. It's fine,' Liu said.

'We need to find a new representative to recruit new students,' Meredith said. 'Gold won't leave his children.'

'Choose someone,' John said.

'Leo,' Liu said.

John leaned back, opened his mouth and closed it again. 'I see.'

'That's very transparent,' I said.

Liu shrugged. 'Immortals aren't known for their duplicity. I'll tell him straight up when I talk to him about the job that it's to give him something to live for: the joy of bringing new students here.'

'It will be interesting to see how he reacts. This could be a measure of how determined he is — whether or not he will take the time to enjoy this post for a while,' John said.

'That's also very transparent,' I said. 'You still have to arrange a day.'

He flipped open his desk diary; he'd scribbled in it to such a degree that it was as chaotic as his desk. 'I'll have to move things around.' He looked up at Liu. 'Anything else?'

'Gold urgently wants to speak to you. I'd be surprised if he isn't outside waiting.'

'Send him in,' John said. He shared a look with me. 'The other three Winds will be in touch soon, asking when I'll be there.'

Liu and Meredith rose, saluted us and went out. As they exited, Gold and Zara — the diamond that had been with Clarissa — came in. Gold's tan suit seemed to complement Zara's completely white hair and golden skin.

Gold sat at the table and laced his fingers together, speaking urgently. 'Zara's been damaged. We looked her over, trying to find the exact time that Clarissa was replaced, and there's a huge corrupt area in her lattice.'

'Someone turned that part of me from diamond to graphite,' she said. 'I feel unclean.'

'When did it happen?'

'From working back through it, we figure it happened about eight weeks ago,' Gold said. 'But that's not the disturbing thing. We found something else. Another part of her lattice was also transformed. Several hours of her trip to Hell in the possession of the Lady Rhonda are missing as well.'

'Rhonda's alive!' I said.

'No, ma'am, that was definitely Rhonda at the coronation,' Gold said. 'There can be no doubt.'

'No, listen,' I said. 'If it was one of the copies that John's only recently detected, then nobody would have been able to sense that it was a demon.'

Gold thought for a moment. 'Didn't the Lady herself say that it was Rhonda?'

I hesitated at that; he was right. 'Is it possible that Kwan Yin was wrong?'

'I know you want Rhonda to be alive,' John said, 'but Kwan Yin is greater than any of us. She is a holy Bodhisattva, and incapable of being incorrect. She may withhold information to balance the nature of the All, but she won't lie to you.'

'I see,' I said.

John looked down at the table. 'I can check the Records, Emma. I can confirm it for you. I have access to the Book.'

'I'd appreciate it, John. I have a nagging doubt — I really want her to be alive.'

'I understand.'

'What is to become of me?' Zara said. 'Will you return me to the Tiger?'

'What would you like to do?' I said.

'I would like to stay here on the Mountain and help you,' Zara said. 'I have grown very fond of Lord Michael and I loved Lady Clarissa very much. I understand that my presence distresses Lord Michael, so if you wish to send me away I will understand.'

'She could temporarily replace the Jade Building Block,' Gold said.

'No, sir, please,' Zara said, desperate. 'I am bad luck when carried as jewellery. If that is the only post you have available for me, I will return to the West.'

'Don't be ridiculous, you're not bad luck. It was just coincidence,' I said.

'I'm sorry, my Lady, but there's no such thing as a coincidence,' Zara said. 'I am not meant to be worn as jewellery. Both times I have done it, my wearer has died. I do not wish to risk anyone else.'

'How about being a personal assistant to the Dark Lord himself?' I said.

'No,' John said.

Zara looked at each of us in turn, her expression bright with hope.

'Before you even think about it, check out his desk,' I said.

She peered around me to see and her expression changed to disbelief. She glanced from John to his desk and back again.

'Would you be willing to deal with an impossible man who not only can generate a mess like that in a very short time, but also will complain bitterly after you've cleaned it up that he can't find anything?' I said.

'But ... he's the Dark Lord. Heaven's greatest Champion, Right Hand of the Jade Emperor ... the Xuan Wu, the power of yin ...'

'The power of chaos,' I said. 'Believe me, this is *tidy*.'

'I'm right here,' John said.

'Yeah, if you were behind your desk, it would be twice as bad already.' I turned to Zara. 'All you have to do is say you'll think about it. I know it's a huge step to take, and I can vouch for the fact that it'll be a frustrating and thankless job.'

'I'm still right here,' John growled.

'John, a stone would be perfect for this. A diamond's lattice is the most efficient memory storage of all the stones; you'll never lose anything as long as you have her.'

'Oh, now you're insulting *me*,' Gold said.

I leaned back and kept my face straight. 'You're mostly quartz, Gold. You're the best timekeeper on the Mountain.'

Zara put her hand over her mouth and collapsed over the table in silent laughter.

'When can you start?' John said.

Zara straightened and bobbed her head. 'Immediately, my Lord.'

'I'll have a desk ornament made for you to sit in, if you like,' I said.

She brightened again. 'You are too kind, ma'am.'

'Gold, arrange it,' John said. 'And now I really must make a move to the other three Bastions. The Winds have been doing the equivalent of swords on rocks in my head since we started talking.'

'I want to see the recordings around Zara's damage,' I said. 'Arrange it for when we return, Gold.'

'Ma'am,' Gold said. 'Also, about me recruiting —'

'Already fixed,' I said. 'We're offering Leo the job.'

'I hope he takes it,' Gold said. He rose and saluted us. 'My Lord. My Lady.'

'May I come with you to the Bastions, my Lord?' Zara said. 'I would like to start assisting you now, if I may. I am eager.'

'Very well,' John said. 'Go ahead of us to the Eastern Palace, warn the Dragon that we're on our way. But before you go, advise the Golden Boy that if he enters our presence again without showing due respect, he will be punished. Dismissed.'

Zara saluted John and disappeared.

Gold fell to one knee and saluted as well, head bowed. 'This small and humble Shen begs his Lord's forgiveness.'

'Lady Emma has been far too lenient with you,' John said. 'Tighten up the protocol. Remember who you are, and where you are.'

'I will never forget, my Lord, because in your service I have come very far.'

CHAPTER 25

We rode a cloud together to the Eastern Palace, which was so high that John had to provide me with air.

The Eastern Palace, home of Qing Long, the Spirit of Wood, was a mighty floating tree a kilometre tall with roots nearly as deep. Its roots held the soil together into a circle of ground two kilometres across, with water constantly streaming from underneath it. The buildings of the Palace stood around the Tree's trunk: glittering pale blue and turquoise glass high-rises, up to thirty storeys high, nestling under its branches. The buildings grew smaller as they spread from the Tree, making it appear as if they were gathering around it. Smaller trees, flower-filled gardens and ponds adorned the ground around the tree, between shining white-tiled pathways edged in blue.

We landed at the end of a wide avenue leading up to the Dragon's own dwelling. In contrast to the modern high rises, it was a traditional Japanese castle, with eight storeys of pitched roofs and upraised corners, white walls and blue tiles. It sat in the centre of a perfectly circular pond, surrounded by maple and mulberry trees. Their leaves were changing colour, providing a spectacular autumn display that was reflected in the water.

The Dragon was waiting for us in Celestial Form at the edge of the Tree's grounds: three metres tall, slim and elegant, his long turquoise hair held in a topknot and floating down to his knees. He was dressed as a Japanese samurai in a wide-sleeved turquoise robe embossed with silver dragons over a pair of broad silver silk pants and soft leather black boots, with the dual swords in his belt. He was flanked by six warriors, similarly dressed, three on either side of him.

As John and I stepped off the cloud, the Dragon and all his retainers fell to one knee in perfect unison and saluted us. 'Ten thousand years.'

'Rise,' John said.

The Dragon stood and bowed to John. 'I thank you for your generosity in visiting my small abode. Please, take tea with me.'

John bowed back. 'Thank you for your kind offer. I would first check your halls and plazas for the presence of demons that only I may detect.'

The Dragon turned side-on and gestured towards the castle. 'Please, then, this way.'

His Retainers formed an honour guard around us as we walked side by side towards the castle.

A smaller version of the Great Tree, thirty metres tall, stood in the centre of the avenue up to the castle. Young dragons, in both human and True Form, lounged on the circular grass garden beneath it.

'Get lost,' the Dragon said loudly as we approached, and they all either flew away or disappeared. 'How is the Princess? Is she well?'

'She is well,' John said. 'The clan of the North fares well. How is your family?'

'My family thrives and prospers; both here and at my undersea Palace.'

I began to wonder if coming along had been such a good idea. Normally when I came to the Eastern

Palace it was to eat with Jade at one of the excellent food outlets — the cold buckwheat soba noodles they made by hand in the Palace were unmatched anywhere — and I didn't have to deal with the tedious protocol.

We approached the Palace, walked across the surface of the pond, and the wooden doors swung open. The Retainers formed a guard outside the door, and we went through a lobby area, traditionally furnished, with a polished wood floor. Living branches of the Tree were embedded in the walls and ceiling, seeming to provide extra structural support. A modern elevator was directly ahead, the steel doors stunningly decorated with gold enamel chrysanthemum flowers each a metre across. The back of the lift was glass, and as we shot upwards we could see out onto a central open atrium the height of the building.

On the top floor, the doors opened and we went out. A kneeling female dragon opened the paper-screened shoji door for us, and we removed our shoes and went inside. The door closed again, and the Dragon waited without moving for her to leave.

I went to the window and looked out. The dragons around the small tree had returned, and the gleaming white avenue was now bustling with life: children running around, families walking together. The canopy of the Great Tree stretched overhead.

I turned back to the room. Large, brightly coloured silk cushions were scattered on the tatami mats around a central coffee table set with tea things. The dragon girl must have gone, because the Dragon strode to John and pulled him into a huge embrace, kissing him on both cheeks.

'God, it is good to have you back, Ah Wu,' he said, his voice thick with emotion. He pulled away, still holding one of John's hands. 'Come and talk with me for a while; then go check for the demons. I'm sure there's none here but you never know.'

He led John to the table by the hand and we all sat around it. The Dragon poured green tea with toasted rice in it for each of us, and raised his cup. 'To the return of the Dark Lord. And about damn time too.'

I raised my cup.

'The Tiger and the Phoenix want me as well, Ah Qing, I can't stay forever,' John said.

'I understand, Ah Wu. We'll have plenty more time like this.' He turned a shy smile to me. 'You did a great job, Emma. Ignore the bullshit; you'll do just fine.'

'Thanks, Ah Qing,' I said. 'Is the Tree awake? I'd love to say hello.'

'Oh yes, she'd like to look at your sword.' The Dragon turned to John. 'Hop out the window and do a quick once-over of the Palace while Emma and I show the Tree her blade. When you come back I'll have some vegetarian sushi for you.'

There was a tap on the screen, and the same young female dragon opened it on her knees.

'I said I was not to be disturbed!' the Dragon yelled at her.

The Tree's human form came in and the Dragon irritably waved for the young woman to close the door.

The Tree wore a Japanese kimono of autumnal colours, embroidered with the same leaves that were falling outside. Her red and gold hair was unbound and fell thick and straight to the floor around her. She bowed elegantly to me, and I stood and bowed in return. She gestured for me to sit again and I did.

'Tree,' John said.

'Turtle,' the Tree said, her voice full of the sound of whispering leaves. 'If you find anything here I will be extremely surprised.'

'I will too,' John said.

372

The Dragon went to the window and slid it open wider. John took a running leap out of it and disappeared. The Dragon returned to the table and poured more tea.

'I hear that my little son Justin has been going out with Simone,' he said. 'She's chosen the smallest and weakest of all the dragons on the Tree, but he's smart and determined and will go far.'

'I'm very impressed with him,' I said. 'Do you know why no dragon traits have emerged in him?'

The Dragon shrugged. 'With a population as large as this, there are bound to be one or two right on the edge of the curve. It happens. He's using his intelligence and common sense to work around it, and making a fine job of it. I just wish the other dragons would cut him some slack.'

'You could tell them to leave him alone,' I said.

He smiled wryly. 'What, and blow my cover? I've built this persona over centuries, Emma. I won't throw it away for one emo kid.'

The Tree interrupted. 'Sorry, but I'd like to see the sword, please.'

'Oh yeah,' the Dragon said. 'Bring it out before the Tree bursts into flames with curiosity.'

I summoned the Murasame and felt the slight hesitation before it obeyed me. It appeared horizontally on my outstretched hands, and I ordered it not to hurt the Tree, then held it out for her.

She raised one slender hand and the sword floated above the table, then the scabbard slid halfway off it.

'Interesting; it is still painful even though there is no physical contact,' she said.

'I can feel it too,' the Dragon said. 'And that's with you telling it to behave?'

'Yes,' I said. 'It's a hundred times worse if I don't give you permission to touch it.'

'Damn,' the Dragon said.

The Tree waved her hands and the sword returned to the scabbard, then fell to rest on the table. 'I have seen enough.'

I touched the sword's handle, told it to go home, and it disappeared.

The Dragon and the Tree spoke in unison. 'I was interested because there's a sword in Osaka ...'

The Dragon raised both hands. 'Sorry, my mistake. I was still connected to the Tree.' He poured more tea for me.

'The sword in the museum in Osaka is supposedly the real Murasame,' the Tree said. 'I honestly thought that your blade was some demon-spawned bastard blade that was the source of much of your grief with your demon nature,' the Tree said. 'I did not want to tell you until I had seen the blade and was sure.'

'And?' I said.

'And the blade you wield is definitely the Murasame itself. It is darker and more destructive than anything a demon could create.'

'I don't know whether I should be pleased or not,' I said.

'Be pleased. One day you may have the chance to use it on the Demon King himself,' the Dragon said.

John flew in through the window, somersaulted and landed on his feet. 'Nothing. Next stop, the West.'

'It's been great to be able to talk to the real you for a change, Ah Qing,' I said. 'Come to the Mountain more often and share tea with us.'

'No, you come here,' the Dragon said. 'Simone and Leo don't know, and I want as few to know as possible. I will not display weakness to anyone except my Lord.'

'You're not being weak, you're being human,' I said.

He smiled slightly. 'Same thing.'

'Wasn't there mention of vegetarian sushi?' John said.

The Tree dropped her head for a moment, and the branches that were integral to the ceiling separated from it and writhed down to us, carrying black lacquer trays bearing a collection of vegetarian sushi: rice and cucumber, pickles, and bean curd rolled in dried seaweed.

'Thank you,' I said as a pair of pointed Japanese chopsticks appeared in front of me.

John didn't bother with chopsticks. He ate the sushi the traditional way, by hand, and with obvious enjoyment.

The Dragon ate one roll delicately, then bent his head without looking away from the table. 'How is Jade?'

'Living the quiet life, working hard, watching her children grow,' I said. 'She has been providing you with visiting rights, hasn't she?'

'Exactly as negotiated.' His expression became wistful. 'That's the only chance I have to see her.'

'It would help a great deal if she knew your true nature, Ah Qing,' I said.

The Dragon fingered his chopsticks, then put them down and placed his palm on the table. 'She does, Emma.'

'But you fathered the babies as your public persona — you said it was a meaningless fling on both your parts, a typical Dragon pairing. Does she prefer your public face? Some women just like assholes.'

'No,' he said. 'She won't marry someone as duplicitous as me.'

'Does she love you, Ah Qing?' John said.

The Dragon tilted his head and smiled slightly at the table.

'Do you love her?'

The Dragon looked up into John's eyes, and John's expression darkened. 'You stupid reptile.'

'I could say the very same thing to you, my brother.'

'Have you spoken to her father of this?' John said. 'I'm sure he would put your case to her.'

'Yes,' the Dragon said. 'The Dragon King ordered her to accept my proposal and she defied him. He's disowned her: she's no longer his eighty-second daughter.'

'What does the Phoenix think?' I said.

The Dragon gestured dismissively. 'She has nothing to do with this. If I choose another wife, that is my business. She only has input after the new bride has been brought into the Tree.'

'No, I mean that maybe the Phoenix could talk to Jade,' I said.

His head shot up and he stared at me. 'What a good idea. But better yet — you are like a sister to her, Emma, and like a sister to me. Would you talk to her?'

'Emma Donahoe, Celestial matchmaker,' John said.

'I don't know if I can morally justify encouraging a friend to marry someone who already has multiple wives.'

The Dragon shrugged. 'You know we do things differently. And dragons do things extremely differently. It's actually unusual for us to be monogamous.' His expression became wistful again. 'But I would for Jade.'

'You'd give up all the others for her?'

He nodded, his eyes dreamy.

'What about the Phoenix? Would you give her up?'

'Nothing to give up; that's a business partnership more than anything. As I said before, it's a marriage of politics, ordered by the Celestial. Jade would understand.'

I leaned over the table to speak intensely to him. 'Would you give up your arrogant façade for her? Would you be your real sweet self in public, if all that's stopping her is your duplicity?'

He leaned back and stared at me for a long time.

'I have cultivated this persona for centuries. If I were to reveal now that it is an act, I would be completely humiliated.'

'You're too proud to give that up for Jade?' I said.

He bent his head. 'I am ashamed to say that I am.'

'Then I don't think I have anything to talk to Jade about.' I turned to John. 'West next?'

John didn't reply; he was gazing with sympathy at the Dragon.

'Thank you for understanding,' Qing Long said.

I rose. 'You break my heart, Ah Qing, you really do.'

John rose as well. 'Talk to her when she brings the little ones. Maybe she can understand too.'

'I live in hope,' the Dragon said.

He rose and embraced us both, and John summoned a cloud to take us to the West.

The Tiger was subdued when he met us at the arched, red-stone entrance to the Western Palace.

'Your parents and sisters would like to see you,' he said to me. 'I should warn you — it's not good.'

John took my hand. 'I'll come along.'

'No,' the Tiger said. 'Go look for demons. Give us ten or fifteen minutes.'

He looked into John's eyes and shared some information.

John released my hand and his face filled with pain. 'I will return for you shortly, Emma, and I will always love you and understand, no matter what you decide.'

'What's going on?' I said. 'Are they that mad with me?'

'They're not angry with you at all,' the Tiger said. He gestured for me to enter. 'Come and talk to them.'

'If they're not mad with me, then what's the problem?' I asked as the Tiger led me towards my parents' villa.

'They want to be the ones to talk this out with you,' the Tiger said. 'I've been told to take you to their house and then leave.'

I dropped my head. 'They must be so done with all this Celestial business.'

'That is exactly the problem.' He opened the gate to the villa's little garden and stopped. 'I'll leave you here. As the Turtle said, whatever choice you make, we will support you.' He turned and walked away without looking back.

I steeled myself and went into the villa.

My parents and my sisters, Jennifer and Amanda, were all waiting in the living room for me. When I entered, they clustered around me, hugging me and holding my hands. They led me to the couch, and my mother went to the kitchen, fussing about with tea and coffee for everybody. Finally, they couldn't postpone it any longer and sat uncomfortably, looking at me.

'Is it really that bad?' I said.

'Yes, it is,' my father said. He took a deep breath. 'We're all tired of being here. We're sick to death of being afraid that someone will attack us, or kill the rest of the kids. It's all right for you, you can defend yourself. He's found you now, like in his oath, so he'll Raise you —'

'He didn't find me,' I said. 'Cheung did.'

'Well, you'll be made into one of these Immortals and you won't have to worry about anything. It's not the same for us, honey.' He shared a look with my mother and sisters. 'We all live in constant fear. Any time, a demon could come and attack us just because we're your family.'

'I'm so tired of having a guard on me twenty-four hours a day,' Amanda said. 'I just want some privacy!'

'Come and live on the Mountain, all of you,' I said. 'You'd be safe there.'

'You just lost a hundred people!' my father said.

That silenced me.

'We've decided to do something like witness protection,' my father said. 'The Tiger offered it to us — actually, we asked. We're all moving to Perth, all our families. We'll take new identities and disconnect ourselves from all of this Celestial bullshit.'

'That won't help,' I said. 'They'll find you.'

'I don't think so, dear,' my mother said. 'Without you to lead them to us, they won't know who or where we are. The Tiger says that he's done it before: there are a few people living on the Earthly in hiding and they've never been bothered.'

'Are you sure that's what you want?' I said, looking around at them.

'Dead certain,' Jennifer said. 'Greg is coming too. He's giving up everything Celestial and changing his appearance. He'll be an ordinary human, like the rest of us.'

'What about me?' I said. 'Can't I come and visit?'

'No,' my father said.

'We love you very much, Emma,' my mother said. 'But we want a clean break from all of this, and frankly you're right in the middle of it. If you want to come down with us and be with your family and be normal, we'd love you to. But if you stay here ... then please, don't come down to visit, because you scare us to death.'

'She doesn't scare us, Barbara, don't be silly,' my father said.

'Yes, she does,' Jennifer said. She broke down and ran out.

'I'm sorry, love, I didn't mean it that way,' my mother said, touching my hand. 'Everything around you scares us to death. John, and the demons, and the fighting — you just take it all for granted. We want to be away from it, to be safe and normal again. We've had enough.' She peered into my eyes, sounding desperate. 'If you come down to visit after we've hidden ourselves away, you'll put us at risk again. They're always after you. Do you understand? Please understand.'

'Come down and join us, Em,' Amanda said. 'Let's all be a normal family again. Wouldn't that be good? Shopping, and camping, and barbecues.' She smiled slightly. 'I'm even giving this opal away to the Tiger.'

'I can't come with you,' I said, my voice thick. 'This is my life.'

'Then I suppose this is goodbye,' my father said.

'What? You're going *now*?'

'Tomorrow. We didn't have much to pack, and we'll have the rest sent along by an ordinary moving firm when we find somewhere to live.' My father glanced around at the family. 'I think it's best for all.'

My mother put her arm around me. 'Let's have a family dinner, all of us together, eh? Allan has the barbecue going in Jennifer's garden; all the kids — well, the rest of the kids — are there. We can have one last dinner in Heaven as a family.'

'Won't you miss the Celestial Plane?'

'What I won't miss is living in fear,' Amanda said with feeling.

I tried to control my voice, but my throat was too thick. 'Please, send me photos, email me updates.' I hugged my mother and held her close, burying my face in her shoulder. 'Keep in touch, Mum, let me know how you are.'

'Don't worry, I will,' she said, her voice as full of tears as mine was. She pulled back and wiped her hand over her eyes. 'No tears, eh? There's a chance the boys are still alive, isn't there?'

I didn't reply; John had said no.

'I live in hope,' Amanda said with forced brightness.

There was a tap at the door and my mother went to open it. It was John. She embraced him and he hugged her back, then came in and shook my father's hand.

'Sit, John, sit,' my father said, gesturing for him to join me on the couch.

He sat next to me and took my hand. 'What have you decided?'

'I'm staying here,' I said.

He exhaled with relief.

'Will they be safe?' I said.

'Yes,' John said. 'With Greg along, they will be. If you or I never visit them, there'll be nothing to link them to us. The demons will have nothing to go on.'

'That means Simone can't visit you either,' I said to my father.

'I know.'

John straightened. 'They think they've found the entrance to the nest, Emma.'

I opened my mouth to say 'Let's go' but changed my mind. 'You go. I'm having dinner here with my family; they're leaving tomorrow.'

'Is this the one that did ... that killed the boys?' my father said.

John and I both nodded.

'I'd come with you myself if I was worth a damn,' my father said.

'John and the Generals can handle it. I'll stay here and keep you updated,' I said.

'How?' John said.

'Give me Zara.'

'Good idea.' He concentrated for a moment, then turned to my father. 'I'm sorry, Brendan, but I'm needed. This Mother is very strong and they want me there to direct.'

'You go, mate,' my father said. He dropped his voice. 'And give them a little extra from me while you're at it.'

John quickly kissed me. 'Gold can relay for me. Zara will let you know what's happening.' He squeezed my hand and was gone.

There was a tap on the door and I let Zara in.

Can I come say goodbye? Simone said into my head.

'Dad, Simone wants to come and have dinner and say goodbye as well,' I said.

'She's most welcome,' my mother said. 'Let's go over to Jennifer's, forget our troubles, and just be a family.'

CHAPTER 26

The dinner was subdued; almost painful. On the one hand, I couldn't wait for it to be over; on the other, I never wanted it to finish.

'They've landed, ma'am,' Zara said as my mother was serving ice-cream.

'Do you mind?' I asked my parents.

'We want to see too,' Amanda said. 'There's a chance Andrew and Mark are in there.'

'It could get ugly,' I said.

'Give me a minute and I'll send the boys to bed,' Jennifer said, rising to escort Colin and David out.

'I can stay, right?' Simone said.

'If Simone can stay, we can stay,' Colin said.

'You can stay,' Amanda said. 'David's too little.' She took David's hand and guided him to the bedroom he was sharing with Colin. He had refused to spend the night in Andrew's room.

'Zara, can you show all of us?' my father said.

Zara's expression went blank and suddenly we were skydiving over Singapore. The house around us disappeared and a three-dimensional image from Gold's viewpoint was projected into the air around us.

'You're seeing through Gold's eyes,' Zara said. 'He's been notified.'

'Damn,' my father said.

'If it becomes difficult or unpleasant, let me know,' Zara said. 'I will disconnect you.'

'Wow, this is just like Covert Ops,' Colin said.

There was even sound with the transmission: the wind whistled past Gold's ears as he, John and the two Generals with them flew down towards Singapore. The land was greener and more open than Hong Kong, with more one- and two-storey buildings, and wide roads bordered by lush grass verges dotted with trees.

'It's near Aljunied,' Gold said. 'Across the freeway from the housing estate, in Kallang.'

'Figures,' I said.

'Why is that, Emma?' Jennifer said.

'That's the red-light district. Aljunied is famous for prostitutes — and temples. There's a mass of temples in that whole area. Kallang is the industrial estate nearby.'

'Coming in. The Dark Lord is guiding us,' Gold said.

They were dropping more than flying, arms spread. John was the lowest, leading the way in Celestial Form, his hair and black robes streaming out behind him. He slid from side to side, then stopped in midair and floated two hundred metres above the ground.

'Zhu,' he said, gesturing without looking back.

'That's Zhu Bei Niang, the Lady of the Shadow Sword,' I said, explaining for my family. Zhu was wearing a black Mountain uniform with armour over the top and her Shadow sword, an unfocused shape of grey, was clipped to her back. Her black hair was tied in a simple ponytail. 'The other guy is General Ma, John's right hand.' Ma's robes and armour had a shifting pattern of flame on them, and his red hair was in a topknot and fell to his waist.

Zhu moved to float next to John, and pulled an ancient-looking, circular mirror out of her sword clip. She held it in front of her and swung it around.

'That's the Thunder Mirror,' I said. 'It sees the truth. It'll show them if there are any demons groundside.'

'It didn't detect the copies?' my father said.

'It saw them as human as well,' I said. 'John suspects that the copies are East-West hybrids and that's why they're undetectable.'

'Like young Tom,' my father said.

'Exactly.'

Zhu spoke. 'Nothing, my Lord. I suggest landing on one of the high rises and checking closer to the ground.'

'The one with the pool on the roof, on the corner nearest to the shophouses,' John said, and leapt from a floating position to freefall again, the Generals and Gold following him.

'Just the four of them?' my father said.

'Each General has a cohort of demon soldiers that they can summon,' I said. 'Until they're sure, they're keeping a low profile.'

John slowed, changed to vertical feet-first, and landed on a white high rise with a swimming pool on the roof. He strode to the edge and crouched, studying the shophouses across the road. Gold's viewpoint followed him, shaky now that Gold was walking, and the view swept over the buildings below.

The shophouses lined the narrow street, pushing hard against each other, their identical pitched roofs making them look like Monopoly houses. Each shophouse was a different colour, but all were two storeys, with an open workshop on the ground floor and a small apartment on the first. Most of them were auto-mechanical workshops, with a couple of metal-fabrication businesses and a tyre retailer. Cars lined the street on both sides, parked under the tired-looking trees.

John stiffened and sniffed the air. Zhu pulled the mirror out again, scanning the shophouses.

'I am relaying for Lady Emma's family,' Gold said softly.

'Hi, Emma,' Ma said behind Gold, sounding as if he was behind me.

John rose and went to the other side of the roof, and again crouched to study the shophouses across the road on the other side. On this side, it was the rear of the buildings on view; most of them had been extended with corrugated iron and tarpaulins, with piles of junk cluttering their concreted drives.

Zhu raised the mirror again and studied it. She went back to the other side of the building and turned the mirror.

'I smell them,' John said without moving. He raised one gloved hand towards the back of the shophouses. 'Down there.'

Zhu quickly joined him and turned the mirror towards the shophouses. 'I can't see anything!' she said, and shook it. 'Batteries must be flat.'

'She's joking, isn't she?' Jennifer said.

'Yes,' I said.

'How can they joke at a time like this?'

'They're Immortals, it's what they do.'

John stood up and flexed his hands. 'Change to plain human form and teleport down.' He disappeared.

The scene shifted and Gold's view was on the ground again. John had made himself short, round and middle-aged; Ma appeared as a teenager; and Zhu was an old woman. The ground crunched beneath their feet and the view shook again as they walked up to the back of the shophouses. John walked along the wall parallel to their backs, and stopped at one with three shipping containers side by side in its lot, a blue tarpaulin tied over them. The door of one of the containers hung open, and a young man leaned against it. He was wearing a stained pair of shorts, no shirt and a cheap pair of flip-flops, a cigarette hanging from his lip.

'You don't know which shop it was,' John said loudly and irritably to Ma. 'I knew I should have checked before we brought Mother.'

'It's all right, son,' Zhu said soothingly in an old-woman voice. 'We'll find it.'

'You, there!' Ma shouted to the young man. 'Where's the Daihatsu shop?'

The young man stuck his thumb over his shoulder towards the next street.

'Xie xie!' Ma waved his thanks, and took Zhu's arm as if she really was his grandmother, leading her away.

'Very strange,' John said as they walked away from the building.

My father saw me fidgeting with impatience. 'You want to be with them, don't you, Emma?'

'More than anything,' I said.

'But you could get killed,' my mother said.

I turned to speak to her. 'Not with John there. Actually, that's right — we only lost students when John wasn't on the Mountain. Now that he's back, it's completely defended. You really would be safe there, I could guarantee it.'

'We'll think about it,' my mother said without looking away from the shophouses.

'Andrew wasn't on the Mountain when he was killed,' Colin said softly.

'We're not sure he's dead, mate, he could still be alive,' Amanda's husband, Allan, said.

John, Gold and the Generals reached the end of the street. John turned to study the shophouses. 'Gold.'

'My Lord.'

'I sense only that one demon at the door; the rest of the above-ground facility is deserted. But I can't sense anything underground. I think this is an empty front.'

387

Zhu raised her mirror as if to tidy her hair. 'I see nothing at all.'

'Tell John it could be the same sort of trick that they used under Kowloon City Park,' I said quickly. 'They have Six's technology with stones and could have made the tunnels invisible to the Inner Eye.'

John's expression cleared. 'That would explain it.' He turned to Gold. 'Can we raid this? What are the terms of the agreement that Emma made with the King?'

'We can't raid anything underground without the Demon King's sanction,' I explained to my family. 'It's his domain, and John has a treaty with him that basically means we have to stay out unless he lets us in.'

'That's ridiculous,' my father said.

'The bureaucracy gets worse,' I said. 'Mortals like me need permission from both the Demon King and the Jade Emperor to enter Hell. So far it's only happened about four times in their entire history — and one of those was Simone, when she went down to get me out.'

'And I didn't have permission,' Simone said with amusement. 'But since I was six years old they waived the punishment. I think I'm still on probation from my suspended sentence.'

'Checking the transcript, my Lord,' Gold said.

'Gold's your lawyer for this stuff as well?' Jennifer said.

'He's the House's lawyer: he oversees both Celestial and Earthly legal matters,' I said.

Gold spoke with my voice: 'How badly do you want the Death Mother and Kitty taken down?' He replied with the Demon King's voice: 'Badly enough to enlist your help.' He returned to his own voice. 'Checking rules of precedent ... Confirmed. That statement can be interpreted as giving us sanction.'

'Follow me,' John said, and disappeared.

Gold reappeared next to John on the roof of the

shophouse, just above the tarpaulin over the containers. They'd returned to Celestial Form. John held one hand out over the roof and a pool of swirling blackness a metre across appeared in it. The blackness disappeared and there was a perfect circular hole where it had been.

'Yin,' Greg said with awe.

'So that's the real thing,' my father said. 'How powerful is that stuff anyway?'

I didn't reply.

'Emma?'

'Even if I did want to answer that question, I couldn't. The information is classified and I can't tell you.'

'You can't even tell your own parents?'

'The short answer is: no,' I said.

'Wow, you really do sound like him,' Greg said.

John had already gone in; Gold went through the hole and landed next to him. The entire row of shophouses, including the shipping containers in the yard, were one single structure housing a vast, empty internal space.

'John was right,' I said. 'An empty front. I hope there's something underneath and they're not wasting their time.'

John raised one hand towards the guard demon, which was frozen where it stood, bound by one of them. He flicked his wrist and it turned into a demon bead, then flew through the air into his hand. He passed the bead to Gold, who shoved it into his head.

'Whoa,' my father said.

'I think I'm going to be sick,' my mother said quietly. 'What did he just do?'

'You know Gold's a stone,' I said. 'His body is just a shell, and he can store stuff inside himself. He probably put it into his head because he's wearing real clothes for a change. The babies must be tiring him out.'

'If you want to have fun with a stone, call them "Tupperware",' Simone said. 'Quality airtight storage.'

'Sorry, Zara,' my mother said.

'Not a problem, ma'am,' Zara said. 'We have many offensive names for you fleshies as well.'

'Zara!' I said with shock.

John took long strides inside the structure, occasionally crouching to put his hands palm-down over the floor.

'I need to spend some serious time down in the Grotto, Emma,' he said softly. 'This weakness thing has been going on for far too long.' He stood up and looked around. 'You've never seen me full strength, and you deserve that before you make the commitment.'

'What's he talking about?' my mother said.

'He may change when he's combined and at full strength,' I said. 'I don't want to commit myself to him until I know what I'm letting myself in for, oath or no oath.'

'That makes sense,' she said.

'Found it,' Zhu said, holding her mirror above the floor in one corner. 'I can see something below here: seems to be demon guards.'

They went to the corner and stood looking at it for a moment.

'Move back,' John said, and yinned the floor, making another hole, this time two metres across.

They dropped through into another area just as large, with a three-metre ceiling. The walls and floor were covered in tan-coloured tiles stained with mould and dirt; the ceiling had bare neon tubes and filthy fans that circled unsteadily.

'They've come out in a wet market,' my father said with wonder.

'Do they do it the same way in Singapore?' my mother said. 'That really looks like the butcher section in a Hong Kong wet market.'

Steel railings lined the side of the room at eye level, with large, vicious hooks holding the meat. The carcases were delivered to each stall in the morning, cut up at the stall, and the pieces hung up ready to be sliced to order for shoppers. Most people bought fresh meat first thing in the morning, so deterioration in the heat wasn't an issue.

'Look, they even have the lungs and liver hanging up near the front, just like they do in Hong Kong,' my father said. 'They must have come out in Central Market or somewhere, one of the big ones. Hardly any beef or goat, though. Why's it all pork?'

'There's the trotters hanging up,' my mother said, then shrieked and ran out of the room. My father followed her.

'Stop the relay,' John said.

The image of human arms dangling hands-down from the rails blinked out.

Zara rested her head in her hands. 'I am so sorry. I thought you were right, and they were in a market.'

Jennifer and Amanda went out too; Allan, Colin and Greg quickly followed them.

'What happened to everybody?' Simone said.

'They've gone off to be sick,' I said.

'That was all the people they copied?' she said.

'Yes.'

'That could have been my cousins' hands, or Clarissa's hands.'

'It could have, yes.'

'Then why aren't I being sick too? Why aren't I affected like them?' She ran her hand over her forehead, desperate. 'What sort of creature am I?'

'Look at me,' I said, and reached to take her hand. 'We're different, Simone. Reptiles, and residents of the Celestial, both of us.'

'I don't want to be different.'

391

'Within the House of the North, you're not. With a bunch of ordinary humans, you are. It all depends on where you stand.' I released her hand and ran my hands through my hair; some of it fell out, clinging to my fingertips. 'There was a time when seeing something like that would have made me pass out from shock. Now look at me.'

Zara interrupted, speaking with Gold's voice. 'We have fought our way through a number of demon guards and located a nest with a Mother. We will update when we have a result.'

My parents returned, both looking drained. They sat on the couches.

'So what's happening now?' my father said.

'They found a demon, and they're about to attack it,' I said. 'Gold will let us know when they know more.'

'Do you still want to be there?' my father said.

'More than anything,' I said. I turned to Zara. 'Can you show just me?'

'Can't you just teleport there?' my mother said.

'Nobody here could manage the speed they travelled at,' I said. 'It'd take a few hours, and by the time I got there, they'd be done.'

'I see.'

'Gold says it is best you do not see this,' Zara said.

'It's all right. I'll tell my parents what's happening.'

'I want to see too,' Simone said.

'Gold says you really don't.'

'Tell Gold that's an order,' I said. 'I want to know what's going on!'

The image appeared in front of me again. They were at the other end of the underground facility, and the tiles had given way to plain concrete. John stood at the edge of the single nest hollow in the middle of the floor, with computer equipment flanking the walls around it. He was embracing a European woman, who was about the

392

same height as me and clutching him as if she'd never let him go. Five eggs, each forty centimetres across, sat in the hollow, tiny demons twitching inside them.

'I'm so glad you came,' the woman said. 'Hold me, don't let me go. I can't believe you're here. Please get me out of this place.'

'Holy shit,' I said softly. The woman was me.

Simone grabbed my arm, wrenched it behind my back, and held me.

'I'm the real Emma, Simone. Your father knows the difference,' I said.

Simone hesitated for a moment, then released me. I worked the muscles of my arm.

'Sorry,' she said.

The copy of me pulled back to smile up at John. He smiled down at her, but his eyes were full of grief.

'I think I've lost my memory,' she said. 'It's all blurry after they took me under Kowloon City Park. Are you back for good? Can we go to the Mountain?'

'I'm back for good,' he said.

She turned in his arms and looked down at the eggs. 'I think I had something to do with these, but I'm not sure. I remember dreaming about them.' She looked back up at him. 'Can we take them with us?'

'We will do whatever you want,' he said.

She buried her head in his chest. 'God, I love you, Xuan Wu.'

He nuzzled her hair. 'I love you too, Emma Donahoe.'

'I will do it,' Ma said. 'Let me.'

'No,' John said.

'Let's go home,' the copy of me said. 'Is Simone okay? Simon Wong had her.'

'Simone is fine, love. I'll take you home now.'

She smiled up at him, then slid her hand around the back of his neck and pulled him down for a kiss. He

393

closed his eyes and kissed her. She went limp in his arms and he gently lowered her to the floor. She changed form to a Snake Mother, the top half still human, and lay motionless with her eyes half-open and a smile on her face.

'Do you want tea or coffee, Emma?' my mother said. 'I'm making a fresh pot.'

I wiped my eyes. 'Tea, please.'

John studied the demon eggs, then pulled a dagger out of its sheath at his side, and crouched to slit one of them open.

'No, Daddy, don't kill them,' Simone said.

'What's happening?' my father said.

The liquid inside the egg spilled out, and along with it came a tiny hairless copy of Michael, only about thirty centimetres long. It blinked its sightless eyes and twitched, then its eyes glazed over and it stopped moving.

'Oh, shit,' Simone said.

John slit open the other four eggs in the clutch to reveal copies of Simone, me and my two demon servants.

'I'm glad I returned when I did,' John said quietly.

'There's a clutch of demon eggs that are copies of me, Michael and Simone,' I told my parents.

My mother tapped my hand and pushed a mug of tea into it.

'Thanks.'

John rose, wiped the dagger on his trouser pants, and put it away. 'Now to find the Mother in charge of all of this.' He looked around. 'I'm glad Emma didn't see that.'

'Uh, my Lord … she did,' Gold said.

John turned to look straight into Gold's eyes. 'What?'

'Tell him I understand,' I said. 'It's the way I would have wanted it.'

394

John shook out his shoulders. 'I will be very happy when I have the real you in my arms.' He raised one hand towards the computers. 'Gold.'

'Already in, my Lord,' Gold said.

'Well?'

'Give me a moment; these disks are seriously fragmented and they don't even have solid state drives. I am sick to death of backwards Earthly technology. Found it.' All the lights on the computer equipment lit up and flashed at the same time as he worked the drives. 'The research on this Mother is in these machines. This facility was mostly created for her; she's the tenth Mother copy of Emma they've made. Each Mother has been better than the one before; this is the best so far, and it's produced five eggs that they're extremely proud of. These Emma copies only last a couple of years at the most; they were running out of genetic material to make them.' His voice went softer. 'Oh, no.'

'What?' John said.

Gold and John shared information telepathically, and John's face filled with even more grief.

'Tell me,' I said.

'I noticed the small wound on your side, Emma. I thought you'd collected it along the way and Edwin had stitched it up,' John said.

'I had that wound when they found me in Lan Kwai Fong ...' I began, and took a deep breath. 'What did they take? ... My right ovary.'

'Your right ovary,' Gold said at the same time.

'Gold ... the other genetic material they were using from me. Tell me it wasn't ...' I took another deep breath and wiped my eyes. 'Tell me it wasn't the left one.'

'It's not the end of the world, Emma,' my mother said.

'It doesn't say, ma'am. I suggest you have yourself checked out tomorrow.'

'Emma, I want you to know that this makes no difference whatsoever to me,' John said.

'It makes an enormous difference to me,' I said.

Gold continued searching the drives. 'There was only one other Snake Mother that would spawn the copies for them: a Mother based on a Chinese woman, but she was killed by One Two Two — by mistake.'

'April,' I said.

'They want to use members of your family, my Lady; apparently your genetic material is somehow superior for their experimentation. They are keeping a record of where your family members are. They want more female members of the family, and there are photographs of your mother and sisters. They also have details and photographs of the other European people — the demon boy and his father.'

'If your family weren't already going into hiding, Emma, I'd be suggesting it anyway,' John said. 'They will be safe with Greg present and no contact from us.'

'The rest of the facility is nearby … there's a …' Gold broke into a barrage of Chinese curses, not bothering to translate it for me.

John raised his eyebrows at Gold. 'It must be something serious to pull that sort of language out of a lump of rock.'

Gold took a step back, nearly treading on Zhu. 'They have established themselves in a Buddhist temple nearby.'

John's expression went rigid with anger. 'Show me.'

They shared the information for a moment, and Ma swore as well.

'Let's go,' John said.

CHAPTER 27

They returned through the hole John had made, again passing the corpses hanging from the butcher's hooks.

'Don't tell me that's a larder,' I said.

'Very well, ma'am,' Gold said.

They travelled vertically about two hundred metres, to where they weren't as exposed. A couple more soldiers had joined the group: the leaders of the two demon cohorts that the Generals commanded.

Gold turned in the air, then pointed past the expressway. 'There.'

They flew over a four-lane main road to another area of narrow streets surrounded by small houses and lawns, then slowed when they came to the correct street.

'It's a street full of temples,' I said.

All the buildings on this street were small, the blocks only ten metres to a side. The first two buildings were two-storey houses; the third was a European-looking two-storey house with an ornate tower — a mosque. Then three more houses, then a Catholic church, and at the end of the street stood a small Buddhist temple.

'I wish the whole world was like that,' I said wistfully. 'Look at them happily coexisting.'

'The Dark Lord just said exactly the same thing,' Zara said in Gold's voice.

397

'They know we're coming,' John said. 'In through the front door.'

He swept down to land in front of the temple. A pair of bollards held a ribbon across the entrance, and a large sign with 'CLOSED' scrawled on it in marker in English and Chinese was stuck to the door. John clasped his hands and bowed in front of it, then stepped over the tape, pushed the door open and strode inside.

Gold followed him, and I gasped when I saw the interior.

The gilt Buddha statue had been overturned and its head torn off, the body splattered with either blood or red paint. The altar had been tipped over and the table smashed, and sticky, fly-covered stains spread over everything in sight.

'Is that urine?' I said.

'It is,' Zara said. 'They urinated on everything — which means there are some extremely high-level demons inside. Only the very biggest can do that.' She dropped her voice. 'Be careful, Gold.'

'Stand back,' John said, and raised his hands towards the toppled Buddha statue. A sphere of water appeared around it, then swept over the smashed furniture, washing it clean. The head of the Buddha reattached itself to the body, and John went to it, set it upright, and knelt to pay homage to it. Now that it was in one piece, I saw that it was an effigy of Kwan Yin herself.

'Go get them, John,' I said softly.

'I cannot bring violence to this place, Emma.'

'So what will you do?'

'Seek.'

He walked past the altar to the back of the building, where the caretaker's office was located. The caretaker — an elderly Chinese man in a plain grey cotton shirt and trousers — lay dead in his office, and had obviously been dead for a long time.

John walked out the back of the building into its tiny yard, and turned around as if sniffing the air. He walked back into the building and scouted around the edge, then stopped and put his hands on his hips. 'Zhu.'

Zhu had already pulled out her mirror and was studying the floor. The floor moved, then heaved upwards, nearly knocking her over, and took the form of a fake stone elemental, towering close to the ceiling. Zhu stepped back, drew her sword and moved into a defensive stance.

John turned his head from side to side. 'I presume this is a fake stone elemental,' he said.

Ma moved next to him. 'Let us handle this one. Stand back, Number Ones.'

The demon commanders moved back, then one took up a post at the front of the building, the other at the rear.

'You presume?' Zhu said, moving to one side so that John was standing between her and Ma.

'I can't see it,' John said.

Ma flipped his left hand and the Seven Stars banner, a shimmering field of black, appeared in it. 'Then let us handle it.'

The stone elemental was a collection of head-sized rocks floating in formation. It turned its faceless head as if it was studying them.

'Put your weapons away. I'll take it down without weapons; this is not the place for fighting,' John said. 'Last time we faced something like this, my Serpent possessed Emma and she took out a few of them single-handed — a sight to see.'

'Scared you all to death,' I said.

'What? What's happening?' my mother said.

'They're in a temple, and they're facing a stone elemental like the ones at Emma's graduation all that time ago,' Simone said.

John turned side-on to the elemental, opened his hands in front of him, then turned on the balls of his feet so that his palms were towards the elemental. He raised his hands slightly, but nothing happened.

The elemental swung at his head and he dodged it easily.

'Ah Wu ...' Ma said.

'Stand back, I have an idea,' John said. 'Give me about two metres.'

Ma and Zhu stood back and watched. Zhu put her sword away, but Ma still held his black banner.

John changed to True Form, his Turtle shape three metres long from its dragon-like head to tiny black tail. He stomped up to the elemental, stretched his head on its long neck, turned it sideways and bit one of the rocks. He proceeded to dismantle the demon rock by rock, spitting each one out, and the elemental seemed unable to do anything about it. When it was just a jumbled pile of rocks, the Turtle changed back to John, and he shook out his shoulders.

'I nearly forgot I could do that, it's been such a long time,' he said.

He kicked some of the rocks to the side and looked down. Gold looked too: the fake elemental had been acting as a combined trapdoor and guard over a tunnel. Gold's vision lurched and flowed across the floor, went into the hole and looked around.

'Geez, Gold,' I said.

'Sorry, stretched my neck out to have a look inside,' Gold said. His vision returned to above-ground. 'There's a long tunnel, heading north. Can't see the end.'

John jumped down into the hole, then stopped and concentrated. 'Again, I can't see anything, but there may be more of those fake elementals on the way.'

He gestured for the others to follow him, then changed into a Turtle again.

'Gold, how much time did he spend in True Form before he was unable to?' I said. 'Will he spend more time as an animal now he can do it?'

'I don't know, ma'am. He'd already made his promise to Lady Michelle when I joined the household.'

The Turtle spoke in John's voice as it led them along the tunnel, the top of its shell brushing the ceiling. 'It depends on the circumstances. Please don't make me swear not to take True Form again, Emma. I think it would kill me.'

'I won't. I think your Turtle form is extremely cute,' I said.

'Wait until you see the combined creature,' Gold said. 'That's never been called cute. First time I saw it, it scared me to death.'

'Quiet. There's something up ahead,' John said. 'Cover your eyes.'

There were a few heavy footsteps up ahead: another stone elemental. John opened his mouth, sending out a stream of shen energy towards the end of the tunnel. The elemental absorbed the shen energy, glowing with white brilliance, until it became too bright to look at and completely shattered.

The ground rumbled and Gold's vision shook.

'They heard us, they're running,' John said.

He changed back to human form and ran to the end of the tunnel, which was unblocked now the elemental was gone. He jumped up to the floor above, the other members of the team following.

'Call the demon soldiers,' John said.

As Gold jumped out of the hole, we saw what appeared to be a warehouse with a series of five-metre-high pitched roofs. Light shone in through windows randomly placed along the wall, and the floor was bare concrete. The space was divided into smaller areas with two-metre high screens, so all that was immediately visible from Gold's view was a three-by-three-metre room with walls, no ceiling and a hole in the floor.

The whole building echoed with the sound of the demons running in terror from John. He jumped high into the air, and Gold followed, floating just below the pitched roof and viewing the interior as if it were a laboratory rat maze. The way the demons were running, it could have been. The tunnel appeared to be the only exit. The demons, in their panic to get away from John and the Generals, were crushing each other in the corners of the building.

'Send the two demon cohorts to round them up,' John said. He raised his voice to cut through the sound of the demons' terror. 'Turn and we will spare you.'

The Celestial demon soldiers started to emerge from the tunnel, causing even more panic.

John rotated in the air. 'Now to find the one who's in charge of all of this.'

'There, my Lord,' Gold said, pointing towards the corner of the building the furthest from them.

A small group was pushing its way out of an ordinary household front door set into a section of wall filled with biotech and computer equipment. The group included Kitty Kwok and the Death Mother, along with a few demon guards.

Simone squeaked when she saw the half-dozen demons they'd left behind. They were unlike anything I'd seen before: three-metre-long, headless snake skeletons; rows of ribs along a central bony spine. They lifted their front ends and rattled at John and Gold, then rushed them.

John didn't mess around; he just raised his hands and sent a blast of chi through them, turning in place to take them all out. He ran through the door, closely followed by the others.

They stopped on the other side: they were in a suburban street. Night had fallen and the streetlights were on. They quickly reduced to human form, and checked up and down the street.

It was one of the enclaves that passed for suburbia in some parts of Asia: tiny two-storey houses, each only four by five metres, packed side by side along narrow streets. All the houses had originally been identical, but many were now painted in gaudy colours or decorated with awnings, stonework and elaborate windows, giving the street a festive air. They all had high steel-spike fences and electric driveway gates, and some had cars parked diagonally to fit in their front yards. Cars lined the street as well, making it only just wide enough to drive through.

The door they'd exited was the front door of one of these houses. It seemed all the houses on that block were joined together inside: a single massive building masquerading as houses. The building's internal light shone from all the windows.

'There,' John said, and took off running down the street.

The Generals sprinted after him, and Gold was hard-pressed to keep up.

John turned right at the end of the street, past a bemused resident who was watering the pot plants in her front yard. Gold reached the corner a few seconds after him, and followed him down another street. John stopped in the middle of the street, and had to jump out of the way of an oncoming car. The Generals pulled up beside him; Gold caught up with them a few seconds later.

'How's the mopping up going?' John said without looking away from the end of the street.

'There are strange hybrids and elementals among the demons, my Lord,' Ma said. He raised one hand. 'I suggest we move off the road before someone hits you and destroys their car.'

They moved to the side.

'Some of these demons are too much for the brigades to handle: we are losing our soldiers,' Zhu said. 'Permission to return and lead them.'

John raised his hand behind him, still not looking away from the end of the street. 'Granted. Return and bolster your armies. Call upon Xun or Zhou if required. I am summoning Guan and Zhao to go with me; these two are moving extremely fast. Gold, stay here. They're running too quickly for you to keep up.'

He shot straight up into the air, leaving a visible blast of dust behind him, and disappeared.

I thumped the arm of the chair. 'Dammit!'

'What, Emma?' my father said.

'Kitty and the Death Mother took off and they're moving too fast for Gold to keep up. John's gone off with Zhao Gong Ming and Guan Yu to take them down, and I can't see what's happening.'

'Those are two of the biggest Generals, aren't they?' my mother said.

'Only Ma himself is bigger than those two guys,' I said. 'It's serious if John has taken Guan off gate duty.'

'Those demons were so gross,' Simone said weakly.

'What did they look like?' Colin said. I hadn't seen him return with the rest of the group.

'Bones,' I said. 'Living snake bones. Horrible.'

Gold turned back and followed Zhu and Ma towards the row of houses that was a front for the Death Mother's operation. They went to the end house and through the front door into the facility, then flew up to hover below the ceiling to get an overview.

The screams of the panicked demons echoed through the building, bouncing off the ceiling. They were trying to escape down the tunnel, and were crushing each other in the stampede. The floor was black with demon essence. Demon warriors from John's army were pulling them out of the crush, clubbing them unconscious and throwing them to one side without destroying them.

Zhu pulled the Shadow Sword from its scabbard and raised it horizontally above her head. Lightning flashed from the sword through the massed demons, knocking them senseless. She did this three more times, each time disabling another wave of demons.

One of the demon officers, in three-metre-tall True Form with black scales and tusks, floated up to Zhu and saluted her. 'Southeast corner, ma'am — Fifty-Seven is having some difficulty there. We can handle these now.'

Zhu turned and flew to the area he'd mentioned: a large open space, twenty metres long and five wide, bounded on two sides by the external walls and on the other two by the internal screens. Rows of benches filled the space.

Ma and Gold joined Zhu, and they flew down to take a look. The benches held octagonal ornamental fish tanks, full of thick, black, bubbling demon essence instead of water. The Generals' demon soldiers were battling a group of water elementals and losing. The water elementals formed water blades that sliced through the demon soldiers, easily destroying them.

Zhu raised her sword and sent a blast of lightning through a couple of elementals. They staggered back then retaliated, shooting balls of ice at the Generals.

'None of us is equipped to deal with these,' Ma said. 'Zhu is thunder and I'm fire; these water things are immune to both of us.'

'Fall back, hold your ground,' I said. 'I'll send Simone.' I turned to speak to her, but she wasn't there. 'Where'd she go?'

'I don't know. She disappeared a while ago,' my father said.

'That's her, there she is,' Gold said.

A screaming sound, like a jet engine, came from outside the row of houses. The demons stopped fighting and cowered as the whole building shook. The roof peeled away and Simone dropped inside, landing in a low defensive stance in front of the fake water elementals. She stood up, raised her hands, and all of the fake elementals turned to ice. She clenched her fists and ripped her hands backwards, and they shattered.

She dropped her hands. 'Anything else I need to worry about?'

A tentacle lashed out of one of the fish tanks, wrapped itself around her throat and jerked her towards the tank. She was pulled along for a moment, then concentrated: the entire fish tank exploded in a shower of glass and demon essence. The tentacle fell, lifeless, from her neck.

'That was some sort of plant hybrid,' I said. 'The Celestial plants will be furious.'

Simone put her hand to the side of her throat and staggered backwards. 'Take care, everybody, those things are poisonous.' She fell to sit on the floor, still with her hand on her throat.

I jumped to my feet. 'Gold she's poisoned.'

'I know, ma'am,' Gold said. He knelt next to her and put his hand on her arm, then concentrated. 'I've never seen anything like this before.'

'It's okay, I learnt how to deal with this in school,' Simone said, then bent over and retched. 'I can handle it.'

Zhu and Ma crouched next to her as well. Another tentacle lashed out of a second tank, but Ma summoned his sword and cut it off before it could touch them. It withdrew into the tank.

Gold's view returned to Simone and I gasped. She was unconscious, her face pale and swollen.

'Call John back,' I said. 'Quickly!'

A deeper, booming scream sounded overhead and John shot through the opened roof to land next to Simone. He pushed Zhu and Ma away, knelt next to her and lifted her head into his lap. He put one hand on her forehead and his expression went grim.

I took half a step forward, but the projection became more difficult to see at close range, so I moved back and sat again, helpless.

John gently lowered Simone to the ground again. Her head lolled, her eyes open but unseeing. He pulled Seven Stars from his back and handed it to Ma, then changed to Turtle.

Zhu jumped up and began searching the benches, carefully staying out of range of the plant demons in the tanks. She found what she was looking for — a glass beaker — and returned to John and Ma.

John raised his front left foot and closed his eyes, his Turtle face serene. Zhu held the beaker below the foot, and Ma cut it off. A stream of blood flowed from the stump and Zhu collected it in the beaker. When it was half-full, she turned and dribbled the blood into Simone's mouth.

'One of the demons poisoned Simone.' I swallowed hard. 'She looks really bad. They're giving her John's blood to drink — it's a healing agent.'

Simone inhaled loudly and gasped, then coughed. John changed back to human form, missing his left hand, and held her. Zhu and Ma cut some strips from Ma's robe, and Gold wrapped them around the stump of John's wrist. John didn't seem aware of them working; he concentrated on Simone.

'Can he grow it back?' I said.

'Sorry; busy,' Gold said.

'I understand.'

Zhu moved to take Simone's head in her lap. John rose, turned, and Ma handed Seven Stars to him. John held it easily in one hand, raised it and loaded it with his chakra energy. The seven holes in the blade sang as they filled with different-coloured lights; then John pointed the blade at the aquariums and dark energy shot out to spread around him, shattering their glass. The demons inside looked like grassy plants: all long, narrow blades, some with yellow flowers. The tentacles weren't visible at first, curled up inside the leaves, but then the demons lashed out towards John, trying to hit him with the tentacles' poisonous spiny ends. John lowered the sword and held out the stump of his left hand towards them, then grimaced and dropped it.

Ma stepped forward, pushed his hands palms out towards the plant demons and enveloped them in a gush of flames. The demons blackened, shrivelled and died.

John turned back to Simone, and Zhu moved out of the way so that he could hold her again. He placed the sword on the ground next to him and put his hand on her forehead.

She opened her eyes and smiled up at him. 'That tasted absolutely awful.'

'I know,' he said. He looked up at Ma, and his eyes unfocused. 'Is that all there is here?'

'No. My commander reports that there are some humans in cages at the other end of the building,' Zhu said.

'Rhonda. Clarissa.' I felt a leap of hope. 'The boys!'

John gazed down at Simone, concerned. 'Can you walk?'

'No, leave me here,' she said.

'Ma, bring her,' John said, and stood up again, collecting his sword. He shook the stump of his left hand. 'I can't grow it back right now, Emma. Either I can wait for it to come back by itself, or visit Court Ten and be renewed. Visiting Court Ten for something as trivial as this is considered a waste of Pao's time, though.'

'I see,' I said.

Ma lifted Simone and carried her, and they rose into the air.

The demon soldiers had finished with the smaller demons that had tried to escape; all had been either destroyed or turned. The ten demons that had turned stood quietly to one side waiting for a Celestial to give them the Fire Essence Pill.

'Put me down, I can fly myself,' Simone said.

'When we're back on the ground,' Ma said.

John led them along the building to the other end. A small partitioned area held four cages, each a metre to a side and two metres tall. I couldn't see from above what was in the cages, and John dropped to examine them.

'Stop the recording before you come down,' he said to Gold. 'I don't care how many orders Emma gives you, she is not to see this. Leave Simone at the other end of the building while we pull them out.'

The recording blanked out.

'But are the boys there?' I said.

My mother rushed to sit next to me. 'They found the boys?'

'I'm not sure,' I said. 'Zara?'

'Yes,' Zara said in Gold's voice. 'Clarissa and the two boys are here. They're in extremely bad shape. We'll clean them up and bring them home.'

Just over an hour later, John rang the doorbell and my family ran to let him in. He stood in the doorway behind Mark and Andrew. Simone was next to him, looking wan and exhausted. The boys had been showered and their clothes changed to Mountain uniforms. They were both gaunt to the point of emaciation, completely bald, with sunken, staring eyes.

Jennifer and Amanda ran to the boys and embraced them, then brought them in and sat them on the couches. Colin and David helped, Colin holding Andrew's hand and David holding Mark's. Their brothers didn't respond.

John came in and knelt in front of Andrew. *What's this one's name again?*

'Andrew,' I said. 'The other one is Mark.'

He touched the side of Andrew's head. 'Andrew.'

Andrew jerked slightly, and seemed to notice John for the first time.

'Andrew, you're at your grandparents' house,' John said, his voice gentle. 'You're home, you're safe, you're with Colin and your mother. They're right here.'

'Mum?' Andrew said, looking around. He saw Jennifer and threw himself into her arms. 'Mum! You're here!'

John went to Mark and did the same thing, touching him lightly on the side of the face. Mark took longer to come around, but he eventually recognised the family as well, and a joyful reunion took place.

John rose and took a few steps back to let us share the moment. Simone collapsed onto a stool at the kitchen bench and leaned her head on her crossed arms.

I went to John and linked my fingers in his right hand; his left was still gone. 'How's Clarissa?'

'In a similar state, but for her it is a hundred times worse. She was convinced that Michael would come and rescue her, and he never did. She feels that he abandoned her.'

'Oh dear Lord, that's awful.'

'She's in the Tiger's hospital here in the West, and refusing to see Michael. She will probably never forgive him. It's quite likely none of them will be able to function completely normally ever again.'

'Did you see Rhonda?'

'No. She is dead, Emma.'

I flopped to sit and put my head in my hands.

'I have something for you,' John said, and held his hand out to me.

I looked in his palm: there was my stone, small, square and green. I took it and turned it in my fingers. 'Hello, stone, welcome back.'

It didn't reply, and I glanced up at John.

'It won't talk to me either,' John said. 'Gold assures me that this is it. Obviously it's been traumatised as well.' He put his arm around me. 'We all have a great deal of healing to do.'

I tried to put the stone back into its setting, but the claws were too close together to slip it in. 'I'll have to ask the Tiger for help. The stone isn't dead, is it?'

'It can't die. I think it's just broken, and it will take some time for it to come back.'

I stroked the stone with my finger. 'I'm glad you're back,' I said to it. 'I really missed you.'

It seemed to pulse under my finger and then went still.

'Will your family still go into hiding?' John said.

'That's the last thing on their minds right now,' I said. 'Provided the boys get a good level of care, I think they will.'

'After this, I don't blame them.'

'What about Kitty and the Death Mother?'

'Zhao and Guan are tracking them. They headed out very fast, north towards Thailand. We will find them.'

I leaned my head on his shoulder and touched the bandage on his left stump. 'Did you really have to cut the whole thing off like that?'

'The Turtle's blood is deep under the surface, and we were in a hurry. It was the only way.'

'You seem to have endless patience with my interminable questions,' I said.

'Do I?' He appeared surprised. 'It's just answers.' He squeezed my shoulders. 'The Tiger says we can stay here tonight and say goodbye to your family tomorrow. He has some things he wants to show us; among them, his hospitality.'

'Do you want to stay here as well, Simone?' I said.

Simone nodded into her crossed arms.

John went to her and put his hand on her shoulder. She raised her head and smiled wanly at him.

Jennifer and Amanda were clutching their sons without speaking. My parents joined John and Simone.

'Would you like a drink or something, Simone?' my father said. 'You look terrible.'

'She was severely poisoned, she nearly died,' John said. 'She just needs to rest.'

'A soft drink would be absolutely awesome,' Simone said. She sat up and took John's hand. 'You saved my life, Daddy.'

My father poured a drink and put it on the bench in front of her. She nodded her thanks and drained it quickly.

'We're staying here in the Western Palace tonight,' John said.

'You should take Emma and Simone to bed then,' my mother said. 'Both of them are exhausted.'

'It's not even nine o'clock,' Simone said.

'You're having trouble staying upright,' I said. 'Mum's right.'

'You don't look too good yourself, John. Do you need that arm seen to?' my mother said. 'That wound is still bleeding.'

John raised his arm; she was right. 'It's minor.'

'Typical. Cut the man's hand off and he says it's minor,' my father said. 'Now you all go and get some rest, and we'll see you at breakfast. And John?'

'Hm?' John said.

My father held out his hand. 'Thanks for bringing the boys back. You have no idea how much that means to us.'

John hesitated for a moment, then shook my father's hand. 'They'll need counselling, Brendan. I won't go into detail about what happened to them, but it wasn't good. They'll never be the same again, and I think you'll be cursing me for many years to come.'

'Probably,' my father said. 'But at least they're alive.'

'Come on, ladies,' John said. 'Let's leave them to it, and return in the morning.'

I hugged my parents before we left, but Jennifer and Amanda didn't seem to be aware that we were going. They were concentrating on their children, and I didn't blame them.

CHAPTER 28

The Tiger showed us to the suite we'd be sharing; it was the same one with the balcony that we'd stayed in all that time ago. Royal blue cushions still decorated the purple couch, and the wind chime sounded gently outside the window.

Simone hugged us both, then took herself straight to bed.

John leaned on the windowsill, then turned to see me. The desert breeze lifted his hair; it had completely come out of its tie again.

'They have seen things no human should see,' he said. 'And they are children.'

I went to him and wrapped myself around him, and he held me close, burying his face in my hair.

There was a tap on the door and he raised his head. 'There's a physician here to tidy up my arm,' he said. 'It hasn't stopped bleeding and he'll close it off.' He released me. 'I suggest you go run a bath or something while we do this; it won't be pretty.'

'Do you need my energy healing?' I said.

He gazed into my eyes with amusement. 'You have a terminal disease and you're offering healing? Go rest yourself, Miss Donahoe, because you're the one who needs it.'

He stroked my arms and I yelped and jumped back; it

felt like a twenty-centimetre red-hot needle had been plunged into my right arm. I unrolled the bandage: there was a streak of normal skin in the centre of the demon essence.

John raised his left arm. 'It was this.'

I carefully edged the black part of my arm towards the stump, and the second it touched I yelped again. Where it had touched, the black had changed to normal human colour.

'My blood is removing the essence,' John said with interest.

The physician tapped on the door again.

'Enter,' John said.

'Can we do the rest of it now?' I said.

'While it causes you that much torment? I don't think so,' John said. 'We'll wait until you're stronger and back on the Mountain, then we'll block the meridians and do it that way. We may even put you under completely.'

The physician came in with a large black doctor's bag, and saluted us on one knee. John nodded to him then returned to me. 'Now go run that bath and wait for me. This shouldn't take long.'

'Won't it hurt you as much as this hurt me?' I said, raising my arm.

'If it did, do you think I'd be talking to you like this?' he said. He pushed me gently away. 'Go, before I die of blood loss and Judge Pao makes me stay on Level Ten for the next six months. He's annoyed enough to do it.'

'No,' I said. 'I want to ask the physician something. Doctor?'

'Bai; I don't use a pseudonym,' the doctor said.

'I had my right ovary removed a few days ago. Is there any way for you to check if the left one is still there?'

'Pull your jeans down a little and lie on the couch, I'll have a feel,' he said.

415

I lay on the couch as directed, and John watched as the doctor massaged my abdomen.

'I need to do an internal to be sure. Is that all right?' the doctor said.

'Sure.'

He took a pair of latex gloves from his bag and slipped them on, and I stood up and pulled my jeans and panties completely off. I lay back on the couch and he slipped his hand inside me to examine me internally. John moved quickly to stop him.

'No,' I said. 'This is normal. Let him.'

He used one hand inside me and the other on the outside of my abdomen to palpate it, feeling for the ovaries. I squeaked as he pushed against the scar on the right side; it was still tender.

'Sorry,' he said, his eyes unfocused. 'That one's definitely gone.' He moved to the left side. 'This one's still here. I can feel it.'

I let out a huge gasping breath of relief. 'Thank you.'

'I suggest you have an ultrasound to confirm; that isn't the most accurate method of identification,' he said, helping me back upright and carefully not watching as I pulled my clothes back on.

'Why couldn't you just feel her pulse like a normal doctor?' John said, obviously distressed.

'Because her ovaries aren't on her wrists,' the doctor said with amusement. He nodded to me. 'Now let me change my gloves and pull out my instruments, and I'll sew up the Dark Lord's arm.'

John came into the bathroom later, looking incongruous with a plastic bag over the end of his arm.

I draped myself over the edge of the bath. 'God of water, can't get his arm wet.'

'I know,' he said. 'It's been so long since my energy has been at full strength that I've forgotten what it's like.'

'I would like to look at you with my Internal Eye and see how big you really are,' I said.

'Go right ahead.'

I opened my Eye on him for the first time since he'd returned. He appeared as a great Turtle, bigger than the building we were in, but so drained that he was only a pale shadow.

'You're vast,' I said with wonder. 'So strong, and still so weak.'

'Not even a trip to Court Ten can fix this,' he said. 'I need to be on my Mountain, undisturbed, for days.'

I hopped out of the tub to help him undress, but he concentrated and lost the clothes before I reached him. I stepped back and admired him.

He saw me looking at him and turned away, knowing full well what the sight of his muscular back and behind did for me. 'Could you tie my hair back? I can't do it one-handed.'

I took a hair tie from the toiletries provided on the bathroom counter and went to him. I smoothed his hair back, then couldn't resist the urge to bury my face in it, relishing the silken feeling and the smell of the sea. I pressed myself into him, breathing in the scent of his hair, and ran my hands down his sides, tracing the muscles over his ribs and abdomen. I slipped my hand lower to stroke him, enjoying his reaction.

He took my hands in his remaining one and held them over his chest. 'Forget the hair tie. I give up,' he said, his voice vibrating through him. He turned around and smiled down at me with his hand and stump low on my back, making the plastic rustle against my skin. 'I guess the hair will have to stay loose.'

As he realised what he was doing, his expression changed and he moved his left arm behind his back. 'That doesn't worry you? If you'd prefer not to be touched with it, I would understand.'

I didn't reply; I just climbed into the shower and pulled him in with me. He pushed his face into the water and ran his remaining hand through his hair, squeezing the water through it with obvious pleasure. I pushed him to turn him around and shampooed his hair for him. He sat so I could massage his scalp, obviously enjoying it.

'Not as dry this time,' I said. 'It's strong and healthy.'

'Wait until I'm at full strength, then it will have a life of its own. It may even stop you from washing it.'

I ran the conditioner through it, revelling in the silken feeling. With him sitting, it touched the shower floor behind him.

'Why do all you traditional Chinese warriors leave your hair long?' I said as I squeezed the conditioner out. 'It must drive you nuts sometimes.'

'My hair is a gift from my ancestors, and it is disrespectful to them to cut it,' he said.

'You're joking.'

'That's why we used to leave it long.' He stood up, took the soap and turned to run it over me. 'Of course, I have no ancestors, but when I took human form, a man's long hair was his ...' He searched for the word. 'His manhood? No. His pride? I don't know.'

'I think I understand. It's a little like shaving prisoners' heads to intimidate them. It's your self-respect.'

'Exactly,' he said.

He slid the soap over me, making me wriggle in response.

'Oh, that's interesting,' he said, rubbing his soapy hand over my back then sliding it onto my breast, making me lean into him and writhe. 'You seem to like this more and more all the time. I just wish I had both hands to do it with.'

'You drive me crazy, you know that, Xuan Wu?' I said as his strong, slick hand roamed over me. He leaned to whisper in my ear as his hand slid between my legs. 'Good. You drive me insane all the time.'

'Last time we were in this room, I wanted to stay here forever,' I said, wrapped around him in the blue and gold bed.

'I remember,' he said. 'We had to return; we had duties to perform.' He turned to see me. 'I hope that isn't the way you feel now.'

'No. I can't wait to be back on our Mountain.'

He touched the side of my face. 'You delight me and terrify me at the same time.'

'Terrify you?'

He stroked my face. 'Please don't be my Serpent. I like having you around.'

I put my hand over his. 'I terrify myself.'

My family were waiting for us on the terrace outside their villa when we returned the next morning. My parents hugged me, and we sat to join them for tea, fruit and pastries.

'Andrew has something he wants to ask John,' my father said.

'Anything, Andrew,' John said.

'I want to know …' Andrew took a deep breath. 'You can mess around with people's heads, can't you?'

'I'm not supposed to, but I can,' John said.

'You want him to erase your memories?' I said.

'Both of us do,' Mark said. 'You know what was down there.' He turned to his mother. 'I think we should talk about this away from you guys. We don't want David to hear what it was like.'

'I'm not little!' David said, protesting. 'I'm nearly thirteen!'

'Can you take the other ones for a walk?' John asked my father.

'No, I want to hear,' Colin said. 'I'm nearly the same age as Simone, and she was there.'

'David, come with me,' my mother said in a tone that brooked no protest. David opened his mouth to argue, then went quiet and left with her.

'There,' Mark said. 'Did you do something to him to make him go with her?'

'No, I didn't,' John said. 'Messing with heads is something we do only in extreme circumstances and in the direst of need, because if we aren't careful we can cause permanent damage.'

Mark's voice went hoarse. 'And you think what we went through down there didn't cause permanent damage?'

John looked him in the eye. 'I know it did.'

'Can you erase our memories back to the moment before we were taken?' Andrew said.

'I want my little brother back,' Colin said, desperate. 'I hate to see him like this.'

'I hate being like this,' Andrew said.

Should I do it, Emma? It would spare them much suffering.

'Yes,' I said. 'It's worth the risk. Despite what you think, John, you're the best telepathic healer that's ever been in my head.'

Mark sagged with relief. 'Thanks, Aunty Emma.'

'Is this what you want as well?' John asked the boys' parents.

'I honestly wish I could join them in forgetting. I don't know how Emma does it,' Allan said.

'I want it too. I want my Andrew back,' Jennifer said.

'Ditto for me,' Amanda said. 'I hate seeing Mark like this.'

'Very well,' John said.

'Yes,' Andrew said softly.

'It will take an hour for each boy. I'll examine them

carefully before I do anything to them,' John said. 'When are you planning to leave?'

'However long you need, take your time,' my father said. 'Do it right.'

'Will it hurt?' Mark said, suddenly unsure.

'No,' John said. 'When I am done, it will be as if all of this had never happened.'

Mark nodded once, sharply. 'Then that's what I want. I'll go first.'

'Finish your food, then we'll go somewhere quiet to do this,' John said.

I'll have to make contact with their heads on both sides and that means removing the bandage, he added silently to me. *They won't see it, but anyone else present will, and that's not good. So I'll do this somewhere out of view.*

'I understand,' I said. I turned to my father. 'He has to be alone and private, and undisturbed, to do it.'

'As I said, whatever it takes,' my father said.

We did Andrew first, in his own bedroom where it would be more reassuring for him. It was a typical boy's room: the floor covered in suspect clothing, school notes and books, with a collection of remote-control cars and Warhammer miniatures neatly lined up on his bookshelves. A set of cardboard boxes sat on the floor, ready for the items to be packed.

John needed me there to help him remove the bandage from his arm. The physician had done a fine job: he'd folded the skin over as much as possible, and sealed the blood vessels. I sat Andrew down in front of John, and John put his hand and stump on the sides of Andrew's head, then dropped his own head.

Andrew jumped as John made the contact.

'Are you okay, Andrew?' I said.

Andrew's face lit up with a sly smile. 'I've never seen his True Form before, Aunty Emma.' His smile widened to a grin. 'He's really ugly!'

'That I am,' John said.

'It's so cold,' Andrew said, more plaintive.

'I am the essence of cold,' John said. 'If I hurt you or I'm too cold, let me know.'

'Okay,' Andrew said.

'I will examine him extensively first,' John said with his eyes closed. 'Then I'll make the changes. I'll call you telepathically when I'm done, Emma. Go talk to your parents.'

Neither of them noticed me walking out.

John didn't call me telepathically when he was finished. Instead, he brought Andrew back into the living room with his arm around Andrew's shoulders. They went to the couch and sat across from the rest of the family.

John leaned forward and put his elbows on his knees, clasping his hand to his roughly bandaged stump. 'I can't do it. I'm sorry.'

'He says it would break me too much,' Andrew said, miserable.

John nodded, his face full of similar misery.

'So what do we do?' Jennifer said.

John glanced up at her. 'Seek counselling for them. I can arrange it for you, if you like.'

'We'll be fine, Mum,' Andrew said with forced brightness.

'I think everybody should leave now so we can pack,' Jennifer said. 'I'll see you all later.' She walked out of the room without looking back.

'You'll all still join us for lunch?' I said.

'We will, don't worry,' Greg said. 'We'll see you at the pool later.'

The Tiger cleared the pool area for us to have lunch together there before my family left. Louise's two children, Simone, and all the parents, including the Tiger himself, came along too.

422

The Australian kids taught Simone and Louise's kids to play Marco Polo in the pool; and they all seemed to be enjoying themselves until Lucas, Louise's son and the youngest there, ran to us to complain.

'Simone's cheating,' he said. 'She can breathe underwater and she won't come up.'

'Don't play with her then,' my mother said.

He opened and closed his mouth a few times, then ran back to the pool.

'He is such a chronic tattle-tale,' Louise said with amusement. She leaned to grin down at the Tiger, who was stretched on the pavers in True Form. 'He gets it from you.'

The Tiger rolled onto his back with his paws in the air. 'Never told a tale in my life; you can ask my boss.' He flicked one paw at John. 'You, Louise, on the other hand ... I seem to recall you running to me when you suspected that one of the harem guards was playing up.'

'Was he?' Amanda said with interest.

'Nope,' the Tiger said, then rolled onto his belly and stretched, scraping his claws on the concrete. 'They know better.'

'I remember,' John said, leaning his chin in his hand over his half-empty plate of barbecued vegetables. 'I remember once, about five hundred years ago, a little tiger thought that one of his neighbours in the Celestial realm had encroached on his boundary. He scurried to the Jade Emperor himself, requesting an audience, and loudly squealed —'

'I don't squeal!' the Tiger said.

John glanced down at him with amusement. 'I didn't say it was you.'

'I know what you're talking about, I remember it too,' the Tiger said.

'He reported to the mighty Jade Emperor that his neighbour's army was massing on his borders.'

'Well, they were,' the Tiger said. 'Black banners and all.'

'The Jade Emperor told the Tiger to return to his Palace, and this time to read the scroll in the red box before sending it back.'

'How was I to know that the damn box had an Edict in it?' the Tiger said.

'Why were you massing on his borders anyway?' Louise asked John, fascinated.

'It was joint exercises,' John said. 'His own army was involved, but they hadn't arrived at the training ground yet.'

'And he never knew?' Louise said, full of mischief.

'Oh, thank you very much,' the Tiger said, and pulled himself lazily to his feet and strolled towards the pool.

'Nope,' John said. 'Completely unaware of what his own army was doing. All the paperwork was sitting on his desk unread.'

The Tiger jumped into the pool and chased the children around, growling at them, his claws carefully sheathed.

John studied them as they splashed. 'They don't seem terribly scared of the Tiger. I wonder what they'd think of a Turtle in there as well?'

'A sea turtle?' I said.

He nodded.

'Can you swim with one flipper missing?'

'I can get around.'

Louise grinned at him. 'Can you give them rides?'

He seemed surprised at that, then smiled gently. 'I suppose I can.'

'Then what's stopping you? They'd love that.'

John didn't reply; he just stood and strode to the pool, changed to a Turtle and slid in. The smaller children squealed when they saw him, then began to argue about climbing onto his back.

424

'Seemed to be a completely new idea to him,' my father said, bemused.

'Probably is,' I said. 'You know how big he is. Louise is probably the first person who's ever had the nerve to ask him.'

'If he'd been the combined creature, they would have been out of the pool in two seconds flat,' Greg said.

'Have you seen it?' Jennifer said.

Greg nodded. 'About thirty or forty years ago, when he returned from Europe. Ask Gold to tell you that story — a very funny thing happened. But the combined creature, the whole Xuan Wu, that is not something a child would ever want to ride.'

There was a rush of air and an explosion near the gates. Michael, in Celestial Form, charged towards us, his golden face a mask of fury. He was two and a half metres tall, his skin was a deep rich gold and his hair shone blinding white in a short ponytail. He was wearing the robe that had materialised on him in Court Ten.

He stopped at the edge of the pool and pointed at John. 'You said she was dead!'

'Get the kids out of the way,' I said, rising to talk to him.

John and the Tiger took human form and floated out of the pool. John stood in front of Michael, his expression full of remorse. 'I did.'

My parents and sisters pulled the kids out of the pool and rushed them out the gates. The Tiger followed them, guarding the rear.

'I'm not going to hurt little kids,' Michael said. 'Who do you think I am?'

'Of course you won't hurt them,' Simone said, climbing out of the pool, still in her pink candy-stripe bikini. 'But we think you'll say some things that they shouldn't hear.'

'Damn straight I will,' Michael said through clenched teeth. He stared directly into John's eyes. 'You told me she was dead. You're the goddamn fucking God of War, you used to be a demon yourself, and you were wrong.'

'I was wrong,' John said. He fell to one knee and bowed his head. 'I most sincerely apologise for my misjudgement, sir, and seek to compensate you.'

'Your head would be a good start,' Michael said. 'She won't even talk to me. She blames me for all of this — she can't even hold a pen! She's living in constant pain and her life is ruined. She'll never work again — hell, she may lose her sight.'

John rose and saluted Michael. 'What can I do to make this up to you?'

I moved to stand next to John. 'Michael, why are you blaming John for this? He didn't do this to her.'

Michael glanced quickly at me. 'I would have gone in for her —'

'And been killed. Multiple times,' I said.

'At least she would know that I tried!'

'Conceded,' I said. 'But the ones to go after are the Death Mother and Kitty Kwok. They're the ones that did this.'

'They're next,' he said.

John spread his hands. 'If you want my head, it is yours.'

'Please don't kill him, Michael, I only just got him back,' Simone said softly.

Michael appeared to see Simone for the first time, and his expression changed when he saw what she was wearing. He pulled himself together. 'It wouldn't achieve anything.'

'That's a good start,' I said.

'And a finish. I'm done with you,' Michael said. He turned and went to the Tiger, who was guarding the gates the families had gone through. He fell to one knee in front of his father. 'I accept the post of Number One. Please use my skills as you see fit.'

The Tiger hesitated for a moment, then said, 'Present yourself to the Quartermaster and the Master at Arms. They have been informed and are expecting you.'

'Can I talk to Clarissa for you?' I called to Michael.

He turned and glared at me. 'Sure. Go ahead and make it worse. Oh, never mind, you *can't.*' He disappeared.

Simone went to her father and put her arm around his waist. 'Well, that ruined that.'

The Tiger came to us. 'Your family have started organising the demons to pack for them. Go to their residences and say goodbye. Michael ruined it for everybody.'

Greg and Jennifer had already finished, and were helping my mother and father direct the demons who were putting everything in boxes for them.

'Oh,' my father said, and pulled out a large photo album. 'This is for you, Emma. Where we're going we're not Donahoes any more, so you might as well take this and do what you like with it.'

I opened the book on the kitchen table. It was the family-tree research that my father had done.

He pointed to a copy of an old document. 'The first Donahoes came over to Australia from Cardiff as free settlers. Oddly enough, they chose Queensland rather than Sydney, where most of the settlers headed.' He turned the page. 'They were originally from Holyhead —'

'There's that place you were talking about,' Simone said with wonder.

'That's right. They were originally from Holy Island, but they seemed to have roots going even further back than that — in Ireland. Anyway, even though they were put on the boat to Australia as free settlers, there was some sort of trial in Holyhead that resulted in them being shipped to Cardiff and then Australia.'

'That doesn't make sense,' I said.

'It gets even stranger,' my father said. 'I finally received the parish records after weeks of waiting for them. There's notice of a trial in the parish register, but the charge isn't listed. Only that the young couple — Iain Donahoe and his wife, Brede — were found guilty of "unnatural acts". The ruling — by Judge Sean MacLaren — says that if they ever returned to Holy Island they'd be hanged.'

'Brede's maiden name was O'Breen,' my mother said. 'We were related to the O'Breens after all.'

I closed the album. 'I'll look further into this. Thanks, guys.'

My mother's voice broke. 'I'll miss you so much, Emma.'

I threw myself into her arms. 'I'll miss you too, Mum. Keep in touch, please. Email if it's safe.' I turned to hug my father. 'Dad. Thanks for putting up with me.'

'I'd put up with anything for my little girl,' he said gruffly into my shoulder. 'Look after her, John, she's very special.'

'I will,' John said. 'I know.'

'I'm going to miss you too,' Simone said, tears running down her cheeks. 'You're the only grandparents I have.' She hugged my mother. 'I love you, Nanna.'

'I love you too, little Simone,' my mother said. 'Be good for your daddy and Emma, okay?'

'Okay,' Simone said, but it came out a gasp.

The Tiger and a few of his sons turned up to take them all down to the Earthly. We had another round of hugs and they were gone.

'Let's go check on Ben and Tom,' I said.

John studied me carefully. 'Are you sure? I would understand if you needed to take some time.'

'They're not dead. I may see them again; things change. They'll be safe. Besides.' I took a deep breath. 'I think I need to keep busy.'

'I do too, I have homework,' Simone said. 'I'm heading home, okay?'

'We'll see you back home later,' John said.

Simone hugged us and was gone as well.

'I'm sure you'll see them again,' John said.

'Funnily enough, I am too,' I said.

CHAPTER 29

The Tiger drove us to his research facility on the Western Plain. John clutched the side of the jeep with his good hand and eventually spoke up.

'You drive like a maniac, Ah Bai.'

'That's because I am one.'

'May I remind you again,' I said from the back seat, 'that I'm a lowly mortal, and if you roll this thing I'm dead.'

He slowed to about a hundred kilometres an hour. 'Keep forgetting. Sorry.' He grinned over his shoulder at me. 'Roll bar will keep you safe, don't worry. I built it myself.'

'Now we have even more reason to worry,' John said.

The Tiger skidded to a halt at the front of the facility and we hopped out.

'Do you have an ultrasound facility here?' I said as we went inside and down to the genetics lab where his son was working on my blood.

'In the hospital, yes,' the Tiger said. He looked sideways at me, then broke into a huge grin and grabbed John's hand to shake it. 'Congratulations! It's about fucking time, you two.'

'I'm not pregnant,' I said. 'Kitty took one of my ovaries for experimenting, and I want to make sure the other one's still there.'

He dropped John's hand and turned away. 'Look after it.'

'After I'm sure it's there,' I said.

'We'll check after we've said hello to your people,' he said. 'One Twenty-Eight can't wait to talk to you. He has a whole lot of shit to tell you that I don't understand. You'll probably get it first time though.'

'Of course she will. She didn't have half her intelligence removed with her right gonad,' John said.

I turned to look at him; he kept his expression carefully neutral.

The Tiger didn't look back. 'I resent the implication that I have intelligence,' he said, opening the door and leading us into the lab.

One Twenty-Eight stood at a laboratory bench surrounded by biological testing pipettes. He turned and grinned his father's grin when he saw us, then fell to one knee and saluted. 'Dark Lord, Dark Lady.'

'Hey, One Two Eight,' I said. 'Where's Ben and Tom?'

'Resting. I put them through some stress tests.' He jumped to his feet, excited. 'Do I have some fascinating findings for you.'

He waved us to the end of the lab where he had a small glassed-in office. He sat behind the desk and spun the monitor so we all could see it.

'Okay. Now, Tom is fairly typical for a high-level demon, but he should be a Number One. He has blood, internal organs — everything.'

'A Number One? There can't be more than one Number One, that's the way it works,' John said, fascinated.

'Not if the other Regions work the same way ours does,' One Twenty-Eight said. 'Each of them could have their own King and Number One.'

'What if another Region didn't have someone as powerful as John to chase the demons underground?' I said.

'Then they're living on the surface and feeding off humans, same as they used to do here,' John said.

'Doesn't seem to be that way in any of the places we've been,' I said.

'That's because we've stayed away from centres of conflict,' John said. 'Where there are demons, there's bloodshed.'

'Oh.'

John leaned on the office wall and crossed his arms over his chest, wincing as he put pressure on the stump. 'Humans aren't killers by nature. You've noticed that.'

'I have,' I said. 'They have to be trained to take life. Murderers are usually mentally unstable.'

'They're happy to get into a scrap, but a lethal blow is usually an accident,' John said. 'As soon as demons interfere, you get killers. Many of them.'

'You make us sound like a bunch of puppies,' I said.

He leaned his head slightly to one side, amused. 'I guess I see humans that way sometimes.'

'Very apt description,' the Tiger said. 'Cute, adorable partners that are as dumb as shit and will bite your hand off as soon as lick it.'

'I'll tell Louise you said that,' I said.

'Pah. I've already told her that one a few times. She just rolls over and asks me to scratch her tummy.'

John raised his hand and stump in defeat. 'How about we let the scientist finish?'

'Oh no, don't mind me, this is fascinating,' One Twenty-Eight said with genuine enthusiasm. 'Insight into the way the deities see us.'

'As dinner, if you don't get a move on,' the Tiger said.

'Anyway,' One Twenty-Eight said, 'Tom, the demon: easily big eighties, but he scans as human on every test we've put him through. The only way of detecting a demon like him is the black reptile over here.'

John bowed slightly in acknowledgement.

'What about Ben?' I said.

'Ben. Now it gets good,' One Twenty-Eight said. 'Tom is a demon: he's tougher than a normal human, can take a hell of a pounding before having to slow down; he's slightly stronger than a human of his size, and of about average intelligence. Ben, on the other hand, is completely human — the Dark Lord confirms this. But he's on the ninety-ninth percentile for intelligence, the one hundred and twentieth percentile for strength —'

'He's inhumanly strong?'

'Exactly. Same for speed: he's about twice as fast as a normal human. I have him generating chi after the third try, and the man's nearly fifty.'

'That's unheard of,' John said, levering himself upright and staring at the graphs on the screen.

'I took blood,' One Twenty-Eight said. 'Tom's DNA seems to be stock-standard human normal — well, what I've unravelled of it anyway. I'm not doing the whole decoding — it would take me years, even using Lord Gold's stone technology. Ben's DNA didn't seem anything different either, until I matched it with Emma's —'

'Oh my,' I said.

'— and found some common strands in their X chromosomes. You need to be female — double-X — for the full coding to come out.'

'And that coding is?' I said.

'Snake. Of course, it's not scientifically possible for your DNA to make you change into a snake, but here we are, able to turn into animals, and we've all given up trying to work out why. You go as far as you can with science, and when the laws start breaking you stop and say, "Okay, not working any more. Celestial bullshit from here on."'

'So my mother or sisters could be snakes too?'

'It seems to have been activated by something to do with him,' One Twenty-Eight said, nodding to John. 'Something about his dark energy has made this particular DNA strand start doing stuff that it never did before. It's not just the DNA; it's the nature of the energy combining with it. Having the strand on both X chromosomes is a prerequisite as well. It's recessive, so you could be the only one in the family with the gene.'

'The demons were right,' I said with wonder. 'Strong inherent snake nature, activated by close personal contact with the biggest snake on the Plane.'

'Why is everybody constantly referring to me as the snake on the Plane?' John said, frustrated. 'It's becoming extremely annoying.'

'What?' the Tiger said, his voice rough with amusement. 'You're sick of being called a motherfucking snake —'

'Oh, shut up, that was old before he even came back,' I said. 'I'll explain later, John. What else do you have for us, One Twenty-Eight?'

He shrugged. 'That's it: a week's work with five assistants summed up in ten minutes.'

'What do we do with Ben and Tom now?'

'Take them to Holy Island,' he said. 'And bring me along as well. I seriously want to have a look at what's living there. No way is that place anything resembling normal. If it's not a gateway to the Western Plane, I'll eat my whiskers.'

'Did Ben know he's close on superhuman?' I said.

'Did you?'

That stopped me. 'No.'

'Never had any reason to test it out,' he said.

'But I sucked at PE.'

John was confused. 'PE?'

'Sport at school,' One Twenty-Eight said. 'I doubt it showed before adulthood. In fact, as a child the nonstandard DNA probably made you weaker than your peers.'

'Yeah, like I said, I sucked at PE.'

'What about schoolwork?'

I snorted with derision. 'I learned damn fast in Montford not to do too well academically. It was an open invitation for a schoolyard thrashing.'

'Your parents would be horrified to hear you say that,' John said with wonder. 'Didn't the school encourage you? Wouldn't they do something about you being bullied for achieving good results?'

'This was during the eighties,' I said. 'Bullying wasn't even a concept, and if it was, everyone pretended that it didn't happen. The teachers didn't give a damn; provided I wasn't getting those schoolyard thrashings, they were out of trouble too. I think they deliberately lowered my grades to help me out.'

'That is unbelievable,' the Tiger said.

'The West is a very strange place sometimes,' One Twenty-Eight said.

'That it is,' John said. 'If we're done here, we should go to the hospital and arrange an ultrasound. I would also like to speak to Clarissa; order her to take Michael back.'

'And you say the West is strange,' I said. 'You don't order someone to take their fiancé back. It's a decision she has to make on her own.'

'A hundred years ago, I could have ordered her to marry him on the spot and she would have had no recourse,' he said. 'It would be considered normal.'

'A hundred years ago, you would not be hoping that your son and his male partner would do something similar.'

'Conceded,' he said. 'The Jade Emperor still won't permit same-sex marriage, and it's about time someone challenged it.' His expression went wistful. 'Maybe we can use the concept of flagrantly defying the Jade Emperor's own rule to tempt Leo to remain alive.' His expression changed to mischief. 'Or I could be female when you and I get married.'

'Oh, I am behind that one hundred per cent,' the Tiger growled.

'Your ongoing slavering over my female human form is bordering on perversity,' John said.

'That's me, a furry old pervert,' the Tiger said, unfazed.

'He only has the hots for you 'cause he can't have you; same as with me,' I said.

'The thought of both of you together in female form keeps me warm at night,' the Tiger said.

John sighed. 'I really don't feel like executing you right now, Ah Bai, so give it up. You're over the line and you know it.'

'Lady Emma executed me forty-three times while you were gone,' Bai Hu said. 'Talk about perversion.'

'That was the main reason for your executions,' I said.

'Let's head to the hospital and do these tests,' John said. 'Then we'll see about lopping the head off this damn cat. Maybe Emma can make it forty-four.'

'Woo-hoo,' the Tiger said without enthusiasm, and led us out.

The ultrasound confirmed it: I still had one ovary left.

The relief turned to grief when we went to visit Clarissa. She was sitting next to the window in a wheelchair in her solitary ward. She ignored us when we came in, and we pulled up chairs to sit with her. She was bald and painfully thin, her eyes were sunken and her collarbones jutted from beneath the hospital robe. Her pale skin was traced with a network of blue veins and her hands were curled up like claws.

'Do you know what they did to us?' she said without looking away from the window.

'The boys won't tell us the details,' John said. 'I know Kitty was feeding off all of you.'

'Kitty and the other one made bets every feeding session on whether or not this would be the one that killed me,' Clarissa said mildly.

I touched her hand. 'You're safe now.'

'I don't feel safe.' She turned and studied my face as if seeing it for the first time. 'When they brought the boys in and put them in the next cage, I was so happy because I had someone to talk to. We shared stories about living on the Celestial Plane.' She smiled slightly. 'Not all it's cracked up to be, actually.' Her face went expressionless. 'She fed off them too. That meant she took less of me, and I would live longer. For some stupid reason, I was glad that I'd live longer.' Her voice gained a desperate edge. 'I was sure Michael would come to get me.'

'I told Michael you were dead,' John said. 'It is my fault he did not come searching for you.'

'I understand that,' she said. She was silent for a long moment, then she said, 'They raped the boys.' Her voice cracked. 'They never touched me, but those bitches raped the boys. They cried and begged them to stop, and the women laughed and kept asking them if they were enjoying it.'

'We didn't know,' I said.

'I need to tell their families,' John said.

'They raped them so systematically and so often — collecting semen — that the boys bled when they did it, but they did it anyway.'

'Genetic material,' John said.

'They made me watch,' Clarissa said, her voice still mild.

'Would you like to talk to them?' I said.

She raised her hands. 'I got out, you know. They tried to make me contribute to one of their little … sessions, and the minute I was out of the cage I took off. I made a run for it, and they caught me and did this to me.' She stretched her fingers slightly, but they remained bent. 'That's as far as they go. They hit me with some sort of black stuff, then they electrocuted me, then they beat me, and then they threw me back in the cage.'

'If it's any consolation, we will find them and stop them,' I said.

She shrugged, making the gown hang off her even more. 'Nope.'

'Would you like to go home to your parents?' John said.

'And watch my dad fool around while Mom's in China again? No, thanks,' Clarissa said. She dropped her hands into her lap. 'I'll stay here for a while, then decide what to do.'

'Michael's heartbroken that you won't see him, Clarissa.'

She looked out the window. 'He's one of them. You're all them. You're just as bad as those women are.' She turned back to speak to John. 'How many did you lose? More than a hundred, and look at you. Not even slightly concerned.'

'I am a general. That is my army. When you go into battle, you expect casualties,' John said. 'My soldiers know that they may have to pay the ultimate price for the safety of those on the Planes. That is what being a soldier is; and I honour them for it.'

'I'm not a soldier,' Clarissa said.

'And by all the rules of engagement, you are a non-combatant and should have remained untouched,' John said.

'Yeah, sure. Right. I see. I'm just collateral damage. A non-combatant caught in the crossfire. Another person trying to keep her head down and getting hit anyway,' Clarissa said. She turned back to the window. 'Could you leave me alone now? I don't think I have anything more to say to you.'

'Let Michael come talk to you,' I said. 'He can help you.'

'He's Immortal now, isn't he?' Clarissa said without looking away from the window.

'That he is,' John said.

'Then I don't think I ever want to see him again. I doubt the mighty Immortal wants to have anything much to do with the little broken human girl.'

'He does,' I said. 'He loves you. He refused Immortality because he thought you were dead.'

'Just go now,' she said, not hearing me. 'I'm tired, and I'm done with all of you. Leave me alone.'

'Can we come back later?' I said, but she ignored me.

She didn't look away from the window as John quietly led me out.

We made a stop at the halls on top of the Mountain before we returned to our offices. A group of seniors was practising hand-to-hand on the square in front of the halls, led by Liu in his saffron robes. John stopped to watch them for a moment, and the students didn't hesitate, continuing the set. John nodded with satisfaction and we moved on.

We went around the edge of the square and up the steps to the entrance of Dragon Tiger. The hall, at fifty metres long, was slightly smaller than Yuzhengong and faced east. Incense smoke and the chanting of the Buddhist nuns floated from inside. The statues of the Three Purities that normally resided in the hall had been moved to Yuzhengong, and rosewood tables were set against its walls. A group of four nuns, bald and tiny in their plain brown robes, knelt at the centre chanting the sutras. They didn't look up when we entered.

The tables on all three sides of the hall held photographs of the dead, with candles either side of them and offerings of food and flowers in front. Similar memorials had been set up in Taoist temples back down on the Earthly. The photographs would remain here, honoured by the sutras, for six weeks, until the Taoist ceremony of passing over with the symbolic travel of the soul to the Higher Plane and the burning of the paper effigies for the next life. Then the photographs would be sent to the families, and red wooden tablets embossed in gold with the students' names would be placed in cabinets in Taoist temples near to the families' homes.

Some of the remains had already been cremated and moved to cemeteries. In Hong Kong, these were multistorey concrete buildings with niches for the ashes, ideally placed for fung shui on hillsides overlooking the water. We had made the decision not to purchase burial plots for any of the students resident in Asia: so many people being buried in the ultra-expensive plots by the same group at once would attract attention.

We stopped inside the temple door and lit incense to place in the large brazier before the nuns, paying our respects to all the dead. Heads bowed, we contemplated the suffering this Heavenly war had caused, then rose, bowed to the nuns — who continued to ignore us — and went to perform the same ritual at Purple Mist, which was also hosting remembrances for the dead.

Jade and Gold were waiting for us at the bottom of the steps as we emerged, and fell into step beside us as we returned to the offices. Jade held a clipboard and spoke as we walked.

'I've arranged all the funerals, my Lord, my Lady. I have written a press release, and I'm in the middle of personally speaking to all the families concerned.'

440

'Any over-enthusiastic media attention?' I said.

'None to report. They're seeing it as "just another earthquake in China".'

'Good.'

'Nothing further?' John said.

'All is handled.'

'Keep us updated on the schedules for the funerals. I would like to attend as many as I can,' I said.

She nodded. 'Ma'am.'

'Dismissed,' John said.

Jade bowed slightly to us and peeled off to return to her office.

'I have Zara in the Dark Lord's office; you said you wanted to see the recordings around her damage,' Gold said.

We passed under a tree in a small courtyard, and a group of juniors who were studying together watched us with awe as we passed, then quickly dropped and saluted us.

John gestured towards the students as he spoke to Gold. 'Let the more junior ones know the protocol, Gold. Someone should have told them.'

Gold nodded. 'Understood.'

When we reached the small courtyard in the centre of the administrative complex, John stopped. He smiled slightly, and Gold and I waited for him.

The quality of the air changed, becoming cooler and softer. Fat snowflakes drifted down among us, and I held my hand out to catch one, its icy coldness stinging my palm. They melted as they touched the ground.

John inhaled deeply and let it out again. 'Now I feel at home.'

He continued to his office, with Gold and me following him through the lightly floating snow.

'Don't waste your energy on weather manipulation,' I said.

He sat at his desk in his office, the French doors on two sides behind him framing the falling snow. 'I didn't. That was natural.'

'Quickly check for your Serpent then,' I said as Gold and I sat across from him.

'Already,' he said, and turned to Zara, who was sitting on his desk in the form of a rough diamond, five centimetres across. 'Is there anything interesting either side of the damage?'

'There is something you should see,' Zara said.

The room expanded and collapsed, and we were in a beautiful indoor garden, where channels of water ran between raised brick planters filled with shrubs. The walls were fifty metres away, white framed with brown wood; and there didn't appear to be a ceiling. It was full of light coming from everywhere at once, but there were no visible light sources. The Demon King and Rhonda were strolling side by side through the garden, talking. He was in his young human form, with blood red hair, wearing a pair of maroon jeans and a black silk shirt. She was wearing a simple sundress of bright coral and turquoise flowers that accentuated her pale beauty.

'There is no need for the sun,' he said, his hands clasped behind his back. 'This part of Hell is a place of joy and light. Take a deep breath.'

She inhaled, and her expression filled with wonder. 'It smells like roses, and freesias, and jonquils. It's lovely.'

He smiled slightly. 'Just for you.'

She stopped and sat on the edge of a planter. 'I know that there are places here that aren't nearly as sweet.'

He stopped as well, still with his hands clasped behind his back. 'That's true. And you never need to see them if you don't wish to.'

She shook her head. 'It won't work, you know.'

He shrugged, smiling wryly. 'Worth a try.' He turned away.

'How many more days do I have here?' she said. 'I'm losing track of them.'

'Only a couple more, my Lady,' the King said. He gestured towards the end of the garden. 'You could always come and spend the night in my villa instead of your own.'

She shook her head. 'You've said that every evening.' She looked up. 'It's never night or day here, is it? It's so artificial.'

'It's night in some parts.'

'I don't want to see them.'

'You never have to.' He bowed slightly to her. 'I bid you good night, madam. And I leave my bedroom door open.'

She sighed. 'Good night, George.'

She turned and went into the villa, and closed the door behind her. She went into the bathroom, changed into bright floral pyjamas, climbed into bed and turned the light off. Nothing happened for a few minutes, then the recording froze.

'Neither of you saw that?' Gold said.

'I didn't see anything,' I said.

'No,' John said.

The recording blinked back to when Rhonda was in bed, and stopped. It moved slowly through the frames: there were two bright flashes, then she was in bed again.

'I saw that,' I said. 'What was it?'

'I will show you at the slowest speed,' Zara said. 'This is right at the edge of the damage to the lattice.'

'One intersection on the lattice is one frame of the recording,' Gold said. 'Zara wasn't keeping the frame rate high — this was just a standard recording for personal use — so it will look a little like film.'

'I should have kept a high frame rate throughout the time I was there,' Zara said ruefully. 'After five days, I relaxed; I thought his intentions were honest.'

She moved the recording back to when Rhonda was in bed. Then came a black frame, half-filled with colour.

'Garbage from the edge of the damage,' Zara said.

A horrible, grinning face filled the entire recording, its eyes level with the top, and black stains over it.

I inhaled sharply. It was Demon Prince Six, the expert at manipulating stones.

'How much time was lost?' I said.

'Four hours,' Zara said. 'I cycled down to rest, and wasn't aware of the lost time.'

'What about your time stamp?' I said. 'That's impossible.'

'It is,' Zara said. 'I have no idea how it happened. Somehow Six managed to blank out my matrix without stopping the time stamp. I was unaware of the lost time until we discovered Clarissa had been taken, and we went through to check.'

'Is there anything like that where Clarissa was taken?' John said.

'I'll show you,' Zara said.

Michael and Clarissa appeared, walking through a factory building on Ap Lei Chau Island on the south side of Hong Kong that had been rented out to stores selling imported Asian furniture and homewares. They wandered through the store, discussing whether they should buy a coffee table made out of a Balinese longhouse door. Clarissa kissed Michael on the cheek, then went out to the lift lobby to the ladies' room. She stopped at the mirror and smiled at her reflection, then went into the cubicle.

'I don't want to see this,' I said. 'That's invasion of privacy.'

'I'll blank out the video; it's the audio you need to hear anyway,' Zara said.

There were the sounds of clothing being adjusted, then water spilling, and Zara slowed the playback, making it deeper. There was a sudden loud screech of noise, then the audio returned to normal. Clarissa came out of the cubicle, rinsed her hands, and returned to Michael.

'That's it?' I said.

'That's it. One-fifth of a second of sound. It has to be: there's damage around that point and nowhere else in my lattice.'

'They are unbelievably skilled,' Gold said. 'Frankly, it's more than a little scary.'

'The Demon King allowed Six into Rhonda's villa,' John said.

'He can't have,' I said. 'While you were gone, I asked the King and he vowed he wasn't in league with them. I had a suspicion he was helping them, but he gave his word he wasn't. Six must have sneaked in by himself.'

'Interesting,' John said.

'I have failed you,' Zara said.

'Yes, you have,' John said. 'But failure in the face of opposition as skilled as this is not cause for discipline. It is cause for retribution. It is time to find these demons and neutralise them.'

'How do we find them?' I said.

'Gold. Take Emma's stone and wake it up. I don't care how you do it. It knows where they are.'

Gold bowed slightly. 'I will do my best.'

'The Tiger just put it back in its setting — take the whole ring,' I said, handing it over.

'Leave it with me,' Gold said. 'I will talk to the people in the Eastern Palace. They may have some high-technology way of waking the stone up.'

'I'm sure they'd be delighted to see you,' I said.

'Dismissed,' John said. After Gold had gone, he leaned back in his executive chair and studied me. 'Lady Emma, I have a request to make of you.'

'Oh no, this sounds formal,' I said.

'I have much to catch up on, my Lady, and I request that you give me an hour until dinnertime to do so. I also request that you take yourself to our residence and rest until dinner, because frankly, my love, you look awful.'

'My in-tray's probably piled higher than yours,' I said.

'Zara,' John said loudly.

'My Lord?'

'Liaise with Lady Emma's secretary, sort through her in-tray and find all tasks that can be done by someone else, and bring them to me,' he said. 'Then find all tasks that must be done by Lady Emma herself, and also bring them to me.'

'My Lord,' Zara said, and disappeared off his desk.

'Now go and have a lie-down, Emma,' John said, rising to guide me out of his office. 'I need you strong.'

I wanted to argue with him, but I didn't have the strength.

CHAPTER 30

Leo didn't join us for dinner that evening; he'd been spending most of his time in Persimmon Tree with Martin. When we'd finished eating, he came to visit us by himself, waiting for us in the Throne Room.

Simone came out of the dining room, stopped in front of him, saw his face and put her hands on her hips. 'You suck.'

'That's why I'm doing this,' he said.

She crouched in front of his wheelchair and put her hands on his knees. 'Is there anything at all I can say to stop you?'

He shook his head, silent.

She stood up, appeared as if she was about to hit him, then sagged, defeated. 'I won't be able to watch.'

'I don't want you to.'

She leaned down to hug him, then broke down and went out.

'You agreed,' Leo said to John. 'Stop putting this off. I want it.'

John concentrated for a moment.

'Don't even think about making another excuse to put it off!' Leo said. 'The nest in Singapore is cleaned out, and you'll soon find Kitty and fix her. You don't need me any more, so stop putting it off and do it already!'

'I was checking my appointments,' John said. 'I have nothing until tomorrow afternoon.'

'Tomorrow morning then,' Leo said, and turned to wheel himself out.

'Leo —' I said, but he cut me off.

'I failed,' he said. 'I've failed systematically and consistently ever since I joined this household. I deserve this.'

'You're family,' I said. 'We love you whatever you do.'

'Then love me enough to let me go.' He nodded to John. 'Tomorrow morning, 9am.'

'Done,' John said. He leaned on the back of the couch. 'You break my heart, Leo. You are one of the finest humans I have ever met.'

'Then I'll be honoured to be one with you,' Leo said, and left.

I went to John, and he wrapped his arm around me, and we stood silently for a while.

In the bathroom later that evening, as we were preparing for bed, I unwound the bandage that I kept on my arm to hide the demon essence, and stopped when I saw it. The essence had seeped through the bandage, and when I touched my arm, my fingers came away black.

'John,' I said, trying to keep the urgency from my voice.

He came in wearing his pyjama pants and carefully studied my arm without touching the essence. He picked the bandage up and used it to mop at the essence; it came away onto the bandage in a sticky stain.

'It's breaking down because you're on the Celestial Plane,' he said. 'It's like a demon exploding on the Plane, but in slow-motion because you're mostly human.'

'How long before I lose my arm?'

'I have no idea,' he said, still focused on the arm. 'Wrap it again, and we will clear it tomorrow for you.' He concentrated on me. 'Does it hurt?'

'No,' I said, finding another roll of bandage.

'If it hurts you during the night, wake me and we will clear it. Otherwise, I think you are safe until morning. It has taken a few days for it to break down this far.'

'Now you're scaring me.'

'You're scaring me,' he said. 'Unlike me, you can't grow it back.'

The pain woke me at 3am. I sat up, looked with horror at my arm, and gently shoved John. 'Wake up. I think we need to do something.'

He rolled over, sat up, saw my arm and concentrated.

We reappeared in the temporary infirmary, and John went around the room switching on the lights. 'Meredith and Edwin will be here shortly.'

I raised my arm: the essence was dripping off it onto the treatment couch, as thick as black tar. John pulled a large examination light towards me and shone it on the arm. It was already a centimetre narrower, and the structure of the bones inside was becoming visible as the external part dissolved.

He glanced up at me. 'Meredith will put you under and we'll do it.'

'Start now,' I said.

'I need Edwin to open me up.'

'Edwin's human, it'll take him a while to get here.' I tried to control the urgency in my voice. 'I'm losing my arm!' My hand was becoming numb, and the pain in the bones was more than I could bear. 'Do something — it's killing me!'

John scrabbled through the medical cabinets until he found a scalpel. He tore the sterile wrapper open with his teeth. 'Sit still and put the arm out.' He ripped the

449

bandages off his left arm with the scalpel, then used it to roughly tear open the stump. He took my right hand with his and held the bleeding stump above the damage. 'Keep very still, and if it hurts too much, I'll stop.'

I closed my eyes and tried to go to a calm place, centring my awareness between my eyes and separating it from the rest of my body, but it didn't help when he touched his blood to my arm. I managed to stay silent, quivering with the shock of each touch, my teeth gritted so hard that my head ached nearly as much as the arm hurt.

I heard Meredith and Edwin come in.

'You should have waited for us,' Meredith said.

'See this and tell me that again,' John said.

Meredith was quiet for a moment, then put her hands on either side of my head. 'Sorry I took so long,' she said gently, and everything faded away.

'You're not weak from blood loss?' Edwin said to John. 'Let me take your blood pressure.'

'You don't need to bother; I know how bad it is,' John said. 'I've sustained more damage than I can handle in the last forty-eight hours. But I can manage. You really don't need to wait. Go back to bed.'

'She's coming around,' Meredith said.

I tried to focus, but everything was blurry. I rubbed my eyes, but my right arm wouldn't move; it was tied down. I ripped it free and jumped off the couch.

'Emma, relax, you're on the Mountain,' John said. 'Find another sling for the arm, Edwin.'

I peered around me, trying to focus, and saw a dark shape. I concentrated on it — it was him. I threw myself at him and he held me.

'Did you save it?' I said. 'I can't see anything.'

He pushed me gently away and his face swam into view. I released him and checked my right arm. It was

450

significantly smaller than it had been; the muscles wasted and the bones visible as shapes beneath the skin. I stepped further back from John and flexed my hand, moving my arm through the air. I settled into my feet and performed a few basic hand-to-hand moves, and the arm worked. I sighed with relief.

'Can we bring it back to the way it was?' I said.

'I don't know,' Edwin said. 'With exercise and physical therapy we may be able to rebuild the muscles. But we've never seen anything like this before —'

'Yeah, I know the drill,' I said. 'Thanks so much for your help, guys. Now go back to bed. We have work to do tomorrow.'

'Both of you need to sleep as well,' Edwin said. 'I'll have your appointments cancelled until lunchtime. Rest.'

'It's freezing out there. Take my hand and I'll carry us home,' John said.

'You should walk!' Edwin said, but it was too late.

John went to the fire in our bedroom and poked the embers until they flared back into life, then crawled into bed next to me. 'Edwin doesn't need to cancel any appointments; we only have one tomorrow morning. Now come here, hold me close, and go to sleep.'

I snuggled into him. 'Yes, sir.' I lifted my head. 'One appointment?'

'One.'

I dropped my head again, my throat thick. 'Damn.'

The next morning dawned bright, clear and cold. The sun was brilliant overhead, making the Golden Temple glow. We did it on the steps just below the Golden Temple, high above the Mountain complex, so there was no chance of John draining anyone but Leo. Leo had agreed to let me and Martin attend; he'd said his goodbyes to everyone else and a small group of distraught students stood on the square in front of Yuzhengong below us.

John sat at the top of the steps in front of Golden Temple while Leo and Martin said goodbye a few steps below him. John's face was expressionless but his eyes were dark with misery.

Leo embraced Martin, and Martin held him like he would never let him go. They kissed, a farewell kiss between lovers, and Martin told Leo softly that he loved him. Leo just smiled, put his hand on Martin's cheek, and turned away.

Leo went to John at the top of the stairs and sat on the steps next to him. I fell to sit as well, my legs weak. Martin came to sit next to me and put his arm around my shoulders, and I leaned into him. He passed me a packet of tissues and I nodded my thanks as I pulled one out to wipe my eyes.

John smiled a sad smile and gazed into Leo's eyes. He ran his fingertips over Leo's face, as if seeing him for the first time, and slid his palm over Leo's neck. Leo closed his eyes with bliss.

'You were like a son to me,' John said, holding the side of Leo's face.

'You are more to me,' Leo said.

'One last time to change your mind.'

'Please make me one with you, John.'

John drew Leo closer and kissed him, and Leo closed his eyes, relishing the touch. Leo pushed the kiss deeper, more passionate, and his Shen energy flared to life, shining so brightly that even the Golden Temple seemed to dim next to it. John's dark nature became visible, a cloud centring on him, and Leo's light was drawn into it, spiralling away inside John. Leo became transparent, then suddenly wrenched his face away from John's and stared at him in horror. 'Not you.'

'John, stop,' I said, standing to go up to them.

Martin held me back. 'He can't, it's too late. Leo's gone.'

John lowered his head and his face became rigid with restraint. He dropped his arms from Leo and clenched his remaining hand to a fist by his side. His face became more and more strained as he raised his head, the dark energy glowing around him. He let loose a roar of anguish, an inhuman sound of agony, and disappeared.

Leo sat there in a daze for a moment, then toppled sideways, hitting the steps hard.

Martin and I rushed to him and lifted him. Martin put Leo's head into his lap and his hand on Leo's forehead. 'Father gave it back,' he said. 'He's still here.'

Leo's eyes snapped open. He grabbed Martin's hand and clutched it. 'I closed my eyes, and it wasn't him, it was you. All this time, I thought I wanted him, and when I finally had him, I wanted it to be you.'

'You have me for as long as you want me, Lion,' Martin said, his voice thick with emotion.

'I can't believe how stupid I've been.' Leo raised one hand from the ground and touched Martin's face, his own full of wonder. 'I love you.'

Martin broke down into silent sobs and I handed back the packet of tissues. He nodded his thanks.

'How do I face everybody now?' Leo said, still prone on the ground.

Martin squeezed his hand. 'By my side.'

'Always,' Leo said. He tried to pull himself upright, and Martin helped him. 'Geez, he could at least have healed my spine.'

'Maybe the Serpent will one day,' I said.

Martin glanced meaningfully at me, and I stood up before he said anything. 'I have places to be. I'll see you guys later.'

I walked back down to the main area, leaving them on top of the Mountain together. The group of students was waiting expectantly for me. Simone was with them.

'He changed his mind,' I said to them, and they whooped and cheered. 'He's alive and he's planning to stay that way.'

One of the students rushed towards the stairs, and I called to stop him. 'Leave them alone, they're having a moment. Wait till they come back down, okay?'

The student stopped, nodded with a huge grin, and returned to the group.

Simone threw her arm around my shoulders, brash with delight. 'We should arrange a wedding for them too.'

'The Jade Emperor won't allow it,' I said.

'Why not? They love each other. They want to be together. Isn't that enough?'

'Not for the Jade Emperor. He defines marriage as between a man and a woman and won't budge on it.'

'My own father spent a week being a woman and the Jade Emperor won't stop you two from getting married. What difference does it make?'

I turned and glanced back at the gleaming golden temple with the dark-clad couple sitting on the steps below it. 'None at all. Hopefully we'll see times change.' I turned back. 'Let's go find something to eat, I'm starving.'

'Daddy's down in the Grotto, and he says pilchards, please.'

'Humph.'

Gold came to us later in the afternoon after trying to revive my stone.

'We can't do anything for it,' he said. 'We hooked it into the Tree's network and got nothing. There are two options now, and both of them are difficult.'

'What are they?' I said, feeling relieved as I slipped the ring back onto my finger. I tapped the stone and it pulsed in response.

'Take it to the Lady Nu Wa — she is its creator and may be able to awaken it. Or take it to the Grandmother herself.'

'I don't think I could make it all the way to Nu Wa by myself right now,' John said. He leaned his chin in his hand. 'And going to the Grandmother is too far to travel in the current circumstances. This may have to wait until everything is dealt with.'

'But it was with me when Kitty and the Death Mother took me to their boat,' I said. 'It knows where they are — we have to get that information out of it.'

John shrugged. 'Keeping our students safe and making sure full respects are paid to our casualties is just as important.'

My mobile phone rang. I pulled it out of my pocket, checked the caller ID and flipped it open. 'Ronnie. Go ahead and tell me that you know exactly what's going on right now. You seemed to know every single other time.'

'I don't, ma'am, and that's why I'm calling you. I haven't known anything for days, since you returned to the Mountain, and I'm concerned for your stone.'

'That bastard was telling you what we were doing?' I said, glaring at the stone.

'No, I wear its daughter as a piece of jewellery...' His voice moved away from the phone. 'Ow! Okay, she doesn't like that. She's actually my partner —'

'And you never told us?' I said.

'She's in hiding ... She pissed off a tree spirit and it wants to chop her up. She's not ready to be a mother, so she's sitting on me until it blows over.'

'I've never seen you wearing a stone as jewellery,' I said.

'She's on a chain around my neck, she looks like a Buddhist medallion.' He moved his mouth away from the phone. 'Talk to them.'

'I don't want to talk to them!' a woman's voice said.

'But how did she know what we were doing?' I said.

Ronnie hesitated for a moment, then said, 'Well, it's her father. She misses the Celestial Plane, so it tells her stories, and sometimes it tells her when you need me.'

'I am going to kill it when it comes around,' I said.

'It's unconscious?'

'Kitty and the Death Mother did something to it. It was in a nest where they were building demon copies and holding humans to feed off. John brought it home, and it's been silent since.'

'Has Gold tried to wake it up?' the female Shen said, her voice still tinny in the background.

'Here, you talk to her,' Ronnie said, and there was the sound of the phone being handed over.

'You are the cause of a huge Heavenly security breach, you know that?' I said. 'Ronnie may have turned, but he's still one hundred per cent demon and he should not have known the details of our Mountain activities.'

'Are you the Dark Lord?' she said.

'No, this is me, Emma Donahoe. The one who's holding your dad. Gold's had a look at the stone —'

'Hi, Jie Jie,' Gold said, joining the call in conference mode.

'Di Di,' she said. 'What have you done with Dad so far? To try to bring him round?'

'If he heard you calling him "he" he'd have an attack,' Gold said. 'I took him to the Tree and plugged him into the network to try to bring him around with an information dump.'

'I've heard they're doing some excellent work over there. Did you get anything?'

'No. Next stop is probably either Nu Wa or Grandma.'

'What about an electric shock? Did you take him to see Thunderbolt?'

Gold's expression went blank, then filled with wonder. 'I never thought of that.'

'That's why you're the runt of the litter,' she said.

'You'll have to go into hiding from Dad too,' Gold said.

'Just take Dad to Thunderbolt, and if that doesn't work try Nu Wa or the Grandmother. But Thunderbolt can probably do it.'

'I think you're right.'

'I thought Thunderbolt had stopped his research with stones when the East took over,' John said.

'He did,' Gold said. 'But knowing him, he probably has all the equipment sitting in his lab gathering dust. We should go have a look.'

'Give me a moment,' John said. 'Very well, I've ordered him to receive you. Head off to the Celestial Palace.'

I returned the ring to Gold, who saluted John and disappeared.

'Does Thunderbolt really have wings and a beak?' I said.

'Yes,' John said. 'Poor fellow, his human form is as unremarkable as his True Form is extreme. The Jade Emperor learned a valuable lesson there: it's all very well to change someone's form to make them a better warrior, but they have to live with the consequences.'

'The Jade Emperor did that to him?'

'It was a long time ago. He helped end the Shang/Zhou — without him it would have dragged on another hundred years and thousands would have died — but he paid the price.' He raised his head. 'Jade is here.'

Jade came in, bowed to both of us, and handed John a piece of paper. 'This is the final schedule for the remaining funerals. Christian ones are so much harder to organise!'

'There are three down at North Point tomorrow,' John said, studying the list. 'We should go. There's nothing urgent here that needs handling.'

The next morning, a bleak autumnal Hong Kong day, we arrived outside the funeral home. I wore a black skirt suit with a black T-shirt under the jacket; John did his usual thing of wearing a black suit with black shirt and tie. Funereal flower arrangements lined the sidewalk: all yellow and white chrysanthemums, with banners showing the names of those who had donated them. We went inside to the lobby, which had green tiles on the floor and walls, with a pair of old lifts in one wall. Jade was waiting for us next to the lifts.

'First one is on the third floor,' she said, pushing the button. 'Nearly done; they've been here the full five days, this is the last day.'

'I'm glad we could make it,' John said, putting his hands into his pants pockets and leaning on the wall of the lift.

On the third floor, three funeral rooms led off from the foyer, each double-doored with the name of the deceased on a stand outside. Jade guided us into the first room. 'Tillie Chung.'

'I remember her,' I said as we went in. 'Talented first year.'

The room was five metres long and four wide: one of the smaller rooms. Chairs were lined up as though in a church, facing the altar which held Tillie's photograph flanked by large candles. Behind the photograph was the glass viewing room, where her embalmed corpse lay. Her family, all wearing the symbolic white of mourning, knelt on a rattan mat to one side. Flower arrangements on bamboo stands lined the walls.

We went to the table to one side of the entrance and paid our respects, signing the guest book and receiving a white packet with a candy to sweeten our sadness. We walked up the aisle to the front row of chairs and one of the officiators moved to stand next to the photograph. He ordered us to bow three times, and we did, with the family carefully not looking at us. Then we bowed once to the family and approached them. They rose to speak to us.

John shook their hands. 'I am John Chen, Master of the Wudang Academy where Tillie was learning. This is my partner, Miss Donahoe.'

'Thank you for coming,' Tillie's father said. 'And for your generosity in providing for the funeral. Your secretary, Jade, has been wonderful.'

'It is the least we could do,' John said.

'My condolences,' I said. 'So many were lost.'

Tillie's mother gestured towards John's arm. 'Did you lose that at the same time?'

'I did, and Miss Donahoe's arm was crushed. The survivors were lucky.'

'Tillie sent us letters. She said you were very special, and she was having a wonderful time, and she wished she could tell us how great it was,' Tillie's father said. 'I'm glad she was so happy.'

Tillie's mother broke down. She pulled a packet of tissues out of her bag, then turned away.

Tillie's father stared up into John's face. 'Tillie said you were something very special, sir. I wonder what she meant.'

'Many of my students say that,' John said. 'I think it is because my students go so far once they have learnt the Arts from us. Many of them go on to successful careers in show business, even if it is behind the scenes.

It is said that my Academy makes up half the film industry here.'

'I understand,' Tillie's father said. He gestured towards the glass viewing area. 'Would you like to see?'

We nodded, and he guided us past the screen in front of the area where the corpse was visible. Tillie's body was glossy and artificial in death, petrified by chemicals. It wasn't her any more. The Tillie I knew had been a joyful student, full of life and wonder, delighted to be doing what she loved every day. What I saw here was a shell; the Tillie I knew was gone.

I pulled a packet of tissues from my bag and wiped my eyes, then couldn't help myself and let go. John put his arm around my shoulders.

'You were right,' I said through the gasps.

'I'm sorry,' Tillie's father said, touching my arm in sympathy.

'She was a lovely girl. We will all miss her,' I said, trying to control my sobs and failing.

Everything has caught up with you, we should take you home, John said.

I shook my head into the tissue.

John led me back to the family, and shook Tillie's father's hand again. 'If there is anything you need, let Jade know.'

Tillie's father nodded to John. 'Thank you.' He touched me on the arm again. 'And thank you.'

John bowed slightly, and led me out.

Jade was waiting outside the room with her clipboard. 'Oh, my Lady,' she said.

'Take her to the side and let her work it out of her system,' John said. 'We should take her home.'

'No,' I said into the tissues. 'Just let me do some deep breathing and I'll be able to continue. Could you get me a bottle of water, Jade?'

Jade went to a corner of the lobby, facing away from us, to conjure the water bottle.

'I don't know how many hundreds of times I have attended events like this,' John said, holding me around the shoulders. 'And every time it is as if it is the first.'

Jade handed me the bottle of water. I took a few sips and nodded that I was okay. 'What's next?'

'Two more here,' she said. 'One on the fifth floor, and one on the sixth. That is all for Hong Kong for today; we have more in other cities.'

'How many?' John said.

'Three in China; one in Shanghai, two in Beijing. One in Kuala Lumpur — a Muslim one, so we have to be there right on time to attend. A Christian one in Singapore — again, we have to be right on time. European and American ones are next week, all Western style.'

'I don't think we'll be able to make them all,' John said.

Jade nodded. 'I don't think anybody would expect you to.'

'I do,' John said.

We went into the lift and Jade pressed the button.

Gold and Thunderbolt were waiting for us outside John's office when we returned later that afternoon. They rose and saluted John, and he waved them into the office with us. Thunderbolt was a small, middle-aged Chinese man with thick glasses and unruly hair, in a pair of plain jeans and a tatty Atari T-shirt.

'Anything major?' John said as he sat behind the desk.

'No, my Lord,' Zara said.

'Good. Out,' John said, and Zara disappeared. He spun in his chair to see Gold and Thunderbolt. 'Well?'

'Could you soak the stone and freeze it while I send a shock through it?' Thunderbolt said.

461

'Will that hurt it?' I said.

'Yes,' Gold said. 'But we need to know where Kitty's base is.'

'How cold?' John said.

'As cold as you can go,' Thunderbolt said.

John smiled slightly. 'I won't destroy the world just to bring a stone back.'

'You can go that cold?' Thunderbolt said with disbelief.

'I can do Absolute Zero,' John said.

Thunderbolt stared at him. 'But that's scientifically impossible.'

'So am I. How cold?' John said.

'Twenty degrees above?'

'Done,' John said. He rubbed his chin. 'Now to find somewhere to do it.'

'North Pole?' Gold said. 'Is that too far?'

'I don't want to go more than a couple of hundred kilometres,' John said.

'Go straight up,' I said. 'Do it in space.'

'Can you do that, my Lord?' Gold said.

John turned to me. 'Want to come? I don't think you've ever been in orbit; it's about time you saw what it's like.'

'Can you keep me alive while you're freezing the stone?'

He hesitated for a moment, then said, 'Let me see.' He raised his hand above the desk and a sphere of water appeared, floating beneath it. He concentrated, and the water shrank slightly, condensation mist coming off it. 'That's supercooled,' he said. 'If you like, I can supercool water around the stone, and we can solidify the water at the same time that you put a shock through it.' The condensation mist around the water sphere disappeared and it hovered, perfectly clear and still.

'How cold is that?' Thunderbolt said.

'A hundred Kelvin at the moment; about minus a hundred and seventy C,' John said. 'I've had to put a vacuum around it; if it touches the molecules in the air it will crystallise.'

'Damn, sir, that's impossible,' Thunderbolt said with awe. His mouth fell open. 'How fast would a silicon processor go at those temperatures?'

'Fastest computer in the world,' Gold said. 'That's going to hurt Dad like hell.'

John snapped his wrist over the sphere and it froze with a loud crack. The air around it filled with ice crystals, which shattered outwards. I quickly ducked to avoid the tiny needles that flew towards me. Just as quickly, they changed to a cloud of warm moisture and disappeared.

'Sorry,' John said. 'Maybe Emma shouldn't come with us.'

'If that doesn't wake Dad up, nothing will,' Gold said.

John shrugged. 'Let's go up and try.'

I followed them out of the office and to the courtyard in front of Yuzhengong. A group of students was practising a tai chi set with Meredith.

John raised one hand towards them. 'We need some space. Move to the side.'

After the students had moved, Gold, Thunderbolt and John all changed to True Form. Gold took his stone shape, and John was a massive black Turtle, four metres from nose to tail. Thunderbolt lost his clothes, grew to three metres tall, and tan-coloured feathers sprang out all over him. He grew a pair of wings with a span of three metres, and a vicious predatory beak replaced his face. The three of them took off vertically and the back blast nearly knocked us over. The ground shook as they broke the sound barrier about half a kilometre above us, and they were gone.

Meredith moved the students back into formation.

'If the Dark Lord broke any windows, his shell is mine,' I said, and went to my office.

They returned an hour later. John came into my office and handed the stone back.

'We couldn't torture it any more,' he said. 'We had to stop. It screamed a couple of times, but apart from that we gained nothing.'

I wanted to give the stone a hug but it was too small. 'So what do we do now?'

'I will contact Nu Wa and the Grandmother. One of them must be able to help us.'

'But both are so far to travel,' I said.

He dropped his head and sighed. 'I know. This may have to wait until I am stronger.'

'It can wait,' I said. 'The demons lost their entire Singapore facility; it will take them a while to rebuild.'

He turned to go out. 'I hope you're right. Dinner in thirty.'

I saluted him. 'Sir.'

CHAPTER 31

Simone was cheerful over breakfast the next morning. 'I've had a major breakthrough with Freddo. I'm going over there after school today, so I won't be home until later this evening — is that all right?'

'What breakthrough?' I said.

She smiled broadly, full of pride. 'Full control of the Implement of Doom. It no longer disobeys him, and stays put when I give him a cuddle.'

'That's good to hear,' I said.

'So it's okay? If I'm a bit late home?' she said, not as confident.

'Not a problem at all.'

'You can bring him here if you like,' John said. 'Put him in the stables in the Northern Heavens.'

She leaned her chin in her hand over her congee bowl. 'Now that we're further along, that sounds like a good idea.' She jumped up and grabbed her schoolbag. 'I have poisons today, and my teacher says that if you see any of those plant demons again, grab a piece. It's something completely new.'

'Hopefully we cleaned them out and there's none left,' John said.

She kissed each of us and disappeared.

'The school principal hasn't pulled me in and laid down the law yet,' John said, musing.

'That's happened before? She's not your first child to attend CH?'

'No, she's the first,' he said. 'She's the first remotely human child I've fathered — or mothered, for that matter —'

'Oh great, now I know about that you're going to keep rubbing it in, aren't you?' I said.

He ignored me. 'But the Tiger's pulled into the school all the time about his children. I was expecting it to happen to me too.'

'She's completely different to the Tiger's kids,' I said. 'And besides, Lord Hong knows we have a lot to deal with right now. He'll probably be in touch when the funerals have settled down.'

'Speaking of today's funerals,' he said, leaning back and retying his hair. 'I request that you do not attend, Miss Donahoe, and stay here to rest. I can handle them alone.'

'But I want to be with you!'

That seemed to surprise him, and he leaned forward to see me more intently. 'I want to be with you too, love. But I'm not strong enough to completely clear the virus from you, and if you don't rest you may develop symptoms. If we don't take care, it could kill you — even here on the Celestial Plane — simply because you try to do too much.'

I tapped the end of my peanut butter knife on the table. 'I have symptoms already. Edwin's handling it.'

'Even more reason for you to stay home and rest,' he said. He reached across the table to take my hand and his cold consciousness swept through me. 'For me? Please?'

'Please don't beg me, sir, you're a Heavenly Emperor. All you have to do is ask.' I raised his hand and kissed the back of it. 'I'll stay home and nap for you.'

He nodded, relieved. 'Thanks, Emma.'

* * *

I was half-asleep and didn't know what time it was when he crawled into bed beside me. I wrapped myself around him and breathed in the scent of the ocean. 'Tell me this isn't a dream.'

'It's not a dream.'

'You're really here?'

'For as long as you want me.'

He kissed the top of my head, pulled me closer, and I went back to sleep.

'I attended four funerals this morning, then I came home and had a nap with you,' John said over a lunch that was so late it was more like afternoon tea. 'I have two more later this evening because of the time difference.'

'I can come for them.'

'Let me look at you first.'

He took my hand and concentrated. After a minute or so, he hadn't come back.

'Is everything all right, John?'

He was still holding my hand but didn't seem to notice. 'Phone call. Give me a minute.'

Five to Throne Room immediately, he said on broadcast mode. *Priority.*

'What?' I said, concerned.

'The Demon King just asked us out on — in his own words — a dinner date,' John said.

'We have to go,' I said. 'We need to pick his brains. Don't you dare ask me to stay behind.'

'I'll need your intelligence beside me,' he said. He rose. 'The Five are here. Good.'

We went into the Throne Room, where the Lius, LK, Martin and Ma were sitting on the couches waiting for us.

'That was quick,' I said.

'We received the same message,' Ma said.

'Dropped what we were doing immediately,' Liu said.

John sat on one of the couches and put his forearms on his knees. 'I want some of you there with us. This may be a trap.'

'If he's behind the Celestial Jade cage business, then it definitely is,' Ma said.

Er Lang appeared just inside the doorway, and came to join us. There wasn't a spare seat for him, so he conjured a simple wooden chair and sat. 'We should go ourselves and leave Ah Wu behind.'

'He has a point, John,' I said. 'You're a fraction of your full strength, you're one-handed, and he wants you in a cage of jade.'

'He's vowed he doesn't want me,' he said. 'Same for you, Emma. Actually, we're the most logical choice to go: he's promised not to hold us.'

'You still think his word is good?' I said.

John hesitated for a long moment, then nodded once, sharply. 'I do. If he wants to ensure our help, then his word must be his bond.' He leaned back. 'We'll meet him as he's asked, and we'll see exactly what he has to say about all of this. Ma, Er Lang, Meredith, come to watch our backs. The rest of you, stay on high alert.'

'Me too,' Martin said.

'Guard the Heavens,' John said.

'I spent time down there. I know him, the way he thinks. Take me.'

John glowered at Martin. 'Guard the Heavens. Yue is not a warrior; you are. Defend my realm, Number One.'

Martin hesitated for a moment, then saluted John. He wiped his eyes, his voice thick. 'My Lord.'

John took my hand. 'Let's go.'

We appeared in the car park underneath the Lo Wu train station, and walked up through the crowds to the Lo Wu Shopping Centre. The shopping centre sat across the road from the train station, so Hong Kong commuters could take the train across the border and walk less than two hundred metres to the Mainland shops. The centre had a large illuminated sign on one side warning people against pickpockets and con artists. Most of the stuff sold there was fake designer gear or copy electrical appliances, but there was also a floor of tailors, hairdressers and nail salons.

We walked past racks of fake designer sports shoes and displays of Mainland silk quilts to the five-star hotel — a distinctive building with its top-floor revolving restaurant. The hotel, still less than a few hundred metres from the border, was for Hong Kongers who chose to stay at Lo Wu overnight. Police guarded the walkways across the busy street, but made no attempt to stop the hawkers selling everything from vegetables to fake Canto-pop CDs.

As we walked along the overpass, I felt it. The more people we passed, the more I felt it. Eventually I had to stop, and the others stopped as well.

'I know you can feel it too,' I said. 'This isn't normal, is it?'

'This is a centre for them,' John said. 'Much crime takes place here. But no, this isn't normal.'

We continued along the overpass until we reached the hotel, and took the stairs down. A ragged young beggar woman sat on one side of the stairs, holding a filthy baby. As we passed, she raised the baby and grinned at me. *An appetiser, missy?* she said into my head.

I hurried past.

It was even worse when we reached street level. They were all demons. As we travelled between the modern high-rise office buildings on one side and the bicycle racks on the other, the people stopped pretending that they weren't watching us. Everybody stared, smiling, as we passed. We were surrounded by a sea of grinning faces. We moved closer together, with John and me in the centre.

We reached the restaurant the Demon King had specified. It occupied the whole building, three storeys high, with a large lobby and sweeping, curved stairs leading up to the second level. It was decorated with salmon and pink carpet and wallpaper that had elaborate details picked out in gold. A huge chandelier hung from the ceiling.

A young woman, a low-level demon appearing in her mid-twenties, stood at the bottom of the stairs. She wore a long skirt and traditional Chinese jacket of salmon silk that matched the wallpaper. She smiled and bowed as we entered.

Without saying a word, she led us up the stairs to the second level. This floor was a single large room with about a hundred tables of various sizes, full of the noise of raised voices and clattering dishes. A small hallway at the far end of the room led to the private dining rooms.

When we reached the top of the stairs, the entire room fell silent. Every diner was a demon, and every demon watched us as we walked through to the private rooms at the end.

The hostess stopped and bowed to us at the end of the hall, then opened the pink double doors to the private room. It held two twelve-seater tables under another large chandelier, and had a television for karaoke in a niche to one side.

The King rose from his seat as we went in. Three other people stood with him: two Mothers and a horse-headed demon Duke, all in human form. The horse-head was in a smart tailored suit and his dyed blond hair was slicked back with gel, making him look like a rich young entrepreneur.

'Honoured Celestial Ambassadors,' the Demon King said, saluting around our group. 'I offer you my hospitality under the banner of truce, that we may speak freely and without fear.'

John stepped forward and saluted him back. 'The terms are acceptable.'

The Demon King swept one hand towards the table. 'Please, everybody take a seat. I'll have the staff bring some delightful,' he cocked his head at me, 'vegetarian dishes.' He grinned at John. 'I have some whale if you want it.'

'I will stay in human form,' John said.

'Oh, come on, Ah Wu, chill,' the King said. 'We're all good friends here. There's XO if you want it, my treat.' The King waved at the demons on his right. 'Mother Number Twenty-Six, Edna; Mother Number Thirty-Two, Lucinda. The brainiest ones I have. The Duke is an ambitious young man who owns the restaurant. They'll be no trouble. I haven't given them permission to talk.'

The Mothers didn't acknowledge our existence; they remained ice-cold and aloof. The Duke waved one hand airily at the waitress and she went out.

As we sat, one of the Mothers opened a bottle of XO cognac and poured it into crystal brandy balloons, then placed them in front of us.

'It's good to have you back, Ah Wu,' the King said, leaning on the table and turning his cognac glass in his hands. 'I know it sounds strange, but I'm counting on you to sort this out for me. I've made a major blunder here and, frankly, if things continue the way they are, I'll lose my throne.'

'Kitty and the Death Mother,' I said. 'But you were helping them.'

'What makes you think I was helping them?' he said.

'We saw what happened to Zara.'

'Who? What?' the King said.

'Six didn't succeed in completely blanking out Zara's memory,' John said. 'We have an image of him on the lattice.'

'From when Rhonda was in Hell,' I said. 'You held her down there, and Six took her for four hours.'

'You're kidding,' the Demon King said, genuinely shocked.

'She was taken from her villa while she slept,' John said.

'I had no idea that happened,' the King said. 'That is scary. I never saw him go in.'

'The same thing happened to Clarissa, who was replaced.'

'Who's Clarissa?'

'Stop playing this game,' John said.

'I swear, Ah Wu, I have no idea who this Clarissa woman is. What's her significance?'

'Michael's fiancée,' I said.

He leaned back and whistled through his teeth. 'And she was replaced? Wait, she was holding the same stone?'

'She was.'

'Okay.' The King put his cognac down. 'Time to put my cards on the table and ask you for help. Freeze.'

The demons with the King stilled, as if time had stopped for them. The noise of the diners outside the room ceased.

'Are you helping them?' I said.

'Of course not. Kitty's turning into something powerful and nasty, and she's human — something I can't touch. I, King of the Demons, have never been involved with them. I never thought she would get this far with what she's done — Simon was a complete moron and he was holding her back. But now she has help from these others. They've gathered together themselves, and it's too big for me to control.'

'And you want us to fix it for you,' John said.

The King leaned forward and gazed into John's eyes. 'It is unbelievably arousing when you say things like that.'

472

John leaned forward and stared back. 'I should let them destroy you.'

'You don't want them on the throne, believe me.'

John placed his remaining hand on the table. 'You have forfeited your right to rule Hell by this stupidity. They have the power to depose you. Give me one good reason why I should stop them.'

'I'm cuter?' the King said.

'Stop wasting our time!' I said.

The King leaned back and his expression filled with bliss. 'I think I'm going to come.'

'You are disgusting,' Meredith said.

'Okay, listen,' the King said, more businesslike. 'Their nest is in Singapore, in Kallang. I think they even had the audacity to desecrate a temple on the Earthly. Look for a closed Buddhist temple with the interior destroyed — that's where the entrance is. Please go in and take them out, or we will all suffer.'

'We cleaned that nest out two days ago,' John said.

The King stared at him. 'What?'

'They ran. They have another base. It's a boat on a lake. Where is it?' I said.

'They have another one?' The King said, aghast. He ran one hand over his forehead; he was sweating. 'Now it's getting scary. And you have no idea where it is? There weren't any leads in the Kallang facility?'

'I was hoping you could tell us,' I said. 'You're in control of all of them; you should know.'

'I lose control of them if they decide to make a grab for the throne,' the King said. He smirked at John. 'You need to bring her up to speed, Ah Wu.' His expression returned to concerned. 'So they're after the throne, and they're powerful, and they have a base somewhere that none of us knows about.' He downed the cognac in one gulp. 'Should I make a will?'

'Do you still want Kitty in a cage of jade?' John said. 'We can imprison her ourselves when we track her down.'

'The jade cage, definitely,' the King said. 'It's ready and waiting for her in Hell. Nothing else will hold her; some of the stuff she's done to herself is very scary.'

'You should have stopped them a long time ago,' I said.

'Yeah. Ordinary weak human, shouldn't be a problem, keep an eye on her and her little boyfriend, he's so stupid they'll be easy to stop.' He shrugged. 'Major miscalculation. When she got too powerful to ignore, I offered her a place in Hell. She turned me down, then disappeared. She has larger plans.'

'What about the Death Mother?' John said. 'Can you see anything she's done?'

The King pushed the glass into the tablecloth, leaving a mark in the soft fabric. 'If you catch that bitch, please give her to me. I want to see her suffer the Thousand Cuts.'

'Can you think of anything that will lead us to their base?' John said. 'There's a large muddy lake, they have a boat on it. From how Emma described it, it sounds like a standard Chinese teak junk. It's in South-East Asia somewhere; they keep running towards Thailand, Laos, Vietnam — one of those places. Think!'

The Demon King shook his head. 'I have nothing. They obviously set this up after they decided to go after my throne. Damn.' He leaned on the table and studied me carefully, his blood-red eyes boring into me. 'Try to remember, Emma. Did they say anything that would give a hint about where that boat is? Did they say "boat at somewhere", anything like that?'

I shook my head. 'I can't remember … It was on a lake.'

'What about your stone? Doesn't it know?'

'Her stone was totally incapacitated by them,' John said.

'And it hasn't recovered?'

'I wish it would,' I said.

'Well, that's that then.' He poured himself some more cognac, a full glass, and drank it in one gulp again. 'I'm glad I cleared the essence from Emma, because the price for your help in this would be higher than I'd probably be prepared to pay, and I'd be done for.' He filled the glass again and leaned on the table, studying the brandy as he turned the glass in his hand. He glanced up at John. 'I have only a small chance of surviving this, and it all depends on you. I cannot ride out with you.' He downed the full glass of cognac again. 'If I lose, remember me well, Ah Wu. You have been a most worthy adversary. Unfreeze.'

The demons in the room with us started breathing again, and the noise outside resumed. The restaurant staff entered with yum cha trolleys holding large dishes of vegetarian food.

'Invite Simone and the Black Lion to join us,' the King said. 'Plenty of food to go around, and you should introduce her to me. If I do survive this, she and I may have more to speak about.'

'When she is older and better able to understand,' John said. He sipped his cognac. 'Leo, for some reason, seems to have taken a dislike to you.'

'Ah well, can't have everything,' the King said. 'So tell me what you've been doing these last few days?'

I touched John's thigh under the table, unable to communicate my unease to him.

We accepted a dinner invitation, he said. *We are bound by rules of courtesy to stay and eat. Listen carefully. I have Zara in my pocket to record, but I want you to take note as well. He sometimes drinks too much and his tongue becomes loose. And don't panic if we have a drinking competition: it's par for the course at these things, and Ma always wins anyway.*

'You look a little uneasy, Emma,' the King said. He raised his glass. 'Drink some cognac, it will make you feel better. And have something to eat. This is the best Cantonese food available in the region; the Duke grows much of it on his own farm at the edge of the province.' He sipped his cognac. 'Don't worry, from here on it's purely social and I won't try a thing.' He raised his glass. 'Demon's honour. Yum sing.'

'Yum sing,' everybody repeated, and took a drink.

They waited expectantly for me and I took a sip. 'Cheers,' I said. 'Now please give me something non-alcoholic. I can't drink alcohol on my medication.'

'Medication? You guys have a lot to tell me about,' the King said enthusiastically.

'I lost my hand in the nest in Singapore,' John said. 'They've built these new plant-like things ...'

The demons brought me soda. This meal was going to be one of the longest of my life.

Simone wasn't there when we returned very much later that evening.

'She's supposed to be with Freddo,' I said. 'Can you check?'

John concentrated a moment, then said, 'She's not answering ... Oh, she's asleep. Freddo says she's staying overnight in the mafoo quarters in the stables; she was too tired to come home tonight. She'll be back tomorrow morning.'

'Double-check with a mafoo or something.'

'Confirmed; the Tiger says he gave her one of the rooms there.'

'Can you talk to the Dragon or the Tree?'

'Why would I want to talk to them?'

'To confirm where Justin is.'

His expression went grim. 'If he's there with her, his head is mine.'

'Just ask where Justin is.'

His face cleared. 'He's in the East. Simone's in a single room in the mafoo quarters.' He retied his hair. 'You gave me a horrible scare just then, Emma.'

'If Justin had been there, I would have stopped you going over anyway,' I said. 'She's old enough to know what she's doing.'

'No, she isn't!'

I linked my arm in his and led him into the Imperial Residence. 'Face it, Xuan Wu, she's going to grow up sooner rather than later.'

'Seventeen is way too young!'

'Wouldn't a girl in China a hundred years ago be married by the time she was thirteen?'

'That was a long time ago.'

I pulled him up the stairs. 'I was fourteen when I had my first sexual experience.'

He stopped and stared at me. 'You were just a child. That is so wrong.'

'It felt right at the time. Wayne was the hottest boy in year nine.'

'You didn't know what you were doing. She's only seventeen, Emma, she's still a child!'

I leaned into him. 'I'm just teasing you, John. Don't worry about her. She's much more mature than I was; I think she'll take her time.'

'I won't get any sleep tonight,' he said, distraught. 'You just scared the living daylights out of me.'

'Typical,' I said. 'Spend the evening with the Host of Hell without batting an eyelid, but freak out when you think your daughter is with a boy.'

'This "being human" business is completely overrated,' he said.

* * *

We both dressed to attend funerals the next morning. Simone wasn't at breakfast. John was about to call her when a demon servant interrupted us.

'There's a horse outside to see you, my Lord.'

We went outside the residence to find Freddo waiting for us.

'Where's Simone?' John said. 'Is she all right? What happened?'

Freddo's voice was unusually strained. 'She ran away. I bit her …' He let loose a sob of misery, full of distress. 'I bit Simone, we had a … ' He took a deep breath and shook his head, choking on the words. 'We had a relapse, a step …' His knees collapsed slightly, then he straightened and spoke quickly, the words cascading out of him. 'A step … backwards … and she ran away, and I don't know where she is, but she probably won't be back for a while … '

'It's all right, Freddo,' I said, running my hand over the crest of his neck. 'You can't be perfect, and she'll be back when she's ready.'

'I'm sure she's all right,' John said. 'You will get there.'

'No!' he said. 'That's not it …' He made a strangled sound of distress and fell to his knees. 'They took her!' He threw his head back and screamed with pain. 'I don't care, I'm telling the truth. They used me! They made me help them! She rode me, and I took her to them.' He grunted a few times, panting with effort. 'They have her …' His front legs collapsed and he fell sideways. 'They took her. I was supposed to tell you a cover story, but I won't! You have to find her … you have to …' He let his breath out in a long gasp and collapsed completely, his hind legs folding under him. 'Find her, please, bring her …' His breath rattled in his throat and his eyes rolled up.

John put his hand on his head. 'You're dying. We can't help you. You have to say the words.'

'Simone made me promise not to,' Freddo said, gasping.

'Simone would want you alive, and you know where they took her! Say the words or you'll die!'

'I can't! I promised!'

'Where is she?' I said.

'I … can't … say …'

'You're her only hope, horse. Say the words. She will understand.'

'Protect me, I am yours,' Freddo said with a huge exhalation of breath, and went still.

John concentrated, feeding the Fire Essence Pill into Freddo.

Freddo's eyes opened. He pulled himself to his feet and lowered his head. 'My Lord. My Lady.'

'She won't understand,' I said.

'I know,' John said without looking away from Freddo. 'Do you know where she is?'

'She's on an island, my Lord,' Freddo said. 'They took her to their island. They had me take her to a big river, and then to a big lake with an island.'

'Show me,' John said, and concentrated on Freddo, then snapped back. 'He knows the general layout but not the exact location. I'll go down and search the Earthly for it,' John said. 'I could sense her when she was underground in Kowloon City Park; I may be able to sense her wherever she is out there. I'll be back when I've found her. I think the Grandmother may have agreed to come help — stay here and see if she turns up.'

'No, it's too big an area to search —' I said, but he was gone.

I called Simone's mobile and it went to voicemail. Freddo stood motionless and attentive, waiting for his next order.

'Go back to the Tiger's stables,' I said. 'Tell the mafoos what happened. Ask them to relocate you into the Northern Heavens.'

He dropped his head. 'My Lady.'

'I'm sorry,' I said softly.

He disappeared.

CHAPTER 32

I was in one of the training rooms doing sword katas when Yi Hao contacted me.

The Grandmother of All the Rocks is here, ma'am.

I quickly put my sword away, grabbed my jacket, and ran to my office. I stopped, out of breath, outside, straightened my suit and went in. The Grandmother appeared as a small, round Aboriginal woman with dark skin and short curly hair. She stood behind my desk with one hand over the computer monitor, the files flashing over the screen faster than the eye could follow.

'Sorry I didn't get here sooner,' she said without looking away from the screen. 'I was napping. Usually takes me a few days to wake up. A lot's happened, eh? Your Turtle's back, and there's some of these demons doing bad stuff to people. Not good. Oh, and you need to update your spam filter, darl. Get your IT people to install something more effective.' She stopped the file feed and put one hand out towards me. 'Let me see.'

I gave her the stone and she concentrated on it, turning it over in her hands. She sat in my desk chair and continued studying it.

She glared at me. 'What have they done to it?'

I sat in one of the visitors' chairs and ran my hand over my forehead. 'Frozen it and electrocuted it.'

Her expression darkened. 'I should take my baby home if they're going to do stuff like that to it.'

'We need to know where these demons are,' I said.

'If you torture my children, you are no better than them!'

'It was Gold's idea.'

'That boy is way too human for my liking,' she said. 'He's been the same gender for years now. It's about time he changed to a girl for a while.'

'He's engaged to Amy and they have three children. He's a father.'

'Humph.' She blew out her dark cheeks. 'Stupid. Now give me a moment and I'll see if I can wake this miserable bastard up.'

A bass sound filled the room, just at the edge of hearing. It filled me with yearning for my Australian home. Then there was a jolt of disorientation and we were next to the Rock herself, in the middle of the desert. The dry, hot air washed over me, full of the crisp smell of desiccated leaves and powdery dust. We rushed towards the Rock, and then were engulfed by darkness as we went inside it.

'Illusion, don't panic,' the Grandmother said. She glanced at me, amused. 'You should come down and see the real thing: I'm quite impressive.'

'You are,' I said with wonder.

The Rock was hollow, and its entire interior stretched before us, with a red-brown sandy floor and a rough interior surface. The air was still dry, but much cooler. Every three metres stood a metre-high stone pedestal with a glowing stone sitting on top.

The Grandmother led me past the pedestals. 'My babies,' she said affectionately, touching one of the stones as she passed it. It sounded a crystalline tone and lit up.

She put my stone on one of the pedestals, and it lit with a soft green glow. 'Now, little fellow, let's see.'

She put her hand over the stone and concentrated: a soft, high-pitched sound came from it. The sound became louder and deeper, more recognisable as a scream of pain. It gained in volume until I nearly had to cover my ears, then abruptly stopped.

'Anchor! They're at anchor!' the stone yelled, and we were back in my office.

'You okay?' the Grandmother said.

'You let them do that to me, Emma? I felt every single thing they did,' the stone said, its voice hoarse with effort.

'I'm sorry, stone,' I said, full of remorse. 'They have Simone.'

The Grandmother came around the desk and handed the ring back to me. 'Never do anything like that to any of my children ever again,' she said. 'I'm going to have a few words with Gold. And this business in the East, making artificial live stones: this must stop.' She narrowed her eyes. 'You'd better care for my children more diligently or I won't let them be a part of this.'

I fell to one knee and dropped my head. 'I sincerely apologise for all the trouble I have caused, Grandmother. I care very much for your children, and I love this stone dearly.'

'Oh, Emma,' the stone said.

'Up you get, no need for that,' the Grandmother said. 'I'll be summoning Gold to me in a day or so, to tell him what's what.'

She touched my stone. 'Take it easy, Jade, you've been through hell. You should take a short nap for a few hundred years.'

'They need me too much,' the stone said.

'Humph. This is altogether too disturbing; you are becoming more and more like these fleshies every day.'

'I care,' the stone said.

'Very disturbing.' The Grandmother sighed and pulled me into a hug, reaching up to kiss me on the cheek. She smelled of back home: the dryness, leaves and dust. 'Go find the little girl. And come visit me.'

She sank into the ground and disappeared.

'Come home, Turtle, I know where they are,' the stone said.

John appeared behind the desk, walked around it and leaned on it. 'Where are they?'

'They told you their location when they were holding you, Emma,' the stone said. 'The boat is at anchor.'

John's face went grim. 'I cannot go there.'

'No, wait,' I said. 'Something's failing with the translation there. What do you mean the boat's at anchor — where's it anchored?'

'Anchor City,' the stone said. 'The ancient palace and temple complex in Cambodia.'

'Oh dear Lord, Angkor Wat? They've taken over that holy place?' I said.

'It's not a holy place,' John said, still grim. 'It's a disaster that I caused, and I cannot go there.' He retied his hair. 'The place is a ruin. The jungle has eaten it. There should be nothing left.' He changed to silent speech. *We've found them. Lius, Ma, Number One: to the Throne Room.*

'They've been restoring it for more than a hundred years now,' I said as we walked back to the Residence.

He didn't look at me. 'I can't go there.'

'What?'

'I vowed I would never return to that awful place. Millions died. Never again.'

We stopped in the entrance lobby of the Residence. Leo was already there, waiting for us.

'Dear Lord, that snake the King was sleeping with that gave him his power — that was you?' I said.

'Not me,' he said, going into the living room and

sitting on a couch, with Leo and me following. 'My daughter. They were in love, and she gave him everything she could. She turned the tiny jungle kingdom into a paradise. They even built a huge lake for me to go visit them. Then they expanded; conquered. They had to stop.' He took a deep breath. 'And it was my job to stop them.'

'So what did you do?' Leo said.

John just glowered at him.

'I don't believe it,' Leo said softly.

'Without her power to hold the kingdom together, the whole population perished the next time their enemies invaded,' John said. 'Millions died, and the kingdom was destroyed. I vowed that I would never return to witness what I had done, and asked the forgiveness of the holy Buddhas.'

'Were you ordered to do this by the Jade Emperor?' I said. 'You must have had no choice.'

'It was my choice,' he said. 'I was not ordered. I made the decision to go in there. And I live with the consequences.'

'Why didn't you just warn them instead of rushing in there and killing everybody?' Leo said fiercely. 'Talk to them instead of murdering them!'

'I did,' he said. 'I warned them. I told them the consequences of their actions if they didn't stop. Her husband thought I wouldn't do it; he thought I could never kill my own child.'

'I used to think the same thing,' I said.

'She should have stopped him,' Leo said.

'This was a different age. Even though they were Shen and human, the husband had power over the wife. She knew I would do it, and I will never forget her eyes when I did.'

'Wasn't there some other way?' Leo said, desperate. 'At least you could have saved the kingdom! All those people!'

'Without her power, it was doomed,' John said. 'She ensured there was sufficient food and water for them; she kept the trading routes clear. Without her, things collapsed quickly.'

'What would have happened if you hadn't stopped them?' I said.

'A thousand years of tyranny. Their kingdom would have invaded and controlled most of Asia, as the Qin did earlier without Divine aid. The Qin only lasted one generation, but with the power of a Shen in the palace, the dynasty would have been unnatural and unstoppable. She was on the way to Immortality; she would have taught him as well, and they would still rule there today. We Shen of Heaven would probably have left the Earthly in the face of such perversion.'

'A change of rule every now and then — a bit of a shake-up — is vital to keep history moving forward,' I said.

'Precisely.'

'I cannot believe you did that,' Leo said gruffly. 'Millions of people. I don't think I want to look at you right now.' He wheeled himself out.

John looked down at his remaining hand. 'My only defence is that it was a long time ago, and that I have changed since then.' He looked up into my eyes. 'I doubt I would be able to do it now.'

'The alternative was worse,' I said. 'You did the right thing.'

'You don't have all those lives weighing on your soul.'

'John, you're Yin. You're death. It's part of what you are.'

'Since I found the Way, it's a very difficult part.'

'Do you ever regret turning?'

He looked me straight in the eye. 'Not for a second.'

The Immortals came in and sat with us.

'Only decision to make is who goes,' Ma said.

'I cannot,' John said. He made a gesture of helplessness. 'I vowed never to go there.'

'But you've died since that vow,' I said. 'Death freed Martin from his agreement with the Demon King.'

'It's part of what he is, Emma,' Ma said. 'He'll never go back on his word. He can't go with us. So who's going?'

'Me,' I said.

Ma smiled slightly. 'I appreciate your enthusiasm, but having Princess Simone in peril is enough to deal with right now. With all due respect, ma'am.' He saluted me. 'Please stay here.'

'I'm not sitting this one out!' I said. 'It was hard enough watching what happened in Singapore. I might have been able to help Simone when she was poisoned. She nearly died, and it cost John his hand. I need to be there.'

'Please stay here where it is safe,' John said. 'I am going as close as I can to take over when they've pulled her out. It will be a great relief if I don't have to be concerned about your safety as well.'

'So who, my Lord?' Ma said.

'Zhao Gong Ming, the Tiger General; Zhou Guang Ze of the Wind Wheel; yourself; Xiao Lei Qiong of the Hours —'

'Good choice, he can manipulate time if necessary,' Meredith said.

'And Bi Tian Hua, the Thunder Marshal. Fire, Wind, Thunder and Time — together with Zhao, who's nearly as chaotic as I am.'

'How close can you go?' Ma said.

'To the edge of the old city. Probably about a kilometre from the main palace.'

'Close enough; you can use your stone to relay. Should we take a stone with us?'

'Take Wang Zhong of the Yellow River Delta,' I said. 'He's an earth spirit — he can talk directly to stones — and he's another element added to the arsenal.'

'Brilliant,' Martin said.

'Obvious,' Ma said. 'Frontal assault, or stealth?'

'We'll pretend to be a bunch of Chinese tourists,' Martin said. 'Blunder around, talk very loudly, and go for a boat ride on the lake while filling our faces with snacks.'

'That is breathtakingly offensive and not like you at all,' I said. 'They'd pick up the stereotype straightaway and know it's you.'

'Emma's right, it'd be too obvious,' Ma said. 'Film crew? Artists?'

'Artists is good,' John said. 'Park a barge and paint the island. Use that as a cover for reconnaissance.'

'That island is supposed to be an Earthly representation of Potakala Island, Kwan Yin's home,' I said. 'It's heartbreaking to think that people have been held and tortured underneath it.'

'No,' John said, 'it's a representation of the Mountain. It's probably eroded down to nearly nothing by now, but it was built to make me feel more at home.'

'Why is the lake a perfect rectangle, if they made it for you?'

'It's on earth. Earth is square, Heaven is round.'

Ma rose to go. 'Anything else?'

'Yes,' I said. 'One more dumb question. They've had her since yesterday morning, so where the hell is the ransom message?'

Ma fell to sit, and looked around at the other Immortals.

'We're not supposed to know yet,' Liu said. 'They're putting stuff together.'

I shook my head. 'That doesn't sound right.'

'Let's just get down there and find out what's happening,' Ma said. He nodded to John. 'My Lord?'

'Round them up, let's go,' John said. He turned to Meredith and Liu. 'Mind the Mountain.' He nodded to Martin. 'Number One, guard the Heavens.' He took my hand and kissed it. 'Stay safe.'

'She is my sister,' Martin said. 'Request permission.'

John hesitated for a moment, then shook his head. 'Guard the Heavens, Number One. That is an order.'

Martin didn't hesitate. 'My Lord.'

Ma and John disappeared.

'I just ordered the entire staff of the Mountain to ignore any request you make to be carried down there, so don't even try it,' Liu said to me. 'Go to one of the temples and meditate, and we'll keep you posted.'

'I'll be doing katas in the training room,' I said. 'And definitely keep me posted.'

They saluted me and went out.

I walked over to the Residence, went into the training area on the ground floor at the back of the house, and pulled a staff from the rack. I did the first twenty or so moves of the staff kata, then put the staff away and wandered into the downstairs bathroom. The minute the door was shut, I leaned on it and pulled out my mobile phone.

'One,' Michael answered.

'Michael, it's Emma. Kitty and the Death Mother have Simone. We know where they are, and they left me behind while they went down.'

'What? How did that ... Where are they?'

'I'll tell you, but you have to take me there. Meet me in the Imperial Residence on the Mountain.'

'You should stay behind.'

'Do you want to go and help?'

'Of course.'

'Then you have to take me; otherwise I won't tell you where she is. Hurry up, they're moving faster than you can!'

'On my way.'

I snapped the phone shut. 'I'm trusting you not to tell them,' I said softly to the stone.

'I want to be down there too. Just take care, dear,' the stone said.

I went out of the bathroom and back into the training room to find Leo waiting for me. He held his hand out. 'Let's go.'

'Michael's coming,' I said. 'Give him a second.'

Michael came through the courtyard and stopped when he saw us. 'We should leave Emma behind, Leo. We're Immortal. She's not.'

'But she's the brains of this outfit,' Leo said. 'Both of us together should be able to keep her safe, and we need to find Simone.' He rose out of his wheelchair and held one hand out to me and the other to Michael. 'Let's go.'

'Not without me,' Martin said, striding across the courtyard.

'Where to?' Michael said.

'Join hands,' I said. 'Martin should take us, he's the biggest.'

We stood in a small circle and linked hands.

'Show me,' Martin said, and touched his mind to mine. I gave him an image of the location of the lake and we were falling high above it through thick clouds.

I released their hands and slowed my fall.

'Cloud under you,' Michael said, and I landed on it.

Michael was standing on the cloud behind me, and we drifted down with Leo and Martin flying beside us, still holding hands.

'Low cloud cover,' Martin said. 'Do you want me to clear it?'

'No, just dip below it; and if you could hide us it would be very helpful,' I said.

We slipped out from the cloud cover and the rectangular lake spread out below us — five kilometres east to west, and two north to south. The rainy season was just ending and the lake was full; during the dry it would be half-empty. A small, eroded island sat in the middle of it, its buildings and structures worn away to nearly nothing. To the east stood the city — a perfect square, two kilometres to a side — eaten now by the jungle. South of the city stood the famous Angkor Wat temple, its five terraced spires clearly visible even from this distance.

'They built this just so Xuan Wu could visit,' I said.

'I can't see anyone,' Martin said.

'Where's your father?'

'I can't see him either. He must be further away.'

'Is the artists' boat still there?'

'No. Stay here,' Martin said, and disappeared.

'He's made himself invisible to have a look around,' the stone said. 'This is strange: the whole area is deserted. There aren't even any tourist or fishing boats on the lake.'

'Damn, I can see the airport and it's tiny compared to this huge lake,' Leo said. 'And the lake is perfectly rectangular.'

'Perfectly aligned east to west, as well,' Michael said. 'Sometimes it's obvious when a Shen is involved in construction.'

Martin reappeared. 'No boat. No sign of anybody.'

'They're either underground or they've been lured away,' I said. 'Can you make us look like tourists and drop us on the island, Martin?'

'Done.'

We landed on the island. It was covered in scrub, with a water-filled track leading up to the main part of the small temple, which was located at the island's centre. All that remained of it was a stone platform, twenty metres to a side, with some tumbledown carved walls and low towers. We walked up to the platform, went under the ruined gate, and stopped to look around.

Martin went to one of the towers, three metres tall and carved with Hindu figures, and nodded. 'Under this.'

We followed him, and found a newly opened trap door with stairs leading down.

'Me on point; Martin with Emma; Michael rearguard,' Leo said.

He summoned his sword, and carefully went sideways down the stairs with his right arm in front, ready to defend.

'I need a light,' I said as I followed him, Martin beside me.

'Touch my back and follow me blind,' Leo said softly. 'I don't want to broadcast our presence. Stone, can you speak for her?'

'Not once we're below ground level, I can only communicate with the one who bears me,' the stone said in similarly soft tones. 'Open your Inner Eye, Emma, use that.'

The stairs widened and curved as they went down, and the rock around us was carved with patterns on nearly every surface. The larger areas showed Hindu gods and heroes dancing, fighting, hunting, and making love.

At the bottom of the stairs we came to a tunnel, three metres wide and the same high, with a light shining from around the corner. We turned the corner into the blinding light and stopped.

A human copy demon was frozen in the process of exploding. The six Generals, facing away from us, were off their feet and flying backwards in the blast. General Xiao of the Hours had his arms raised to each side and his head lowered: he had stopped time. The corridor behind the exploding demon was full of more human copies, lined up and expressionless. A demon two metres back from the blast had just begun to detonate, and another one two metres behind it had a surprised look on its bright red face. The rest of the demons stood silent and immobile.

Leo made to race to the Generals and I grabbed him and held him back.

'They were hit by a big explosion and Xiao stopped time,' I said. 'But he can't hold it forever so we have to get out of here.'

'We need to take them with us,' Leo said, and reached towards Ma. 'We can just —'

I stopped him. 'You enter the time field, you're frozen too, and just as dead as they are.'

'Is it just me, or is it still moving?' Michael said.

He was right: the explosion had shifted towards us, so minutely that it was almost undetectable.

'He didn't stop time, he just slowed it,' I said. 'Let's get out of here. This will blow up in our faces.'

Martin grabbed my hand and teleported me directly up from the island, floating about a hundred metres above it.

'Sideways too, we're directly above the shock —' I began, but it was too late.

The demons exploded one by one, about a second apart, under the ground, causing a visible shockwave through the island's surface. The ground shook, then a cloud of dust came shooting out of the tunnel entrance. The blast hit us a few seconds later, and we were blown twenty metres back.

Martin was knocked free of my hand and I fell towards the water. He quickly dropped to collect me again, then guided me back onto the island.

We went back down the stairs, once again in near complete darkness. I opened my Eye and the walls around us became visible in shades of grey: something was affecting my vision.

'Incoming,' Michael said softly behind me. 'Shen. A dragon and a stone … Oh, it's Jade and Gold. What are they —'

I turned to see; it was Jade and Gold, both in human form.

'We came as soon as we heard,' Jade said.

I can see all of you. Go home right now. Another group of Generals is on its way; they'll be there in less than an hour, John said.

'All in favour of ignoring His Highness?' I said.

'We are in so much trouble,' Jade said. She moved forward to peer down the corridor. 'This tunnel is damaged. Gold, can you make sure it doesn't collapse on us?'

'Already,' Gold said. 'I can't see what's at the end.'

'Simone is,' I said. 'Let's go.'

Emma, please, John said.

'Can anyone talk to him?' I said.

'I can,' Jade said. She flinched. 'Please don't make me.'

'I will,' Martin said.

'Tell him we'll be careful.'

'I already did.'

I ask you again, my Lady, please do not do this.

I ignored him.

The tunnel had been severely damaged by the explosions: the carvings shattered to pieces; rocks and dust covering the floor. We travelled with care, as a group, with me in the middle.

Doors at the end, the stone said. *Can't see what's on the other side.*

We approached the doors as silently as we could. They were three by three metres: the width and height of the passage. They opened before us and a brilliant green light shone from the other side.

'Come on in, Emma,' Kitty Kwok said. 'I've been waiting for you.'

CHAPTER 33

We moved carefully as a group to the doors and looked through into a stone chamber, fifty metres to a side with a domed ceiling. It had carvings on the walls similar to those in the tunnel. Simone was sitting on a stone throne on the other side of the room. I nearly ran to her, but stopped. A pair of large demons stood on either side of her — the same demons that had flanked Kitty at the Convention Centre. One held a blade at Simone's throat; the other held a blade over her heart.

The Death Mother, in True Form and unconscious, lay chained to what was obviously a stone sacrificial table in the centre of the room. Kitty stood between the table and the far wall, appearing relaxed.

'Oh, look, Emma finally did as she was told and bought a suit,' she said. 'Come on in, I want to make a deal.'

The carvings on the walls, thrown into relief by the rippling green glow from overhead, weren't of Hindu gods and heroes; instead, they depicted demons in the acts of torturing and killing humans and animals. The table the Death Mother was chained to had a large demonic face with huge tusks and bulging eyes carved into its side. Its arms were outstretched and holding daggers in each hand. The table had grooves around its edges to collect the sacrificial blood, channelling it to a cup that sat below the mouth of the face. I looked up: the green glow lighting the room came from ooze demons, shining fluorescent green as they slid across the ceiling in a nauseating image of fluidity.

'Simone, are you okay?' I said.

Simone stared at me dully. Her eyes were half-closed and she sagged in the chair, a strand of drool hanging from one side of her mouth.

'She's drugged, but she looks okay,' Leo said. 'That has to be her. No demon could possibly be that big inside.'

'Oh, it's her all right,' Kitty said. 'I know better than to mess around with so much at stake. She's full of heroin; it's the only thing that would keep her passive enough to control. I want to do a straight-up deal in good faith. I know when I'm in serious trouble.'

She moved slightly to the side, towards the Death Mother's head, and a statue came into view behind her. Jade hissed when she saw the statue: a depiction of the Hindu goddess Kali, bringer of destruction. The goddess was painted black with a wide, demonic face and a huge red mouth full of tusks. A necklace of skulls sat over her bare breasts, and she had six arms: two held swords, two held human heads, and two held the impaled corpses of dead babies.

Kitty saw Jade's reaction and smiled slightly. 'You know, Emma, some of your people in the West worship Kali as the personification of female empowerment? Stupid.'

'She's not real. Tell me she's not real,' I said softly.

'Three Demon Kings ago, the King liked to take female demonic form and tear the guts out of anything he touched,' Martin said. His voice dropped with emotion. 'That was a bad time.'

'Uh, Emma,' Gold said urgently. 'Those demons on the ceiling — they're glowing with radiation.'

'How long do I have?'

The Shen with me were silent.

'Nobody here's done any work with radiation?'

'I can see what it is. I don't know how much of a dose you're getting,' Gold said.

'What about Simone?'

'She's so big it probably bounces right off her.'

'I'd better tell you the deal fast, and we can get on with it,' Kitty said, moving to the Death Mother's head and stroking her skinless scalp. 'I'm sacrificing my little sister here as a demonstration of good faith.' She shrugged. 'And because I don't need her any more.'

She walked around the table and leaned on it facing us with her hands on either side of her. 'I know you agreed to take me to the King. I'll give you Simone and come along quietly if you'll agree to do one thing for me.'

'What's that?'

'Leave the cage door open. Let me out again once you've put me in. You'll have completed your agreement with the King, and I'll be able to have a little chat with him.'

'That's all?' I said with disbelief.

'Thoroughly doable, eh? Give me your word, and I'll come quietly.'

'Do you really think you can take down the Demon King?'

She smiled slightly. 'You'd be surprised.'

She pulled a dagger from the side of the table and moved to stand behind the Death Mother's head. She wrenched the Mother's head back, plunged the blade sideways into her throat, then ripped it towards the ceiling, still holding it horizontally. The Mother didn't dissipate; she burst into a fountain of black demon essence, which gathered in the channels around the table. Her snake tail lashed from side to side, so powerful it chipped the stone where it hit, and her arms strained against the chains binding her. Eventually she stopped thrashing and dissolved slowly, her structure melting into more demon essence, like thick oil.

Kitty went to the side of the table and lifted the cup full of demon essence. She held it out towards us.

My stomach lurched with nausea as the smell of the demon essence hit me.

Jade turned away with her hands over her mouth.

'She cannot do this,' Martin said in disbelief.

'No way,' Gold said.

Kitty raised the cup with both hands and drank the demon essence, then lowered the cup and wiped her mouth. She placed the cup back on the table, then grinned at me. 'Watch this, Emma, this is very good.'

She dropped her head and concentrated and a pale blue nimbus grew around her head.

'Holy shit, she can do it too,' I said.

'What is she doing?' Martin said.

Kitty threw her head back, her expression filled with bliss and she generated a ball of black energy over her hands. She spun faster than the eye could follow and shot the black essence at each of Simone's guard demons in turn, destroying them.

She turned back to me. 'That will destroy the King.'

'A human can't take over Hell,' I said.

'She's not human any more, Emma,' Martin said. 'She's turned. She's demon.'

I inhaled sharply. 'She's changed into a demon?'

Kitty dismissed the black energy. 'I've done enough of the right stuff —'

'Atrocities!' Jade said.

'— and I'm more powerful than I ever was,' Kitty went on. 'But I need a lift down to Hell, and you can provide me with one — straight into the arms of the King.'

'The Demon King has control over you now,' I said. 'You've sacrificed your free will for power.'

'Not if I decide to make a try for the throne,' Kitty said. 'Let's go down and pay him a visit.'

'The Demon King loves it when you humans turn,' Martin said. 'He gains control over what was once a human; and if you try to take his throne, he can destroy you.'

'I hope he's ready for you, because I really don't want you to win,' I said to Kitty.

'Do we have an agreement?' she said.

'I vow to leave the cage door open when I put you into it.'

She raised her hands, palms out. 'I'm all yours. You can tie me up if you like — we can play some bondage.' She smiled slightly. 'Take me to Hell. I want to say hello to the King.'

I went to Simone and checked her; her pupils were huge. 'Can you hear me, Simone?'

She made some guttural noises, trying to speak and failing. She changed to silent speech but just generated static.

Leo came and checked the pulse in her neck. 'God, she's ice-cold. We have to get her home.' He looked around at everybody. 'Who goes and who stays?'

'Has anyone updated John?' I said.

'Doing it now, ma'am,' Jade said.

A boat is waiting for you next to the dock on the island, John said. *Send Simone home with Jade and Gold. Leo, Michael, Martin, stay with Emma. As soon as you are far enough away from the city, I will join you and take you all to Hell.*

'Even both of us together cannot carry the Princess, she is too big,' Gold said.

'I'll take her,' Michael said, bending to see into Simone's face. 'Simone, it's me. You're safe. I'll take you home.'

Simone raised her head and peered at him. 'Michael?'

He put one hand on the side of her face. 'It's me. I'm here.'

She raised her arms and tried to hug him, but failed, dropping them again. He put his hands under her arms and lifted her into an embrace, and she clutched him.

'Michael, stay with me. Please don't go away.'

'I'm here,' he said, his voice thick with emotion.

'My Michael,' she whispered, limp in his arms. 'Stay with me always.'

Michael, take her. Jade and Gold, retreat with them, you are too small.

'I'm bigger than Michael!' Jade said, protesting.

Michael is now Number One of Bai Hu and big enough. You and Gold are both parents. Jade, Gold, Michael, escort Simone to Wudang and notify me immediately upon arrival. Emma, Leo, Martin, go up to the dock, and if the boat goes anywhere except the far western shore of the lake, leave it.

'We've done a deal,' I said to Kitty. 'The Dark Lord's not too far away, so I suggest you don't go back on it. The three of us here are more than a match for you.'

'I didn't know he couldn't come to Angkor. If I had known, I would have established the whole setup here,' Kitty said. 'I'll keep that in mind in future, when I am King.'

Leo and I moved away from Simone and Michael, who were still locked in an embrace. Jade and Gold stood one on either side of them, and all four disappeared.

Kitty came to me and threw her arm around my shoulders, hugging me. I pulled away.

'Come on, Emma, let's go have some fun with the King,' she said. 'This should be quite a show.'

We walked back along the tunnel, bringing back unpleasant memories of a walk along a tunnel in

Kowloon City Park that hadn't led to the promised freedom. Leo and Martin were ahead of me, on either side of Kitty. I felt a lurch of nausea. It was possible that she would break the deal again, and the three of us together couldn't stop her. I had to trust their Immortal reflexes to keep me safe.

'Don't worry, I won't try anything,' Kitty said. 'So far everything is going the way I want it, so I'm not going anywhere. Isn't it a tremendous feeling when everything goes exactly to plan? So rare when that happens.'

Now I'm really worried, Leo said. *I can't hold this much longer, I'll need a chair soon.*

The same Chinese junk that Kitty had taken me to before waited for us at the dock. We boarded it. A human cast us off and drove us across the lake.

'Are we going in the right direction?' I asked.

'Yes,' Martin said.

Leo went into the stateroom and fell to sit on one of the chairs. My stomach lurched again and I rushed into the boat's bathroom. After a couple of minutes, Martin rapped on the door.

'Sorry to disturb you, Emma, but the Dark Lord says this is important. Do you have vomiting and diarrhoea?'

'Go away,' the stone said loudly as I clutched the toilet. 'We both know what it is and I have the network looking it up right now.'

'How bad is it, stone?' Martin said.

'I'm right here,' I growled, then retched again, but nothing came up. I'd puked myself dry.

'Find some drugs to control the symptoms,' the stone said. 'She needs to be able to put Kitty in the cage, then we can get her home.'

Realisation hit me. I hadn't eaten anything on the Earthly Plane, so it couldn't be food poisoning. And any stomach bug I'd picked up here wouldn't show

501

symptoms this quickly. 'Radiation poisoning, right?' I said.

'We can fix it,' the stone said.

'And now you're lying to me. Why is it displaying like a stomach bug?'

'The cells in the lining of your digestive system are particularly sensitive to ionising radiation and they've been severely damaged.'

'I see.' I collapsed to sit on the floor next to the toilet and leaned on the wall, which seemed to be falling away from me. 'Wow, this is really bad.'

'If it's bad enough, we'll give you a cupful of Turtle blood and that will fix it.'

'We'll have to time that very carefully, stone.'

'Let's just get this done and worry about that later.'

The sound of the boat's engines changed, and we slowed. We'd reached the western side of the lake.

'Is Simone okay?' I said.

'She is on the Mountain. That was close to a fatal dose of heroin and she'll need intensive care for a couple of days. But she's tough, she'll be fine. She's out of danger and on a ventilator.'

'Good.'

I used the wall to heave myself to my feet, then clutched the cistern of the toilet. I desperately wished for a mint: my mouth tasted horrible. I was drenched in sweat, and my insides were still spasming. I hoped they found something to control this, otherwise I wouldn't be able to leave the bathroom.

'They have,' the stone said. 'Martin is outside the door with Stemetil and Lomotil for you. Out you go.'

I washed my hands and went out. Martin handed me a couple of foils of pills and a bottle of water. 'One of each now. If the symptoms are still bad, take another.'

I pushed the pills out and swallowed them, then leaned against the wall. 'Is Simone damaged by the radiation?'

502

'No, it didn't seem to affect her,' Martin said. 'You're the only one that it hurt.'

I took a deep breath and went up the stairs onto the deck of the boat. Leo and John were there with Kitty. John quickly came to me and pulled me into a hug.

'Don't worry, we will heal you,' he said into my ear. 'Let's finish this. I am interested to see which one of these monsters will win.' He pulled back to speak to Martin. 'Take Emma. I will take this demon. Let's go.'

'I don't want you touching me,' Kitty said. 'Someone else.'

'How stupid you are to have forsaken your humanity,' John said. 'While all the world strives to attain the Tao, you have taken a huge leap backwards. The King will enjoy destroying you.'

'How about we go see?' Kitty said. 'But not you; you can kill me with a touch. Have the black one or the stupid one take me.'

'I'm both,' Leo said.

'So am I,' Martin said.

'Then both of you,' Kitty said.

John took my hand and raised it. Leo and Martin went to either side of Kitty and put a hand on her shoulder.

'Follow,' John said.

We landed in a huge, brightly lit, oval-shaped hall. The walls were faced with tan-coloured stone etched all around with gold filigree. The ceiling appeared to be glass and open to the sky: blue with clouds, which had to be an illusion. The hall was twenty metres long and fifteen wide, and the stone floor was decorated with more gold filigree in the shapes of plants and flowers. The jade cage stood in the middle of the hall, also oval; it looked like a giant barred egg lying on its side, three metres long, two high, and two wide, with a full-sized door that hung open. The bars were each three centimetres wide, spaced at three-centimetre intervals.

'This can't be Celestial Jade,' John said. 'There has never been any piece of Celestial Jade that large.'

'Six was very talented indeed,' the Demon King said, emerging from the other side of the cage and patting its side. 'He could join pieces of Celestial Jade together using the blood of living stones. Six used quite a few to make this for Simon; it would be a shame if they had died for no purpose.' He gestured towards the door. 'Put her in.'

Martin and Leo still held Kitty's shoulders. They turned to put her in the cage.

'No, Emma and I need to do it, as promised,' John said. 'Stand down.'

John and I took her, one arm each, and guided her into the cage. She didn't fight us. The King closed the door on us.

I quickly tried to open it, but it was locked. The jade latch was brittle, but I couldn't break it.

'It's Celestial Jade, you can't open it,' John said.

'You vowed to let us go!' I yelled through the bars at the King.

'I'm not holding you, honey, you can teleport out,' the King said. 'Both of you can. Bring her out, Turtle.'

Something blasted me from behind, slamming my head into the jade and stunning me. The floor flew up to meet me, hitting my head hard, and I couldn't breathe. The jade around me turned black and I realised Kitty had hit me in the back with the black energy.

John knelt next to me and held me. 'Hold on, Emma, I'll take you out.'

'She's too weak to teleport out, Turtle,' Kitty said from a safe distance. 'She's dying. What will you do?'

John glared up at the King. 'Let us out!'

'I'm not holding you in,' the King said. 'You can teleport out anytime. I promised I didn't want you, and I meant it. Out you come, you two.'

John lifted my head slightly and I moaned at the movement; my head was throbbing with agony.

'I can't teleport her out,' John said. 'You have to open the door and let her out! You vowed you wouldn't hold her.'

'Just change to Turtle and give her some of your blood,' Kitty said. 'That'll fix her right up, and you can teleport out.'

John hesitated for a moment, thinking about it.

I clutched his arm. 'Don't take True Form,' I said, trying to suck the breath in. 'You'll be trapped.'

'I don't need True Form,' he said.

Leo and Martin were at the edge of the cage; I could see their faces at the corner of my eye.

'Get me a blade,' John said to them. 'Cut open my arm.'

He lowered me gently to the floor and reached out. Martin summoned a dagger and tried to push it through the bars of the cage, but it wouldn't fit.

'I can't,' he said. 'The bars are too close together.'

John dropped his head and concentrated, his jaw clenched with effort.

'You're too weak to be doing this,' I said. 'Take yourself out.'

'Not without you,' he said.

A dagger appeared in his hand and he slashed at the stump of his left arm, crying out with pain as he did it. Blood flowed, and he dug the point of the knife into the wound, widening it. I tried to breathe, but he was fading and my ears were full of roaring. Something huge and black and cold appeared behind him, and he turned to see. It was his Serpent.

'Hello, Emma,' it said in John's female voice. 'You're very hurt. Can I help?'

John's eyes went black and he held his arm out towards it.

I grabbed the dagger from John's hand, but my right arm was too weak and wasted to use it. I quickly passed it to my left hand and plunged it with all my remaining strength into John's right eye.

'No!' Kitty and the Demon King yelled at the same time.

John looked at me, shocked, for a long horrible moment with the dagger handle jutting from his eye socket, then he collapsed on top of me and disappeared.

'Shit!' Kitty yelled. 'So close!'

She stormed up to me, her appearance changing from female to male. My vision turned into a dark tunnel with her outline at the end of it. She kicked me in the abdomen a few times, then the Serpent grabbed her in its mouth and tossed her aside.

The Serpent turned back to me. 'What have they done to you?'

I tried to reach up to touch it, but I couldn't move my arms. I wanted to speak, but the words didn't come out.

The stone spoke for me. 'Radiation poisoning, AIDS, and just generally being thrown around. You should not be in here, Serpent, this cage isn't for you.'

'I'm trapped,' it said. It touched its nose to me. 'But you need healing.'

Its ice-cold fire shot through me and I screamed.

'Sorry,' it whispered. 'You are close to death.'

'Shit shit shit shit shit,' the Demon King said, hitting the jade and making it ring with each word. I couldn't see him, but I could hear that his voice was coming from the other side of the cage where Kitty was. 'So close, and she had to go and do that.'

'It was you!' Leo yelled, his voice deep with fury. 'All along, it was you!'

The Serpent's healing eased and I panted, trying to suck in air.

'That's the second time you've come when I needed you,' I said to it.

'And she thinks the test run was an accident!' the King yelled.

The Serpent touched its nose to me again. 'I'll always come when you need me.' It raised its head and looked around. 'Or not. I appear to be stuck now; this is not good.' It spoke to the Demon King, who I now saw was pacing the interior of the cage. 'You did this.'

The King lowered his head and disappeared, reappearing on the outside of the cage. Too weak to move, I watched him walk to where Martin and Leo were staring at him with horror. Before he reached them, he passed an exact copy of himself also standing outside the cage.

'Leave my dominion immediately,' he said to Martin and Leo.

They disappeared.

The demon that had represented the Demon King while he was Kitty Kwok changed its form. It was the blond horse-head from the restaurant in China.

'Well,' the King said, pacing around the outside of the cage. 'What do I do with you? I've achieved half of what I wanted, so I suppose it was worth the effort.'

The Serpent raised its head to see him. 'You vowed that you had nothing to do with these demons.'

'I vowed that I as Demon King had nothing to do with them. I didn't say anything about me as Kitty Kwok.' The King shrugged. 'Having my word unconditionally trusted is an asset I've built over many years, Ah Wu.' He leaned towards the cage. 'Seeing you in there now, it was an asset well worth the cost.'

I pulled myself to sit upright, and the Serpent coiled protectively around me.

'You vowed to let me out,' I said. 'Will you go back on that as well?'

'I'll still let you out,' the King said. 'I have half the prize. Well, less than half, actually. Babies from you and young Mr O'Breen would have been a nice bonus, but that didn't work out either. You keep as many suits in your hand as you can, but eventually you draw one tile that forces you to decide which suit you'll go for.' He slammed one fist on the jade, making it ring. 'Number One, go in and teleport her out.'

The blond demon shifted his feet and moved back. 'That snake thing will eat me.'

'I will not eat you,' the Serpent said. 'If you take her out and return her to the Celestial side, I will not hurt you.' Its voice dropped to silky menace. 'But beware, because you are the very last demon that I will not hurt. I have vowed to destroy you all.' It raised its head to speak to the King. 'Did you do this to me? Did you split me into two pieces?'

The King raised his hands. 'Nothing at all to do with me, I swear.'

'Your word is worth nothing,' I said.

'I vowed as Demon King. I made no such vow as Kitty Kwok,' he said. 'As King of the Demons, I have never gone back on my word.'

'Yeah, you said that,' I said, and coughed. The Serpent pulled its coils more protectively around me. 'Always masking your meaning with words.'

'I got what I wanted, Emma,' the King said kindly. 'The Turtle isn't trapped; Number One will take you out; everything I vowed to do, I've done.'

'You were a lousy boss when you were Kitty, you know that?'

'He still is,' Number One said.

'Was there ever a real Kitty Kwok?' I said, running my hands over the Serpent's smooth scales.

'I killed her and her husband at the same time,' the King said. 'A very long time ago. That little group of demons were so useful, doing all that research for me.' He gestured towards the cage. 'And now I have this. It nearly wasn't ready in time; Ah Wu was back and it wasn't complete. I had to keep you occupied until it was ready.' He patted the cage. 'But we got there.'

Number One sidled up to the bars, obviously terrified of the Serpent, then teleported into the cage as far from the Serpent as he could get. His expression was a mixture of fear and loathing.

'Come on then,' he said to me.

The Serpent dropped its huge head next to my face and spoke silently. *Go and find the Turtle. Both of you may be able to find a way to get me out. And my daughter needs you.*

Can it use a phone from down here? I asked the stone.

No, the stone said. *This room is the same stone stuff.*

Can you stay with it and relay for us?

No, not underground.

I wrapped my arms around the Serpent's coils and held it. 'I don't want to leave you, John.'

'Go to the Turtle,' the Serpent said. 'Find my other half. You did the right thing to kill him before he could merge with me.'

'Didn't think she had it in her,' the Demon King said, close to us on the other side of the bars. 'They say you kill the one you love, eh?'

'Go, Emma,' the Serpent said. It squeezed me gently with its coils. 'I love you.'

I threw my arms around its neck and put my forehead against its snout. 'I love you too, John.'

'Look after my Turtle. It's not nearly as smart as I am.'

I brushed my hands over its head. 'I know.'

It gently butted me with its nose. 'Now go.'

I rose, a little unsteady but okay. I went to Number One and held my hand out. He took it, and we were outside the cage.

'Okay, take her to the Celestial side,' the King said.

'One more thing,' I said.

'Don't tell me.' He raised his hands with delight. 'You want me to tell you what you are. You mean you still don't know?'

'I'm a Western Shen mix of some sort.'

'See? You do know. A child of the Shen of the West, the Serpent people. As long as they mixed their blood with humans, it didn't come out. You're a descendant of two very stupid people who combined their heritage.' He raised one hand, palm up, towards me. 'The first one to show the Serpent nature in a thousand years. I've been watching you for a very long time, Miss O'Breen-Donahoe. I thought the Xuan Wu would like you, and here you are.'

'That's not ironic.'

He laughed out loud. 'But you're that as well!' he said with delight, pointing at the Serpent. 'One day, it'll take you over and you'll be gone. Won't that be a day to mark on the calendar? Imagine your most powerful adversary kneeling before you, asking what it is.' He spread his hands. 'That was one of the finest days of my life, and here we have another one. The Xuan Wu is cut in half, and I own the smart bit of it. Bring the Turtle down here and try to get it out, Emma: the cage is plenty big enough for the combined creature. And then we'll have some real fun.' He turned away. 'Take her out. I'm done here.' He put his hands on his hips, studying the Serpent. 'I have some things I want to do with you.'

'Do your worst,' the Serpent said. 'Go ahead and kill me, then I'll be free.'

'Don't worry, Ah Wu, I have every intention of keeping you alive,' the King said.

I moved between the King and the cage. 'Take me instead. Change me to demon, fill me with essence — I'm clear of the AIDS now. Make babies with me. I'll do whatever you like, I'll even be your Queen, just let the Serpent go.'

'Oh, well said, my Lady.' He bowed slightly. 'And here you are in a suit and everything — an image that gave me a shocking hard-on every time I pictured it. I pushed you so hard when I was Kitty to wear one for me, and you're finally in one and I don't even get to take it off you.' He looked away. 'Go home.'

'You've always wanted me; you said you would forsake your kingdom for me. Here's your chance.'

'You believed that? Really?' He snorted with contempt. 'I don't want something as small and useless as you. Go to the West, Emma; they'll probably eat you the minute they see you. The Serpent part of you is ...' He shrugged. 'Kind of useful — it kept Ah Wu busy. You were a great potential spy, but you're a mix of mostly human and a small part Shen and, frankly, not even worth trying to keep. Compared to having the Serpent, you're nothing.' He waved one hand dismissively towards Number One. 'I have her right ovary already, I don't need the rest of her. Take her home.'

Number One took my hand, and we were on the Celestial side of Hell, outside Court Ten.

'One day I'm going to kill that bastard and take his throne,' Number One said. 'You know where to find me.' He disappeared.

511

CHAPTER 34

I was weak, but still able to walk. I headed for the courtroom building to find John. The demons on either side of the door stopped me.

'Let me in,' I said. 'I'm Emma Donahoe, First —'

'No, you aren't, sorry, ma'am,' one of the demons said. 'You aren't First any more, and you cannot enter.'

'Tell Judge Pao I am here to see him.'

'He knows, ma'am, and he says to wait.'

'Yeah, I know,' I said. 'He says, "Too bad".'

I curled up at the bottom of the steps, leaning against the wall of the courtroom building, and closed my eyes. I was jerked awake later by someone saying my name. It was Er Lang, on one knee before me.

'Are you all right?' he said. 'I heard what happened.'

'Where's John?'

He gestured with his head towards the building. 'In there. It will take a while: Judge Pao is working through every single legal technicality.' He put his hand out, still on one knee. 'Take my hand and I'll carry you home.'

I took his hand. 'Do you know how Simone is?'

'No,' he said, and we were back on the Mountain. 'I have to go: the Jade Emperor has summoned me. The news of what has happened is causing something close to hysteria on the Celestial Plane. The Xuan Wu being imprisoned in Hell is very disturbing.' He glanced around. 'Can I leave you here?'

'Go,' I said. 'I'll be fine.'

He disappeared, and I walked alone from the square at the front of Yuzhengong back to the Imperial Residence. The Mountain was quiet; even the mess hall wasn't echoing with its usual noise of chatter and laughter.

I arrived at the Imperial Residence and looked around; nobody was there. I changed out of my sweat- and blood-stained suit, pulled on a comfortable Mountain uniform, and went to the temporary infirmary to find Simone. I desperately needed a shower, but this came first.

Simone was in a training room that had been converted to a two-bed ward; she was its only occupant. The ventilator whispered softly, its hoses snaking into her mouth. Michael lay asleep on the floor in tiger form.

I sat next to the bed and took her hand.

Edwin came in and stood behind me.

'Is she all right?' I said softly.

Michael heard me and jumped up, banging his head on the underside of the bed. He changed to human and stood up, rubbing his head. 'Ow,' he whispered.

'She is recovering quickly,' Edwin said. 'The heroin nearly stopped her respiratory system, but we'll be taking her off the ventilator very soon.'

'Is there any danger of her being addicted to the heroin?' Michael said.

Edwin leaned on the back of my chair. 'They say that many addicts experience such a profound rush on the first try that they spend the rest of their lives seeking that rush again. In Simone's case, the drug was inflicted on her in a place full of horrific images. It's possible that instead of a high, she experienced what they call a "bad trip". We'll have to see when she wakes up.' He put his hand on my shoulder. 'I need to check you over, Emma; and the rest of the Celestial wants to know what happened. The Dark Lord has passed on word that the Serpent part of him is held in Hell.'

'Oh no, they got the Serpent,' Michael said.

'I was the bait,' I said. 'They nearly killed me, and the Serpent came to heal me. But I was in a cage of Celestial Jade, so it was trapped.'

'What happened to Kitty Kwok?' Michael said. 'Did that bitch finally get what was coming to her?'

'She grew them all, and helped them all, and then killed them one by one when she'd finished with them. Then we put her in a jade cage as promised, and she nearly killed me and used me as bait to trap the Serpent.' I nearly moaned with misery. 'But she was the Demon King.'

'What?' Michael said, loudly enough to make Simone stir. He dropped his voice. 'You're kidding me. No way. I thought he vowed he wasn't working with her or those other demons.'

'He vowed that he as Demon King wasn't working with her; he claims Kitty was a different persona and so the vow didn't apply to her. He's been keeping his word for centuries so everybody came to trust him, and today he broke it to get what he wanted.' I shrugged. 'Nearly. He didn't get all of the Xuan Wu. I killed John to stop him from merging with the Serpent.'

'*You* killed him?'

'I don't want to talk about it.'

'Let me look you over, Emma,' Edwin said. 'They say you had a near-fatal dose of radiation.'

I went to sit on the other bed in the ward. 'Check me over, but you'll find there's nothing wrong with me; the Serpent cured me. It may even have been able to clear the AIDS.' I wiped my eyes and my voice thickened. 'And at what a price.'

514

'What will the King do with the Serpent?' Michael said.

I dropped my head, my throat even thicker. 'Play.'

'Lie down and let me take some blood,' Edwin said, rifling through the cupboard. 'I want you to stay here overnight for observation.'

'I'll be right next door in the Residence.'

'No.' He patted the mattress. 'Here.'

He took the blood, and went out to put it into the collection vials. Michael came to sit in a chair next to my bed.

'I didn't know,' he said.

'You didn't know what?'

He gestured with his head towards Simone.

'You don't have to do anything,' I said.

'I don't intend to.' He leaned his elbows on his knees and looked down at his hands. 'She's only seventeen, Emma. She's much younger than me and she should be with a boy of her own age, if she's with anyone at all.' He glanced up at me. 'I'm not coming back to work for you. I'm staying as Number One.'

'I understand.'

He studied me. 'You do?'

I nodded a reply.

'Well, if you do understand, could you explain it to her when she wakes up tomorrow and I'm gone?'

'Nothing to explain, Michael. She doesn't expect anything from you.'

'It's just because I'm here, and I'm older than her, and I understand what it's like,' he said. 'That's all. That's all it's ever been. I have Clarissa back in the West, and I'll wait for her.'

I leaned back on the pillows. 'Oh yeah, you owe me ten yuan.'

'They've broken up already?' he said with disbelief.

'They called it quits within five days.'

Michael looked around, then jumped up and fished through his pockets. He found his mobile phone and held one hand over it. A flurry of tiny glowing particles drifted out of the phone and coalesced into a gold coin. He held the coin out to me. 'There's usually about five US dollars worth of gold in a phone — that should cover it.'

I nodded to him. 'Thank you.'

Edwin came back. 'Stop talking to the patient, please. If you would return to the bedside of the Princess like the fairytale prince you are ...'

Michael poked Edwin in the chest with his index finger. 'Call me Prince Charming one more time and I will call you out.'

'Just go home, man,' Edwin said.

The two of them embraced quickly, and Michael disappeared.

Edwin sighed and shook his head. 'Do you need anything, Emma?'

'A shower, a really big mug of tea and something to eat. I'm still covered in blood and grit, and I haven't had anything to eat in ages. Being healed by the Serpent makes me starving.'

'Blood?' He took my hands to examine them.

'Not mine,' I said.

'All right, you can go back to the Residence. But I want you here first thing in the morning when I have the results of the tests.'

I hopped down off the bed and clutched it as the room swirled around me. 'I'll be here.'

He stopped me with a hand on my arm as I was leaving. 'Just let me say — I understand completely why you did what you did, and I'm behind you all the way.'

'Oh dear, that doesn't sound good,' I said. 'Thanks for your support.'

* * *

The next morning I woke to the sound of the fountain in the courtyard below and the gentle noises of the demons going about their work downstairs. I was alone in the house; John hadn't returned.

I rose and dressed and went down to the dining room to find Er Lang sitting at the table with a pot of Chinese tea and a bowl of congee in front of him.

I saluted him and sat. 'Tell me the worst.'

His expression was very grim. 'Half the Celestial is demanding both your heads.'

'Only half?'

'The other half are pushing for him to be thrown from Heaven, and a long sentence for both of you to be carried out on the Earthly Plane.'

'I'm sure a lot of people will be extremely happy to see the uppity human bitch get what's coming to her. When's the trial?'

'No trial. The Jade Emperor will wait until the Dark Lord returns to plead your case before he passes judgement. Until then you are under house arrest.'

'House arrest — does that mean the Residence or the Mountain?'

'It is open to interpretation.'

'Okay, Mountain. What do you think our chances are?'

He sighed and leaned his chin in his hand. 'A month ago I would have been delighted at the concept of your execution.'

My stomach fell out. To come so far and finally gain John back, only to lose everything because of my own stupidity.

'Stomping around being arrogant won't help at all in this case, will it?' I said.

'Absolutely not. Handle this with humility.'

'I intend to; it's the way I really feel. If I'd never gone down there, none of this would have happened.'

He put his teacup down. 'And now I must return to the Celestial and try to minimise the hysteria.'

'Any idea when John will be back?'

'Probably tomorrow at the earliest. Judge Pao is as pissed as everybody else.'

I held my hand out and we clasped hands as comrades-in-arms. 'Thank you, Rob.'

He nodded to me. 'No problem.'

I went straight to Simone when I arrived at the infirmary. She was off the ventilator and appeared to be sleeping normally.

'Did she wake up?' I said.

'She woke, used the bedpan, asked after the Dark Lord, you and Michael, then went back to sleep,' Edwin said. 'She's recovering quickly and she'll probably be out of here in a few days.'

He led me into his office and sat me on the other side of his desk. He pulled out the test results.

'Well?' I said.

'Radiation damage is difficult to quantify; we usually go by symptoms. Well, those who are experienced with it do — I had to contact some specialists, who will probably spend weeks trying to establish where the top-secret leak occurred. Are you experiencing any symptoms?'

'No.'

'Good. We'll play that by ear, but since you're free of the HIV I think we can safely say the Serpent cured you of everything.' He put the results on his desk. 'I can see why everyone constantly complains about it not being here. If it was here, I would probably have nothing to do.'

'You'll always have something to do, Edwin, you're a fine doctor.' I corrected myself. 'No, if anybody asks, tell them that I was rude to you and always put your skills down, and you really disliked me.'

'Oh, absolutely; it's the truth after all.' He shrugged. 'You're free to go, clean bill of health. Take it easy; you've been through a lot.'

'Let me know if Simone wakes up,' I said, rising to go out.

'Sure thing.'

I left the infirmary and headed for my office. Classes had started, and several groups occupied the squares and training areas, practising the Arts in near-perfect unison. As I neared the administration section, I passed Chang in one of the gardens. He wore the brown working robe of a Buddhist monk and cheap cotton work gloves, and he was on his knees, pulling weeds and throwing them into a bamboo basket.

He waved to me. 'I've been seconded here to help out with the autumn clean-up.'

'Happy?' I said.

He stood up and studied his work. 'Always.'

'That's good to hear.'

He turned to see me. 'I did not know that the woman the demons were working with was the King of the Demons himself. If I had known I would surely have told you.'

'I know that, Chang. I should have worked it out myself a long time ago. Everything I did against them was always too easy. Having the Dark Lord back forced their hand.'

'Will you be punished?'

'Probably.'

'If you are sent to the Earthly, I would like to come with you, look after you.'

'If I'm sent to the Earthly, they'll probably wipe my memory.'

'Still.'

'Chang.' I reached out and touched his arm. 'If anyone asks you, tell them that you never liked me, and

519

that working in the garden is ten times better than working for me.'

He straightened. 'I will not lie.'

'That's not a lie — well, the bit about the garden anyway.'

He hesitated for a moment, then grinned broadly. 'You're right.'

I nodded to him and continued towards the offices. 'Stay happy, Chang.'

'I choose to, therefore I am,' he said, and knelt to return to the weeding. 'I am free of needs and cares and my spirit is light.'

When I arrived at my office, Yi Hao wasn't at her desk. I went in and saw that my desk was immaculately tidy and my in-tray was empty. I checked my email and there was nothing that needed doing.

'This is ridiculous,' I said.

'You needed to rest,' the stone said.

'I need something to do!'

'Just a sec, I'm finding your secretary.' The stone made a soft sound of amusement, like stones clicking together. 'She's parked herself in the coat cupboard in the reception area.'

I went out to the waiting room and opened the cupboard door. The stone was right: Yi Hao stood there silent, unmoving and unbreathing, as if she was dead.

'Yi Hao,' I said, and she snapped into life, her eyes wide.

She jumped out of the cupboard and hugged me gently. 'Ma'am, welcome back. I had given up ...' She wiped her eyes. 'I am so glad you're back!'

'I've only been gone less than a day.'

'I haven't seen you in *days*, ma'am.'

'Well, I'm back now. What do we have?'

'Your diary is empty, the Dark Lord cleared it. The

only thing you have is Lord Gold's wedding day in six weeks.'

'Classes I'm teaching?'

She cringed. 'All cleared, ma'am. You have nothing. You are supposed to be resting. You're sick, remember?'

'Not any more. The Xuan Wu Serpent cured me of everything.'

She studied me carefully. 'You don't look well. Your face is very pale.'

'I'm still weak, but I need something to do. I suppose I'll just have to wait until the Dark Lord is back and we can divide up the tasks. I'm sure his in-tray is overflowing.'

'What happened?' she said.

'Come and sit down,' I gestured for her to take the visitor's chair, 'and I'll tell you the whole ridiculous story.'

I ate lunch alone in the Residence; I didn't want to face the questions in the mess. Afterwards, I went back to the infirmary. Simone was still sleeping, so I decided to visit Jade in her office to check on the wedding preparations.

I found her running around her office holding a large sheet of pale pink paper. 'This is the wrong colour!' she said to one of her assistants. 'I wanted salmon for the menus!'

She saw me, dropped the paper onto a table, and quickly hugged me. 'You should be in the infirmary, shouldn't you, Emma? I thought you'd need at least a day's rest after that.'

'I'm okay, just bored,' I said.

Jade looked around the office. It was a complete disaster, with menus, ribbons, flowers and CDs strewn all over the desks. 'I'm having the time of my life.'

'Can I help?'

She thought for a moment, then shook her head. 'You don't know the story so far, so I'm afraid you can't really be of any help to me.' She put her hands on my arms. 'Go rest. Everything is under control, and the Dark Lord will be home soon.'

I sighed and nodded. We embraced again and I went out.

I was sitting with Simone later that afternoon when Martin and Leo came into the infirmary. They sat down on the other side of her bed.

'Has she woken up yet?' Leo said, touching her hand.

I held her other hand; it was ice-cold. 'She wakes up, talks for a bit, goes to the bathroom, and goes back to sleep. It's like she doesn't want to wake up.'

'She's waiting for her father,' Martin said. He concentrated for a moment, then snapped back and shook his head. 'She's closed in on herself.'

'Will she be all right?' Leo said.

'Meredith says to let her take her time,' I said. 'She'll probably come around when John is back.'

'Has anybody checked with Judge Pao?' Martin said. 'As Father's Number One I have precedence so I can check on proceedings, but if it's already been done it would be a bad idea.'

'Er Lang says tomorrow.'

Martin nodded understanding.

'Do you get a ceremony to confirm you as Number One?' I said.

Leo put his arm around Martin's back and smiled proudly at him.

Martin shrugged. 'I was already in the position, so I don't think it's necessary. It's a return to work after being temporarily stood down.'

'I think we should have one anyway,' I said.

'Me too,' Leo said.

'It's not really necessary.'

'After Gold and Amy's wedding maybe. Speaking of weddings, have you two ...?'

'We asked each other,' Martin said with amusement. 'We both said yes at the same time.'

'But the Jade Emperor won't permit it; we checked,' Leo said. He shrugged. 'So that's that.'

Martin gazed at Leo with pride. 'The Celestial suggested we have a ceremonial handfasting rather than a true marriage.'

'I hope you told him where to go,' I said.

Martin seemed even prouder. 'Leo did. He told the Jade Emperor that I'm Number One of the First Heavenly General, and I deserve better than a mock marriage.'

'And Martin said I'm the Black Lion and I deserve the real thing,' Leo took Martin's hand. 'The Jade Emperor actually said he'd think about it.'

'John'll speak to the Jade Emperor when he comes back. We're on your side, and you're right. You deserve better than that.'

'We have to go choose rings,' Martin said. 'And we know better than to have anything to do with sentient stones.'

'Hey,' Leo said. 'Come and have dinner at our place tonight. Our treat. We'll cook for you.'

'You cook?' I said.

Martin grinned. 'We've been teaching each other.'

'It's a date. I can't wait to see what you've done with Persimmon Tree.'

'We nearly killed each other over the décor,' Leo said. 'I wanted traditional Chinese and he wanted modern Western. We arrived at a compromise, and I think it's neat. The rosewood table with the pine chairs works surprisingly well.'

'He actually suggested Ikea,' Martin said with scorn. 'I love modern Western, but there is a limit!'

'God.' Leo ran his hand over his bald head. 'I was just joking, Ming, get over it.'

Martin glowered at him. 'Never.'

'Now I really can't wait,' I said.

The next morning I heard voices as I passed John's office and felt a shot of delight — he was back. I walked towards his office, then stopped when I heard what they were talking about.

'She may be profoundly changed,' John said. 'She may wake up and not be the Emma we know.'

'We have no choice, we have to do it,' Martin said.

'We all know that. The choice we have to make is: do we tell her before we do it, or just put her under without her knowing?'

'She would want the chance to say goodbye,' Leo said.

'It is kinder if she does not know,' Martin said.

'She's gone through so much,' John said, his voice full of remorse. 'So many times she's suffered for our love. And we have to ask her to suffer again. I don't think I can do this any more.'

'So you'll wipe her memory, change her face, and drop her back with her parents?' Leo said. 'That's even worse than not telling her.'

'She knew what she was getting into: Kwan Yin warned her,' Meredith said. 'The hardest decision is the right one to take in this circumstance. Tell her, and then let her say goodbye.'

'That means we have to wait until Simone is out of the infirmary. I can't do that to Simone — have her wake up and see Emma changed.'

I went to the doorway and leaned on the frame. They all went quiet.

'Well, there's that decision made for us,' Meredith said.

'How much have you heard?' John said.

'Enough.'

He sighed and ran his hand over his forehead. 'We've been ordered to do this by the Jade Emperor. He is concerned that you may be an agent of the Demon King.'

'I see. Exactly what have you been ordered to do?'

Meredith turned in her chair to see me. 'We've looked inside you before, Emma, but nobody's really made a thorough inspection, particularly to see if you've been modified by the Demon King. We found that snake thing when the Tiger really dug deep, but there are still depths to you that nobody's seen properly. We have to burrow very deeply into your psyche and see exactly what the King's done to you. We know that Kitty Kwok messed with your head when you were working for her in the kindergarten: she made you oblivious to the strange things happening in the Dark Lord's household all that time ago. Then she broke your memory and dropped you in Lan Kwai Fong. She's had a great deal of opportunity to mess around inside your head, and we need to be sure that she isn't still in there. He,' she corrected herself.

'He's had plenty of opportunity to modify me,' I said. 'I used to work for him, and he was turning me into a demon. I'd be surprised if that's all he's done.'

'He could have controlled you and made you go down to Angkor,' John said. 'It's really not like you to do something so —'

'Stupid,' I finished for him.

'You took the smallest and weakest of all the Shen at your command and rushed in blindly after six of the biggest Heavenly Generals had been destroyed.'

'Yes, stupid,' I said. 'You think the King was influencing me to do that?'

He didn't reply.

'Then we need to look inside me and see if he has control over me.'

'You could be changed, Emma.'

'My parents said that I had changed.'

'If we find something, we will remove it. I don't know how much will be left.'

I tapped my head on the doorframe. 'I'd rather you did it right now and be done with it.'

'We can if you like, but Simone will be very upset if she wakes up and you are changed.'

'As soon as she's conscious enough for me to tell her, we do it. You said you'd put me under?'

'The pain this would cause is too much for you to bear conscious,' Meredith said.

'Who would do it? John?'

John nodded once.

I turned to go. 'I'll be in the Residence doing katas. Let me know when she wakes up and I'll say goodbye to everybody.'

After half an hour of katas, I gave up and went around the Mountain to say my goodbyes. Everybody knew already; it was an uncomfortable couple of hours.

John, Leo, Martin and I had lunch together in the Residence. At the end of the mostly uneaten meal, John took my hand. 'She's awake and eating. Time to go.'

'Good luck, Emma,' Leo said.

I embraced both him and Martin, and went over to the infirmary with John.

Simone was sitting up, but she'd been crying. I sat on the bed and hugged her.

'Is there any way we can avoid this, Daddy?' she said.

John just shook his head.

'Do you mind if I go out for a while then, while you do it?' she said. 'I need to be somewhere else.'

'Go for a walk,' I said. 'Go and sit in one of the

pagodas, or check out Leo and Martin's house.' I turned to John. 'How long will this take?'

John brushed his unbound hair out of his face; he'd already lost the hair tie. 'It depends on whether you've been modified, and if so, how much. I really don't know.'

'I'll go and visit Freddo then,' Simone said. 'He's probably worried sick.'

'Uh, Simone,' I said, but John was ahead of me. He concentrated on Simone and told her telepathically.

'No,' Simone said softly, then yelled it. 'No!' She disappeared.

John rose and put one hand out to me. 'Stone, we need you to assist. Meredith and Edwin are waiting in the other room. Hopefully, we will be finished in an hour or so and there will be no difference to our lives.'

In the second temporary ward, Meredith and Edwin had set up a full intensive-care unit.

'What's the crash cart for?' I said as I moved behind the screen and changed into a hospital gown to give Edwin easier access to my vitals. 'I know a defibrillator's useless if my heart stops.'

Edwin shrugged. 'You may go into fibrillation. I want to be ready for anything.'

'But they do it all the time on the television,' John said. 'Someone dies, they shock them alive again.'

'It doesn't work like that in real life,' I said. 'A defibrillator's only useful if your heart is palpitating. If it's stopped, you're dead.'

'Fascinating,' John said. He gestured towards the bed. 'The sooner we have this finished, the sooner I can take you into the Residence and give you a thorough lesson in double sword. Your technique is terrible.'

'Blame my husband,' Meredith said. 'He is far too soft on her.'

I climbed onto the bed. Edwin clipped a blood-oxygen monitor to my finger and a couple of ECG wires to my chest. He checked that the equipment was working correctly, then moved back out of the way.

'Stone, next to her feet, but keep contact and watch her. Meredith on that side, me on this side; you put her under first and then we'll look inside,' John said.

'Let me sit at the base of her throat, that's the best place to monitor her,' the stone said.

'Done.'

They moved into position and I felt a rush of panic. Then I looked up into John's eyes and calmed.

I love you, he said, and Meredith put her hands on either side of my head.

CHAPTER 35

My head hurt more than it had ever hurt in my life. Every heartbeat was a throbbing agony.

'Emma,' John said.

I opened my eyes, and quickly closed them again at the lancing pain of the light.

'Turn down the light, it hurts like anything,' I said.

'Try now,' Edwin said.

I peeled open my eyes; the room was much dimmer. 'Thank you.' I took John's hand. 'I know who you are, which is a good start.'

'Do you know where you are?'

'Temporary infirmary on the Mountain. Stone, move off there, it's uncomfortable. You weigh ten times more than you should.'

The stone lifted off my throat and the suffocating sensation disappeared.

'All signs are normal,' Meredith said. 'She doesn't appear to be damaged.' Her voice broke. 'Oh God, I was sure that would hurt her, but she seems okay.'

'I am hurt,' I said. 'My head is killing me.' I took a deep breath as I remembered. 'Did you find anything?'

They were silent.

'You did.'

I felt my reactions: I loved John. I loved Simone. Leo

was my best friend, and I was delighted that he didn't want to die. The Demon King, on the other hand …

'I don't feel any different,' I said. 'What did he change?'

'It was unbelievably subtle,' John said. 'It took us more than four hours to find it. Your Serpent nature, now that we know what it is, is absolutely fascinating and I have collected a vast amount of extremely interesting data on it.'

'But what did the Demon King do to me?'

'He's been doing it right from the start, when you were working for him as Kitty Kwok,' Meredith said. 'The changes were so subtle and so elegant.'

'But what were they?' I said, frustrated.

'He enhanced your maternal instinct, your natural love of children, so that you are immensely protective of them. I'm surprised you let Simone go out by herself,' John said. 'He raised your courage so you are almost completely unafraid of anything, to the point of reckless self-endangerment. He made you only notice strange happenings if they were brought directly to your attention — well, we knew that, and it was quickly short-circuited by living with me. Same with the conditioning to obey him in his Kitty form: you broke that almost immediately. And he planted a death wish in you.'

'I don't have a death wish,' I said.

'Yes, you do, Emma,' Meredith said. 'Your conscious mind can argue it down, and you have Simone and Lord Xuan to live for, but if you ever lost them, you'd kill yourself immediately. We shouldn't have worried about you going to the Earthly with your parents — you were incapable of leaving Lord Xuan and Simone.'

'Basically, he implanted in you the instinct to throw yourself thoughtlessly into any dangerous situation where Simone is threatened, and to stay with us no matter what the circumstances,' John said. 'And to self-destruct if your purpose of being with us is removed.'

'Did you remove the changes?' I said.

'We spent a long time arguing about whether those things made you what you are,' John said. 'Your courage, your love for Simone, your complete selflessness when it comes to her being in danger.' He clasped his hands. 'The very things I find most appealing about you.'

'That's beside the point. This is my personality we're talking about, and I should be the real me.' I dropped my voice. 'I just hope you'll still love me.'

'We removed the modifications to your personality,' Meredith said. 'Do you feel different?'

'No,' I said with wonder.

'It will probably show the first time you're faced with a dangerous situation,' John said. 'Although I have to admit, a more healthy reflex towards self-preservation will be reassuring.'

'So how long have we been here?' I said.

'Six hours,' Meredith said. 'But there was something else.'

My heart sank. 'What?'

'When he had you this last time, he inscribed a message onto your mind after he broke it and before he dropped you in Lan Kwai Fong. He was obviously expecting us to do this eventually.'

'What does the message say?'

'I'll show you,' the stone said. 'It's your mind; you have a right to see.'

The stone projected a floating two-dimensional image, bright with light, next to the bed. The Demon King stood in the middle of the frame, in his normal mid-twenties human form. He smiled wryly and waved one hand. 'Hi, guys. About time you had a look inside her. Isn't she fascinating? Look deeper and you'll find a whole lot more that's been there all along.' He leaned in to the camera and grinned. 'You fell in love with a construct, Ah Wu.' He leaned back. 'I'm about to drop her off in Lan Kwai Fong, but you'll find her, I know you will. It's in your oath. I've planted the name of the location in her head ...'

'Boat at anchor,' I said.

'And left clues in Singapore on where I am ...'

'We never found any of them,' John said. 'We didn't look hard enough.'

'... so she'll lead you to me very soon. If my plan works out, I'll have the Serpent at the very least, and there's a remote chance I'll have all of you.' He punched the table in front of him. 'Yes. Now know this: I will put you in a cage of jade, Xuan Wu.' He dropped his voice menacingly. 'I will find Kwan Yin in her guise of the Little Grandfather and I will lock her up and throw away the key — in Hell, she's mine.'

'I already warned her,' John said.

'I will put you in a cage of jade, and then I will ride out with my army and reclaim ...' His face filled with fury and he yelled the words. 'My world! Our world! We were here long before these humans, and we will take it back, and control them all.' He calmed. 'And then we will take an army of the humans that you love so much and we will march on the Heavens. We will destroy everything, and control everything, and we will cage all of you.' He spread his hands and grew larger, turning black as he changed to his male Snake Mother form. 'I have already destroyed half your army on the Mountain with my demon copies. Fair warning, Xuan Wu: I am coming for you.'

The image blinked out.

'Rest now,' John said. 'Six hours being probed like that will leave some severe bruising.'

'I want to rest in the Residence with you,' I said. 'You're back and I want to be with you.'

John looked at Edwin, who nodded.

'I'll carry you,' John said.

'Not by teleport!' I said.

'No, I'll carry you.' He stood, wrapped the hospital blanket around me and lifted me like a child. 'Let's take you home.'

'Is Simone okay?' I said as he carried me out into the crisp autumn night. 'Oh! It's snowing.'

Soft, fat flakes drifted down around us, and this time they didn't melt when they touched the ground.

'Simone is at home,' John said. 'She cried for a long time about Freddo. She's happy that you haven't changed much. And she said, "Always knew you were an idiot rushing into stuff, Emma."'

'She knows me so well.' I cuddled into John. 'Knew me so well. I'll be changed. I hope you will still love me.'

'I will always love you,' he said, his voice warm and low. 'Bedtime.'

'You just said some of the finest words ever said in the history of the world.'

'You're not serious,' he said as he carried me up the stairs in the Residence.

'Sleep,' I said.

'That's more like it. I was wondering if we had to go back in and check the sex drive. You have the headache from hell, you shouldn't be wanting anything.'

'Not tonight,' I said.

'Perfectly understandable.' He laid me on the bed. 'I need to build the fire. Go to sleep.' He pulled the covers over me and I wriggled down under them.

'How is it you can do magic but you can't make fire?' I said.

'If you want a fireplace full of hot water,' he said, 'then I can do that no problem at all.'

I drifted off to the sound of logs being piled in the fireplace, and was only vaguely aware of him joining me and holding me close.

Simone, Leo and Martin joined us for breakfast the next day.

'I'm sorry about Freddo,' I said.

Simone didn't look at me. 'Better than dead, I suppose. Freddo's father is being investigated; it looks like he was a plant too.'

'Do you feel different, Emma?' Leo said. 'You don't sound different.'

I shook my head. 'It will probably show the first time we're in a dangerous situation. I'll experience fear for the first time in a very long time.'

'It'll be good for you,' Martin said. 'Fear is a healthy reaction. Overcoming it is courage. Knowing when to run away is intelligence.'

John studied Martin, then nodded once.

'John,' I said, 'I have nothing to do! You took all my work away. I'm dying of boredom. For God's sake, put something in my in-tray before I go mad.'

'I'll put you back on the teaching roster as well,' he said.

'So what's the plan for today?'

They all shared a look and the room went very quiet.

'Uh-oh. What's up?'

'You have to face trial by the Jade Emperor.'

'Oh shit,' I said softly. 'I forgot about that.'

'Emma!' Leo said. He pointed at Simone with his fork. 'In front of the children. Really!'

'Yes, I'm damaged for life, I'll turn out a total delinquent now,' Simone said. 'Any of that paint left over, Dad? I'll go spray graffiti all over the Celestial Palace.'

'You may need more colours to do it right, I used most of it,' John said.

'Come and help me knock over an art shop then.'

He shrugged. 'Only if I can do some graffiti too.'

I studied my toast. I knew what they were doing, but it wasn't working. Half the Celestial was after our heads.

John took me to the Celestial Palace himself, riding on a cloud. I wore a simple Mountain uniform; he was in ordinary human form, similarly dressed.

I leaned back into him and he put his arms around me. 'Any idea what will happen to us?' I said.

'None whatsoever. We'll have to take it as it comes.'

'You won't have to ...' I took a deep breath, '... execute me if that's ordered, will you?'

He was silent.

'Oh, John.'

'It's unlikely your execution will be ordered,' he said. 'You were changed by the Demon King; you were not fully in control of your faculties. You have a legitimate defence.'

'No, I don't. I did something stupid and your Serpent is imprisoned because of it.' I took another deep breath and wiped my eyes. 'I've never been so terrified in my life. Is this the new me?'

He didn't reply.

'I'm not sure I like it.'

'Too bad, I love it,' he said, pulling me tighter.

We landed outside the gates, and he raised one hand to open them. We went inside. Again, the courtyard was deserted.

'Every single Shen in the Heavens will be up there waiting for us,' I said. I squared my shoulders. 'Let's give them a show they won't forget.'

'There's your natural courage coming through,' John said with satisfaction. 'I knew you had it in you.'

We linked hands, said the words and took a step forwards. The Door Gods were waiting for us outside the hall.

'Hey, guys, heard what happened; that sucks,' General Qin said. 'Organise yourselves to go get your Serpent out, please. We need the combined Xuan Wu back. The Celestial is way too long on pretty and extremely short on ugly.'

'We have you,' General Wei said to him.

General Qin nodded. 'True.' He patted us on the shoulders. 'In you go, guys, and remember that some of us are on your side.'

'We appreciate it,' John said, and we followed them into the hall.

The hall was fuller than I had ever seen it. The Shen crowded around the gold carpet, watching us with a mix of curiosity and malice.

'Lord Xuan Wu and Lady Emma Donahoe,' General Qin said.

'John, you didn't take Celestial Form,' I said softly.

'I'm doing this human,' he said.

We walked side by side down the carpet towards the dais. The Jade Emperor was in Celestial Form; the first time I'd seen it. He appeared as a slim, elderly gentleman, three metres tall, glowing with shen energy.

We stopped at the base of the dais and knelt as warriors. 'Ten thousand times ten thousand years.'

'Rise,' the Jade Emperor said.

We stood and faced him side by side.

Er Lang was in Celestial Form as well: three metres tall wearing scaled armour of green and gold. He unrolled a scroll and read from it. 'The Lord Xuan Wu and the Lady Emma Donahoe are accused of recklessly endangering the Celestial by walking into a trap set by the Demon King without adequate military intelligence and support.'

We're basically accused of doing something stupid, John said.

I shrugged almost imperceptibly. *Tell him, guilty as charged*, I said to the stone.

Yep. Time to be brave, John said.

'Lord Xuan. You had a whole army and thirty-five mighty Generals at your command,' the Jade Emperor said. 'Why did you rush in with the weakest of your Retainers after six of the most powerful Generals had just been destroyed?'

'My daughter was held by the demons,' John said. 'There is nothing on any Plane that will keep me from her when she is in peril.'

'No, it was me, I was rushing in,' I said, interrupting. 'He tried to stop me, Majesty, but when Simone is in danger nothing will stand between me and her.'

'Did you try to stop her, Xuan Wu?' the Jade Emperor said.

For God's sake, make him tell the truth, I said.

He must anyway in this place, the stone said. *You just did him a huge favour.*

John hesitated for a long moment, then dropped his voice and said, 'Yes, I did. I asked her repeatedly not to do it, and gave up and went along when it was apparent that she was determined.'

There was a ripple of consternation through the hall.

'There are mitigating circumstances, Majesty,' John said. 'The Demon King held her for years before she came to me, and her personality was altered so that she would do exactly as she has done. She was changed so that if my daughter was in danger, she would rush in without thought or fear to assist her.'

The Jade Emperor glared at John. 'You allowed a creature modified by the Demon King to enter your household?'

'The modifications were almost undetectable, and enhanced her courage and love for my daughter,' John said. 'They only made her a stronger ally.'

'Did the Demon King at any time have control over her actions?'

'No, Majesty.'

'So she has done this stupid thing, disobeyed you and rushed in unprepared, entirely of her own accord?'

There was another rustle of noise through the hall.

'She loves my daughter more than her life. She would risk anything to protect Simone.'

'And I love her,' Simone said from somewhere in the crowd to the left of us.

'If she had not thought quickly and killed my Turtle half, both of me would be imprisoned,' John said.

'That will be taken into consideration,' the Jade Emperor said. 'Lord Xuan, you are not to be corrected, but be warned that if this happens again your position will be in jeopardy.'

John fell to one knee beside me. 'I understand, Majesty.'

The Jade Emperor raised one hand towards me. 'Lady Emma. Plead your case. Give me one good reason not to execute you.'

The hall went very still and quiet. I started to talk, but my voice wouldn't come out. I gulped and coughed, then started again.

'I do not defend my actions,' I said. 'I will do anything to protect Simone. I admit that I've done something stupid that has imprisoned Xuan Wu and put all the Celestial at risk. Punish me as you see fit, Majesty.'

No, Emma, John said.

I ignored him. 'I take full responsibility. He tried to stop me and I rushed in regardless, arrogantly over-confident in my abilities. The Demon King has been assisting me all along, and I was unprepared when faced with the real threat. I am a small human in a world of mighty demons and Shen, and I have been given a fast, hard lesson in humility.'

'Oh, Emma,' Simone said.

'You are a profound demonstration of the value of

538

the Tao — the way of detachment — in making us better able to deal with matters of importance,' the Jade Emperor said.

'I will spend more time in meditation upon the Way, Majesty.'

'That is certain, madam, because you will not be doing anything else.' The Jade Emperor held out his hand and a scroll appeared in it. He passed the scroll to Er Lang, who opened it to read it.

'Emma Donahoe,' he said, his voice fierce.

I dropped so that I was on both knees with my hands in my lap and my head bowed. 'This small human is present and honoured, my Lord.'

'You are hereby removed from all duties. You will have no title, no responsibility, no seniority, and no position on the Celestial at all. You may not teach, attend or contribute to the administration of either Wudangshan or the Northern Heavens. You may not advise the Dark Lord in matters of policy or protocol. You may not sit as his rightful partner until your marriage to him is formalised. Until then you are to take the position of servant to the Dark Lord in all public engagements. You are stripped of all rank and precedence, and banished from the Court until further notice.' He rolled up the scroll. 'Ten thousand years.'

'Not enough. We want her head!' someone shouted from the back of the hall.

I touched my forehead to the floor and tried to keep my voice steady. 'This small human thanks his Majesty for his merciful correction of her erroneous ways.'

'Dismissed,' the Jade Emperor said.

'Ten thousand years,' John and I said in unison, then rose and backed out of the hall.

Our staff gathered protectively around me outside the Hall. Occasionally, a Shen hissed something threatening as they went past.

'I really don't know what I'm going to do with you,' John said. 'There was absolutely no need for that.'

'We need to get her out of here before she's lynched,' Gold said.

'I'll take her,' John said. 'Let's go back to the Mountain.'

Simone moved in front of me and put her hands on my arms. 'Are you okay, Emma? You look like you're about to pass out.'

I ran my hands through my hair and retied my ponytail. 'New me, I guess. I honestly thought I'd be executed.' My eyes filled with tears and I wiped them. 'I just want to go home.'

John crushed me into a fierce hug and teleported me down to the gates. Once we were through them, he summoned a cloud and we took off.

'You have the choice,' he said. 'I can wipe your memory, change your face, and you can return to your parents as if you had never met me. It would be as if all of this never happened.'

I took his hands and wrapped them around me. 'Do you still want me, Xuan Wu?'

'More than anything.'

'And I want to be with you. More than anything. I miss my family, but I want to be with you.'

He relaxed behind me. 'I don't think you've changed that much.'

'I was completely terrified in there.'

He squeezed me gently. 'So was I. For a moment I thought he would order your execution.'

I leaned back into him. 'Enforced holiday. What am I going to do with myself?'

'Do your PhD. They keep sending you letters offering one.'

'Fat lot of good that will do me when I can't work with you.'

'The sentence isn't forever, Emma. One day you'll be able to take your place by my side assisting me to run Wudang, and that is a day to heartily look forward to. Take this as an opportunity to gain mastery of the Arts and the Throne. Because the minute I've Raised you, you're standing next to me.'

'Will the Jade Emperor still let you do that?'

'Of course. I promised. It will be.'

'You still have to find me.'

'I already did.'

'You sure that was it? Cheung was the one who really found me.'

He was silent for a moment and I knew I was right.

'Whatever,' I said, holding his hands. 'Minor setback. We'll get there. And when the Demon King comes to try to take over, we'll fight him and take him down.'

'You haven't changed at all,' he said with quiet delight.

We approached the Mountain, and John slowed the cloud so we could admire it. The banners snapped on top of the walls: half of them plain black, the other half black with the Seven Stars motif. The black buildings and green pines were covered in a light dusting of snow, making them gleam in the sunlight. A fresh breeze, full of the scent of the snow and pines, lifted our hair.

'That is so beautiful,' I said.

'I am so glad I can share it with you,' he said.

'It's home,' I said. 'Home with you and Simone.' I squeezed his hands where he held me. 'Let's go home.'

CHAPTER 36

Gold, John and I were in John's office discussing the limits on my activities when there was a commotion outside.

'I don't care if he's in a meeting, he's seeing me now!' Qing Long yelled.

The double doors flew open and the Dragon planted himself just inside. He pointed at me, his finger quivering with rage. 'This ... thing is your downfall, Turtle, and you need to stand down. You are no longer capable of running the Heavens, and I do not acknowledge you as Sovereign.'

John rose, his voice mild. 'Ah Qing, think carefully before —'

Qing Long cut him off. 'You should be thrown from Heaven! Do you know how many of us are signing a petition to the Jade Emperor?'

'Gold,' John said, 'go and check this with the Celestial bureaucracy, please? Find out the details of the petition.'

'My Lord,' Gold said, and went out.

'Come now, old friend, there's no need for this,' John said, closing the office doors.

The Dragon moved to John, quickly embraced him and kissed him on both cheeks. Then he moved back to the doorway and yelled, 'Don't tell me to calm down!'

He came to me and patted me on the back. 'Don't look like that. I know what I'm doing.'

'What *are* you doing?' I said.

'It's a petition to have him thrown from Heaven and you executed,' Qing Long said, lowering his voice so that only we could hear. 'Based on the argument that you're an agent for the Demon King and he let you into his household fully aware of it.'

'That'll be thrown straight out of court, because we have proof that I'm not an agent for the Demon King.'

'Precisely,' the Dragon said. 'And no other petitions can be put forward while this one is grinding slowly through the wheels.'

'Brilliant,' John said. 'I owe you.'

The Dragon moved back to the door to yell again. 'I will see you thrown from Heaven and this bitch executed. Any Sovereign is better than you — hell, I'd rather serve the Demon King himself. You have failed, Turtle.'

The doors flew open to show a large group of horrified spectators standing outside.

Jade stormed in to stand in front of the Dragon and glared up at him, furious. 'You are petitioning to have the Dark Lord thrown from Heaven?' She looked from the Dragon to me. 'And Lady Emma executed?'

'Lady Emma no more,' the Dragon said, glowing blue against her green. 'They are a disgrace to the Celestial and need to be removed.'

'Come on, everyone, there's no need to fight like this,' I said, closing the doors again.

Jade took the Dragon's hands in hers. 'I'll marry you,' she said. 'I'll come and live with you in the East. Anything. Just don't do this to them, please. Haven't they suffered enough?'

His expression softened as he gazed down at her, holding her hands for a long moment. 'And now she says yes,' he said with heart-breaking gentleness.

'He doesn't mean it,' I said. 'He's creating a dummy petition that will automatically fail so that no real ones can go up.'

Jade's mouth opened into an 'O' and stayed there.

He lifted her hands. 'Will you still say yes?'

She didn't reply; she just threw her arms around his neck, pulled him down and kissed him hard.

I had to interrupt them after a couple of minutes. 'Uh, we can't leave you two alone without opening the doors. And then everybody will see you.'

They broke apart and gazed into each other's eyes for a long time, still holding each other.

'Is that a yes?' the Dragon said.

'Let me think about it,' Jade said. She turned and went out of the office, closing the doors behind her.

'I will do this!' the Dragon shouted. 'The Winds will have a new Sovereign and you will return to Hell!'

'I think that's enough,' John said.

The Dragon quickly embraced both of us and left. We could hear him shouting as he made his way through the crowd.

'There goes a true friend,' John said as he returned to sit behind the desk. 'Gold is on his way back with the petition.' He smiled slightly. 'He says it will be thrown out of court. What a shame.'

Gold and Amy's wedding was held midwinter, and the day was clear and bright. The dragons resident on the Mountain had ensured that the weather was fine for the wedding of one of their own. The Mountain's paths and courtyards were cleared of snow, but the trees, roofs and peaks were covered in a white blanket. Jade had decorated the Hall of Purple Mist for the wedding ceremony: it was bedecked with wide red ribbon with rosettes on every corner and pillar holding gold 'double happiness' circular motifs.

Gold was in human form, wearing a Mountain uniform, with red ribbons draped across his chest and held with a rosette in the middle. He waited at the top of the stairs with John and the parents: my stone in human form, and Amy's mother and father. Amy's father, a dragon, was in human form: a short, round middle-aged Chinese man with a jolly smile. Her mother was human, an art gallery owner from Sydney; she was slender and elegant in a beautifully tailored pale blue suit. My stone had outdone itself; it wore a green embossed silk Chinese robe, which highlighted its pale European skin and shock of white hair.

The palanquin holding Amy arrived, also decorated with red ribbons and gold 'double happiness' motifs and carried by dragons, one in front and one behind, both brilliant crimson with gold fins and tails. Jade walked alongside the palanquin in True Form: a glittering green dragon, four metres long, with gold fins and tail.

Meredith and I were on babysitting duties for Amy and Gold's little ones. I was holding Richard up to see the spectacle, and he seemed to be enjoying it, crowing loudly with delight at the dragons. Little Jade, in Meredith's arms, was fast asleep.

The palanquin stopped at the bottom of the stairs and Amy stepped out. The students of the Mountain burst into spontaneous applause when they saw her, and she blushed. She wore a traditional wedding dress: a slender, fitted red silk cheongsam that featured a dragon on one side and a phoenix on the other, each brilliantly embroidered in gold, silver and brightly coloured thread. She wore a similarly embroidered short red silk jacket over the top — against the cold — but had broken with tradition in not wearing a red silk veil over her face. Her hair was pinned up into a bun decorated with red beads and silk flowers.

Jade changed to human form, in a plain green cheongsam, and guided Amy to the top of the stairs. She bowed to John and the parents, then went back down the stairs.

John stood at the front of the terrace to face the gathered crowd, with Amy and Gold on his left and the parents on the right.

'Amy Wu, child of Richard and Veronica, has agreed to wed the Golden Child of the Jade Building Block.' He nodded towards my stone. 'Do you agree to this union, Jade Building Block?'

'I agree. They are well matched,' the stone said with pride.

'Master Richard, Madam Veronica, do you agree to your daughter undertaking this union?'

'I agree,' Richard said.

'I'm not a Madam,' Veronica said with dignity. 'And I agree.' She wiped her eyes. 'He is a fine young man.'

'Uh …' John approached her and said something softly to her.

'A thousand years old?' Veronica said loudly with shock. 'A thousand?'

Gold winced, and Amy put her hand on her forehead.

'I still agree regardless,' Veronica said. She glared at Amy. 'And we are talking about this later.'

John moved back and waved one hand, and ebony Ming-style wooden chairs with red silk cushions appeared behind himself, the stone and Amy's parents. They all sat. Jade floated up the stairs holding a tray containing four teacups. She gave the tray to Gold, kissed him and Amy on the cheek, said something inaudible to them, then floated back down the stairs.

Amy and Gold held the tray between them and went to stand in front of John. John's face was full of delight as he accepted the tea from Amy and Gold. They knelt before him, he took a cup and sipped it, then they stood again. They turned to serve tea to Amy's parents, who sat with their hands on their knees, both obviously bursting with pride.

As Amy and Gold were serving tea to my stone, John's face went completely ashen and he toppled sideways off his chair.

Amy and Gold stood there stricken. The stone went to John and knelt next to him.

He's severely injured, the stone said in broadcast mode. *Get medical help.*

Meredith and I raced up the stairs, and quickly handed the babies to Amy and Gold. I pushed my way through to John. His breath was short and shallow and he didn't seem able to see us.

Someone turned him onto his back and we all gasped: his side was black with blood. I opened the top of his robe to see, but the toggles and loops wouldn't open far enough. I caught a glimpse of what looked like a burn on his side, but the robe wouldn't open, and it went all the way down to his feet so I couldn't pull it up.

'What happened?' Meredith said.

'Don't worry about what happened, get him to the infirmary,' the stone said.

A few people lifted him and carried him quickly to the infirmary, the rest of us following. He made a few soft noises of pain as they moved him, and I nearly cried out with him.

'How did this happen?' I said as we entered the makeshift ward. 'John, what happened to you?'

Edwin pushed us aside as soon as John was on the bed. He cut away John's robe and pulled his cotton pants down slightly over his slim hips to see the damage. One side of his body, all the way down the side of his abdomen, was blackened as if burnt to a depth of two to three centimetres. The skin of his chest and upper arms was covered in shallow cuts, some fresh and bleeding, some half-healed.

I sank into a chair, dizzy with shock.

Edwin hissed when he saw the injuries and quickly put himself in John's face. 'Are you in pain, Lord Xuan?' he said urgently. 'Do you require painkillers?'

John nodded, his face a fierce mask of concentration.

Edwin turned to the drugs cabinet and quickly pulled out a vial and a syringe. He injected John and then waved us all back. 'Emma and Meredith can stay. I want everybody else out.'

'Come on, Simone,' Leo said.

'I want to stay with Daddy!' Simone yelled.

'I need space to work. I'll call you back in when I'm done,' Edwin said, and Simone went out with Leo.

'Thanks,' I said, moving to sit next to John's head and hold his hand. 'John, what happened?'

He spoke through his teeth. 'Demon King ... playing ... with a blowtorch.'

'Oh, dear Lord,' Meredith said. She moved closer to John. 'We can send you down to Court Ten —'

'No!' John raised his head then dropped it again. 'If you kill me now, while the Serpent is in so much pain, I'll rejoin with it. You have ... to keep me ... alive!'

'I'll do my best, my Lord,' Edwin said. He put a saline bag on a drip stand and inserted the needle into John's arm. 'These don't look mortal.'

John yelled with pain and arched his back, then threw himself onto the side that wasn't burnt. He gasped a few times, breathing heavily, then stopped. He flopped onto his back again and I saw that the scorched area had grown. The room filled with the smell of burnt flesh.

'I can manage,' he said.

Edwin ran out of the room. Meredith and I sat together, stricken, watching John. Edwin returned with some damp sheets of what appeared to be skin. He sprinkled antibiotic powder over the burns and then put the sheets over them.

'Thank you,' John said. 'I think he's finished for now. Any more and the Serpent will die too.'

I touched John's chest, making sure to stay well away from the burns. He was covered in small cuts. 'He's been torturing you for a while.'

'Yes. His timing is impeccable, to do this during the wedding.'

'Would he know the wedding was on?'

'The whole of the Celestial is out for it; he'd know.' He cried out and arched his back again. 'He just kicked me in the burns. Damn!' He panted a few times, his eyes closed. 'He had to open the door to the cage and come inside to do that, but I'm too incapacitated to get myself out. I can't move worth a damn.' He relaxed slightly. 'Whatever Edwin gave me isn't working too well.'

'Should he give you enough for the Serpent too?' I said.

'No, that'd probably kill me.' He stiffened and his eyes snapped open.

'Stay with us, John,' I said, clutching his hand.

'I'm trying.' He smiled but it was almost a grimace. 'He's worried now: he may have killed the Serpent. I die, and it's all for nothing.' He relaxed. 'Oh no, just leave me here and let me die. No need to treat it; I won't hold it against you. No hurry, take your time.'

'We won't let you —' I began, but Meredith stopped me.

'That's the Serpent speaking,' she said.

John continued without hearing us. 'Feel free to leave the door open when you go out.' He appeared to be looking at something that wasn't there, and winced a few times, then breathed out a huge sigh. 'That's better. I don't suppose a painkilling injection would be on offer

549

as well? Sure. Heads. Oh, I hadn't thought of that; I'll ask one of the vets on the Celestial and see.' He came back to us. 'That is a very unusual feeling. I need to find out what sort of painkillers work on snakes. I won the toss, but human pain relief probably doesn't work on a reptile.'

'You should have told us, my Lord,' Meredith said.

'I didn't think he'd take it this far. He was having fun just slicing at me through the bars,' John said. 'Getting a blowtorch was a stroke of genius: the flame goes all the way through the cage and I can't move away from it.'

'Are you in that close contact with your Serpent?' I said.

'When it's hurting this bad, yes,' John said. 'Otherwise ...' His face twisted with pain. 'Can I explain the details of being two creatures at another time?'

I kissed his hand. 'Sorry.'

'Close down your consciousness,' Meredith said. 'Rest and heal.'

Simone rushed in. 'Daddy? Edwin said I can come in now.'

'Simone,' John said. 'I'm in a lot of pain, but I'll live. I'll always live, you know that.'

Meredith moved so Simone could sit next to John on the other side. Simone studied the covered wounds closely. 'What's this? How did this happen? You were burnt?'

Meredith told Simone silently and she stared at John, stricken. 'That's so horrible!' She jumped to her feet. 'I am going down there right now to yin that monster!'

'What with?' John said with amusement through the pain.

Simone fell to sit again. 'Give me back my yin.'

He gasped with the effort of speaking. 'Not until I'm sure you won't destroy the world.'

'Well then, you go down and yin him.'

'The minute I enter Hell, he'll do something like this again and I'll be flopping around on the floor helpless,' John said. 'Let's train our army, and when he heads up here we'll give him a fight he won't forget.'

She raised his hand. 'Sounds like a plan.'

'Let him rest, Simone,' I said.

'Can I stay?'

'No, go to the wedding, both of you,' John said. 'I'm fine. He's leaving me alone now, and I'll just be lying here unconscious anyway.'

'They can finish the wedding without me,' I said without moving.

'You need to be there, Emma,' John said.

'Shut up and go down,' I said. 'Close up and heal.'

'And we'll be here when you wake up,' Simone said. 'Gold and Amy will understand.'

Of course we understand, Gold said.

'See? Now do as you're told and close down your mind,' I said, holding his hand. 'We'll look after you.'

Simone held his other hand. 'Always.'

'I am so glad I have you …' he said, but didn't finish.

The Serpent lies in a cage of jade,
the demons laugh and poke it.
It does not cry.

The Turtle lies on a hospital bed
unconscious in a haze of pain,
dreaming of being whole.

They want to be one
and know it cannot be.

GLOSSARY

The Chinese language is divided by a number of different dialects and this has been reflected throughout my story. The main dialect spoken in Hong Kong is Cantonese, and many of the terms I've used are in Cantonese. The main method for transcribing Cantonese into English is the Yale system, which I have hardly used at all in this book, preferring to use a simpler phonetic method for spelling the Cantonese. Apologies to purists, but I've chosen ease of readability over phonetic correctness.

The dialect mainly spoken on the Mainland of China is Putonghua (also called Mandarin Chinese), which was originally the dialect used in the north of China but has spread to become the standard tongue. Putonghua has a strict and useful set of transcription rules called pinyin, which I've used throughout for Putonghua terms. As a rough guide to pronunciation, the 'Q' in pinyin is pronounced 'ch', the 'X' is 'sh' and the 'Zh' is a softer 'ch' than the 'Q' sound. Xuan Wu is therefore pronounced 'Shwan Wu'.

I've spelt chi with the 'ch' throughout the book, even though in pinyin it is qi, purely to aid in readability. Qing Long and Zhu Que I have spelt in pinyin to assist anybody who'd like to look into these interesting deities further.

Aberdeen Typhoon Shelter: A harbour on the south side of Hong Kong Island that is home to a large number of small and large fishing boats. Some of the boats are permanently moored there and are residences.

Admiralty: The first station after the MTR train has come through the tunnel onto Hong Kong Island from Kowloon, and a major traffic interchange.

Amah: Domestic helper.

Ancestral tablet: A tablet inscribed with the name of the deceased, which is kept in a temple or at the residence of the person's descendants and occasionally provided with incense and offerings to appease the spirit.

Anime (Japanese): Animation; can vary from cute children's shows to violent horror stories for adults, and everything in between.

Bai Hu (Putonghua): The White Tiger of the West.

Bo: Weapon — staff.

Bodhisattva: A being who has attained Buddhist Nirvana and has returned to Earth to help others achieve Enlightenment.

Bo lei: A very dark and pungent Chinese tea, often drunk with yum cha to help digest the sometimes heavy and rich food served there.

Bu keqi (Putonghua) pronounced, roughly, 'bu kerchi': 'You're welcome.'

Buddhism: The system of beliefs that life is an endless journey through reincarnation until a state of perfect detachment or Nirvana is reached.

Cantonese: The dialect of Chinese spoken mainly in the south of China and used extensively in Hong Kong. Although in written form it is nearly identical to Putonghua, when spoken it is almost unintelligible to Putonghua speakers.

Causeway Bay: Large shopping and office district on Hong Kong Island. Most of the Island's residents seem to head there on Sunday for shopping.

Central: The main business district in Hong Kong, on the waterfront on Hong Kong Island.

Central Committee: Main governing body of Mainland China.

Cha siu bow: Dim sum served at yum cha; a steamed bread bun containing barbecued pork and gravy in the centre.

Chek Lap Kok: Hong Kong's new airport on a large swathe of reclaimed land north of Lantau Island.

Cheongsam (Cantonese): Traditional Chinese dress, with a mandarin collar, usually closed with toggles and loops, and with splits up the sides.

Cheung Chau: Small dumbbell-shaped island off the coast of Hong Kong Island, about an hour away by ferry.

Chi: Energy. The literal meaning is 'gas' or 'breath' but in martial arts terms it describes the energy (or breath) of life that exists in all living things.

Chi gong (Cantonese): Literally, 'energy work'. A series of movements expressly designed for manipulation of chi.

Chinese New Year: The Chinese calendar is lunar, and New Year falls at a different time each Western calendar. Chinese New Year usually falls in either January or February.

Ching: A type of life energy, ching is the energy of sex and reproduction, the Essence of Life. Every person is born with a limited amount of ching and as this energy is drained they grow old and die.

Chiu Chow: A southeastern province of China.

Choy sum (Cantonese): A leafy green Chinese vegetable vaguely resembling English spinach.

City Hall: Hall on the waterfront in Central on Hong Kong Island containing theatres and a large restaurant.

Confucianism: A set of rules for social behaviour designed to ensure that all of society runs smoothly.

Congee: A gruel made by boiling rice with savoury ingredients such as pork or thousand-year egg. Usually eaten for breakfast but can be eaten as a meal or snack any time of the day.

Connaught Road: Main thoroughfare through the middle of Central District in Hong Kong, running parallel to the waterfront and with five lanes each side.

Cross-Harbour Tunnel: Tunnel that carries both cars and MTR trains from Hong Kong Island to Kowloon under the harbour.

Cultural Revolution: A turbulent period of recent Chinese history (1966–75) during which gangs of young people called Red Guards overthrew 'old ways of thinking' and destroyed many ancient cultural icons.

Dai pai dong (Cantonese): Small open-air restaurant.

Daisho: A set of katana, wakizashi, and sometimes a tanto (small dagger), all matching bladed weapons used by samurai in ancient times.

Dan tian: Energy centre, a source of energy within the body. The central dan tian is roughly located in the solar plexus.

Daujie (Cantonese): 'Thank you', used exclusively when a gift is given.

Dim sum (Cantonese): Small dumplings in bamboo steamers served at yum cha. Usually each dumpling is less than three centimetres across and four are found in each steamer. There are a number of different types, and standard types of dim sum are served at every yum cha.

Discovery Bay: Residential enclave on Lantau Island, quite some distance from the rush of Hong Kong Island and only reachable by ferry.

Dojo (Japanese): Martial arts training school.

Eight Immortals: A group of iconic Immortals from Taoist mythology, each one representing a human condition. Stories of their exploits are part of popular Chinese culture.

Er Lang: The Second Heavenly General, second-in-charge of the running of Heavenly affairs. Usually depicted as a young man with three eyes and accompanied by his faithful dog.

Fortune sticks: A set of bamboo sticks in a bamboo holder. The questioner kneels in front of the altar and shakes the holder until one stick rises above the rest and falls out. This stick has a number that is translated into the fortune by temple staff.

Fung shui (or feng shui): The Chinese system of geomancy that links the environment to the fate of those living in it. A house with good internal and external fung shui assures its residents of good luck in their life.

Gay-lo (Cantonese slang): gay, homosexual.

Ge ge (Putonghua): Big brother.

Guangdong: The province of China directly across the border from Hong Kong.

Guangzhou: The capital city of Guangdong Province, about an hour away by road from Hong Kong. A large bustling commercial city rivalling Hong Kong in size and activity.

Guanxi: Guanxi is a social concept where people have built a network of others that they can call upon to help them when needed. The more guanxi you have, the more others will be willing to assist you when you are in need.

Gundam (Japanese): Large humanoid robot armour popular in Japanese cartoons.

Gung hei fat choy (Cantonese): Happy New Year.

Gweipoh: (lit: 'foreign grandmother') The feminine form of 'gweiloh', suggesting a female foreign devil.

Gwun Gong (or Guan Gong): A southern Chinese Taoist deity; a local General who attained Immortality and is venerated for his strengths of loyalty and justice and his ability to destroy demons.

H'suantian Shangdi (Cantonese): Xuan Tian Shang Di in the Wade-Giles method of writing Cantonese words.

Har gow: Dim sum served at yum cha; a steamed dumpling with a thin skin of rice flour dough containing prawns.

Hei sun (Cantonese): Arise.

Ho ak (Cantonese): Okay.

Ho fan (Cantonese): Flat white noodles made from rice; can be either boiled in soup or stir-fried.

Hong Kong Jockey Club: a private Hong Kong institution that runs and handles all of the horseracing and legal gambling in Hong Kong. There can be billions of Hong Kong dollars in bets on a single race meeting.

Hungry Ghosts Festival: It is believed that once a year the gates of Hell are opened, and all the ghosts who do not have descendants to care for them are free to roam the Earth. Offerings of food and incense are left on roadsides, and in towns operas are performed to entertain the spirits.

Hutong (Putonghua): Traditional square Chinese house, built around a central courtyard.

ICAC: Independent Commission Against Corruption; an independent government agency focused on tracking down corruption in Hong Kong.

Jade Emperor: The supreme ruler of the Taoist Celestial Government.

Journey to the West: A classic of Chinese literature written during the Ming Dynasty by Wu Cheng'En. The story of the Monkey King's journey to India with a Buddhist priest to collect scriptures and return them to China.

Kata (Japanese): A martial arts 'set'; a series of moves to practise the use of a weapon or hand-to-hand skills.

Katana: Japanese sword.

KCR: A separate above-ground train network that connects with the MTR and travels to the border with Mainland China. Used to travel to towns in the New Territories.

Kitchen God: A domestic deity who watches over the activities of the family and reports annually to the Jade Emperor.

Koi (Japanese): Coloured ornamental carp.

Kowloon: Peninsula opposite the Harbour from Hong Kong Island, a densely packed area of high-rise buildings. Actually on the Chinese Mainland, but separated by a strict border dividing Hong Kong from China.

Kowloon City: District in Kowloon just before the entrance to the Cross-Harbour Tunnel.

Kwan Yin: Buddhist icon; a woman who attained Nirvana and became a Buddha but returned to Earth to help others achieve Nirvana as well. Often represented as a goddess of Mercy.

Lai see (Cantonese): A red paper envelope used to give cash as a gift for birthdays and at New Year. It's believed that for every dollar given ten will return during the year.

Lai see dao loy (Cantonese): 'Lai see, please!'

Lantau Island: One of Hong Kong's outlying islands, larger than Hong Kong Island but not as densely inhabited.

Li: Chinese unit of measure, approximately half a kilometre.

Lo Wu: The area of Hong Kong that contains the border crossing. Lo Wu is an area that covers both sides of the border; it is in both Hong Kong and China.

Lo Wu Shopping Centre: A large shopping centre directly across the Hong Kong/Chinese border on the Chinese side. A shopping destination for Hong Kong residents in search of a bargain.

Love hotel: Hotel with rooms that are rented by the hour by young people who live with their parents (and therefore have no privacy) or businessmen meeting their mistresses for sex.

M'goi sai (Cantonese): 'Thank you very much.'

M'sai (Cantonese): Literally, 'no need', but it generally means 'you're welcome'.

Macau: One-time Portuguese colony to the west of Hong Kong in the Pearl River Delta, about an hour away by jet hydrofoil; now another Special Administrative Region of China. Macau's port is not as deep and sheltered as Hong Kong's so it has never been the busy trade port that Hong Kong is.

Mafoo (Cantonese): Groom.

Mah jong: Chinese game played with tiles. The Chinese play it differently from the polite game played by many

Westerners; it is played for money and can often be a cut-throat competition between skilled players, rather like poker.

Manga: Japanese illustrated novel or comic book.

Mei mei (Putonghua): Little sister.

MTR: Fast, cheap, efficient and spotlessly clean subway train system in Hong Kong. Mostly standing room, and during rush hour so packed that it is often impossible to get onto a carriage.

Na Zha: Famous mythical Immortal who was so powerful as a child that he killed one of the dragon sons of the Dragon King. He gained Immortality by unselfishly travelling into Hell to release his parents who had been held in punishment for his crime. A spirit of Youthfulness.

New Territories: A large area of land between Kowloon and Mainland China that was granted to extend Hong Kong. Less crowded than Hong Kong and Kowloon, the New Territories are green and hilly with high-rise New Towns scattered through them.

Nunchucks: Short wooden sticks held together with chains; a martial arts weapon.

Opium Wars: (1839–60) A series of clashes between the then British Empire and the Imperial Chinese Government over Britain's right to trade opium to China. It led to a number of humiliating defeats and surrenders by China as they were massively outclassed by modern Western military technology.

Pa Kua (Cantonese): The Eight Symbols, a central part of Taoist mysticism. Four of these Eight Symbols flank the circle in the centre of the Korean flag.

Pak Tai: One of Xuan Wu's many names; this one is used in Southern China.

Peak Tower: Tourist sightseeing spot at the top of the Peak Tram. Nestled between the two highest peaks on the Island and therefore not the highest point in Hong Kong, but providing a good view for tourist photographs.

Peak Tram: Tram that has been running for many years between Central and the Peak. Now mostly a tourist attraction because of the steepness of the ride and the view.

Peak, the: Prestigious residential area of Hong Kong, on top of the highest point of the centre of Hong Kong Island. The view over the harbour and high-rises is spectacular, and the property prices there are some of the highest in the world.

Pipa: A Chinese musical instrument, shaped like a mandolin, but played vertically with the body of the instrument held in the lap.

Pocky: A popular Japanese snack, which is a box of stick-shaped biscuits dipped in flavoured sweet coating.

Pokfulam: Area of Hong Kong west of the main business districts, facing the open ocean rather than the harbour. Contains large residential apartment blocks and a very large hillside cemetery.

Putonghua: Also called Mandarin, the dialect of Chinese spoken throughout China as a standard language. Individual provinces have their own dialects but Putonghua is spoken as a common tongue.

Qing Long (Putonghua) pronounced, roughly, Ching Long: The Azure Dragon of the East.

Ramen (Japanese): Instant two-minute noodles.

Repulse Bay: A small swimming beach surrounded by an expensive residential enclave of high- and low-rise apartment blocks on the south side of Hong Kong Island.

Salute, Chinese: The left hand is closed into a fist and the right hand is wrapped around it. Then the two hands are held in front of the chest and sometimes shaken.

Sashimi (Japanese): Raw fish.

Seiza: Japanese kneeling position.

Sensei (Japanese): Master.

Seppuku: Japanese ritual suicide by disembowelment: hari-kiri.

Sha Tin: A New Territories 'New Town', consisting of a large shopping centre surrounded by a massive number of high-rise developments on the banks of the Shing Mun River.

Shaolin: Famous temple, monastery and school of martial arts, as well as a style of martial arts.

Shen: Shen has two meanings, in the same sense that the English word spirit has two meanings ('ghost' and 'energy'). Shen can mean an Immortal being, something like a god in Chinese mythology. It is also the spirit that dwells within a person, the energy of their soul.

Shenzhen: The city at the border between Hong Kong and China, a 'special economic zone' where capitalism has been allowed to flourish. Most of the goods manufactured in China for export to the West are made in Shenzhen.

Sheung Wan: The western end of the Hong Kong Island MTR line; most people get off the train before reaching this station.

Shoji (Japanese): Screen of paper stretched over a wooden frame.

Shui (Cantonese): Water.

Shui gow: Chinese dumplings made of pork and prawn meat inside a dough wrapping, boiled in soup stock.

Shroff Office: A counter in a car park where you pay the parking fee before returning to your car.

Sifu (Cantonese): Master.

Siu mai: Dim sum served at yum cha; a steamed dumpling with a skin of wheat flour containing prawn and pork.

Sow mei (Cantonese): A type of Chinese tea, with a greenish colour and a light, fragrant flavour.

Stanley Market: A famous market on the south side of Hong Kong Island, specialising in tourist items.

Star Ferry: Small oval green and white ferries that run a cheap service between Hong Kong Island and Kowloon.

Sticky rice: Dim sum served at yum cha; glutinous rice filled with savouries such as pork and thousand-year egg, wrapped in a green leaf and steamed.

Sun Wu Kong (Cantonese): The Monkey King's real name.

Tae kwon do: Korean martial art.

Tai chi: A martial art that consists of a slow series of movements, used mainly as a form of exercise and chi manipulation to enhance health and extend life. Usable as a lethal martial art by advanced practitioners. There are several different styles of tai chi, including Chen, Yang and Wu, named after the people who invented them.

Tai chi chuan: Full correct name for tai chi.

Tai Koo Shing: Large enclosed shopping mall on the north side of Hong Kong.

Tai Tai (Cantonese): Lit: 'wife' but in this context it refers to a wealthy middle-aged Hong Kong woman who spends all her time shuffling between designer clothing stores, expensive lunches, and beauty salons.

Tao Teh Ching: A collection of writings by Lao Tzu on the elemental nature of Taoist philosophy.

Tao, the: 'The Way'. A perfect state of consciousness equivalent to the Buddhist Nirvana, in which a person becomes completely attuned with the universe and achieves Immortality. Also the shortened name of a collection of writings (the Tao Teh Ching) on Taoist philosophy written by Lao Tzu.

Taoism: Similar to Buddhism, but the state of perfection can be reached by a number of different methods, including alchemy and internal energy manipulation as well as meditation and spirituality.

Tatami (Japanese): Rice-fibre matting.

Temple Street: A night market along a street on the Kowloon side in Hong Kong. Notorious as a triad gang hangout as well as being one of Hong Kong's more colourful markets.

Ten Levels of Hell: It is believed that a human soul travels through ten levels of Hell, being judged and punished for a particular type of sin at each level. Upon reaching the lowest, or tenth, level, the soul is given an elixir of forgetfulness and returned to Earth to reincarnate and live another life.

Teppan (Japanese): Hotplate used for cooking food at teppanyaki.

Teppanyaki (Japanese): Meal where the food is cooked on the teppan in front of the diners and served when done.

Thousand-year egg: A duck egg that's been preserved in a mixture of lime, ash, tea and salt for one hundred days, making the flesh of the egg black and strong in flavour.

Tikuanyin (Cantonese; or Tikuanyum): Iron Buddha Tea. A dark, strong and flavourful black Chinese tea. Named because, according to legend, the first tea bush of this type was found behind a roadside altar containing an iron statue of Kwan Yin.

Tin Hau (Cantonese): Taoist deity, worshipped by seafarers.

Triad: Hong Kong organised-crime syndicate. Members of the syndicates are also called triads.

Tsim Sha Tsui: Main tourist and entertainment district on the Kowloon side, next to the harbour.

Tsing Ma Bridge: Large suspension bridge connecting Kowloon with Lantau Island, used to connect to the Airport Expressway.

Typhoon: A hurricane that occurs in Asia. Equivalent to a hurricane in the US or a cyclone in Australia.

Wakizashi: Japanese dagger, usually matched with a sword to make a set called a daisho.

Wan Chai: Commercial district on Hong Kong Island, between the offices and designer stores of Central and the shopping area of Causeway Bay. Contains office buildings and restaurants, and is famous for its nightclubs and girlie bars.

Wan sui (Putonghua): 'Ten thousand years'; traditional greeting for the Emperor, wishing him ten thousand times ten thousand years of life.

Wei? (Cantonese): 'Hello?' when answering the phone.

Wing chun: Southern style of Chinese kung fu. Made famous by Bruce Lee, this style is fast, close in ('short') and lethal. It's also a 'soft' style where the defender uses the attacker's weight and strength against him or her, rather than relying on brute force to hit hard.

Wire-fu: Movie kung-fu performed on wires so that the actors appear to be flying.

Won ton (Cantonese): Chinese dumplings made mostly of pork with a dough wrapping and boiled in soup stock. Often called 'short soup' in the West.

Won ton mien (Cantonese): 'won ton noodles'; won ton boiled in stock with noodles added to the soup.

Wu shu (Putonghua): A general term to mean all martial arts.

Wudang (Putonghua): A rough translation could be 'true martial arts'. The name of the mountain in Hubei Province; also the name of the martial arts academy and the style of martial arts taught there. Xuan Wu was a Celestial 'sponsor' of the Ming Dynasty and the entire mountain complex of temples and monasteries was built by the government of the time in his honour.

Wudangshan (Putonghua): 'Shan' means 'mountain'; Wudang Mountain.

Xie xie (Putonghua): 'Thank you.'

Xuan Wu (Putonghua) pronounced, roughly, 'Shwan Wu': means 'Dark Martial Arts'; the Black Turtle of the North, Mr Chen.

Yamen: Administration, as in Yamen Building.

Yang: One of the two prime forces of the universe in Taoist philosophy. Yang is the Light: masculine, bright, hot and hard.

Yang and yin: The two prime forces of the universe, when joined together form the One, the essence of everything. The symbol of yang and yin shows each essence containing a small part of the other.

Yellow Emperor: An ancient mythological figure, the Yellow Emperor is credited with founding civilisation and inventing clothing and agriculture.

Yin: One of the two prime forces of the universe in Taoist philosophy. Yin is Darkness: feminine, dark, cold and soft.

Yuexia Loaren (Putonghua): 'Old Man Under the Moon'; a Taoist deity responsible for matchmaking.

Yum cha (Cantonese): Literally 'drink tea'. Most restaurants hold yum cha between breakfast and mid-afternoon. Tea is served, and waitresses wheel around trolleys containing varieties of dim sum.

Yuzhengong (Putonghua): 'Find the True Spirit'; the name of the palace complex on Wudang Mountain.

Zhu Que (Putonghua) pronounced, roughly, Joo Chway: the Red Phoenix of the South.

CULTURAL NOTES

Animals on the edge of the roof:

Traditional Chinese buildings have upturned roofs and on official buildings there is always the same series of creatures. The point of the roof holds a man riding a chicken (or phoenix), and he is followed by a series of mythical creatures, with a dragon's head at the very back. The more creatures behind the man, the higher the building is in the Imperial hierarchy. Buildings in the Forbidden City have nine animals; in a small province there would be only one between the man and the dragon. The small vignette is a reminder and a warning to those working inside the building, that whatever they do, all of the mythical creatures on the roof are watching them, and will pounce on them and devour them if they stray from their official duty.

Ah Ting:

Part of the legend of the 'Creation of the Gods' involves the raising of all concerned to the Celestial. When it came time to choose the person for the job of Jade Emperor, the leader of the winning side graciously and politely didn't immediately take the position, he just said 'Ting, ting.' ('Wait, wait.') Legend has it that a rogue by the name of Ting jumped up and loudly accepted the post of Jade Emperor, and as it was what the leader had said, he was given the post.

FURTHER READING

I have expanded my library considerably while researching for the second trilogy, *Journey to Wudang*, and I have delved deeper into the mythology, as well as the texts and scriptures, of Taoism. Here is a list of some of the works that I have added to my collection, and may be of interest:

A Selected Collection of Mencius, Sinolingua, Beijing, 2006

A Selected Collection of the Analects, Confucius, Sinolingua, Beijing, 2006

Anecdotes about Spirits and Immortals (in two volumes) by Gan Bao, translated into English by Ding Wangdao, Foreign Languages Press, Beijing, 2004

Creation of the Gods (in four volumes), Xu Zhonglin, translated by Gu Zhizhong, New World Press, Beijing, 2000

Early Taoist Scriptures, Stephen R Bokenkamp, University of California Press, Berkeley, 1997

Journey to the North, Gary Seaman, University of California Press, Berkeley, 1987

Journey to the West, Wu Cheng'En, translated by W J F Jenner, Foreign Languages Press, Beijing, 1993

Secret of the Golden Flower, Lu Yen, NuVision E-book, 2004

Selected Chinese Tales of the Han, Wei, and Six Dynasties Periods, translated by Yang Xianyi and Gladys Yang, Foreign Languages Press, Beijing, 2001

The Origin of Chinese Deities, Cheng Manchao, Foreign Languages Press, Beijing, 1995

The Scripture on Great Peace: the Tai Ping Jing and the Beginnings of Taoism, by Barbara Hendrischke, University of California Press, Berkeley, 2006

To Live as Long as Heaven and Earth, a Translation and Study of Ge Hong's Traditions of Divine Transcendents, Robert Ford Campany, University of California Press, Berkeley, 2002